U0360300

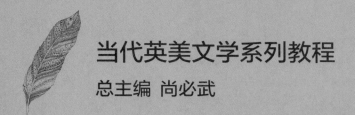

当代英美文学系列教程

总主编 尚必武

当代西方文学理论导读

An Introduction to Contemporary Western Literature Theories

主 编：陈后亮

编 委：隋红升 丁兆国 李 锋
　　　马 特 刘芊玥 陈 萃

上海交通大学出版社
SHANGHAI JIAO TONG UNIVERSITY PRESS

内容提要

本书为"当代英美文学系列教程"之一,主要对 20 世纪 60 年代以来西方文学理论发展历程中的 15～20 篇名作(论文或著作节选)进行分析介绍,既涵盖结构主义、解构主义、性别研究、新历史主义、后现代主义等理论热时期的主导思潮,也涉及自 20 世纪 80 年代以来随着反理论运动以及所谓"后理论"时期的到来,西方文论出现的新动向、新思潮。全书共分为 9 章,每章集中于一种思潮或流派,选择 2～3 篇代表性作品,单篇选读篇幅在 5 000～10 000 词左右,每篇附有约 5 000 字的分析导读。本教材侧重于理论的思辨性而非实用批评价值,特别是借助于反理论运动和 21 世纪以来的"后理论"背景,对每一种文学批评思潮的兴起动因、价值和功能进行深入反思。本书适合外国文学专业方向的博士、硕士研究生作为教材使用,也适合文学爱好者使用。

图书在版编目 (CIP) 数据

当代西方文学理论导读／陈后亮主编. -- 上海:
上海交通大学出版社,2024. 8 --(当代英美文学系列教
程／尚必武总主编). -- ISBN 978 - 7 - 313 - 31225 - 9

Ⅰ. I106

中国国家版本馆 CIP 数据核字第 20245XW794 号

当代西方文学理论导读
DANGDAI XIFANG WENXUE LILUN DAODU

主　　编:	陈后亮		
出版发行:	上海交通大学出版社	地　　址:	上海市番禺路 951 号
邮政编码:	200030	电　　话:	021 - 64071208
印　　制:	上海万卷印刷股份有限公司	经　　销:	全国新华书店
开　　本:	889 mm×1194 mm　1/16	印　　张:	12.25
字　　数:	307 千字		
版　　次:	2024 年 8 月第 1 版	印　　次:	2024 年 8 月第 1 次印刷
书　　号:	ISBN 978 - 7 - 313 - 31225 - 9		
定　　价:	59.00 元		

　　2012 年，国务院学位委员会第六届学科评议组在外国语言文学一级学科目录下设置了 5 大方向，即外国文学、语言学与应用语言学、翻译学、国别与区域研究、比较文学与跨文化研究。2020 年起，教育部开始大力推进"新文科"建设，不仅发布了《新文科建设宣言》，还设立了"新文科研究与改革实践项目"，旨在进一步打破学科壁垒，促进学科的交叉融合，提升文科建设的内涵与质量。在这种背景下，外语研究生教育既迎来了机遇，同时又面临新的挑战，这就要求我们的研究生培养模式为适应这些变化而进行必要的改革与创新。在孙益、陈露茜、王晨看来，"研究生教育方针、教育路线的贯彻执行，研究生教育体制改革和教育思想的革新，研究生专业培养方案、培养计划的制定，研究生教学内容和教学方法的改革，最终都会反映和落实到研究生教材的建设上来。重视研究生教材建设工作，是提高高校研究生教学质量和保证教学改革成效的关键所在"。[①] 从这种意义上说，教材建设是提高外语研究生教育的一个重要抓手。

　　就国内外语专业研究生教材而言，上海外语教育出版社推出的"高等院校英语语言文学专业研究生系列教材"占据了主要地位。该系列涵盖语言学、语言教学、文学理论、原著选读等多个领域，为我国的外语研究生培养做出了重要贡献。需要指出的是，同外语专业本科生教材建设相比，外语专业研究生教材建设显得明显滞后。很多高校的外语专业研究生课堂上所使用的教材基本上是原版引进教材或教师自编讲义。我们知道，"教材不仅是教师进行教学的基本工具，而且是学生获取知识、培养能力的重要手段。研究生教材是直接体现高等院校研究生教学内容和教学方法的知识载体，也是反映高等院校教学水平、科研水平及其成果的重要标志，优秀的研究生教材是提高研究生教学质量的重要保证"。[②] 上海交通大学外国语学院历来重视教材建设，曾主编《研究生英语教程》《多维教程》《新视野大学英语》《21 世纪大学英语》等多套本科和研究生层次的英语教材，在全国范围内产生了较大影响。

---

① 孙益、陈露茜、王晨：《高校研究生教材建设的国际经验与中国路径》，载《学位与研究生教育》2018 年第 2 期，第 72 页。
② 同上。

　　为进一步加强和推动外语专业,尤其是英语专业英美文学方向的研究生教材建设,助力研究生培养从接受知识到创造知识的模式转变,在上海交通大学出版社的大力支持下,上海交通大学外国语学院发挥优势,携手复旦大学外文学院、上海外国语大学英语学院、华中科技大学外国语学院、北京科技大学外国语学院、东北师范大学外国语学院、中南财经政法大学外国语学院、山东师范大学外国语学院等兄弟单位,主编"当代英美文学系列教程"。本系列教材重点聚焦20世纪80年代以来的英美文学与文论,由《当代英国小说教程》《当代美国小说教程》《当代西方英国戏剧教程》《当代美国戏剧教程》《当代英国诗歌教程》《当代美国诗歌教程》《当代西方文学理论导读》《当代叙事理论教程》8册构成。

　　本系列教材以问题意识为导向,围绕当代英美文学,尤其是21世纪英美文学的新类型、新材料、新视角、新话题,将文学作为一种直面问题、思考问题、应对问题、解决问题的重要途径和方式,从而发掘和彰显文学的能动性。在每册教材的导论部分,首先重点概述20世纪80年代以来的文学发展态势与特征,由此回答"当代起于何时"的问题。在此基础上,简述教材内容所涉及的主要命题、思潮、样式、作家和作品,由此回答"新在哪里"的问题。本系列教材打破按照时间顺序来划分章节的惯例,转而以研究问题或文学样式来安排各章。例如,教材纳入了气候变化、新型战争、族裔流散、世界主义等问题与文学样式。在文学作品的选择标准上,教材以类型和样式的标准来分类,如气候变化文学、新型战争文学等。每个门类下均选取数篇具有典型性的作品,并对其主题特色、历史背景及其相关文学特质进行介绍,凸显对文本性敏锐的分析能力以及对相关文学研究视角及理论知识的掌握。除此之外,教材还有意识地呈现当代英美文学新的创作手法、文学思潮和文体特征。教材的每章集中一种文学样式、类型、思潮或流派,选择2～3篇代表性作品,单篇选读篇幅在5 000～10 000词(英文)左右,每篇附有5 000字(中文)左右的分析导读以及若干思考题。教材对作家或理论家及其著作的选取,不求涵盖全部,而是以权威性、代表性和重要性为首要原则,兼顾年代、流派、思潮等因素。本系列教材适合国内高校外国文学尤其是英美文学专业的博士研究生、硕士研究生、高年级本科生、文学研究者与爱好者使用。

　　本系列教材在编写过程中得到了上海交通大学外国语学院、上海交通大学出版社以及国内外同行专家学者的关心、帮助与支持,特此谢忱!

尚必武

2023年3月

在本教材的绪论部分,我们分析比较了两种主要的教材编写理念——理论作为一种批判性话语与理论作为一套批评方法,同时讨论了文学理论的根本属性及其主要功能。因此,我们对当代文学理论教材的编写有以下几点认识。第一,文学理论教材应当尽可能突出理论的思辨性,要把它作为一种生动活泼的思考方式,而非僵化的理论知识。第二,文学理论教材可以重视其对批评实践的指导性,甚至可以提供案例分析,但应该尽可能避免把工具化价值作为理论学习的主要意义。第三,在编写体例上,我们认为应该以经典理论著作的篇章选读为主,同时辅之以较为全面且有一定深度的理论导读,这样有利于学生在对文学理论有一个总体认识的基础上,细致深入地剖析具体理论文本,循序渐进地做到见树又见林。第四,具体到中文语境下的西方文学理论教材编写工作,我们建议还是要以"我"为主,要充分考量国内学界在西方文学理论教学、研究、教材编写等方面取得的成就和形成的传统,同时还要考虑学生的学术背景以及知识语境,在实事求是的原则下,适度融入中国文学理论的学术话语,真正让我们的西方文学理论教材既具有知识上的创新性,又具有实践上的灵活适应性。当然,无论哪一种教材编写方式都不可能是尽善尽美的。在具体的教学实践中同时使用多部教材,取长补短,也不失为一种合理的策略。

在本教材的编写过程中,我们也力图把以上认识贯彻进来。也就是说,我们的目的不是讲授最新的批评方法,而是介绍近几十年来,尤其是理论热渐渐消退以后英美文学批评界所出现的几种新思潮,包括新历史主义、后殖民主义、解殖民研究、生态批评、性别研究、白人性研究、情动理论、数字人文研究、反理论等。它们有的是对语言学转向和后结构主义的进一步承续和拓展,延续了理论的政治性特征和社会介入的旨趣,比如新历史主义、后殖民主义、解殖民研究、性别研究、白人性研究等等;有的则是在人文学科危机大背景下对文学研究的范式进行批判性反思并寻求新合法性辩护的尝试,比如情动理论、数字人文研究和反理论。它们有的可以对我们的文本解读提供新思路、新启发,有的则有助于我们对文学批评的学术惯例、现实规制、社会意义、价值功能等进行反思。本教材编写的一个根本理念是：理论可以对文学研究产生积极的帮助作用，但绝不可被化简为机械僵硬的批评公式。

自 20 世纪末以来，西方理论界又出现了相当多的新热点、新思潮，但受编者能力所限，本教材仅选择介绍其中 9 种。具体编写分工如下：新历史主义（李锋教授，中国海洋大学），后殖民主义（丁兆国教授，山东财经大学），解殖民研究（陈萃副教授，山东大学），生态批评（马特副教授，中央财经大学），性别研究（隋红升教授，浙大城市学院），情动理论（刘芊玥博士，苏州大学），白人性研究、数字人文研究和反理论（陈后亮教授，华中科技大学）。每章分为两节，第一节是一万字左右的概论，第二节是 2~3 篇经典文献选读。此外，每章还设置了几个思考题，并提供了 20 个左右的推荐阅读文献。每一章的编写者皆在该领域有多年深入研究，取得过重要的研究成果。每章概论部分都由相应编者撰写，尽可能涵盖该领域重要的理论家和文献，提供一幅鸟瞰式的导览图，有助于读者对该思潮的整体了解。需要说明的是，尽管后殖民主义研究和解殖民研究有诸多相似的学术渊源，也存在一些交叉点，但在基本理念和批评旨趣上又存在很大差异。因此，我们在本书中还是把它们分开来写，这样也有助于读者从中看出它们的异同之处。虽然我们在每章概论中尽量做到客观描述，但也不可避免地带有编写者的一些主观判断，甚至是偏见。当然这也是理论带给我们的启迪之一，即完全不带偏见的客观认识几乎是不可能的。这也要求读者在阅读本书的过程中小心甄别，避免被编者的主观判断所干扰，同时也要对自己的认识的主观性保持反省。最后我们还要对本书的注释体例稍作说明：一方面，我们在导论中力图涵盖更多文献，提供的文献注释比较多且详尽，但同时也尽量做到精简，删除不必要的信息，对重复出现的文献也做了简化处理；另一方面，我们在文献选读部分删除了原文出现的注释。

国内目前已经出版了很多优秀的当代西方文论教材，我们在编写过程中也参考学习了这些教材，受益良多，在此不再一一致谢。参考教材皆在文献注释中列出。受编者能力所限，本书不可避免地存在一些瑕疵，恳请学界同仁批评指正！

Contents | **目录**

绪　论

　　自 20 世纪 70 年代以降,理论以前所未有的姿态强势进入文学批评领域,成为显著的在场之物,各种批评理论迅速崛起,以至于到了 80 年代之后,英美学界的文学研究出现所谓的"范式转换",从以批评为基础变为以理论为基础,或者说批评工作不再是"文本细读",而是有关语言、阐释本身、性别、文化、社会等的理论思辨,理论成了被广为接受的批评实践模式——一种被完全许可的范式。① 在此情况下,理论学习成为文学研究者的必修课,然而理论之晦涩也是众所周知的。人们急需一种深入浅出的文学理论教材,以在短时间内对那些复杂的理论有全面的认识,从中获得启发并将其转化为实践工具和批评方法。于是,文学理论教材编写的第一轮热潮也紧跟理论热出现。包括特里·伊格尔顿(Terry Eagleton)、乔纳森·卡勒(Jonathan Culler)在内的很多著名理论家,以及劳特里奇(Routledge)出版社、布莱克维尔(Blackwell)出版社、牛津大学出版社等著名学术出版社也都加入文学理论教材编写和出版的热潮中。尤其像伊格尔顿的《文学理论导论》(*Literary Theory: An Introduction*)和卡勒的《文学理论入门》(*Literary Theory: A Very Short Introduction*),它们早已成为世界范围内的文学理论经典教材,惠及无数学者,其影响之大难以估量。

　　可以说,理论之所以能在 20 世纪 80 年代产生广泛影响,在相当程度上是因为大量高质量理论教材的推出。它们使得那些深奥的理论更容易被讨论、学习和讲授,进而被很多人接受。所以华莱士·马丁(Wallace Martin)早在 1982 年就提出:"在批评史、学术史和教学史中,教材都值得被单列一章进行研究,它们的内容和销量最直接地证明了这一点。"②这些教材并非删繁就简的二流读物,而是普通读者与高深理论之间的桥梁,对理论的普及传播起到巨大作用。但或许也正是这些教材在编写理念和方法上的不足之处导致了人们对理论的误读或者过度期待,为后来的理论危机埋下了伏笔。因此,我们在这里首先对过去几十年间被广泛采用、同时也最有影响力的几部文学理论教材进行对比分析,寻找可为我们这本教材的编写提供借鉴的地方,在向它们致敬的同时,也特别关注其编写理念(而非具体编写内容),进而思考不足的编写理念带来了哪些后果。

---

① Jeffrey Williams, "Packaging Theory," *College English* 3 (1994), pp.282 - 283.
② Wallace Martin, "Literary Theory in/vs. the Classroom," *College Literature* 3 (1982), p.177.

第一节 理论作为一种批判性话语

在众多理论教材中,伊格尔顿的《文学理论导论》①无疑是最有影响力的一部。作为当今英国乃至全世界"最杰出的文学理论家、文化批评家和马克思主义理论家"之一②,伊格尔顿本人的学术生涯与现代批评理论的发展历程基本平行甚至重合。他于 20 世纪 80 年代前后在西方理论界奠定了自己的学术地位,彼时恰逢理论鼎盛时期,他的成名在很大程度上得益于这部教材在全世界范围内的广泛传播。其实在此之前,英美国家的文学院系并没有通用的理论教材,理论课程也不受重视。人们要想学习文学理论,要么读原著,要么就使用极少数的理论选集,比如哈泽德·亚当斯(Hazard Adams)的《柏拉图以来的批评理论》(Critical Theory since Plato)。随着文学理论越来越成为文学专业学生的必修课程,人们急需一本导论性的理论入门读物。伊格尔顿的这一著作可谓应时而生。作为公认的第一部理论教材,《文学理论导论》从一问世便引起巨大反响。在出版后的 5 年时间内,包括乔纳森·卡勒、迈克尔·瑞安(Michael Ryan)、拉曼·塞尔登(Raman Selden)、琳达·哈琴(Linda Hutcheon)等一流理论家在内的 20 多位学者先后为其撰写书评,称赞其为"现有最好的文学理论导读作品"③以及"伊格尔顿最好的著作"④。这部著作的发行量之大、传播和影响范围之广,恐怕至今没有其他同类著作可以比拟,并且其不断再版、重印,被翻译成几十种不同语言发行。也正是因为这个原因,伊格尔顿在书中所采用的对待理论的基本观点、研究路径和批评态度深刻影响了其读者,塑造了很多人对待理论的基本认识和元立场。

作为现代文学理论教材的开山之作,伊格尔顿的这本书与此后其他类似著作有一个很大的不同。它虽名为导论,实际上却"并非通常意义上的文学理论导论"⑤。尽管他的文风生动活泼,他也尽可能清晰地梳理出每一种理论流派的来龙去脉,但初学者在阅读时还是感到十分困难。其实,伊格尔顿的写作意图与其说是帮助初学者领略理论王国的基本面貌,不如说是要从根本上破除他们对理论以及传统文学批评的误解。他开篇第一个命题不是理论是什么,而是文学是什么。在对英国文学的兴起做了系统深入的考察之后,他得出的结论是:文学就是一种意识形态,它与种种社会权力问题有着最密切的关系,英国文学在 19 世纪兴起就是为了代替原来的宗教,继续承担意识形态任务。⑥ 也就是说,文学研究从一开始就不是像它所宣称的那样超然,而是服务于一定的国家意图,受阶级意识形态控制。非但如此,新批评之后的每一种或激进或保守的批评理论都是某种意识形态的代理,尽管它们都以不同面纱遮住本来面目。他说:"我从头至尾都在试图表明的就是,现代文学理论的历史是我们时代的政治和意识形态历史的一部分。从雪莱到霍兰德,文学理论一直与种种政治信念和意识

---

① 本书第一版于 1983 年由明尼苏达大学出版社出版。中文版标题被修改为《二十世纪西方文学理论》(伍晓明译,北京:北京大学出版社,2007 年)。

② 参见王宁为本书外研社影印版(2004 年)所写的导言。

③ Michael Ryan, "*Literary Theory: An Introduction* by Terry Eagleton(Book Review)," *Substance* 3/4 (1984), p.134.

④ Jonathan Culler, "*Literary Theory: An Introduction* by Terry Eagleton(Book Review)," *Poetics Today* 1 (1984), p.149.

⑤ Raman Selden, "*Literary Theory: An Introduction* by Terry Eagleton(Book Review)," *The Modern Language Review* 2 (1985), p.396.

⑥ Terry Eagleton, *Literary Theory: An Introduction*. Beijing: Foreign Language Teaching and Research Press, 2004, pp.20-21.

形态价值标准密不可分……与其说文学理论本身就有权作为理智探究的一个对象,还不如说它是观察我们时代的历史的一个特殊角度。"①伊格尔顿并非谴责理论的意识形态本质,他只是反对理论和文学批评以各种方式逃避或掩盖对自己的政治立场或意识形态的认识,即反对那种缺少反思的盲目性。凡是期望从伊格尔顿这里获得具体批评方法的读者必然会失望而归,因为伊格尔顿从头至尾都不是把理论作为文本解读的工具方法来理解的。对他来说,文学理论从根本上来说不过是"对批评的批评反思"②,它让人们能够洞察一切有关文学的讨论在背后是如何涉及阶级、性别、种族等政治问题的,也能够让人们自我检视,尽可能认识到自己的批评实践受何种价值支配,并且服务于何种意图。

伊格尔顿的著作以《文学理论导论》为标题,最终却又解构了理论甚至文学本身。他告诉人们文学和理论都不过是幻觉,它们都不是具有某种本体论意义上的价值的事物,而是"种种意识形态的一个分支"③。既然如此,文学批评和理论也就不必遮遮掩掩,而只需公开承认其意识形态属性,直言不讳地袒露自己通过谈论文学而最终要达到的非文学目的,也就是走向他所倡导的政治批评。因此,伊格尔顿的这本书与其说是理论导论,不如说是对整个文学批评事业的批评综述。他从未具体告诉读者这些理论有哪些功用,以及如何帮助他们加深对作品的理解,而是以宏阔而深邃的视角揭示了文学理论的非文学面目。他明确告诉读者,关于文学理论,"首先要问的并非对象是什么,或我们应该如何接近它,而是为何应该研究它"④,"你在理论上选择与拒绝什么取决于你在实际中试图去做什么"⑤。与其他教材相比,伊格尔顿的这部作品没有把理论庸俗化为实用批评工具,而是始终把理论作为反思文学批评活动本身的一种话语实践,这是其最突出的特征。不过正如彼得・巴里(Peter Barry)所评价的,伊格尔顿的长处是其"整体的能量、睿智和思想活力,以及对整个庞大思想体系的巧妙总结……这些更能打动同行,却并不适合寻求初始启蒙的学生"⑥。

由卡勒撰写的《文学理论入门》是另外一部影响巨大的理论教科书。这本著作被纳入"牛津通识读本"系列。正是因为以通识为目标,所以它是一部只有130多页的小32开本著作,力求言简意赅。值得一提的是,该书首次出版时间是1997年。与伊格尔顿的《文学理论导论》问世时的语境不同,此时的理论热已基本结束,对理论的质疑之声此起彼伏,"理论的终结""后理论"等说法已经甚嚣尘上。在这样的背景下,卡勒作为法国理论在美国最重要的传播者和研究者之一,他的著作就具有特殊意义。他必须以最简洁的语言告诉人们理论是什么,消除人们对理论的误解,以为理论的复苏注入活力。由于这部书的主要内容都基于他在康奈尔大学文学理论导论课程的讲稿,因此具有很强的实用性。他在前言部分特别提到自己力求避免一个做法,即避免像大多数文论教材一样,把"理论"呈现为不同的批评流派,在那些教材中,"理论被当作一系列相互竞争的'批评路径',每一种都有其理论立场和旨归"⑦。伊格尔顿的《文学理论导论》也是以这种框架写成的,但卡勒认为这种写作方式过多强调了不同理论流派之间的

---

① Eagleton, *Literary Theory: An Introduction*, p.169.
② Ibid., p.172.
③ Ibid., p.178.
④ Ibid., p.183.
⑤ Ibid., p.184.
⑥ Peter Barry, *Beginning Theory: An Introduction to Literary and Cultural Theory*. Manchester：Manchester University Press, 2009, p.271.
⑦ Jonathan Culler, *Literary Theory: A Very Short Introduction*. Oxford：Oxford University Press, 1997, "Preface".

差异,而没有看到它们有很多共通之处。因此他认为:"如果介绍理论,讨论其共同的问题和主张要好过考察理论流派。更好的做法是讨论那些重要的论题,这些论题并没有把不同流派彼此对立起来,却又能显示出彼此之间的显著分歧。"①换句话说,卡勒认为真正重要的是作为一种思考方式的、不可数的"理论",而非具体的、复数的、不同理论流派的集合。他在《文学理论入门》的第一章中首先就厘清了"什么是理论"这个问题。他从四个方面给出回答,概括出理论的主要特征,如"跨学科性""分析性和思辨性""对常识和自然观念的批判""自我反思性"等。因此,他的重点不是理论的工具性效用,而是围绕"什么是文学""文学与文化研究""语言、意义和阐释""修辞、诗学和诗歌""叙事""操演性语言""身份、认同与主体"七个议题,穿插讨论不同理论视角在这些问题上的看法,以及对文学常识的动摇。

拉曼·塞尔登的《当代文学理论导读》(*A Reader's Guide to Contemporary Literary Theory*)是一部极具影响力的文学理论教材。该书在塞尔登去世以后,于 1997 年出了修订版,并由彼得·威多森(Peter Widdowson)和彼得·布鲁克(Peter Brooker)两人合作补写了部分篇章。正如该书中国影印版导读中所说的,它不像特里·伊格尔顿的《文学理论导论》那样深奥,也不像乔纳森·卡勒的《文学理论入门》那样随便。它以全面、准确、可靠、流畅等诸多优点赢得了读者,自问世以来受到广泛欢迎。在同类教材中,它是再版次数最多的一本。② 塞尔登没有像伊格尔顿和卡勒那样花费很大笔墨去批判性地剖析不同流派的见解,而是充分考虑到大部分初学者的阅读期待,致力于梳理过去 30 年间最具挑战性的、最有影响力的理论趋势,为初学者提供一张作为基础指南的素描,使初学者更快速地熟悉 20 世纪文学理论的基本面貌。③ 与伊格尔顿一样,塞尔登等人也没有把理论当作批评方法来讲述,但同时他们也认为理论学习会对文学批评有多方面益处。大体说来,理论主要可以在两方面发挥作用:一是理论可以颠覆我们有关文学的幼稚理解,让我们知道一切文学话语都是有理论假定的;二是理论非但不会让我们的文学阅读变得枯燥乏味,反倒会"重新激活"我们与文本之间的关系。④ 在对待文学批评的根本特征上,该书与伊格尔顿所持观点很接近,即认为一切文学批评活动都是有理论支撑的,所有理论也都是有意识形态的。为了在最小篇幅内涵盖最多的内容,该书有一个不可避免的缺陷,就是过于简化和压缩了对不同理论流派的介绍,读者只能对最具代表性的理论家和论著有一个初步认识。

本节所描述的这三本理论导读著作都有一个共同特征,即它们都没有把理论等同于文学批评方法,而是更强调理论的思辨性。理论可以指导人们更好地理解和分析文本,但更重要的是可以帮助人们对批评活动本身进行反思。这几本教材的优点是避免了那种把理论简化为批评工具的庸俗方法,让理论保持活力,但缺点是让理论远离了实践,让那些真正借助这几本教材学习理论的初学者感到理论只是一种批判性话语,好像与文学批评实践的关系不大。人们期待另一种让理论更具操作性的教科书,一种可以帮助他们把理论付诸批评实践的教科书。

---

① Culler, *Literary Theory: A Very Short Introduction*,"Preface".
② 参见周小仪为拉曼·塞尔登等著的《当代文学理论导读》(外研社 2004 年影印版)所作的中文导读,第 1 页。
③ Raman Selden, et al., *A Reader's Guide to Contemporary Literary Theory*. Beijing: Foreign Language Teaching and Research Press, 2004, p.3.
④ Ibid., p.4.

第二节　理论作为一套批评方法

与上述这种更具有研究评述性质的著作不同,还有一类理论教材应用非常广泛。它们不是把理论当作对实践的反思,而是把理论当作更具有操作性的批评方法。这类教材的作者们都清楚,对多数普通读者来说,他们更关心的不是理论是什么,而是理论有什么用、如何借助理论工具改进批评实践或写出更好的文章等。这类教材有很多,其中最有代表性的一本当属由威尔弗雷德·L. 古尔灵(Wilfred L. Guerin)等人编写的《文学批评方法手册》(*A Handbook of Critical Approaches to Literature*)。此书初版于 20 世纪 60 年代中期,当时主要介绍的还都是形式主义、新批评、精神分析等相对"传统的"批评方法,1999 年修订后的第 4 版添加了有关 60 年代以后的现代批评理论的内容。

在伊格尔顿等人的理论教材出现之前,这本教材的使用范围也非常广。正如该书标题所显示的,它所介绍的与其说是文学理论,不如说是"批评方法",而且它还是便于上手操作、易于模仿的"手册",具有十分鲜明的实用性。它所面对的主要是文学专业的本科生,他们虽然熟悉传统研究方法,却对 20 世纪中叶以来的诸多理论缺乏了解,而这些理论都是"最有启发性的批评技巧"[1],所以本书的目的就是帮助学生提高文学分析能力,产生一种更加专业化、学术化的文学批评。为此,作者们在编写方法上开创了一种典型的理论教科书模式,即每一章开头都是对某一种理论流派的简单综述介绍,然后是定义,再辅以一篇批评范文,尤其是在不同章节运用不同理论方法反复解读剖析同一篇文本,以展示这些方法的有效性。它带给学生的总体印象就是:一种理论就是一种方法、一个套路、一条进入文本的路径。虽然本书作者也告诫读者不可过于操切地运用理论分析文本,但它还是为日后那种庸俗和僵化的批评实践埋下了伏笔。

彼得·巴里的《理论入门:文学与文化理论导论》(*Beginning Theory: An Introduction to Literary and Cultural Theory*)也很典型,它同样把理论当成方法。该书于 1995 年初版,因为通俗易懂,对理论的介绍深入浅出,所以特别受理论初学者欢迎。该书介绍了 20 世纪的绝大多数理论流派,对 90 年代以来的后理论话题也有涉及。作者在前言部分坦言,出于现实教学所需,他写了这本书,因为他发现很多学生抱怨理论难学,或者抱怨自己头脑笨,学校又没有提供足够好的理论教学,这导致理论学习成了让人望而生畏的精英知识游戏。但巴里认为,那些理论被书写的形式使得理论看上去很艰深,"理论并非在本质方面很难,文学理论中很少存在从内里来说就很复杂的思想,相反,被称为'理论'的著作,大都基于几十条思想,它们都不太难"[2]。真正难的不过是法语思维以及过于忠实于原文的英文翻译。他认为,理论要想有长远未来,就必须被改造为适合本科教学的批评技巧。如果理论只是少数学者玩的知识游戏,那么注定会被人们抛弃。因此他编写的这部教材就定位于教学实践,为学生和教师提供一本"工作手册",他还说:"理论不只是明星们玩的游戏,观众也不只是观众,而应参与进来。"[3]该教材与之前的其他同类教材的最大区别就在于其他教材"平均全面地涵盖了整个理论领域,却相对较少地涉及具体实

---

[1] Wilfred L. Guerin, et al., *A Handbook of Critical Approaches to Literature*. Beijing: Foreign Language Teaching and Research Press, 2004, p.ii.

[2] Barry, *Beginning Theory: An Introduction to Literary and Cultural Theory*, p.7.

[3] Ibid., p.2.

践应用……（它们都是）对理论的摘要复述而非导论，且往往大多从哲学而非文学的角度出发"①。与之相反，巴里的这本书不求全面，而是试图实现节奏变化，选择有重点的问题和关键论文进行细读。巴里认为现有文学理论教材最大的问题就是不关心教与学，而教与学对本科生来说才是最重要的。因此，这本教材的目标就是要成为"一部现实意义上的教学大纲，而非一本理想化了的教材"②。为了让学生更容易理解理论的意义，他在第 1 章特别论述了理论兴起之前的自由人文主义批评理念，这些理念实际上正是被人们普遍接受的基本共识和假定，它们就是未被说明的"理论"，人们从来没有去质疑它们。而现代批评理论在一定程度上正是源自对这些未被阐明的自由人文主义批评观的反叛和纠正。如此一来，读者便可看到，理论不是凭空出现的新事物，它与之前的东西之间存在关联。

该书的另一个独到之处是在第 14 章专门以 10 次重要的文学理论"事件"为节点，把它们串联起来，勾勒出理论在半个世纪内从兴起到鼎盛再到衰退的全过程，让初学者得以历时性地通览理论的概貌，这有助于破除那种把理论奉若不变真理的错误观点。总体上来说，巴里这本教材的最大特点就是简洁明了、通俗易懂，尤其适合本科教学。初版在 8 年内连续 9 次重印，2002 年修订版也连续 7 次印刷。但这也不可避免地带来一个消极后果，即他对理论的过度简化让初学者误以为理论不过如此，容易导致一知半解却过度自信的理论乐观主义。比如在他看来，一切理论都可被归结为 5 个基本要点，即"政治无处不在；语言是建构性的；真理是有限定条件的；意义是偶然的；人的本质是一个神话"③。这虽然可以帮助学生在最短的时间内抓住理论的某些要害，但显然也容易导致学生对理论的本质主义的、绝对化的误解，与理论真正倡导的那种对知识的反思和批判精神相悖。

由基思·格林（Keith Green）和吉尔·勒比汉（Jill LeBihan）合作编写的《批评理论与实践教科书》（*Critical Theory and Practice: A Coursebook*）同样直接源自两位作者的本科教学实践。他们发现，在 20 世纪 80 年代前后出现的大量理论和教科书中，"老师和学生都很难找到一条连贯的路径"④，即这些理论和教科书不能被有效地运用于课堂教学。学生们真正需要的不是一套僵化的"主义"，而是有关如何阅读和评价理论的具体指导。为此，该教材的具体编写方法和巴里的方法很相似，即在每一章的开头部分先给出一个指导性评价，然后辅助以具体的批评实践案例，再提出大量开放式的问题并设置思考练习，以帮助读者更好地理解和掌握这些理论。此外，该教材并未像通常做法那样按照流派来划分章节，而是和卡勒的做法类似，即以几个主要话题为焦点，包括"语言、语言学与语文学""文学的结构""文学与历史""主体性""心理分析与批评""阅读、写作与接受""女性主义、文学与批评""文化身份、文学与批评"等，分析不同理论在特定话题上的阐发力度，其重心同样是引导学生运用理论工具来帮助批评实践。

最后一部值得一提的理论教材是格雷戈里·卡斯尔（Gregory Castle）编写的《布莱克维尔文学理论指南》（*The Blackwell Guide to Literary Theory*），本书出版之时早已是所谓的后理论时代，但这绝不意味着已经没有学习理论的必要；恰恰相反，理论已然成为从事文学研究的基础知识。卡斯尔认为以前的教科书都不够理想，它们"都把理论的本质问题、文学文本的本质问题复杂化了"⑤。在他看来，理论不过是有关文学批评的原理和概念，是用于指导批评实践的策略和方法，因此本书的主要目的就是为教师

---

① Barry, *Beginning Theory: An Introduction to Literary and Cultural Theory*, p.2
② Ibid., p.4.
③ Ibid., p.35.
④ Keith Green and Jill LeBihan, *Critical Theory and Practice: A Coursebook*. New York：Routledge, 2001, p.xvi.
⑤ Gregory Castle, *The Blackwell Guide to Literary Theory*. Malden：Blackwell Publishing Ltd, 2007, p.2.

和学生提供有关理论和批评实践的基础知识,帮助学生、教师和普通读者从不同角度熟悉文学理论,包括它的历史和诸多表现。[①] 为了防止初学者把理论奉为绝对的知识权威,作者刻意在第一章用很大篇幅讲述理论的兴起过程,从而告诉人们文学理论的历史就是关于阅读和阐释观念如何变化的历史。文学理论和文学一样,是一定历史条件下的产物,这些条件包括既有的观念语境、知识传统、学术惯例、社会政治关系和各种力量的复杂交织等。因此,"文学理论并不拥有关于文学本质意义和价值的绝对标准,它所拥有的只是一套被运用于文本阅读的原理和假定"[②]。归根结底,在本书作者看来,理论不过是给读者提供的"研究工具",能够有效助益于文本批评实践。在本书的最后部分,他还给出了很多具体的批评案例,分别运用不同的理论解读同一部作品,比如从后殖民主义、后现代主义等角度解读萨尔曼·拉什迪的《午夜的孩子》,从批判理论、马克思主义和后现代主义等角度解读塞缪尔·贝克特的《终局》,从女权主义、精神分析、解构主义等角度解读弗吉尼亚·伍尔夫的《到灯塔去》等,"以展示用不同理论得出不同结果的应用技巧"[③]。

与第一节讨论的几本教科书不同,本节提到的这4部教科书都是把理论作为批评工具来对待的,具有突出的实用主义特征。其作者虽大都不是像伊格尔顿和卡勒那样的一流理论家,却都来自教学一线,熟悉学生和教师们的现实需求,他们编写的教材也就更有针对性,因此被广泛采用。这些教材在普及理论知识、提高学生的理论修养方面发挥了巨大作用,但其缺陷也十分明显。它们在根本上都把理论视为批评工具,并且还都给出了非常具体的批评实践案例,这就很容易导致对理论的化简式的模仿运用。理论被化简为僵化的批评公式,"从某某角度解读某某作品"几乎成为一种标准操作范式,所谓的"灌香肠机"[④]"曲奇压花模"[⑤]都是常被人们用来形容化简式批评的隐喻。原本有机的文学"谷物"和"糕点"被研究者用机械蛮力粗暴加工、碾磨和压榨,制作成千篇一律的产品。虽然导致理论热消退的原因有很多,但是这种化简式批评是最常被人们诟病的理论的弊端。

第三节　文学理论到底有什么功能?

自从理论于20世纪80年代被广泛传播开来之后,文学专业的学生们就不得不去面对这样一个多少有些异质性的存在。各种新理论、新思潮不断涌现,它们让文学批评有了更好的反思意识和理论自觉,理论所提供的新思想、新视角也让整个人文学科焕发出无限活力,极大地促进了文学研究的方法创新和知识生产。21世纪以来,理论热逐渐消退,后理论时代被宣告来临。于是很多人便认为理论已然终结,无须再去了解和掌握那些已经过时了的东西。这显然是一种错误认识。理论热的消退有很多原因,既有它本身创新能力下降,需要调整节奏、整合资源、重新定位等内部原因,也有众多外部原因。但

---

① Castle, *The Blackwell Guide to Literary Theory*, p.12.
② Ibid., p.10.
③ Ibid., p.12.
④ Martin McQuillan, et al., "The Joy of Theory," *Post-theory: New Directions in Criticism*. Eds. Martin McQuillan, et al. Beijing: Foreign Language Teaching and Research Press, 2018, p.xxvi.
⑤ Gerald Graff and J. R. Di Leo, "Literary Theory and the Teaching of Literature: An Exchange," *Symplokē* 1/2 (2000), p.113.

无论如何,理论热的消退都不是因为它已经被时代证明是错误的。事实上,理论从来就不关心事物的对错问题,它更关心的是那些促使我们做出各种价值判断的背后的观念和假定。在后理论时代,我们需要做的工作不是抛弃理论,而是更好地学习和运用理论,因为它已经深深地植入当今文学研究的血脉中,成为学科体制不可或缺的一部分。而要想学好理论,理论教科书的编写就是非常重要的事情。因为对大部分人来说,他们接触理论的首要途径并不是阅读理论原著,而是阅读各种理论教材。一部好的教材能够让读者顺利进入理论的大门,并从中看到绚丽的风景,产生更多的兴趣和期待;相反,不恰当的教材则会让人们对理论产生误解或感到失望。可以说,理论之所以在后来受到那么多批评,被认为是导致人文研究陷入危机的罪魁祸首,在很大程度上是因为理论教学方式不当。有人把理论当成高深莫测的思想知识,对理论望而却步。更多的人则把理论化简为批评工具,当成改进批评实践的灵丹妙药,认为得其一点便可"化石成金"。这两种讲述理论的方法都是值得商榷的。

通过分析可以看到,理论教科书的编写背后涉及对有关理论的基本认识。理论究竟是什么? 它又有哪些功用? 对这些问题的不同看法决定了编写教材的不同路径。伊格尔顿、卡勒等人把理论视为一种与意识形态密切相关的话语实践,一种对一切文学和文化现象进行关注的反思式批判活动,所以他们的教科书更强调理论的思辨性,认为理论是能够把我们从各种缺乏自觉的错误信念中解放出来的革命性话语。而巴里等人则把理论具体化为文学批评工具,认为理论是能够发挥实际效能的阐释技巧,掌握的技巧越多,就越有可能创新地解读文本。他们虽然让理论成了大部分人易于接受的事物,增加了理论的可操作性,却也为僵化教条的庸俗批评实践创造了可能。

文学理论不同于科学意义上的"理论"。科学理论大多是对实践经验的归纳和总结,其主要目的是服务于实践。文学理论虽然也不能脱离文学批评实践,却并非对实践活动的归纳概括,而是对它的反思,甚至是批判。理论当然也应该对批评实践具有启发和指导作用,但其功能绝非局限于此,它应该有助于提升文学研究活动的自我反思意识。正如威廉·斯潘诺思(William Spanos)所说,仅仅强调理论能够被用来帮助学生掌握阐释技巧还远远不够,这遮蔽了理论真正强大的功能。它可以揭示貌似超然的传统文学研究和制度性工具如何支持和再生了其背后的现实观念结构,因此"理论教学不应该以教授阐释技巧为目的,而应该以激活'批判意识'为目的。把学生以及老师从看不见的霸权话语实践的压迫下解放出来,使其摆脱那些在历史上被处于主导地位的社会秩序建构出来、却被想当然地接受的观念思想"[1]。史蒂文·厄恩肖(Steven Earnshaw)也认为:"从总体上来说,理论的思想前提是,它是一种逻辑练习。"[2]理论可以带给我们新颖的视角和更敏锐的洞察力,但这可能不是因为理论本身有多么大的工具性,而是因为它解放了我们此前的旧知识信念,可以让我们对文本中的诸多问题更加敏感。比如女性主义让我们更敏感地注意到男权结构,生态批评和动物研究让我们反思了人类中心主义,后殖民主义暴露了西方话语霸权等。

---

① William Spanos, "Theory in the Undergraduate English Curriculum: Towards an Interested pedagogy," *boundary 2*, 2/3 (1989), p.46.

② Steven Earnshaw, *The Direction of Literary Theory*. London: Macmillan, 1996, p.110.

第一章
新历史主义

第一节　概　论

　　二战之后，传统的历史批评受到了来自新批评(以及随后的结构主义、解构主义等)的严重冲击；到了20世纪70年代末，这股重形式、轻历史的风气又开始发生转向，源自美国高校的新历史主义登上舞台，其主旨非常明确，就是让文本重新呈现出其应有的历史维度。1982年，哈佛大学教授、莎士比亚研究专家斯蒂芬·格林布拉特(Stephen Greenblatt)在给《文类》(*Genre*)杂志的一期专刊号所写的前言中提出了"新历史主义"(New Historicism)，并在随后通过大量有关文化研究和文艺复兴研究的著述推广相关理念(尽管当时他并未将之视为一种专门的批评方法)；他还参与创办了文学与文化期刊《表征》(*Representations*)，使之成为传播新历史主义思想的重要阵地。通过一众批评家的努力，新历史主义很快便在学术界占得一席之地，并在20世纪80年代至90年代风行一时，影响十分广泛。

　　除格林布拉特之外，同时期的代表人物还有路易斯·A. 蒙特罗斯(Louis A. Montrose)和凯瑟琳·加拉格尔(Catherine Gallagher)——前者是格林布拉特的好友，他提出的"文本的历史性"和"历史的文本性"几乎成为界说新历史主义的标志性语句；后者则始终是新历史主义的倡导者和身体力行者，她与格林布拉特合著的《实践新历史主义》(*Practicing New Historicism*)是21世纪初新历史主义的代表作，该书对此前的各种质疑做出了积极回应。

　　H. 阿拉姆·威瑟(H. Aram Veeser)虽然并没有提出太多原创性的观点和方法，但对新历史主义也贡献良多——由他主编的《新历史主义》(*The New Historicism*)和《新历史主义读本》(*The New Historicism Reader*)颇为难得地汇集了对该"流派"的各种不同论述，其中既有上述新历史主义代表人物的论述，也有历史学家海登·怀特(Hayden White)、马克思主义批评家弗雷德里克·詹姆森(Fredric Jameson)、文化批评家加亚特里·C. 斯皮瓦克(Gayatri C. Spivak)等人的论述。这两本文集采众家之长，甚至允许不同的声音针锋相对，呈现出一幅新历史主义的全景图，尤其是威瑟在导言处提出的新历史主义的5条基本假设，已成为相关研究和批评的重要依据。

　　在其发展历程中，新历史主义受到了马克思主义、新左派、后结构主义、文化人类学等学科和流派的影响。它秉承20世纪50年代思想史研究的精神，将历史重新纳入文学研究的视野，并将其置于中心地位，但这种"回归"绝非对原先的历史主义的重复，而是呈现出质的不同——它既反对形式主义将文本孤悬于历史语境之外的做法，亦不认可旧历史主义视文本为历史产物、对其进行简单的"语境化"（contextualization）处理的方式，而是融通两者的研究方法，使得文学作品（text）与历史语境（context）在同一层面上互相观照，甚至对两者不加区分地一视同仁，将一切社会现象都视为文化现象，进而将一切文化现象都视为文本（此即新历史主义区别于旧历史主义的"新"之所在）。

新历史主义的核心历史观主要受惠于后结构主义，尤其是米歇尔·福柯（Michel Foucault）的思想。例如，新历史主义对所谓"历史真实性"的质疑就来自福柯"一切知识都是权力关系的产物"的观点，这一理念戳破了"客观知识"（其中包括历史知识）的虚假面具——由于史学家在分析历史时，必然受到其所处时空和自身视角的局限，只能选取某个具体角度进行观察，根据有限材料做出个体化的解读，所以绝对客观、完整、可靠的历史研究是断难发生的；而且，权力除了产生知识，还具有产生"现实"的能力，以至于诸多现实可以同时并存，或者说本就没有一个"单一而正确的现实"，存在的仅仅是我们恰好能够体验到的那个版本而已。既然现实是复数的，历史自然也应当是复数和开放的，里面不应只有主流势力的话语，边缘势力的声音和权力形态也是不容忽视的；所谓"统一和谐的文化"，只不过是强加到历史头上的一个神话，是统治阶级为维护自身利益所做的宣传。于是，原本单一、线性的"大历史"（History）被拆解成了许多断断续续、彼此矛盾的个体历史（histories），这些个体历史相互指涉，形成互文。

在新历史主义看来，既然单一的客观事实并不存在，那么我们在历史探索中也就没必要试图去恢复历史原貌、追究事实本身，即"当初发生了什么"（what），而是应当关注所发生的事件究竟是如何被选择、记录和阐释的（how），并进一步思考阐释者所处的心理状态和时代背景，以及相关阐释的接受状况（即它如何影响其他人，以及如何反过来被这些人所影响和塑造）。由于这里明显涉及对历史阐释的再度理解和阐释，所以新历史主义具有一种类似詹姆森提出的"元评论"（meta-commentary）的属性。

事实上，不仅"历史真实性"本身不存在，历史的呈现方式也同样无法做到客观真实，这是因为对历史的讲述同文学叙事之间并无本质差异，两者都包含主观想象与艺术加工的成分——怀特认为，历史学家并不是冷静、沉着地看待事实，而是通过特定的叙事体裁和文学修辞来展现事实，以此创造意义；蒙特罗斯在提出"历史的文本性"时也认定"没有任何知识可以存在于叙事、书写和话语的国度之外"[1]，意即作为文本的历史有着与生俱来的文学叙事属性。既然历史是一种叙事，那么叙事者在讲述过程中必然会带有个人的种种偏见、曲解，甚至杜撰，这就使得历史记述具有相当的虚构性（fictionality）。以上观念瓦解了历史话语的客观性基础，也彻底拆除了历史话语与文学话语之间的传统藩篱。

一、批评思路与方法

新历史主义（在纵向上）将过去和当下有机串联，（在横向上）将文本和语境充分融合，有效拓展了文学批评的思路和格局——由于将作品和产生/接受作品的语境视若等同，新历史主义模糊了内容与形式、文学与非文学、文本与历史之间的疆界，将一切都归为广义的文本，因而极大地扩展了研究对象的范围，使得各种资料和事件统统进入批评家的视野。这其中当然也包括历史——历史不再是某个文本赖以依托的稳定背景，历史本身即是文本，是关于过去的故事，并且同其他的各种文本形成互文关系。于

---

[1] John Brannigan, "History, Power and Politics in the Literary Artifact: New Historicism," *Introducing Literary Theories: A Guide and Glossary*. Ed. Julian Wolfreys. Edinburgh: Edinburgh University Press, 2006, p.170.

是，我们在批评实践中便可以合法地将"语境"作为一种特殊的文本进行阐释(同时关注阐释者在其中扮演的角色)，同时"以史为鉴"，反思现实的问题(即关注过去在当今的意义，而不是仅关注孤立的过去本身)，以此来联通过去与当下、融合文化与社会。这无疑有利于寻觅历史的空白点、挖掘出原先隐秘的矛盾(尤其是意识形态信息和权力运作的痕迹)，或是得到不同于以往的结论，从而丰富我们对作品及其政治条件与文化气候的理解。无怪乎霍米·K.巴巴(Homi K. Bhabha)指出："格林布拉特不仅仅建立了一个批评流派，还为文学批评创造了一种思维习惯。"[1]

如上所述，新历史主义关注的核心问题始终是历史与文本的关系，它消解了两者之间传统意义上的对立，使其互为参照、彼此揭示，从而为文学和文化批评提供了不同于以往的视角和切入点。[1] 既然历史是一种文本，我们不妨采用文学批评的方法来阐释历史资料，尤其是尝试把原先受到压制的那一部分语焉不详的历史叙事(比如边缘群体和琐细事件)挖掘出来，彰显其意义所在。这一点跟马克思主义(对受压迫阶级的关注)和巴赫金的对话主义有相通之处。[2] 反过来，文学也被"消解"到了历史的复合体之中，我们可以透过历史的视角来重新审视文学作品和文学事件，即把文学文本视为一种特殊的历史话语，对其进行上下文关联的考古式处理，分析它与其他历史话语(包括作品反映的历史话语、作品产生以及接受过程中蕴含的历史话语)之间的相互影响，及其同当下之间的对应关系，揭示出其中的权力结构。鉴于这种双向的靠拢与融合，新历史主义可以说是一种将历史带入文学，又将文学进行历史化处理的批评方式。

比如说，伊丽莎白·福克斯-吉诺维斯(Elizabeth Fox-Genovese)在《文学批评与新历史主义政治》("Literary Criticism and the Politics of the New Historicism")一文中就指出，要想真正把握美国内战爆发之前的文学史与文化史，批评家应当广泛阅读当时的各种文本，这其中既包括北方作家的作品，也应当包括逃跑的黑奴的作品，甚至南方亲奴隶制的作家的作品(后者往往是被相对忽略的)，因为他们都同属一个彼此交织的世界；而且，只是阅读作品本身还不够，我们还应当格外关注将这些不同的文本维系在一起的纽带。[2]

由此可见，就研究对象和方法而言，由于新历史主义并不像传统的历史批评那样，去考察文本如何"反映"其背后的作者意图或者时代精神，而是集中关注文本与语境之间的紧密互动，所以研究者常常将文学文本与同时期的其他文本(如日记、回忆录、街谈巷语、档案资料、新闻报道、商品广告等)有机结合起来，挖掘彼此的互文关系，以丰富我们对人类体验的认识。这种做法承袭了文化人类学家克利福德·格尔茨(Clifford Geertz)提出的"厚描法"(thick description)，厚描法将人类行为本身连同"行为背景"一同作为描述和解释的对象。就研究范围而言，新历史主义批评呈现出两个明显的"延伸"——纵向来看，其肇始于对文艺复兴(特别是莎士比亚)的研究，但在随后延伸到了其他国家和历史时期(特别是英国浪漫主义和维多利亚时期，以及美国现实主义时期)；横向来看，其研究对象从文学文本延伸到几乎一切文本(甚至包括一切文化现象和人类活动)。

基于以上原因，新历史主义批评呈现出相当程度的跨学科性，除了显而易见的文学和艺术史之外，它还涉及政治、经济、人类学、符号学等多个领域。例如，大量来自经济学和市场的语汇，如"资本"

---

① Homi K. Bhabha，"Praise for *The Greenblatt Reader*," *The Greenblatt Reader*. Ed. Michael Payne. Malden：Blackwell，2005.

② Elizabeth Fox-Genovese，"Literary Criticism and the Politics of the New Historicism," *The New Historicism*. Ed. H. Aram Veeser. New York：Routledge，1989，p.221.

(capital)、"交易"(exchange)、"流通"(circulation)、"协商"(negotiation)等,频繁出现在新历史主义批评中,这些隐喻性的表达,形象地展现出各种文化权力和象征性资本、各种无形的社会有利条件(有如货币一般)在其流通过程中的行迹和作用,我们借此便可以直观地体会到个人地位和声誉如何相当于他所持有的某种社会资产、艺术如何给当事人带来最大化的象征性收益等。

需要指出的是,不管面对的是何种文本,采用的是哪些学科概念,新历史主义强调的是对话语实践进行意识形态解读;而且,批评家应当清醒地意识到自己在思想立场和文化体验上的局限,并坦承这一局限所造成的偏见,以尽量减少对读者潜在的误导。

二、存在的问题与未来走向

凡事皆有两面:新历史主义的上述包容性导致其难免有些杂糅,缺乏一定的系统性——它虽然名义上是一种"理论",实则并没有非常统一的理论架构和方法论,而是高度倚赖具体的批评实践以及批评家个人的性情旨趣和思维方式,所以我们可以看到,同属新历史主义批评的学者,其思路和结论居然可以大异其趣甚至相互冲突,以至于它成了一个缺乏统一战线、"没有确切指涉的措辞"。[1] 格林布拉特和加拉格尔对此亦不避讳,两人在合著的《实践新历史主义》一书中对新历史主义遭受的各种质疑进行了回应,坦承了自身的定位,即新历史主义本就是一种富于热情的学术实践,它不受抽象理论的桎梏,亦无意追求连贯一致,从而撇清了不该承担的理论责任。[2]

除了缺乏统一的理论框架之外,新历史主义受到的学界质疑主要还包括:① 它否认历史的宏大叙事,执迷于对一些边角文本和逸闻的解读,因此缺乏专业史学的科学性和严谨性;② 过度专注文本的意识形态属性和是否"政治正确",以至忽略了文学原有的艺术性,甚至使文学沦为历史的脚注;③ 它在否认客观知识和普遍价值的同时,容易罔顾事实,陷入似是而非的相对主义(甚至历史修正主义和虚无主义)误区。就连其颇为得意的"厚描法",也被人批评是在屏蔽外部世界。这些批评质疑未必都正确,但我们从中可以看到,新历史主义最初的创新与价值所在,其实正是其最易受诟病之处——它用共时性的文化文本取代了原本历时性的历史文本(即把时间空间化),虽力图顾及方方面面,却难免出现宽泛化和浅表化的趋向。

事实上,新历史主义在问世之后经历了一个"出奇守正"的发展轨迹——它在初始阶段并不自认为是一个专门领域,但多数实践者以代言边缘群体和受压制声音、充满颠覆精神而自居,被一些保守学者指控为"萦绕于人文学科头上的新历史主义幽灵"[3];然而随着声誉日隆,它却一步步跻身正统,成为设定规则、供人效仿的"流派",这就难免破坏了自己当初的"出师之名",甚至无可避免地陷入它所批判的范式当中,这也是相当一部分新历史主义者对其"流派"或"运动"的存在予以自我否认的原因之一,尤其是格林布拉特,他始终不情愿被贴上新历史主义的标签,而更愿将新历史主义称为"文化诗学"(Cultural Poetics)。近 20 年来,新历史主义已呈式微之势,但其精神主旨依然体现在各种批评实践(如女性主义、性别研究、族裔研究、后殖民主义、读者反应批评等)中。

---

① H. Aram Veeser, "Introduction," *The New Historicism*. Ed. H. Aram Veeser. New York: Routledge, 1989, p.x.
② Catherine Gallagher and Stephen Greenblatt, *Practicing New Historicism*. Chicago: The University of Chicago Press, 2000, pp.1–19.
③ Edward Pechter, "The New Historicism and Its Discontents: Politicizing Renaissance Drama," *PLMA* 102 (1987), p.292.

需要指出的是,新历史主义在理论导向和操作方式上跟大致同时期兴起于英国的文化唯物主义(cultural materialism)极为相近,后者由英国左翼批评家雷蒙·威廉斯(Raymond Williams)提出,该方法基于法兰克福学派的批判传统,结合了马克思主义分析与左翼文化研究的特征,力图通过对历史材料的分析,重现某一特定历史时刻的时代精神。同新历史主义一样,文化唯物主义格外强调历史语境与文本分析,重视其中的意识形态和权力关系,而且在这些方面比新历史主义有过之而无不及——它比新历史主义具有更加鲜明的当下性和政治性,更倾向于批判社会现状、关注边缘势力,并呼吁对现状的改变,无怪乎文化唯物主义的另一创始人格雷厄姆·霍尔德内斯(Graham Holderness)干脆将其界定为一种政治化的史学形态。除威廉斯和霍尔德内斯之外,乔纳森·多利莫尔(Jonathan Dollimore)和艾伦·辛菲尔德(Alan Sinfield)也是该领域的代表人物,两人合编的论文集《政治的莎士比亚:文化唯物主义论》(*Political Shakespeare: Essays in Cultural Materialism*)几乎成为文化唯物主义的纲领性文件。

未来的新历史主义将向何处去,我们很难确知——威瑟在《新历史主义读本》的导言结尾处曾抛出这样的问题:"新历史主义到底是历史,还是文学?是垃圾,还是宝藏?也许回答这些问题还为时尚早。"[①]将近 30 年过去了,文学理论界在这段时间里经历了巨大变化,对于威瑟当初的发问,我们似乎依然无法给出确切回答,但新历史主义的思维方式和批评精神将长期具有启示意义,指引我们更为透彻地看待文学和文化,以及我们身处其中的这个世界。

第二节 经典文献选读

本章共有两篇选文。第一篇节选自蒙特罗斯的《声言文艺复兴:文化的诗学与政治》("Professing the Renaissance: The Poetics and Politics of Culture")一文。尽管格林布拉特被广泛视为新历史主义的开创者,但在介绍新历史主义主旨的代表作中,蒙特罗斯的这篇文章似乎更像是一篇开宗明义的新历史主义提纲。作者在文中清晰地阐述了语言形式与社会/历史之间的有机关系,进而梳理了新历史主义的发展脉络和主要特征,纠正了其中一些常见的误解,作者对"文本的历史性"和"历史的文本性"的解释尤其重要,该文章堪称把握新历史主义精神的必读文献。第二篇选自罗伊丝·泰森(Lois Tyson)所著的《当代批评理论实用指南》(*Critical Theory Today: A User-Friendly Guide*),系作者为该书第九章"新历史主义与文化批评"所提供的案例分析,文章结合盛行于现代美国的"白手起家者"神话,对文学名著《了不起的盖茨比》进行了新历史主义解读,其分析通俗易懂,展示出非凡的文本阐释力。

一、《声言文艺复兴:文化的诗学与政治》选读[②]

There has recently emerged within Renaissance studies, as in Anglo-American literary studies

① H. Aram Veeser, ed., *The New Historicism Reader*. New York: Routledge, 1994, p.28.
② Louis A. Montrose, "Professing the Renaissance: The Poetics and Politics of Culture," *The New Historicism*. Ed. H. Aram Veeser. New York: Routledge, 1989, pp.15-36.

generally, a renewed concern with the historical, social, and political conditions and consequences of literary production and reproduction: The writing and reading of texts, as well as the processes by which they are circulated and categorized, analyzed and taught, are being reconstrued as historically determined and determining modes of cultural work; apparently autonomous aesthetic and academic issues are being reunderstood as inextricably though complexly linked to other discourses and practices—such linkages constituting the social networks within which individual subjectivities and collective structures are mutually and continuously shaped. This general reorientation is the unhappy subject of J. Hillis Miller's 1986 Presidential Address to the Modern Language Association. In that address, Miller noted with some dismay—and with some hyperbole— that "literary study in the past few years has undergone a sudden, almost universal turn away from theory in the sense of an orientation toward language as such and has made a corresponding turn toward history, culture, society, politics, institutions, class and gender conditions, the social context, the material base". By such a formulation, Miller polarizes the linguistic and the social. However, the prevailing tendency across cultural studies is to emphasize their reciprocity and mutual constitution: On the one hand, the social is understood to be discursively constructed; and on the other, language-use is understood to be always and necessarily dialogical, to be socially and materially determined and constrained.

Miller's categorical opposition of "reading" to cultural critique, of "theory" to the discourses of "history, culture, society, politics, institutions, class and gender" seems to me not only to oversimplify both sets of terms but also to suppress their points of contact and compatibility. The propositions and operations of deconstructive reading may be employed as powerful tools of ideological analysis. Derrida himself has recently suggested that, at least in his own work and in the context of European cultural politics, they have always been so: He writes that "deconstructive readings and writings are concerned not only with...discourses, with conceptual and semantic contents...Deconstructive practices are also and first of all political and institutional practices". The notorious Derridean aphorism, "*il n'ya pas de hors-text*", may be invoked to abet an escape from the determinate necessities of history, a self-abandonment to the indeterminate pleasures of the text; however, it may also be construed as an insistence upon the ideological force of discourse in general and of those discourses in particular which reduce the work of discourse to the mere reflection of an ontologically prior, essential or empirical reality.

[…]

A couple of years ago, I attempted briefly to articulate and scrutinize some of the theoretical, methodological and political assumptions and implications of the kind of work produced since the late 1970s by those (including myself) who were then coming to be labelled as "New Historicists". The focus of such work has been upon a refiguring of the socio-cultural field within which canonical Renaissance literary and dramatic works were originally produced; upon resituating them not only in relationship to other genres and modes of discourse but also in relationship to contemporaneous social institutions and non-discursive practices. Stephen Greenblatt, who is most closely identified with the label "New Historicism" in Renaissance literary studies, has himself now abandoned it in favor of "Cultural Poetics", a term he had used earlier and one which perhaps more accurately represents the critical project I have described. In effect, this project reorients the axis of inter-textuality, substituting for the diachronic text of an autonomous literary history the synchronic text of a cultural system. As the conjunction of terms in its title suggests, the interests and analytical techniques of "Cultural Poetics" are at once historicist and formalist; implicit in its project, though perhaps not yet adequately articulated or theorized, is a conviction that formal and historical concerns are not opposed but rather are inseparable.

Until very recently—and perhaps even now—the dominant mode of interpretation in English Renaissance literary studies has been to combine formalist techniques of close rhetorical analysis with the elaboration of relatively self-contained histories of "ideas", or of literary genres and topoi—histories that have been abstracted from their social matrices. In addition to such literary histories, we may note two other traditional practices of "history" in Renaissance literary studies: one comprises those commentaries on political commonplaces in which the dominant ideology of Tudor-Stuart society—the unreliable machinery of socio-political legitimation—is misrecognized as a stable, coherent, and collective Elizabethan world picture, a picture discovered to be lucidly reproduced in the canonical literary works of the age; and the other, the erudite but sometimes eccentric scholarly detective work which, by treating texts as elaborate ciphers, seeks to fix the meaning of fictional characters and actions in their reference to specific historical persons and events. Though sometimes reproducing the methodological shortcomings of such older idealist and empiricist modes of historical criticism, but also often appropriating their prodigious scholarly labors to good effect, the newer historical criticism is *new* in its refusal of unproblematized distinctions between "literature" and "history", between "text" and "context"; new in resisting a prevalent tendency to posit and privilege a unified and autonomous individual—whether an Author or a Work—to be set against a social or literary background.

In the essay of mine to which I have already referred, I wrote merely of a new historical *orientation* in Renaissance literary studies, because it seemed to me that those identified with it by themselves or by others were actually quite heterogeneous in their critical practices and, for the most pan, reluctant to theorize those practices. The very lack of such explicit articulations was itself symptomatic of certain eclectic and empiricist tendencies that threatened to undermine any attempt to distinguish a new historicism from an old one. It may well be that these very ambiguities rendered New Historicism less a critique of dominant critical ideology than a subject for ideological appropriation, thus contributing to its almost sudden installation as the newest academic orthodoxy, to its rapid assimilation by the "interpretive community" of Renaissance literary studies. Certainly, some who have been identified as exemplary New Historicists now enjoy the material and symbolic tokens of academic success; and any number of New Historicist dissertations, conferences, and publications testify to a significant degree of disciplinary influence and prestige. However, it remains unclear whether or not this latest "ism", with its appeal to our commodifying cult of the "new", will have been more than another passing intellectual fancy in what Fredric Jameson would call the academic marketplace under late capitalism. "The New Historicism" has not yet begun to fade from the academic scene, nor is it quietly taking its place in the assortment of critical approaches on the interpreter's shelf. But neither has it become any clearer that "The New Historicism" designates any agreed upon intellectual and institutional program. There has been no coalescence of the various identifiably New Historicist practices into a systematic and authoritative paradigm for the interpretation of Renaissance texts; nor does the emergence of such a paradigm seem either likely or desirable. What we are currently witnessing is the convergence of a variety of special interests upon "New Historicism", now constituted as a terminological site of intense debate and critique, of multiple appropriations and contestations within the ideological field of Renaissance studies itself, and to some extent in other areas of the discipline.

If Edward Pechter dubiously assimilates New Historicism to Marxism on the grounds that it insists upon the omnipresence of struggle as the motor of history, some self-identified Marxist critics are actively indicting New Historicism for its evasion of both political commitment and diachronic analysis—in effect, for its failure to be genuinely *historical*; while some female and male Renaissance scholars are fruitfully combining New Historicist and Feminist concerns, others are representing these projects (and/or their practitioners) as deeply antagonistic in gender-specific terms; while some see New Historicism as one of several modes of socio-criticism engaged in constructing a theoretically informed, post-structuralist problematic of historical study, others see it as aligned with a neo-pragmatist reaction against all forms of High Theory; if some see New Historicist preoccupations with ideology and social context as threatening to traditional critical concerns and literary values, others see a New Historicist delight in anecdote, narrative and what Clifford Geertz calls "thick description" as a will to construe *all* of culture as the domain of literary criticism—a text to be perpetually interpreted, an inexhaustible collection of stories from which curiosities may be culled and cleverly retold.

Inhabiting the discursive spaces traversed by the term "New Historicism" are some of the most complex, persistent, and unsettling of the problems that professors of literature attempt variously to confront or to evade: Among them, the essential or historical bases upon which "literature" is to be distinguished from other discourses; the possible configurations of relationship between cultural practices and social, political and economic processes; the consequences of post-structuralist theories of textuality for the practice of an historical or materialist criticism; the means by which subjectivity is socially constituted and constrained; the processes by which ideologies are produced and sustained, and by which they may be contested; the patterns of consonance and contradiction among the values and interests of a given individual, as these are actualized in the shifting conjunctures of various subject positions—as, for example, intellectual worker, academic professional, and gendered domestic, social, political and economic agent. My point is not that "The New Historicism" as a definable project, or the work of specific individuals identified by themselves or by others as New Historicists, can necessarily provide even provisional answers to such questions, but rather that the term "New Historicism" is currently being invoked in order to bring such issues into play and to stake out—or to hunt down—specific positions within the discursive spaces mapped by these issues.

The post-structuralist orientation to history now emerging in literary studies may be characterized chiastically, as a reciprocal concern with the historicity of texts and the textuality of history. By *the historicity of texts*, I mean to suggest the cultural specificity, the social embedment, of all modes of writing—not only the texts that critics study but also the texts in which we study them. By *the textuality of history*, I mean to suggest, firstly, that we can have no access to a full and authentic past, a lived material existence, unmediated by the surviving textual traces of the society in question—traces whose survival we cannot assume to be merely contingent but must rather presume to be at least partially consequent upon complex and subtle social processes of preservation and effacement; and secondly, that those textual traces are themselves subject to subsequent textual mediations when they are construed as the "documents" upon which historians ground their own texts, called "histories". As Hayden White has forcefully reminded us, such textual histories necessarily but always incompletely constitute in their narrative and rhetorical forms the "History" to which they offer access.

In *After the New Criticism*, Frank Lentricchia links "the antihistorical impulses of formalist theories of literary criticism" with monolithic and teleological theories of "history". I assume that among the latter belongs not only the great code of Christian figural and eschatological history but also the classical Marxian master-narrative that Fredric Jameson characterizes as "history now conceived in its vastest sense of the sequence of modes of production and the succession and destiny of the various human social formations"; and which he projects as the "untranscendable horizon" of interpretive activity, subsuming "apparently antagonistic or incommensurable critical operations, assigning them an undoubted sectoral validity within itself, and thus at once cancelling and preserving them". Against an unholy alliance of unhistoricized formalisms and totalized History, Lentricchia opposes the multiplicity of "histories", history as characterized by "forces of heterogeneity, contradiction, fragmentation, and difference". It seems to me that the various modes of what could be called post-structuralist historical criticism (including modes of revisionist or "post" Marxism, as well as "New Historicism" or "Cultural Poetics") can be characterized by such a shift from History to histories.

二、《当代批评理论实用指南》选读①

The Discourse of the Self-made Man:
A New Historical Reading of *The Great Gatsby*

F. Scott Fitzgerald's *The Great Gatsby* (1925) was published during one of America's greatest periods of economic growth. As the nation expanded its borders and developed its industries between the end of the Civil War in 1865 and the stock-market crash in 1929, many private fortunes were made. Everyone in America knew the success stories of millionaires like John D. Rockefeller, Jay Gould, Jim Fisk, Andrew Carnegie, J. P. Morgan, Philip Armour, and James J. Hill. Even Gatsby's father, an uneducated and unsuccessful farmer, is aware of these stories. He says of his son, "If he'd of lived he'd of been a great man. A man like James J. Hill. He'd of helped build up the country." With the exception of J. P. Morgan, the son of a wealthy banker, all of these millionaires were self-made men: from very humble beginnings they rose to their position at the top of the financial world. And popular belief held that any poor boy in America with the right personal qualities could do the same.

Thus, a dominant discourse of the period was the discourse of the self-made man, which circulated in the "success manuals" of the period; in the self-improvement speeches and essays composed by the self-made millionaires of that era; in the Horatio Alger novels; in the McGuffey Readers, which were used throughout the nation to teach young children to read; and in the biographies of famous self-made men. Fitzgerald's novel participates in the circulation of this discourse, I think, in at least two significant ways. It reflects the major tenets of the discourse and, I would argue, it embodies one of its central contradictions: the discourse of the self-made man, while it claims to open the annals of American history to all those who have the ambition and perseverance required to "make their mark", is permeated by the desire to "escape" history and to transcend the historical realities of time, place, and human limitation.

Let's begin by examining the ways in which *The Great Gatsby* reflects the major tenets of the discourse of the self-made man. Of course, readers frequently notice the similarities between Gatsby's boyhood "schedule"—in which the young man divided his day among physical exercise, the study of electricity, work, sports, the practice of elocution and poise, and the study of needed inventions—and the self-improvement ideology found in the autobiography of Benjamin Franklin, America's original self-made man. Obviously, Gatsby hoped, indeed planned, to live the "rags-to-riches" life associated with the self-made millionaires of his day. However, the characterization of Gatsby draws on the self-improvement tradition more thoroughly than some readers today may realize.

---

① Lois Tyson, *Critical Theory Today: A User-Friendly Guide*. New York: Routledge, 2006, pp.301 - 311.

[...]

Clearly, *The Great Gatsby* reflects the discourse of the self-made man circulating in so many of the texts that both shaped and were shaped by American culture during the final decades of the nineteenth century and the early decades of the twentieth. For ideology does not observe boundaries between "high" and "popular" culture: a discourse circulating in such practical and mundane texts as success manuals, children's readers, and didactic formula-novels can also saturate the pages of one of the era's most sophisticated artistic productions.

However, the novel also serves as a comment on the discourse of the self-made man to the extent that it reveals one of its central contradictions, which concerns the relationship of that discourse to history. Although the discourse of the self-made man claims to open the annals of American history to all those who have the ambition and perseverance required to "make their mark" on its pages, the discourse is permeated by the desire to escape history, to transcend the historical realities of time, place, and human limitation.

This contradiction appears in many of the autobiographical stories of the self-made millionaires mentioned above. Although self-made men often spoke of the harsh historical realities they experienced as children, particularly of their poverty, they did so only to celebrate how far they had come. And the form that celebration took, I would argue, constitutes a denial of historical reality because it was a way of reinventing the suffering self-made men saw in their youth as nothing but a prelude to their success. Looking back on their lives, they saw their boyhood selves as "future millionaires in training", so to speak, being honed in the workshop of "hard knocks" and fired in the kiln of poverty. Such an ideology didn't permit them to see the debilitating effects of the poverty they escaped on those who didn't manage to do the same.

Among the general population of America's impoverished, relatively few, in any generation, have become millionaires. According to the discourse of the self-made man, those who didn't rise to the top had only themselves to blame, which implies, of course, that poverty and the degrading influence of tenement life (not to mention the almost insurmountable obstacles raised against business opportunities for women and people of color) are no excuse for the failure to rise in the business world. Such failure was defined as a failure of one's character, pure and simple. This is why many self-made millionaires refused to give money to charity, confining their philanthropy to endowing libraries, museums, and universities, which could, they reasoned, help only those who were willing to help themselves and not encourage the slothful behavior that charity would, they believed, encourage.

For example, in his autobiography, Andrew Carnegie describes the happy family life he enjoyed as a child of poor immigrant parents. He notes, in addition to his family's economic hardship, how politically active his relatives were, how education was valued by his parents, and how he was trained by his home environment to engage in rigorous debate on the issues of the day. Indeed, Carnegie observes that the economic poverty he suffered in childhood was richly compensated by the training and support he received in the bosom of a strong family. Yet he was apparently unable to realize that many other poor youngsters in his own neighborhood—for example, the sons of parents who did not understand the value of education or the sons of drunken, abusive parents—did not have the same advantages he had and therefore could not be expected to raise themselves up as readily as he did. That is, in Carnegie's desire to focus on his own transcendence of historical reality, he ignores those aspects of history that cannot be overcome so readily.

The Great Gatsby reflects this same desire to transcend history in Gatsby's efforts to deny his true origins. Gatsby's "parents were shiftless and unsuccessful farm people", but "his imagination had never really accepted them as his parents at all". Instead, Gatsby invented a family, an Oxford education, and an inheritance in order to convince himself and others that he was born to wealth and social position. That is, Gatsby wants to deny the historical realities of socioeconomic class to which he had been subjected all his life. As Nick puts it, "Jay Gatsby...sprang from his Platonic conception of himself." A Platonic conception is one that, by definition, is outside history: it exists in a timeless dimension untouched by daily occurrences in the material world. And this is the dimension in which Gatsby wants to live.

Gatsby's claim that Daisy's love for Tom "was just personal", a statement that confuses Nick as well as many readers, makes sense in this context. In Gatsby's eyes, Daisy's love for Tom exists within history, within the domain of the personal, and is thus no competition for the love she and Gatsby share, which exists in a timeless dimension beyond history. Similarly, Gatsby's belief in our power over the past makes sense only if he conceives of his own life outside the bounds of historical reality. His conviction that the three years Daisy has spent married to Tom can be "obliterated" by her telling Tom that she never loved him, and that they can "repeat the past" by "go[ing] back to Louisville and be[ing] married from her house—just as if it were five years ago" is a conviction one can hold only from a place outside history, a place where the past is repeatable because it is timelessly preserved, forever accessible.

The discourse of the self-made man also "erases history" in choosing to ignore or marginalize the enormous character flaws of many famous self-made men while simultaneously defining self-made success as a product of one's character rather than of one's environment. The success manuals from this period offered very little, if any, practical advice about business matters. All of their advice focused, instead, on attributes of character—from honesty and integrity in the workplace to frugality and sobriety in the home—because it was believed that success comes from within the man. Therefore, character, rather than education or business acumen, was considered the foundation of the self-made man. Yet some of the moral failings of self-made millionaires were the very factors that enabled them to rise to the top by enabling them to ruthlessly and often unethically destroy their business rivals. Of course, this aspect of historical reality was absent from the proliferation of texts that extolled the virtues of the self-made man, or it was recast, in the popular imagination, as a capitalist virtue: competitiveness, aggressiveness, toughness.

It is interesting to note in this context that since the publication of *The Great Gatsby*, the majority of critical response to the novel's title character has romanticized him much as American culture has romanticized the self-made man, by idealizing his desire to succeed and ignoring or marginalizing the means by which he fulfilled that desire. What an early reviewer said of Gatsby in 1925 has continued to represent the feeling of a good many readers over the course of the novel's reception: Gatsby's "is a vitality...the inner fire [of] which comes from living with an incorruptible dream, even if extraordinary material corruption has been practised in its realization". In 1945, William Troy describes Gatsby as the "projected wish fulfillment" of the "consciousness of a race". And Tom Burnam argues in 1952 that Gatsby "survives sound and whole in character, uncorrupted by the corruption which surrounded him". In 1954, Marius Bewley writes that Gatsby is "all aspiration and goodness": "an heroic personification of the American romantic hero", who represents "the energy of the spirit's resistance" and "immunity to the final contamination" of "cheapness and vulgarity". And Barry Edward Gross suggests in 1963 that "Gatsby's dream is essentially 'incorruptible'" because it "is essentially immaterial", which is why "he turns 'out all right at the end'". Similarly, in 1978 Rose Adrienne Gallo argues that Gatsby "maintained his innocence" to the end, or as André Le Vot puts it in 1983, Gatsby never loses his "fundamental integrity, his spiritual intactness". Even when the protagonist's darker side is acknowledged, it is excused. As Kent Cartwright argues in 1984, "Gatsby can be both criminal and romantic hero because the book creates for him a visionary moral standard that transcends the conventional and that his life affirms". Or as Andrew Dillon sums up, in 1988, what he sees as the protagonist's merger of worldliness and spirituality, Gatsby is "a sensual saint".

Finally, the connection between the discourse of the self-made man and the desire to transcend history can be seen in the McGuffey Readers. In the self-improvement discourse that informs the bulk of the material in the Readers there is a striking absence of reference to historical reality. Even during the period directly after the Civil War, when poems and songs about the war abounded, the only "historical" piece included isn't historical at all: it's a sentimental poem called "The Blue and the Gray" (1867) in which soldiers from both sides are glorified in terms such that they could be soldiers from almost any war fought during almost any historical period. In other words, the poem creates a timeless world that remains untouched by historical events.

[...]

There is a striking similarity between the overblown sentimentality of the McGuffey Readers and the "appalling sentimentality" of the autobiographical narrative Gatsby offers Nick, a sentimentality that removes Gatsby's life, just as it removed the McGuffey Readers, from the realities of history. Gatsby tells Nick,

> My family all died and I came into a good deal of money…After that I lived like a young rajah in all the capitals of Europe…collecting jewels, chiefly rubies, hunting big game, painting a little…and trying to forget something very sad that had happened to me long ago.

Gatsby's autobiographical sketch sounds more like an outline for a staged Victorian melodrama than a narrative about an actual life. As Nick puts it, "The very phrases were worn so threadbare that they evoked no image except that of a turbaned 'character' leaking sawdust at every pore." But it is this sentimental "translation" of his life—which he offers, Nick says, in a "solemn" voice, "as if the memory…still haunted him"—that allows Gatsby to escape historical reality into a "larger-than-life" fairy tale.

[…]

Clearly, *The Great Gatsby*'s embodiment of the complexities and contradictions of the discourse of the self-made man reveals the complexities and contradictions that informed the attitude of Fitzgerald's America toward the achievement of financial success. Without the discourse of the self-made man, Fitzgerald's best-known novel would not be possible. For the character of Jay Gatsby would simply be the "cheap sharper"—just another criminal—he fears people will see in him. It is this discourse, as much as his devotion to Daisy and his boyish optimism, that makes it possible for Gatsby to remain the romantic figure he is today.

Fitzgerald's novel also shows us how the circulation of discourses has very personal implications for all of us. For it illustrates the ways in which cultural discourses are the raw materials from which we fashion our individual identities. Nick Carraway may think that Gatsby "sprang from his Platonic" ahistorical "conception of himself", a belief Gatsby clearly shares, but Gatsby's personal identity did not so originate. As we have seen, James Gatz's creation of Jay Gatsby drew heavily on the discourse of the self-made man, one of the dominant discourses circulating in the culture in which he lived. And like Jay Gatsby, all of us do the same. We each may draw on different discourses, and we each may draw on them in different ways, but it is through the discourses circulating in our culture that our individual identities are formed, are linked to one another, and are linked to the culture that both shapes and is shaped by each of us.

三、思考与讨论

1. 新历史主义首先兴起于 20 世纪 80 年代初的美国高校,除了当时重形式、轻历史的学术风气正在发生改变之外,是否还有其他的外部因素起作用?

2. 为什么霍米·巴巴认为格林布拉特的新历史主义"不仅仅建立了一个批评流派,还为文学批评创造了一种思维习惯"？这样一种"思维习惯"是否也适用于文学批评以外的其他研究领域(如对社会、文化、艺术的批评)？

3. 针对新历史主义的各种弊端(如缺乏专业史学的科学性和严谨性,过分关注意识形态,忽略文学原有的艺术性,容易陷入似是而非的相对主义等),我们在运用这一方法进行文学批评时,应当注意什么问题？

4. 新历史主义与文化唯物主义的肇始都跟莎士比亚研究紧密相关,为什么会出现这样一种"巧合"？同样是对莎剧(及其背后的历史语境)进行考察和分析,两者有什么异同之处？

本章推荐阅读文献

［1］Brook Thomas. *The New Historicism*. Princeton：Princeton University Press，1991.

［2］Catherine Gallagher and Stephen Greenblatt. *Practicing New Historicism*. Chicago：The University of Chicago Press，2000.

［3］Frank Kermode. *Pieces of My Mind: Essays and Criticism 1957-2002*. New York：Farrar，Straus and Giroux，2003.

［4］Gina Hens-Piazza（ed.）. *The New Historicism*（*Guides to Biblical Scholarship Old Testament*）. Minneapolis：Fortress Press，2002.

［5］H. Aram Veeser（ed.）. *The New Historicism*. New York：Routledge，1989.

［6］H. Aram Veeser（ed.）. *The New Historicism Reader*. New York：Routledge，1994.

［7］Jeffrey N. Cox and Larry J. Reynolds（eds.）. *New Historical Literary Study: Essays on Reproducing Texts*，*Representing History*. Princeton：Princeton University Press，1993.

［8］John Brannigan. *New Historicism and Cultural Materialism*. New York：St. Martin's Press，1998.

［9］Jonathan Dollimore and Alan Sinfield. *Political Shakespeare: Essays in Cultural Materialism*（2nd edition）. Manchester：Manchester University Press，1994.

［10］Jürgen Pieters. *Moments of Negotiation: The New Historicism of Stephen Greenblatt*. Amsterdam：Amsterdam University Press，2001.

［11］Louis Adrian Montrose. "'The Place of a Brother' in *As You Like It*：Social Process and Comic Form," *Shakespeare Quarterly* 32.1（1981），pp.28-54.

［12］Neema Parvini. *Shakespeare and Contemporary Theory: New Historicism and Cultural Materialism*. New York：Bloomsbury，2012.

［13］Neema Parvini. *Shakespeare and New Historicist Theory*. New York：Bloomsbury，2017.

［14］Neema Parvini. *Shakespeare's History Plays: Rethinking Historicism*. Edinburgh：Edinburgh University Press，2012.

［15］Philippa Kelly. *The Touch of the Real: Essays in Early Modern Culture in Honour of Stephen Greenblatt*. Crawley：University of Western Australia Press，2002.

［16］Stephen Greenblatt. *Hamlet in Purgatory*. Princeton：Princeton University Press，2001.

［17］Stephen Greenblatt. *Renaissance Self-Fashioning: From More to Shakespeare*. Chicago：The University of Chicago Press，1980.

［18］Stephen Greenblatt. *Shakespearean Negotiations: The Circulation of Social Energy in Renaissance England*. Berkeley：University of California Press，1988.

［19］Stephen Greenblatt. *Shakespeare's Freedom*. Chicago：The University of Chicago Press，2010.

［20］Stephen Greenblatt. *Will in the World: How Shakespeare Became Shakespeare*. New York：W. W. Norton & Company，2004.

［21］Tamsin Spargo（ed.）. *Reading the Past: Literature and History*. New York：Palgrave，2000.

第二章
后殖民主义

第一节 概 论

作为西方当代文学文化批评思潮之一,后殖民主义自 20 世纪 80 年代兴起,随后渐成体制化的显学。后殖民主义具有显著的跨学科特点,其影响遍及哲学、经济学、政治学、人类学、历史学等众多领域。如果没有学科跨界,后殖民主义仍将局限在文学文化领域,其在两种情况下的影响力不可同日而语。[①]

后殖民主义思潮的源头常被追溯到爱德华·W. 萨义德(Edward W. Said)的《东方学》(*Orientalism*)。[②] 后殖民主义作为理论话语在 20 世纪八九十年代英美学界的兴起,得益于英国漫长的殖民史及其强大的国家体系。欧洲的海外殖民扩张伴随着领土占有、政治宰制和经济剥削,而被殖民地区对殖民主义的抵抗也从未止息。20 世纪五六十年代,亚非拉三大洲的殖民地纷纷开展了反殖民主义民族解放斗争,大量的殖民地获得政治独立,建立新的民族国家。然而,政治独立并不意味着非殖民化的完成,在新殖民主义时期,殖民主义所遗留的问题长期困扰着前殖民地国家,经济和文化独立迫在眉睫。因此在一定程度上可以说,后殖民主义是第三世界国家独立后反殖民主义民族解放运动在思想理论领域的延伸。

历史学家最初用“后殖民”(post-colonial)一词来描述前殖民地独立后的时期,但作为学术话语的后殖民主义强调殖民主义对前殖民国家和前殖民地社会文化持续至今的影响,而非殖民主义的终结或与殖民主义政治、经济、文化遗产的历史断裂。阿里夫·德里克(Arif Dirlik)认为后殖民这个术语包含了三种意义:“一是对前殖民地社会现实状况的描述,具有明确的指称对象,如后殖民社会或后殖民知识分子;二是对殖民主义之后的全球状况的描述,缺乏具体所指,意义抽象模糊,如同第三世界的概念一样;三是指描述上述全球状况的话语,其认识论和心理倾向是全球状况的产物。”[③]后殖民主义应该是他说的第三种意思。对罗伯特·J. C. 扬(Robert J. C. Young)来说,后殖民是一个辩证的概念,一方面指非殖民化的历史事实和前殖民地国家的政治独立,另一方面也指这些国家和人民所处的帝国主义经济和政治宰制的情境,其阐明了前殖民地国家随着政治情境的改变而产生的文化形态。“后殖民性”强调的

---

① Vivek Chibber, *Postcolonial Theory and the Spectre of Capital*. London: Verso, 2013, p.1.
② Gayatri C. Spivak, *Outside in the Teaching Machine*. London and New York: Routledge, 1993, p.56; Robert J. C. Young, *Postcolonialism: An Historical Introduction*. Oxford: Blackwell, 2001, pp.383 - 384.
③ Arif Dirlik, "The Postcolonial Aura: Third World Criticism in the Age of Global Capitalism," *Critical Inquiry* 20 (1994), pp.328 - 356.

是经济、物质和文化条件,这些条件决定了后殖民国家必须在其中运作的全球体系,而这一体系服务于国际资本和七国集团的利益。后殖民主义体现了在这种压迫环境下进行积极干预的理论和政治立场,结合了后殖民时期认识论上的文化创新和对后殖民性的政治批判。①

后殖民主义的理论渊源具有多元化的特点。近现代以来,欧洲内部存在着反思和批判自身思想和理论的传统,如马克思主义、女性主义、后现代主义、后结构主义等,这些传统成为后殖民主义的重要理论来源。扬认为后殖民主义起源于国际主义的非殖民化斗争,得益于马克思主义理论和后结构主义思想的强化②;里拉·甘地(Leela Gandhi)认为后殖民主义的"主要来源是后结构主义和后现代主义,以及它们与马克思主义纠缠不清的矛盾关系"③。根据其不同的理论背景,后殖民主义可以分为三种流派:一是以萨义德、斯皮瓦克和巴巴为代表的"三剑客"后结构主义流派;二是以钱德拉·T. 莫汉蒂(Chandra T. Mohanty)为代表的后殖民女性主义流派,该流派从第三世界女性的独特身份和际遇角度出发批判西方女性主义的本质主义和白人中心主义;三是以阿吉兹·阿罕默德(Aijaz Ahmad)为代表的马克思主义流派。这种划分表明,后殖民主义理论家的思想谱系和研究方法具有多样性和异质性,他们对各种理论兼收并蓄,往往互相引证,"构成了后殖民主义内部最富于戏剧性的理论张力"。④

"三剑客"后结构主义流派代表了后殖民主义发展的不同方向和理论谱系。萨义德早年为美国学界引介以福柯等人为代表的后结构主义,其《东方学》受益于福柯的话语/权力理论,但他一开始批判后结构主义的文本主义倾向和非历史的哲学思维,转而以相对传统的历史方法挖掘文本的世俗性,倡导"世界、文本、批评家"三位一体的"世俗批评"。他继承了反殖思想家的激进人文主义,如"历史主义、意识和身份"等观念⑤,以"世俗批评"在西方殖民国家的理论与反殖话语分析之间寻求契合点⑥。相比之下,巴巴和斯皮瓦克更加倚重后结构主义,其理论主张代表了后殖民主义发展的其他方向和路径。巴巴受雅克·拉康(Jacques Lacan)的精神分析理论和雅克·德里达(Jacques Derrida)的解构主义影响,提出模仿、矛盾性、混杂性等后殖民概念;斯皮瓦克则借用马克思主义、后结构主义和女性主义阐述属下与策略本质主义,分析全球资本主义背景下的国际劳动分工。

一、萨义德：世俗性与身份政治

作为萨义德批评思想的关键词,世俗性(worldliness)或世俗批评反对文学批评脱离政治和历史的倾向,强调具有批判意识的知识分子应该超越狭隘的专业界限,参与对抗实践。⑦ 世俗性也是萨义德批判本质主义身份政治(identity politics)的基础。他认为,民族主义建构拜物教式的民族认同往往使人产生准宗教情感,进而否定人类历史的世俗性,因此我们不能把复杂的人类生活完全归为"民族认同的

---

①　Young, *Postcolonialism: An Historical Introduction*, pp.57-58.
②　Ibid., p.18.
③　Leela Gandhi, *Postcolonial Theory: A Critical Introduction*. New York: Columbia University Press, 1998, p.25.
④　罗钢、刘象愚:《后殖民主义文化理论》,北京:中国社会科学出版社,1999年,第3页。
⑤　Simon Gikandi, "Poststructuralism and Postcolonial Discourse," *The Cambridge Companion to Postcolonial Literary Studies*. Ed. Neil Lazarus. Cambridge: Cambridge University Press, 2004, p.101.
⑥　Benita Parry, "The Institutionalization of Postcolonial Studies," *The Cambridge Companion to Postcolonial Literary Studies*, p.69.
⑦　Edward W. Said, *The World, the Text, and the Critic*. London: Faber and Faber, 1984, p.4, p.292.

范畴"①。

萨义德以世俗性批判身份政治,但他并不否认跨文化阐释的有效性,阐释政治与其从属的情境和阐释者的意图有关。如何摆脱封闭的文化身份建构、跨越文化边界来理解其他文化和社会正是《东方学》集中论述的问题:"我们如何再现其他文化? 什么是另一种文化? 一种独特的文化(或种族、宗教、文明)观念是有用的吗? 或者它涉及的要么是自我夸耀(当人们谈论自己的文化时),要么是敌意和侵犯(当人们谈论"其他"文化时)吗? 文化、宗教和种族差异比社会经济或政治历史范畴更重要吗?"②针对再现这一文化批判的难题,他强调,对人类社会的研究是基于具体的人类历史和经验的,而不是建立在学究式抽象、晦涩的规律或武断的制度之上的。《东方学》的批判焦点是西方的身份政治,其目的不是提出与东方主义相对的西方主义,而是批判作为权力话语和意识形态的东方主义"无法与人类经验相认同"③。

萨义德批判本质化的东方观念以及自我再现的排他性:"我一直认为'东方'本身就是一个建构的实体,而这种观念则不无争议:在地理空间里生活着非常'不同'的本土居民,可以用某些符合那一地理空间的宗教、文化或种族本质来定义他们。我当然不相信那种只有黑人才能写黑人、穆斯林才能写穆斯林的狭隘说法。"④据此,东方是以地理、宗教、文化和种族的异质性建构的,即使是东方人也不能以排他性的身份政治宣称文化再现的特权。《东方学》通过否弃本质主义的身份建构,强调东方和西方范畴不过是基于一系列固定的、本质化的本体论和认识论差异的一种思维方式,"它与魔法和神话一样,具有封闭系统的自我包含和自我强化的特征"⑤。东方主义以刻板形象和化简范畴再现东方,"显露了随之而来的误现和虚假,以及产生与理解'东方'或'西方'这类事物的权力共谋方式"⑥,而体制权力结构则不断地利用和强化这些形象和范畴。

建构历史文化的集体认同是后殖民抵抗的策略,但萨义德的身份政治批判并不赞同纯粹的本土身份建构,因为民族主义可能发展为原教旨主义或本土主义。族裔或民族性的本土主义建构会延续殖民主义造成的种族和政治分裂,离开历史的世界去追求本质的形而上学,就是放弃历史去追求本质化,这种本质化使人类互相对立,一旦背弃了世俗世界,人们往往不假思索地接受帝国主义鼓吹的刻板印象、神话、仇恨和传统,而这也违背了后殖民抵抗运动所设想的目标。⑦ 显然,本质化的身份建构否弃了历史的世俗性,萨义德的身份政治批判既针对西方关于东方的再现,又质疑在后殖民抵抗中建构本质主义的族裔或民族身份。

萨义德批判身份政治,但并不否认民族主义在反殖解放运动中的历史进步作用:"任何人都无须提醒,在非殖民化时期,这样或那样的民族主义推动了抗议、抵抗和独立运动……我不希望被人误解为持简单的反民族主义立场。民族主义作为一种动员的政治力量,在欧洲以外的世界各地激发并推动了反对西方统治的斗争,这是历史事实。"⑧因此,作为民族认同主张,前殖民地国家的民族主义可以看作对

① Michael Sprinker, ed., *Edward Said: A Critical Reader*. Cambridge, Mass.: Blackwell, 1992, p.233.
② Edward W. Said, *Orientalism*. New York: Vintage Books, 1979, pp.325 - 326.
③ Ibid., p.328.
④ Ibid., p.322.
⑤ Ibid., p.70.
⑥ Ibid., p.347.
⑦ Edward W. Said, *Culture and Imperialism*. New York: Knopf, 1993, pp.228 - 229.
⑧ Ibid., pp.216 - 218.

殖民主义的积极回应。

　　萨义德借鉴弗朗茨·法农(Frantz Fanon)批判民族主义的身份政治,认为民族主义意识很容易导致僵化,用有色人种统治者取代白人统治者"不能保证民族主义官员不会重拾旧制度"[1]。解殖有赖于民族意识向社会意识的转变,正如法农讨论"民族意识的陷阱"时所言:"使人民奋起抵抗压迫者的伟大的民族主义之歌,在宣布独立之日戛然而止,动摇了,最后消亡了。民族主义不是政治教义,也不是纲领。如果你真希望你的国家能避免倒退,或不那么糟糕地停止前进,就必须迅速把民族意识转化为政治和社会意识。"[2]萨义德批判本土主义和民族主义是为了重构殖民者与被殖民者的相互关系,这种重构提供了他称为"对位阅读"的方法。"对位"以及"重叠的领土和交织的历史"体现了萨义德的解放构想:解殖民需要基于殖民相遇历史过程的相互性做出政治选择,不能以孤立的方式审视宰制和抵抗的经验,这样才能建构容纳殖民者和被殖民者的非强制性的共同体。

　　萨义德以世俗性批判身份政治,试图拆解殖民者/被殖民者、中心/边缘等二元对立问题,从而把民族意识转化为社会意识,借以构想自由和谐的人类社会共同体。他认为,"尽管西方的殖民史充满痛苦和暴力,法农作品的全部意义在于迫使欧洲大都市在殖民地历史中思考自身的历史,从帝国统治的残酷、麻木和凌辱的无为状态中觉醒"[3]。对萨义德来说,后殖民抵抗政治可以促使西方反思和重构自己的历史,将西方人和非西方人都纳入其中。这一宏伟的解放构想对人类社会的未来愿景不无意义,但如果我们没有忘记反殖独立后新生民族国家的困境与幻灭,面对当前全球资本主义背景下资源和财富的不平等分配和新的国际劳动分工,这种解放构想难免带有乌托邦的性质。

二、巴巴:矛盾性与混杂性

　　巴巴批判萨义德的《东方学》建构了同质性、总体化的东方话语,认为显性与隐性的东方主义二元对立削弱了话语的有效性,因为殖民主体与殖民话语的关系微妙而复杂。他指出:"萨义德的著述似乎始终表明殖民者完全占有殖民权力和殖民话语,而这是对历史和理论的简化。"[4]巴巴强调主体化意味着被殖民主体和殖民主体都进入殖民话语的定位,而萨义德的隐性东方主义具有封闭性,其殖民主体简化了权力/知识观。通过批判萨义德的东方主义话语概念,巴巴意在探讨殖民话语的矛盾性(ambivalence)和混杂性(hybridity)。

　　作为精神分析术语,矛盾性描述同时想要某物及其对立面的持续心理波动,意指"同时对某物、某人或某行为的吸引和排斥"[5]。巴巴借用了拉康的这一概念描述殖民者与被殖民者的复杂关系:被殖民者与殖民者并非完全对立,反抗和共谋同时存在于殖民主体中,因为殖民话语既压制又培育被殖民主体,如同福柯的权力概念那样既具有限制性又具有生产性。殖民话语的矛盾性使殖民者的权威产生不稳定性:殖民话语试图生产被殖民主体,而被殖民主体往往会复制殖民话语的观念和价值。这与巴巴的模仿(mimicry)概念有关:"作为一个几乎相同但不完全相同的主体,殖民模仿是对一个经过改造的、可识

①　Said, *Culture and Imperialism*, p.214.
②　Frantz Fanon, *The Wretched of the Earth*. Trans. Constance Farrington. London: MacGibbon and Kee, 1965, p.164.
③　Edward W. Said, "Representing the Colonized: Anthropology's Interlocutors," *Critical Inquiry* 15 (1989), p.314.
④　Homi K. Bhabha, "The Other Question," *Screen* 24 (1983), pp.24-25.
⑤　Robert J. C. Young, *Colonial Desire: Hybridity in Theory, Culture and Race*. London: Routledge, 1995, p.161.

别的'他者'的欲望。也就是说,模仿话语是围绕矛盾性而构建的;为了做到有效,模仿必须不断地产生不足、过剩和差异。因此,我称之为'殖民话语模式的权威被不确定性侵袭并出现了表现差异的模仿',而它本身就是一个否认和拒绝的过程。"①由此看来,殖民话语的矛盾性产生了矛盾的被殖民主体,被殖民主体以嘲讽的口吻模仿殖民者,模仿的效果侵扰了殖民话语的权威,因为在使被殖民主体标准化和文明化的过程中,标准化和文明化的知识否定了他者的差异,但同时产生了异化文明话语假设的威权形式。

模仿与嘲讽之间的矛盾性场域构成了一个话语空间,它不仅打破了殖民话语,而且将殖民主体转化为不完整的在场。因此,在写作和重复的过程中,被殖民主体意欲通过模仿成为殖民者那样的人,兼具相似性和威胁性:"殖民威权的矛盾性不断地从模仿——几乎没有差异但又不完全相同——转变为威胁——几乎完全不同但又并非完全不同。"②模仿的威胁在于其双重视野通过暴露殖民话语的矛盾性,颠覆了殖民话语的权威。但这是否意味着没有被殖民者的抵抗能动性,殖民威权也可以自动瓦解? 对此,巴巴强调:"抵抗不一定是带有政治意图的对抗行为,也不是简单地否定或排斥另一种文化的内容,就像人们曾经认识到的差异那样。它是在主流话语的认知规则中产生的一种矛盾性效果,因为殖民话语清晰地表达了文化差异的迹象,并将其重新纳入等级制、标准化、边缘化等殖民权力的顺从关系中。"③这显示了殖民话语与殖民关系的矛盾性:希望被殖民者变得与殖民者几乎一样,但不完全一样,这种吸引和排斥之间的波动构成了殖民话语的内在逻辑,有助于产生矛盾性空间,打破其权力假设。因此,抵抗脱离了被殖民者的主观能动性和政治意图,成为殖民话语和殖民关系的"矛盾性效果"。

由此看来,巴巴的后殖民抵抗政治不是通过在殖民话语的运作之外建构独立的本土族裔或民族认同来对抗殖民主义的,而是坚持认为抵抗产生于殖民话语的矛盾性空间,因为殖民者和被殖民者总是紧密相连。这与巴巴的混杂性概念有关。他借助混杂性提出了"第三空间"(Third Space)概念,进而"挑战我们对文化的历史身份感,即文化作为一种同质化、统一的力量,被本源的过去所证实,在人们的民族传统中保持着活力"④。这种理论认识有助于我们构想基于文化差异的国际文化,而文化差异的产生是建立在文化混杂性的表达假设之上的。巴巴论述了混杂性与文化差异的联系:"殖民混杂性不是两种不同文化之间的谱系或身份问题,不是以文化相对主义就能解决的问题。混杂性是殖民表征和个体化的问题域(problematic),它逆转了殖民主义的否认效果,使其他'被否认'的知识进入主导话语行列,离间权威的基础,即它的认知规则。"⑤换言之,文化差异否定了殖民相遇后文化身份的孤立性,而文化多样性则肯定了文化身份作为一个封闭而连贯的反殖抵抗而存在。殖民话语的混杂性所产生的"第三空间"超越了纯粹的文化对立,为从内部颠覆殖民权威提供了介入场地。

马克思主义批评家认为,巴巴的混杂性过度重视殖民话语内在的相互关系,忽视了社会历史和现实中被殖民者的对立和反抗。他们反对把混杂性看作共同的后殖民状态,因为混杂性体现了殖民话语分

---

① Homi K. Bhabha, "Of Mimicry and Man: The Ambivalence of Colonial Discourse," *The Location of Culture*. London: Routledge: 1994, p.86.
② Ibid., p.91.
③ Homi K. Bhabha, "Signs Taken for Wonders: Questions of Ambivalence and Authority under a Tree Outside Delhi, May 1817," *The Location of Culture*, pp.110 - 111.
④ Homi K. Bhabha, "Commitment to Theory," *The Location of Culture*, p.37.
⑤ Bhabha, "Signs Taken for Wonders: Questions of Ambivalence and Authority under a Tree Outside Delhi, May 1817," p.114.

析的倾向,即在具体的时间、空间、地理和语言语境中对文化的去历史化,进而忽视了具体的文化差异。混杂性将社会政治简化为心理问题,用后结构主义的语言运作取代社会历史的解释①,如果后殖民批评家不顾及霸权问题和新殖民主义的权力关系,一味颂扬混杂性本身,那就说明他们似乎认可了殖民暴力的既成事实②。这些批评不无道理,殖民话语的混杂性和矛盾性难免带有抽象化、普适化的文本主义色彩,对反殖抵抗的特定历史政治情境关注不够。

与马克思主义批评不同,扬认为混杂性可以从历史、地理、政治、军事等角度为我们提供理解殖民主义的框架。不管是对殖民话语分析来说,还是对殖民主义自身来说,殖民话语这一媒介都是必需的,因为"用来描述或分析殖民主义的语言并不是透明的、清白的、非历史的,也不仅仅是工具性的,而且殖民主义文本也不只是文献或证据"③。可以说,巴巴的矛盾性和混杂性为后殖民抵抗政治提供了理论思路,模仿和"第三空间"隐含的反话语实践可以为破坏殖民权威奠定基础。然而,巴巴将混杂性和矛盾性作为产生抵抗的基础,把模仿作为产生嘲讽的反话语手段,这忽视了被殖民者在反殖斗争中的主体意志和能动性。

三、斯皮瓦克:属下与策略本质主义

在《属下能说话吗?》("Can the Subaltern Speak?")一文中,斯皮瓦克以解构主义的问题化方式审视属下(subaltern)阶层的能动性,论述了"帝国认知暴力"、后殖民知识分子的定位及代表/再现问题。在安东尼奥·葛兰西(Antonio Gramsci)看来,属下指那些受统治阶级霸权统治的农民、工人等社会群体,其历史必然是零散而时断时续的,很少能通过文化资本或社会机构代表/再现自我。④ 印度属下研究小组以属下描述南亚社会在阶级、种姓、年龄、性别、职位等从属关系上的总体特点,认为印度史学受制于殖民主义和资产阶级精英的民族主义,需通过审视属下概念来批判精英阶层的角色。⑤ 在斯皮瓦克看来,属下主体的异质性是无可避免的,没有一种方法论既能确定属下的构成,又能避免本质主义:"对于'真正的'属下群体来说,他们的身份就是他们的差异,并不存在任何能认识和言说自我但无法被代表的属下主体;知识分子的解决办法不是放弃代表属下主体。问题在于,尚未有人追寻主体的踪迹,从而引起代表他们的知识分子的注意……即使我们能调查人民的政治,但我们如何能触及他们的意识?属下又能用什么声音意识说话?"⑥由此看来,如同其他宏大词汇,属下充其量只是一种误用修辞(catachresis),即一个没有适当指涉的词。如果考虑到强加于殖民主体的殖民和帝国认知暴力,而且考虑到"只有反暴动的文本或精英文献才能给我们关于属下意识的信息"⑦,那么我们就能知道纯粹本真的属下意识是不可复原的,作为精英主导的话语效果,属下并非独立的意识或主体。

① Dirlik, "The Postcolonial Aura: Third World Criticism in the Age of Global Capitalism," p.333.
② Ella Shohat, "Notes on the 'Post-Colonial'," *Social Text* 31-32 (1992), p.109.
③ Young, *Colonial Desire: Hybridity in Theory, Culture and Race*, p.163.
④ Antonio Gramsci, *Selections from the Prison Notebooks of Antonio Gramsci*. Eds. and trans. Quintin Hoare and G. Smith. London: Lawrence and Wishart, 1971, pp.52-54.
⑤ Ranajit Guha, ed., *Subaltern Studies 1: Writings on South Asian History and Society*. Delhi: Oxford University Press, 1982, p.vii.
⑥ Gayatri C. Spivak, "Can the Subaltern Speak?" *The Post-colonial Studies Reader*. Eds. Bill Ashcroft, Gareth Griffiths, and Allen Tiffin. London: Routledge, 1995, p.27.
⑦ Gayatri C. Spivak, *The Spivak Reader: Selected Works of Gayatri Chakravorty Spivak*. Eds. Donna Landry and Gerald MacLean. London: Routledge, 1996, pp.203-204.

　　把属下作为纯粹意识难免有本质主义之嫌,但斯皮瓦克对属下异质性的批判"在不可通约性的框架下近乎神化了差异性"①,而我们往往"需要普适性的话语来批判性地解读社会不公现象"②。她的属下阐述似乎陷入了后殖民抵抗政治的困境,但不能因此断言斯皮瓦克的思想完全缺乏对属下阶层反叛和抵抗的思考,因为她提出文学文本可以为女性属下的反抗提供修辞场地。③ 实际上,斯皮瓦克不愿"在一种积极而纯粹的状态中发现(属下)意识……"④,这暴露了她在后殖民语境中自相矛盾的思想立场。由于属下不可还原的异质性以及殖民话语对它的预先建构,代表/再现属下阶层的善意企图可能会侵占和盗用属下阶层的声音,并因此使他们沉默。

　　通过分析马克思的名言"他们不能代表自己,他们必须被代表"⑤,斯皮瓦克强调属下研究小组应该注意代表/再现的双重含义,而不是通过总体化的权力和欲望概念引入个人主体。福柯和吉尔·德勒兹(Gilles Deleuze)认为被压迫者可以自由地代表自我。对此,斯皮瓦克认为他们混淆了代表/再现(representation)的两种意义:一是作为政治代言的"代表"(vertreten),二是作为艺术或哲学的"再现"(darstellen)。把属下看作具有自我代表能力的主体,最终会使属下的主体能动性屈从于声称代表他们说话的声音。因此,艺术或哲学上的再现,即把属下作为独立主体的象征表现,往往被误认为是他们自己欲望和权力的清晰表达。⑥ 知识分子如果想当然地认为自己只是客观地报道那些未被代表的主体,而不把他们自己视为"权力和欲望的隐秘主体",他们则无法对寄身其中的主流话语和体制实践保持批判意识,而成为"国际分工剥削者的一方"。⑦

　　斯皮瓦克一方面认识到为他人代言的困难和危险而诚惶诚恐,承认很难"想出减轻这种恐惧的策略"⑧,另一方面则提出"策略本质主义"(strategic essentialism)和"积极性共谋关系"。她在采访中说:"先认为自己的本体论义务难免会受到价值编码的审视,然后假定一个误用修辞的名义来奠定我们计划和调查的基础,这样我们就可以保持彻底的经验主义,而不必成为盲目的本质主义者。"⑨这显然透露了斯皮瓦克后殖民批判的总体方法论,即策略性地结合解构主义的认识论与马克思主义的本体论:在认识论上借用解构主义的策略,对属下意识构成和知识分子代表/再现假定的透明性进行问题化批判;在本体论上借用马克思主义的观点,承认"策略本质主义"和"积极性共谋关系"的必要性。

　　斯皮瓦克既认为属下突出不可化简的差异和主流话语的效果,又强调策略本质主义对抵抗殖民主义和帝国主义宰制与压迫的必要性。对她来说,策略与理论的区别在于:"策略通过不断地对理论进行建构/解构性的批判而发挥作用,而且作为具有争议的概念隐喻,策略与理论不同,其前身并不是无关利害和普适的。"⑩她同时强调:"至于本质,至少我觉得它很有用。对于理论,我觉得,就目前而言,至少对

① Neil Lazarus,"Introducing Postcolonial Studies," *The Cambridge Companion to Postcolonial Literary Studies*,p.10.
② Dipesh Chakrabarty,*Provincializing Europe: Postcolonial Thought and Historical Difference*. Princeton:Princeton University Press,2000,p.254.
③ Stephen Morton,*Gayatri Chakravorty Spivak*. London:Routledge,2003,p.55.
④ Gayatri C. Spivak,*In Other Worlds: Essays in Cultural Politics*. New York:Methuen,1987,p.198.
⑤ Karl Marx,*The Eighteenth Brumaire of Louis Bonaparte*. New York:International Publishers,1963,p.124.
⑥ Gayatri C. Spivak,*A Critique of Postcolonial Reason: Toward a History of the Vanishing Present*. Cambridge:Harvard University Press,1999,p.256.
⑦ Ibid.,pp.264-265.
⑧ Gayatri C. Spivak,*The Post-colonial Critic: Interviews,Strategies,Dialogues*. Ed. Sarah Harasym. New York:Routledge,1990,p.63.
⑨ Spivak,*Outside in the Teaching Machine*,p.16.
⑩ Ibid.,p.3.

我来说,最好与之保持距离,将其视为理论自身的生产实践。即便如此,我不明白为什么本质主义有时会与经验主义相混淆。"①她反思自己的解构主义方法论,认为反对本质主义话语完全切中目标,但在策略上我们却做不到,"从根本上说我关注那种异质性,但我在那场运动中选择了普适话语,因为我觉得与其说自己否定普适性——因为普适化、终结化是任何话语都不可化简的——不如说我把自己看作具体的而不是普适的,我应该发现普适化的话语中哪些是有用的,然后继续发现那种话语在那一领域内的局限和挑战所在。我认为我们必须再次做出策略选择,不是选择普适话语,而是选择本质主义的话语……实际上,我必须时不时地说自己是一个本质主义者。"②由此来看,斯皮瓦克的策略本质主义与萨义德的民族主义批判不无相通之处。

借助解构主义方法论,斯皮瓦克批判后殖民知识分子在主流话语和体制权力结构中的矛盾定位。她认为解构主义并不否认主体、真理和历史的存在,而是对人们不得不要的东西进行持续批判,虽质疑研究主体的权威,但又不使其失去行动能力,持续把不可能的条件转变为可能。③因此可以从解构主义哲学立场解读后殖民性。后殖民批评家既批判帝国结构,但又紧密地栖居其中。④斯皮瓦克借此把自我定位阐述为"不那么强调地方主义,而是在细微的分析中有成效地承认共谋关系"⑤,从而承认自己作为后殖民知识分子在西方学术话语和体制中心的共谋关系,展示了一种思想成熟、富有道德勇气的后殖民批判立场。

批评界往往认为斯皮瓦克的后殖民理论过于依赖解构主义方法论,忽视了被殖民主体的抵抗能动性,但她从属下和策略本质主义角度分析被殖民主体的异质性和知识分子定位问题,有助于我们以问题化的方式审视后殖民主体和身份观念,揭示后殖民文本重写可能导致复制帝国权力结构和使属下阶层无法言说的困境。

第二节　经典文献选读

本章共有三篇选文。第一篇节选自萨义德的《东方学》导言,从西方的学科研究和西方再现东方的总体形象角度阐述了东方主义,提出东方主义的话语表征与其说是关于东方的真实历史、文化和人,不如说表现了西方自身及其对东方的幻想和权力欲望。第二篇《论模仿与人:殖民话语的矛盾性》("Of Mimicry and Man: The Ambivalence of Colonial Discourse")选自巴巴的论文集《文化的定位》(*The Location of Culture*),在分析殖民话语矛盾性的基础上,强调可以通过模仿改写殖民话语来建构殖民主体的混杂身份。第三篇节选自斯皮瓦克的《后殖民理性批判:正在消失的当下的历史》(*A Critique of Postcolonial Reason: Toward a History of the Vanishing Present*),即她修订后的著名论文《属下能说话

---

① Spivak, *Outside in the Teaching Machine*, pp.15 - 16.
② Spivak, *The Post-colonial Critic: Interviews, Strategies, Dialogues*, p.11.
③ Spivak, *The Spivak Reader: Selected Works of Gayatri Chakravorty Spivak*, pp.27 - 28, p.210.
④ Gayatri C. Spivak, "The Making of Americans, the Teaching of English, and the Future of Culture Studies," *New Literary History* 21 (1990), p.794.
⑤ Spivak, *A Critique of Postcolonial Reason: Toward a History of the Vanishing Present*, p.xii.

吗?》,通过分析印度的女性属下阶层,论述了全球资本主义背景下后殖民知识分子的定位、代表/再现等问题。

一、《东方学》选读①

Introduction

[...]

The Orient is not only adjacent to Europe; it is also the place of Europe's greatest and richest and oldest colonies, the source of its civilizations and languages, its cultural contestant, and one of its deepest and most recurring images of the Other. In addition, the Orient has helped to define Europe (or the West) as its contrasting image, idea, personality, experience. Yet none of this Orient is merely imaginative. The Orient is an integral part of European *material* civilization and culture. [...]

It will be clear to the reader [...] that by Orientalism I mean several things, all of them, in my opinion, interdependent. The most readily accepted designation for Orientalism is an academic one, and indeed the label still serves in a number of academic institutions. Anyone who teaches, writes about, or researches the Orient—and this applies whether the person is an anthropologist, sociologist, historian, or philologist—either in its specific or its general aspects, is an Orientalist, and what he or she does is Orientalism. Compared with *Oriental studies* or *area studies*, it is true that the term *Orientalism* is less preferred by specialists today, both because it is too vague and general and because it connotes the high-handed executive attitude of nineteenth-century and early-twentieth-century European colonialism. Nevertheless, books are written and congresses held with "the Orient" as their main focus, with the Orientalist in his new or old guise as their main authority. The point is that even if it does not survive as it once did, Orientalism lives on academically through its doctrines and theses about the Orient and the Oriental.

Related to this academic tradition, whose fortunes, transmigrations, specializations, and transmissions are in part the subject of this study, is a more general meaning for Orientalism. Orientalism is a style of thought based upon an ontological and epistemological distinction made between "the Orient" and (most of the time) "the Occident". Thus a very large mass of writers, among whom are poets, novelists, philosophers, political theorists, economists, and imperial administrators, have accepted the basic distinction between East and West as the starting point for elaborate theories, epics, novels, social descriptions, and political accounts concerning the Orient, its people, customs, "mind", destiny, and so on. This Orientalism can accommodate Aeschylus, say, and Victor Hugo, Dante and Karl Marx. [...]

---

① Said, *Orientalism*, pp.1 – 13.

The interchange between the academic and the more or less imaginative meanings of Orientalism is a constant one, and since the late eighteenth century there has been a considerable, quite disciplined—perhaps even regulated—traffic between the two. Here I come to the third meaning of Orientalism, which is something more historically and materially defined than either of the other two. Taking the late eighteenth century as a very roughly defined starting point Orientalism can be discussed and analyzed as the corporate institution for dealing with the Orient—dealing with it by making statements about it, authorizing views of it, describing it, by teaching it, settling it, ruling over it: in short, Orientalism as a Western style for dominating, restructuring, and having authority over the Orient. I have found it useful here to employ Michel Foucault's notion of a discourse, as described by him in *The Archaeology of Knowledge* and in *Discipline and Punish*, to identify Orientalism. My contention is that without examining Orientalism as a discourse one cannot possibly understand the enormously systematic discipline by which European culture was able to manage—and even produce—the Orient politically, sociologically, militarily, ideologically, scientifically, and imaginatively during the post-Enlightenment period. Moreover, so authoritative a position did Orientalism have that I believe no one writing, thinking, or acting on the Orient could do so without taking account of the limitations on thought and action imposed by Orientalism. In brief, because of Orientalism the Orient was not (and is not) a free subject of thought or action. This is not to say that Orientalism unilaterally determines what can be said about the Orient, but that it is the whole network of interests inevitably brought to bear on (and therefore always involved in) any occasion when that peculiar entity "the Orient" is in question. How this happens is what this book tries to demonstrate. It also tries to show that European culture gained in strength and identity by setting itself off against the Orient as a sort of surrogate and even underground self.

[...]

I have begun with the assumption that the Orient is not an inert fact of nature. It is not merely *there*, just as the Occident itself is not just *there* either. We must take seriously Vico's great observation that men make their own history, that what they can know is what they have made, and extend it to geography: as both geographical and cultural entities—to say nothing of historical entities—such locales, regions, geographical sectors as "Orient" and "Occident" are man-made. Therefore, as much as the West itself, the Orient is an idea that has a history and a tradition of thought, imagery, and vocabulary that have given it reality and presence in and for the West. The two geographical entities thus support and to an extent reflect each other.

Having said that, one must go on to state a number of reasonable qualifications. In the first place, it would be wrong to conclude that the Orient was *essentially* an idea, or a creation with no corresponding reality. [...] There were—and are—cultures and nations whose location is in the East, and their lives, histories, and customs have a brute reality obviously greater than anything that could be said about them in the West. About that fact this study of Orientalism has very little to contribute, except to acknowledge it tacitly. But the phenomenon of Orientalism as I study it here deals principally, not with a correspondence between Orientalism and Orient, but with the internal consistency of Orientalism and its ideas about the Orient (the East as career) despite or beyond any correspondence, or lack thereof, with a "real" Orient. [...]

A second qualification is that ideas, cultures, and histories cannot seriously be understood or studied without their force, or more precisely their configurations of power, also being studied. To believe that the Orient was created—or, as I call it, "Orientalized"—and to believe that such things happen simply as a necessity of the imagination, is to be disingenuous. The relationship between Occident and Orient is a relationship of power, of domination, of varying degrees of a complex hegemony. [...]

This brings us to a third qualification. One ought never to assume that the structure of Orientalism is nothing more than a structure of lies or of myths which, were the truth about them to be told, would simply blow away. I myself believe that Orientalism is more particularly valuable as a sign of European-Atlantic power over the Orient than it is as a veridic discourse about the Orient (which is what, in its academic or scholarly form, it claims to be). [...] Orientalism, therefore, is not an airy European fantasy about the Orient, but a created body of theory and practice in which, for many generations, there has been a considerable material investment. Continued investment made Orientalism, as a system of knowledge about the Orient, an accepted grid for filtering through the Orient into Western consciousness, just as that same investment multiplied—indeed, made truly productive—the statements proliferating out from Orientalism into the general culture.

Gramsci has made the useful analytic distinction between civil and political society in which the former is made up of voluntary (or at least rational and noncoercive) affiliations like schools, families, and unions, the latter of state institutions (the army, the police, the central bureaucracy) whose role in the polity is direct domination. Culture, of course, is to be found operating within civil society, where the influence of ideas, of institutions, and of other persons works not through domination but by what Gramsci calls consent. In any society not totalitarian, then, certain cultural forms predominate over others, just as certain ideas are more influential than others; the form of this cultural leadership is what Gramsci has identified as hegemony, an indispensable concept for any understanding of cultural life in the industrial West. It is hegemony, or rather the result of cultural hegemony at work, that gives Orientalism the durability and the strength I have been speaking about so far. Orientalism is never far from what Denys Hay has called the idea of Europe, a collective notion identifying "us" Europeans as against all "those" non-Europeans, and indeed it can be argued that the major component in European culture is precisely what made that culture hegemonic both in and outside Europe: the idea of European identity as a superior one in comparison with all the non-European peoples and cultures. There is in addition the hegemony of European ideas about the Orient, themselves reiterating European superiority over Oriental backwardness, usually overriding the possibility that a more independent, or more skeptical, thinker might have had different views on the matter.

[...]

Therefore, Orientalism is not a mere political subject matter or field that is reflected passively by culture, scholarship, or institutions; nor is it a large and diffuse collection of texts about the Orient; nor is it representative and expressive of some nefarious "Western" imperialist plot to hold down the "Oriental" world. It is rather a *distribution* of geopolitical awareness into aesthetic, scholarly, economic, sociological, historical, and philological texts; it is an *elaboration* not only of a basic geographical distinction (the world is made up of two unequal halves, Orient and Occident) but also of a whole series of "interests" which, by such means as scholarly discovery, philological reconstruction, psychological analysis, landscape and sociological description, it not only creates but also maintains; it is, rather than expresses, a certain *will* or *intention* to understand, in some cases to control, manipulate, even to incorporate, what is a manifestly different (or alternative and novel) world; it is, above all, a discourse that is by no means in direct, corresponding relationship with political power in the raw, but rather is produced and exists in an uneven exchange with various kinds of power, shaped to a degree by the exchange with power political (as with a colonial or imperial establishment), power intellectual (as with reigning sciences like comparative linguistics or anatomy, or any of the modern policy sciences), power cultural (as with orthodoxies and canons of taste, texts, values), power moral (as with ideas about what "we" do and what "they" cannot do or understand as "we" do). Indeed, my real argument is that Orientalism is—and does not simply represent—a considerable dimension of modern political-intellectual culture, and as such has less to do with the Orient than it does with "our" world.

Because Orientalism is a cultural and a political fact, then, it does not exist in some archival vacuum; quite the contrary, I think it can be shown that what is thought, said, or even done about the Orient follows (perhaps occurs within) certain distinct and intellectually knowable lines. Here too a considerable degree of nuance and elaboration can be seen working as between the broad superstructural pressures and the details of composition, the facts of textuality. Most humanistic scholars are, I think, perfectly happy with the notion that texts exist in contexts, that there is such a thing as intertextuality, that the pressures of conventions, predecessors, and rhetorical styles limit what Walter Benjamin once called the "overtaxing of the productive person in the name of...the principle of 'creativity'", in which the poet is believed on his own, and out of his pure mind, to have brought forth his work. Yet there is a reluctance to allow that political, institutional, and ideological constraints act in the same manner on the individual author. [...]

二、《论模仿与人：殖民话语的矛盾性》选读①

The discourse of post-Enlightenment English colonialism often speaks in a tongue that is forked, not false. If colonialism takes power in the name of history, it repeatedly exercises its authority through the figures of farce. For the epic intention of the civilizing mission, "human and not wholly human" in the famous words of Lord Rosebery, "writ by the finger of the Divine" often produces a text rich in the traditions of *trompe-l'œil*, irony, mimicry and repetition. In this comic turn from the high ideals of the colonial imagination to its low mimetic literary effects mimicry emerges as one of the most elusive and effective strategies of colonial power and knowledge.

Within that conflictual economy of colonial discourse which Edward Said describes as the tension between the synchronic panoptical vision of domination—the demand for identity, stasis—and the counter-pressure of the diachrony of history—change, difference—mimicry represents an ironic compromise. If I may adapt Samuel Weber's formulation of the marginalizing vision of castration, then colonial mimicry is the desire for a reformed, recognizable Other, as a subject of a difference that is almost the same, but not quite. Which is to say, that the discourse of mimicry is constructed around an ambivalence; in order to be effective, mimicry must continually produce its slippage, its excess, its difference. The authority of that mode of colonial discourse that I have called mimicry is therefore stricken by an indeterminacy: mimicry emerges as the representation of a difference that is itself a process of disavowal. Mimicry is, thus the sign of a double articulation; a complex strategy of reform, regulation and discipline, which "appropriates" the Other as it visualizes power. Mimicry is also the sign of the inappropriate, however, a difference or recalcitrance which coheres the dominant strategic function of colonial power, intensifies surveillance, and poses an immanent threat to both "normalized" knowledges and disciplinary powers.

The effect of mimicry on the authority of colonial discourse is profound and disturbing. For in "normalizing" the colonial state or subject, the dream of post-Enlightenment civility alienates its own language of liberty and produces another knowledge of its norms. The ambivalence which thus informs this strategy is discernible, for example, in Locke's Second Treatise which *splits* to reveal the limitations of liberty in his double use of the word "slave": first simply, descriptively as the locus of a legitimate form of ownership, then as the trope for an intolerable, illegitimate exercise of power. What is articulated in that distance between the two uses is the absolute, imagined difference between the "Colonial" State of Carolina and the Original State of Nature.

It is from this area between mimicry and mockery, where the reforming, civilizing mission is

---

①　Bhabha, "Of Mimicry and Man: The Ambivalence of Colonial Discourse," pp.122 – 131.

threatened by the displacing gaze of its disciplinary double, that my instances of colonial imitation come. What they all share is a discursive process by which the excess or slippage produced by the ambivalence of mimicry (almost the same, but not quite) does not merely "rupture" the discourse, but becomes transformed into an uncertainty which fixes the colonial subject as a "partial" presence. By "partial" I mean both "incomplete" and "virtual". It is as if the very emergence of the "colonial" is dependent for its representation upon some strategic limitation or prohibition within the authoritative discourse itself. The success of colonial appropriation depends on a proliferation of inappropriate objects that ensure its strategic failure, so that mimicry is at once resemblance and menace.

[...]

The absurd extravagance of Macaulay's "Minute" (1835)—deeply influenced by Charles Grant's "Observations"—makes a mockery of Oriental learning until faced with the challenge of conceiving of a "reformed" colonial subject. Then, the great tradition of European humanism seems capable only of ironizing itself. At the intersection of European learning and colonial power, Macaulay can conceive of nothing other than "a class of interpreters between us and the millions whom we govern—a class of persons Indian in blood and colour, but English in tastes, in opinions, in morals and in intellect"—in other words a mimic man raised "through our English School", as a missionary educationist wrote in 1819, "to form a corps of translators and be employed in different departments of Labour". The line of descent of the mimic man can be traced through the works of Kipling, Forster, Orwell, Naipaul, and to his emergence, most recently, in Benedict Anderson's excellent work on nationalism, as the anomalous Bipin Chandra Pal. He is the effect of a flawed colonial mimesis, in which to be Anglicized is emphatically not to be English.

The figure of mimicry is locatable within what Anderson describes as "the inner compatibility of empire and nation". It problematizes the signs of racial and cultural priority, so that the "national" is no longer naturalizable. What emerges between mimesis and mimicry is a writing, a mode of representation, that marginalizes the monumentality of history, quite simply mocks its power to be a model, that power which supposedly makes it imitable. [...]

What I have called mimicry is not the familiar exercise of dependent colonial relations through narcissistic identification so that, as Fanon has observed, the black man stops being an actional person for only the white man can represent his self-esteem. Mimicry conceals no presence or identity behind its mask: it is not what Césaire describes as "colonization-thingification" behind which there stands the essence of the *présence Africaine*. The menace of mimicry is its double vision which in disclosing the ambivalence of colonial discourse also disrupts its authority. And it is a double vision that is a result of what I've described as the partial representation/recognition of the colonial object. Grant's colonial as partial imitator, Macaulay's translator, Naipaul's colonial politician as play-actor, Decoud as the scene setter of the opéra bouffe of the New World, these are the appropriate objects of a colonialist chain of command, authorized versions of otherness. But they are also, as I have shown, the figures of a doubling, the part-objects of a metonymy of colonial desire which alienates the modality and normality of those dominant discourses in which they emerge as "inappropriate" colonial subjects. A desire that, through the repetition of partial presence, which is the basis of mimicry, articulates those disturbances of cultural, racial and historical difference that menace the narcissistic demand of colonial authority. It is a desire that reverses "in part" the colonial appropriation by now producing a partial vision of the colonizer's presence; a gaze of otherness, that shares the acuity of the genealogical gaze which, as Foucault describes it, liberates marginal elements and shatters the unity of man's being through which he extends his sovereignty.

[...]

What is the nature of the hidden threat of the partial gaze? How does mimicry emerge as the subject of the scopic drive and the object of colonial surveillance? How is desire disciplined, authority displaced?

If we turn to a Freudian figure to address these issues of colonial textuality, that form of difference that is mimicry—almost the same but not quite—will become clear. Writing of the partial nature of fantasy, caught inappropriately, between the unconscious and the preconscious, making problematic, like mimicry, the very notion of "origins", Freud has this to say: "Their mixed and split origin is what decides their fate. We may compare them with individuals of mixed race who taken all round resemble white men but who betray their coloured descent by some striking feature or other and on that account are excluded from society and enjoy none of the privileges." Almost the same but not white: the visibility of mimicry is always produced at the site of interdiction. It is a form of colonial discourse that is uttered *inter dicta*: a discourse at the crossroads of what is known and permissible and that which though known must be kept concealed; a discourse uttered between the lines and as such both against the rules and within them. The question of the representation of difference is therefore always also a problem of authority. The "desire" of mimicry, which is Freud's "striking feature" that reveals so little but makes such a big difference, is not merely that impossibility of the Other which repeatedly resists signification. The desire of colonial mimicry—an interdictory desire—may not have an object, but it has strategic objectives which I shall call the metonymy of presence.

Those inappropriate signifiers of colonial discourse—the difference between being English and being Anglicized; the identity between stereotypes which, through repetition, also become different [...]. They are strategies of desire in discourse that make the anomalous representation of the colonized something other than a process of "the return of the repressed", what Fanon unsatisfactorily characterized as collective catharsis. These instances of metonymy are the non-repressive productions of contradictory and multiple belief. They cross the boundaries of the culture of enunciation through a strategic confusion of the metaphoric and metonymic axes of the cultural production of meaning.

In mimicry, the representation of identity and meaning is rearticulated along the axis of metonymy. As Lacan reminds us, mimicry is like camouflage, not a harmonization of repression of difference, but a form of resemblance, that differs from or defends presence by displaying it in part, metonymically. Its threat, I would add, comes from the prodigious and strategic production of conflictual, fantastic, discriminatory "identity effects" in the play of a power that is elusive because it hides no essence, no "itself". [...]

From such a colonial encounter between the white presence and its black semblance, there emerges the question of the ambivalence of mimicry as a problematic of colonial subjection. For if Sade's scandalous theatricalization of language repeatedly reminds us that discourse can claim "no priority", then the work of Edward Said will not let us forget that the "ethnocentric and erratic will to power from which texts can spring" is itself a theatre of war. Mimicry, as the metonymy of presence is, indeed, such an erratic, eccentric strategy of authority in colonial discourse. Mimicry does not merely destroy narcissistic authority through the repetitious slippage of difference and desire. It is the process of the fixation of the colonial as a form of cross-classificatory, discriminatory knowledge within an interdictory discourse, and therefore necessarily raises the question of the authorization of colonial representations; a question of authority that goes beyond the subject's lack of priority (castration) to a historical crisis in the conceptuality of colonial man as an object of regulatory power, as the subject of racial, cultural, national representation.

"This culture [...] fixed in its colonial status," Fanon suggests, "[is] both present and mummified, it testified against its members. It defines them in fact without appeal." The ambivalence of mimicry—almost but not quite—suggests that the fetishized colonial culture is potentially and strategically an insurgent counter-appeal. What I have called its "identity-effects" are always crucially split. Under cover of camouflage, mimicry, like the fetish, is a part-object that radically revalues the normative knowledges of the priority of race, writing, history. For the fetish mimes the forms of authority at the point at which it deauthorizes them. Similarly, mimicry rearticulates presence in terms of its "otherness", that which it disavows. There is a crucial difference between this colonial articulation of man and his doubles and that which Foucault describes as "thinking the unthought" which, for nineteenth-century Europe, is the ending of man's alienation by reconciling him with his essence. The colonial discourse that articulates an interdictory otherness is precisely the "other scene" of this nineteenth-century European desire for an authentic historical consciousness.

The "unthought" across which colonial man is articulated is that process of classificatory confusion that I have described as the metonymy of the substitutive chain of ethical and cultural discourse. This results in the splitting of colonial discourse so that two attitudes towards external reality persist; one takes reality into consideration while the other disavows it and replaces it by a product of desire that repeats, rearticulates "reality" as mimicry.

[...]

Such contradictory articulations of reality and desire—seen in racist stereotypes, statements, jokes, myths—are not caught in the doubtful circle of the return of the repressed. They are the effects of a disavowal that denies the differences of the other but produces in its stead forms of authority and multiple belief that alienate the assumptions of "civil" discourse. If, for a while, the ruse of desire is calculable for the uses of discipline soon the repetition of guilt, justification, pseudo-scientific theories, superstition, spurious authorities, and classifications can be seen as the desperate effort to "normalize" formally the disturbance of a discourse of splitting that violates the rational, enlightened claims of its enunciatory modality. The ambivalence of colonial authority repeatedly turns from mimicry—a difference that is almost nothing but not quite—to menace—a difference that is almost total but not quite. And in that other scene of colonial power, where history turns to farce and presence to "a part" can be seen the twin figures of narcissism and paranoia that repeat furiously, uncontrollably.

三、《后殖民理性批判：正在消失的当下的历史》选读①

Can the Subaltern Speak?

[...]

An important point is being made here: the production of theory is also a practice; the opposition between abstract "pure" theory and concrete "applied" practice is too quick and easy. But Deleuze's articulation of the argument is problematic. Two senses of representation are being run together: representation as "speaking for", as in politics, and representation as "re-presentation", as in art or philosophy. Since theory is also only "action", the theoretician does not represent (speak for) the oppressed group. Indeed, the subject is not seen as a representative consciousness (one re-presenting reality adequately). These two senses of representation—within state formation and the law, on the one hand, and in subject-predication, on the other—are related but irreducibly discontinuous. To cover over the discontinuity with an analogy that is presented as a proof reflects again a paradoxical subject-privileging. *Because* "the person who speaks and acts... is always a multiplicity", no "theorizing intellectual... [or] party or... union" can represent "those who act and struggle". Are those who act and *struggle* mute, as opposed to those who act and *speak*? These immense problems are buried in the differences between the "same" words: consciousness and conscience (both *conscience* in French), representation and re-presentation. The critique of ideological subject-constitution within state formations and systems of political economy can now be

---

① Spivak, *A Critique of Postcolonial Reason: Toward a History of the Vanishing Present*, pp.256 – 274.

effaced, as can the active theoretical practice of the "transformation of consciousness". The banality of leftist intellectuals' lists of self-knowing, politically canny subalterns stands revealed; representing them, the intellectuals represent themselves as transparent.

If such a critique and such a project are not to be given up, the shifting distinctions between representation within the state and political economy, on the one hand, and within the theory of the Subject, on the other, must not be obliterated. Let us consider the play of *vertreten* ("represent" in the first sense) and *darstellen* ("re-present" in the second sense) in a famous passage in *The Eighteenth Brumaire of Louis Bonaparte*, where Marx touches on "class" as a descriptive and transformative concept in a manner somewhat more complex than Althusser's distinction between class instinct and class position would allow. This is important in the context of the argument from the working class both from our two philosophers and "political" third-world feminism from the metropolis.

[...]

The reduction of Marx to a benevolent but dated figure most often serves the interest of launching a new theory of interpretation. In the Foucault-Deleuze conversation, the issue seems to be that there is no representation, no signifier (Is it to be presumed that the signifier has already been dispatched? There is, then, no sign-structure operating experience, and thus might one lay semiotics to rest?); theory is a relay of practice (thus laying problems of theoretical practice to rest); and the oppressed can know and speak for themselves. This reintroduces the constitutive subject on at least two levels: the Subject of desire and power as an irreducible methodological presupposition; and the self-proximate, if not self-identical, subject of the oppressed. Further, the intellectuals, who are neither of these S/subjects, become transparent in the relay race, for they merely report on the nonrepresented subject and analyze (without analyzing) the workings of (the unnamed Subject irreducibly presupposed by) power and desire. The produced "transparency" marks the place of "interest"; it is maintained by vehement denegation: "Now this rôle of referee, judge and universal witness is one which I *absolutely refuse* to adopt." One responsibility of the critic might be to read and write so that the impossibility of such interested individualistic refusals of the institutional privileges of power bestowed on the subject is taken seriously. The refusal of sign-system blocks the way to a developed theory of ideology in the "empirical". [...]

Edward W. Said's critique of power in Foucault as a captivating and mystifying category that allows him "to obliterate the rôle of classes, the rôle of economics, the rôle of insurgency and rebellion", is pertinent here, although the importance of the name of "power" in the sub-individual is not to be ignored. I add to Said's analysis the notion of the surreptitious subject of power and desire marked by the transparency of the intellectual.

This S/subject, curiously sewn together into a transparency by denegations, belongs to the exploiters' side of the international division of labor. It is impossible for contemporary French intellectuals to imagine the kind of Power and Desire that would inhabit the unnamed subject of the

Other of Europe. It is not only that everything they read, critical or uncritical, is caught within the debate of the production of that Other, supporting or critiquing the constitution of the Subject as Europe. It is also that, in the constitution of that Other of Europe, great care was taken to obliterate the textual ingredients with which such a subject could cathect, could occupy (invest?) its itinerary—not only by ideological and scientific production, but also by the institution of the law. However reductionistic an economic analysis might seem, the French intellectuals forget at their peril that this entire overdetermined enterprise was in the interest of a dynamic economic situation requiring that interests, motives (desires), and power (of knowledge) be ruthlessly dislocated. To invoke that dislocation now as a radical discovery that should make us diagnose the economic (conditions of existence that separate out "classes" descriptively) as a piece of dated analytic machinery may well be to continue the work of that dislocation and unwittingly to help in securing "a new balance of hegemonic relations". In the face of the possibility that the intellectual is complicit in the persistent constitution of the Other as the Self's shadow, a possibility of political practice for the intellectual would be to put the economic "under erasure", to see the economic factor as irreducible as it reinscribes the social text, even as it is erased, however imperfectly, when it claims to be the final determinant or the transcendental signified.

Until very recently, the clearest available example of such epistemic violence was the remotely orchestrated, far-flung, and heterogeneous project to constitute the colonial subject as Other. This project is also the asymmetrical obliteration of the trace of that Other in its precarious Subject-ivity. It is well known that Foucault locates one case of epistemic violence, a complete overhaul of the episteme, in the redefinition of madness at the end of the European eighteenth century. But what if that particular redefinition was only a part of the narrative of history in Europe as well as in the colonies? What if the two projects of epistemic overhaul worked as dislocated and unacknowledged parts of a vast two-handed engine? Perhaps it is no more than to ask that the subtext of the palimpsestic narrative of imperialism be recognized as "subjugated knowledge", "a whole set of knowledges that have been disqualified as inadequate to their task or insufficiently elaborated: naive knowledges, located low down on the hierarchy, beneath the required level of cognition or scientificity".

This is not to describe "the way things really were" or to privilege the narrative of history as imperialism as the best version of history. It is, rather, to continue the account of how one explanation and narrative of reality was established as the normative one. [...]

Let us now move to consider the margins (one can just as well say the silent, silenced center) of the circuit marked out by this epistemic violence, men and women among the illiterate peasantry, Aboriginals, and the lowest strata of the urban subproletariat. According to Foucault and Deleuze (in the First World, under the standardization and regimentation of socialized capital, though they do not seem to recognize this) and mutatis mutandis the metropolitan "third world feminist" only interested in resistance within capital logic, the oppressed, if given the chance (the problem of representation cannot be bypassed here), and on the way to solidarity through alliance politics (a Marxist thematic is at work here) *can speak and know their conditions*. We must now confront the following question: On the other side of the international division of labor from socialized capital, inside and outside the circuit of the epistemic violence of imperialist law and education supplementing an earlier economic text, *can the subaltern speak?*

We have already considered the possibility that, given the exigencies of the inauguration of colonial records, the instrumental woman (the Rani of Sirmur) is not fully written.

Antonio Gramsci's work on the "subaltern classes" extends the class-position/class-consciousness argument isolated in *The Eighteenth Brumaire*. Perhaps because Gramsci criticizes the vanguardistic position of the Leninist intellectual, he is concerned with the intellectual's rôle in the subaltern's cultural and political movement into the hegemony. This movement must be made to determine the production of history as narrative (of truth). In texts such as *The Southern Question*, Gramsci considers the movement of historical-political economy in Italy within what can be seen as an allegory of reading taken from or prefiguring an international division of labor. Yet an account of the phased development of the subaltern is thrown out of joint when his cultural macrology is operated, however remotely, by the epistemic interference with legal and disciplinary definitions accompanying the imperialist project. When I move, at the end of this essay, to the question of woman as subaltern, I will suggest that the possibility of collectivity itself is persistently foreclosed through the manipulation of female agency.

The first part of my proposition—that the phased development of the subaltern is complicated by the imperialist project—is confronted by the "Subaltern Studies" group. They *must* ask, Can the subaltern speak? Here we are within Foucault's own discipline of history and with people who acknowledge his influence. Their project is to rethink Indian colonial historiography from the perspective of the discontinuous chain of peasant insurgencies during the colonial occupation. This is indeed the problem of "the permission to narrate" discussed by Said. As Ranajit Guha, the founding editor of the collective, argues,

The historiography of Indian nationalism has for a long time been dominated by elitism—colonialist elitism and bourgeois-nationalist elitism...shar[ing] the prejudice that the making of the Indian nation and the development of the consciousness—nationalism—which confirmed this process were exclusively or predominantly elite achievements. In the colonialist and neo-colonialist historiographies these achievements are credited to British colonial rulers, administrators, policies, institutions, and culture; in the nationalist and neo-nationalist writings—to Indian elite personalities, institutions, activities and ideas.

Certain members of the Indian elite are of course native informants for first-world intellectuals interested in the voice of the Other. But one must nevertheless insist that the colonized subaltern *subject* is irretrievably heterogeneous.

Against the indigenous elite we may set what Guha calls "the politics of the people", both outside ("this was an autonomous domain, for it neither originated from elite politics nor did its existence depend on the latter") and inside ("it continued to operate vigorously in spite of [colonialism], adjusting itself to the conditions prevailing under the Raj and in many respects developing entirely new strains in both form and content") the circuit of colonial production. I cannot entirely endorse this insistence of determinate vigor and full autonomy, for practical historiographic exigencies will not allow such endorsements to privilege subaltern consciousness. Against the possible charge that his approach is essentialist, Guha constructs a definition of the people (the place of that essence) that can be only an identity-in-differential. He proposes a dynamic stratification grid describing colonial social production at large. Even the third group on the list, the buffer group, as it were, between the people and the great macro-structural dominant groups, is itself defined as a place of in-betweenness. The classification falls into: "dominant foreign groups", and "dominant indigenous groups at the all-India and at the regional and local levels" representing the elite; and "[t]he social groups and elements included in [the terms 'people' and 'subaltern classes'] represent[ing] *the demographic difference between the total Indian population and all those whom we have described as the 'elite'"*.

"The task of research" projected here is "to investigate, identify and measure the *specific* nature and degree of the *deviation* of [the] elements [constituting item 3] from the ideal and situate it historically". "Investigate, identify, and measure the specific": a program could hardly be more essentialist and taxonomic. Yet a curious methodological imperative is at work. I have argued that, in the Foucault-Deleuze conversation, a post-representationalist vocabulary hides an essentialist agenda. In subaltern studies, because of the violence of imperialist epistemic, social, and disciplinary inscription, a project understood in essentialist terms must traffic in a radical textual practice of differences. The object of the group's investigation, in this case not even of the people as such but of the floating buffer zone of the regional elite—is a *deviation* from an *ideal*—the people or subaltern—which is itself defined as a difference from the elite. It is toward this structure that the research is oriented, a predicament rather different from the self-diagnosed transparency of the first-world radical intellectual. What taxonomy can fix such a space? Whether or not they themselves perceive it—in fact Guha sees his definition of "the people" within the master-slave dialectic—their text articulates the difficult task of rewriting its own conditions of impossibility as the conditions of its possibility. "At the regional and local levels [the dominant indigenous groups]...if belonging to social strata hierarchically inferior to those of the dominant all-Indian groups *acted in the interests of the latter and not in conformity to interests corresponding truly to their own social being*." When these writers speak, in their essentializing language, of a gap between interest and action in the intermediate group, their conclusions are closer to Marx than to the self-conscious naivete of Deleuze's pronouncement on the issue. Guha, like Marx, speaks of interest in terms of the social rather than the libidinal being. The Name-of-the-Father imagery in *The Eighteenth Brumaire* can help to emphasize that, on the level of class or group action, "true correspondence to own being" is as artificial or social as the patronymic.

It is to this intermediate group that the second woman in this chapter belongs. The pattern of domination is here determined mainly by gender rather than class. The subordinated gender following the dominant within the challenge of nationalism while remaining caught within gender oppression is not an unknown story.

For the (gender-unspecified) "true" subaltern group, whose identity is its difference, there is no unrepresentable subaltern subject that can know and speak itself; the intellectual's solution is not to abstain from representation. The problem is that the subject's itinerary has not been left traced so as to offer an object of seduction to the representing intellectual. In the slightly dated language of the Indian group, the question becomes, How can we touch the consciousness of the people, even as we investigate their politics? With what voice-consciousness can the subaltern speak?

[...]

Within the effaced itinerary of the subaltern subject, the track of sexual difference is doubly effaced. The question is not of female participation in insurgency, or the ground rules of the sexual division of labor, for both of which there is "evidence". It is, rather, that, both as object of colonialist historiography and as subject of insurgency, the ideological construction of gender keeps the male dominant. If, in the contest of colonial production, the subaltern has no history and cannot speak, the subaltern as female is even more deeply in shadow. [...]

四、思考与讨论

1.萨义德对"东方主义"的定义是什么？如何结合他的世俗性和身份政治批判来理解这种定义？能否据此举例分析东西方文化再现的具体现象，如英美文学文化中的中国形象？

2.通过批判萨义德同质性、总体化的东方话语，巴巴提出了矛盾性、混杂性、模仿、第三空间等概念，强调通过模仿改写殖民话语来建构殖民主体的混杂身份。如何认识这些概念在后殖民主义抵抗政治中的有效性？能否以后殖民文学作品举例说明？

3.斯皮瓦克如何以解构主义的方法论述属下与后殖民主义的代表/再现这一难题？

本章推荐阅读文献

[1] Aijaz Ahmad. *In Theory: Classes, Nations, Literatures*. New York: Verso, 1992.

［2］Ania Loomba. *Colonialism／Postcolonialism*. London：Routledge，2015.

［3］Arif Dirlik. *The Postcolonial Aura: Third World Criticism in the Age of Global Capitalism*. Boulder：Westview Press，1997.

［4］Bart Moore-Gilbert. *Postcolonial Theory: Contexts，Practices，Politics*. London：Verso，1997.

［5］Benita Parry. *Postcolonial Studies: A Materialist Critique*. London：Routledge，2004.

［6］Edward W. Said. *Culture and Imperialism*. New York：Knopf，1993.

［7］Edward W. Said. *Orientalism*. New York：Vintage Books，1979.

［8］Edward W. Said. *The World，the Text，and the Critic*. London：Faber and Faber，1984.

［9］Frantz Fanon. *Black Skin，White Masks*. Trans. C. L. Markmann. New York：Grove Press，1967.

［10］Frantz Fanon. *The Wretched of the Earth*. Trans. Constance Farrington. London：MacGibbon and Kee，1965.

［11］Gayatri C. Spivak. *A Critique of Postcolonial Reason: Toward a History of the Vanishing Present*. Cambridge：Harvard University Press，1999.

［12］Gayatri C. Spivak. *In Other Worlds: Essays in Cultural Politics*. New York：Methuen，1987.

［13］Gayatri C. Spivak. *Outside in the Teaching Machine*. London and New York：Routledge，1993.

［14］Graham Huggan（ed.）. *The Oxford Handbook of Postcolonial Studies*. Oxford：Oxford University Press，2013.

［15］Homi K. Bhabha. *The Location of Culture*. London：Routledge，1994.

［16］John McLeod. *Beginning Postcolonialism*. Manchester：Manchester University Press，2010.

［17］John McLeod（ed.）. *The Routledge Companion to Postcolonial Studies*. London：Routledge，2007.

［18］Leela Gandhi. *Postcolonial Theory: A Critical Introduction*. New York：Columbia University Press，1998.

［19］Neil Lazarus. *The Postcolonial Unconscious*. Cambridge：Cambridge University Press，2011.

［20］Peter Childs and Patrick Williams. *An Introduction to Post-Colonial Theory*. London：Prentice Hall，1997.

［21］Robert J. C. Young. *Postcolonialism: An Historical Introduction*. Oxford：Blackwell，2001.

第三章
解殖民研究

第一节 概 论

21世纪以来,解殖民研究(Decolonial Studies)在学术界逐渐升温,涉及文学、哲学、政治学、人类学、社会学、历史学、教育学、传播学、心理学等多个领域。简单地说,解殖民研究是为构建真正的多元化和多极化世界而对现代性及其隐暗面殖民性(coloniality)进行再审视、再批评的理论思潮和文化实践。与注重政治语境和意识形态分析的后殖民理论不同,解殖民研究聚焦现代性/殖民性,并提出了一系列新的观点:第一,1492年哥伦布发现新大陆标志着"现代/殖民世界体系"(modern/colonial world system)的诞生,多中心的非资本主义世界被排他性的单一世界取代;第二,现代性的宏大叙事遭到质疑,现代性不再被认为是"一个普遍的全球进程"①;第三,现代性和殖民性是同一枚硬币的两面,殖民性是现代性的隐暗面,"没有殖民性就没有现代性"②;第四,"现代性、资本主义和殖民性是同一套控制系统的不同方面"③,殖民性以殖民权力矩阵(the colonial matrix of power)的方式影响着现代世界的诸多分类,比如政治、经济、宗教、认知、审美、主体性等,并渗透到各个领域④;第五,跨现代性(transmodernity)旨在从认知和审美层面与现代性/殖民性"脱钩"(delinking)⑤。总体而言,解殖民研究者认为,要想建立一个真正的多元化和多极化世界,就需要对西方现代性进行"祛魅",他们还主张从非西方的文化传统和生活实践中发掘知识财富,进行认识论重构和审美重构,最终实现彻底的去殖民化。

解殖民研究与20世纪的全球去殖民化活动密切相关。其中,1955年万隆会议的召开标志着解殖民性正式进入公众视野。瓦尔特·米尼奥罗(Walter Mignolo)认为:"后殖民主义和(解)殖民性都是万隆会议的结果……解殖民性作为一系列没有中心的、但却相互关联的全球项目亦自此起航。"⑥值得注

---

① Walter Mignolo,"Delinking:The Rhetoric of Modernity, the Logic of Coloniality and the Grammar of De-coloniality," *Cultural Studies* 21.2-3(2007),p.463.
② Ibid.,p.464.
③ Walter Mignolo,"Introduction:Coloniality of Power and De-colonial Thinking," *Cultural Studies* 21.2-3(2007),p.162.
④ Walter Mignolo, *The Idea of Latin America*. Malden:Blackwell Publishing,2005,p.xiii.
⑤ Mignolo,"Delinking:The Rhetoric of Modernity, the Logic of Coloniality and the Grammar of De-coloniality," p.450.
⑥ 转引自 Walter Mignolo,"Modernity and Decoloniality," *Oxford Bibliographies*.[2017-05-05].

意的是,解殖民研究根植于拉美经验,比如"拉美的土著激进主义以及非裔加勒比和非裔安第斯社区的斗争"[1],并深受拉美思想界的影响,尤其是 20 世纪下半叶的各种理论思潮(包括"60 年代和 70 年代的解放神学,拉美哲社领域围绕解放哲学和自治社会科学的辩论及依赖理论,80 年代拉美关于现代性和后现代性的辩论,90 年代人类学、传播学和文化研究中关于杂糅性的讨论以及美国拉美庶民研究"[2]等)。但是,解殖民研究并非局限在拉美场域。解殖民研究不仅关注现代性/殖民性在亚非拉第三世界国家的具体表现形式,而且也重视其在欧美国家的相关体现。目前,解殖民研究已辐射到不同学科领域,探讨殖民权力矩阵如何渗透到世界各个领域,其最终目标是打破现代性迷思(myth of modernity),实现认知和审美的彻底去殖民化。下面我们就从解殖民研究的缘起开始,围绕现代性迷思、殖民性、跨现代性等重要议题展开介绍。

一、解殖民研究的缘起

虽然解殖民研究在 21 世纪初才逐渐发展为热点,但解殖民思想历史久远。美国罗格斯大学的解殖民研究者纳尔逊·马尔多纳多-托里斯(Nelson Maldonado-Torres)认为,解殖民思想产生于 15、16 世纪发现和征服美洲的殖民活动之中,而影响更大、更深刻的解殖民思想出现在 20 世纪。[3] 美国黑人知识分子 W. E. B. 杜波依斯(W. E. B. Du Bois)、法属马提尼克黑人运动领袖艾梅·塞泽尔(Aimé Césaire)和法属马提尼克反殖民运动思想家法农均认为去殖民化活动不应局限在政治和经济领域,也应从思想观念上推动去殖民化进程。20 世纪末,面对新的世界秩序,秘鲁社会学家和人文思想家阿尼巴尔·基哈诺(Aníbal Quijano)在其文章《殖民性与现代性/理性》("Colonialidad y Modernidad/Racionalidad")中首先提出了殖民性的概念,认为殖民性依旧是当今世界最普遍的统治形式。[4] 他强调当下应从认知层面上继续推进去殖民化进程,抛弃殖民性的原有知识结构和认知方式。他发现,虽然民族独立运动摧毁了作为外部政治秩序的殖民主义,但殖民性依旧是西方掌控世界的主要方式,因为争取民族独立等去殖民化活动并未消除殖民主义的剥削和控制,只是令其变得更加隐晦而已。换言之,去殖民化活动结束后,殖民性并未消失,而是变得更加隐晦。同时,围绕现代性的文明话语却越发凸显,并为西方知识生产方式贴上新奇、高级、先进等标签。隐晦的殖民性与外显的现代性继续合谋,将西方知识生产方式作为唯一权威向全世界推广,以确保世界依旧处于殖民掌控之下。因此,基哈诺提出,应当批判这种西方中心主义色彩浓厚的认知方式,并通过"认知重组"(epistemological reconstitution)来实现彻底的去殖民化。由此可见,基哈诺不但指明了现代性与殖民性的密切关系,还提出从认知层面去殖民化的观点,因此,基哈诺被认为是解殖民研究的理论先驱,奠定了解殖民研究的理论基础。

[1]　Nelson Maldonado-Torres, "Colonialism, Neocolonial, Internal Colonialism, the Postcolonial, Coloniality, and Decoloniality," *Critical Terms in Caribbean and Latin American Thought: Historical and Institutional Trajectories*. Eds. Yolanda Martínez-San Miguel, Ben. Sifuentes-Jáuregui and Marisa Belausteguigoitia. Hampshire: Palgrave Macmillan, 2016, p.76.

[2]　Arturo Escobar, "Words and Knowledges of Otherwise: The Latin American Modernity/Coloniality Research Program," *Cultural Studies* 21.2–3 (2007), pp.179–180.

[3]　Nelson Maldonado-Torres, "Thinking through the Decolonial Turn: Post-continental Interventions in Theory, Philosophy, and Critique—An Introduction," *TRANSMODERNITY: Journal of Peripheral Cultural Production of the Luso-Hispanic World* 1.2 (2011), pp.1–2.

[4]　Aníbal Quijano, "Colonialidad y modernidad/racionalidad," *Perú Indígena* 13.29 (1992), pp.11–20.

《文化研究》(Cultural Studies)2007年第2期和第3期"全球化与解殖民选择"专刊标志着解殖民研究的兴起。该专刊是阿根廷裔杜克大学文学和文化人类学教授米尼奥罗与哥伦比亚裔美国人类学家阿图罗·埃斯科瓦尔(Arturo Escobar)共同筹划的现代性/殖民性工作坊的阶段性成果,作者均为解殖民研究领域的重要学者,如米尼奥罗、基哈诺、埃斯科瓦尔、美国加州大学的拉蒙·格罗斯福格尔(Ramón Grosfoguel)、安第斯西蒙·玻利瓦尔大学(基多分校)的凯瑟琳·沃尔什(Catherine Walsh)、马尔多纳多-托里斯、哥伦比亚哲学家圣地亚哥·卡斯特罗-戈麦斯(Santiago Castro-Gómez)等。米尼奥罗在专刊导言《权力殖民性和解殖民思维》中宣称该专刊旨在"将解殖民思维作为一种特殊的批评理论"[①]。该专刊的主要目的就是挑战西方批评理论的权威地位,即打破将西方批评理论作为唯一正统理论的现状,并寻求从认识论和知识生产的角度批判西方现代性的可能性。其中米尼奥罗的文章《脱钩:现代性话术、殖民性逻辑和解殖民性语法》("Delinking:The Rhetoric of Modernity, the Logic of Coloniality and the Grammar of De-coloniality")的影响最大。在这篇文章中,米尼奥罗主要揭示了西方现代性话术,揭露了现代性的隐暗面——殖民性——的运行逻辑,指出了解殖民研究最重要的任务是反思西方化所推动的现代/殖民世界体系,并探讨了从认识、审美等方面进行去殖民化的可能性。自此,解殖民研究将解殖民思维引入各个领域,向西方现代性发起了持久进攻。

二、现代性迷思

伴随着欧洲殖民活动遍及世界各地,代表着"理性"和"进步"的西方现代性也随之在全球"兜售"。在围绕现代性的西方话语中,西方文明优越性的论调非常普遍,欧洲文明常被认为是世界上最先进、最高级的文明,而非欧洲文明则常被降格为未开化的、异教的、野蛮的文明,应当被西化或被清除。此类现代性迷思早在欧洲移民征服美洲的殖民活动中就已经清晰可见,并为血腥暴力的殖民扩张罩上了崇高的光环。哲学家恩里克·杜塞尔(Enrique Dussel)认为,自哥伦布发现新大陆伊始,西方殖民者便为现代性的良善编制了一套话术。为了使其暴力行为合法化,殖民者声称他们之所以诉诸暴力是因为需要帮助原住民走向理性、进步的文明之路,同时,殖民者还以无辜受害者自居,宣称自身亦饱受诸多来自野蛮原住民的暴力。[②] 值得注意的是,这种现代性话术不但在西方异常流行,而且也得到了原住民的认可。现代性迷思让人们相信所有人都可以平等自由地享用西方现代性带来的种种好处。事实上,就在人们"享受"现代性成果的同时,现代性不仅使殖民地灾难重重,而且在西方世界内部也引发了诸多问题,其中最为凸显的当属两次世界大战的爆发。因此,对现代性的批判势在必行。

早在19世纪后期,西方思想界就已经开始批判现代性。当时席卷欧洲的文化悲观主义氛围为现代性的批评提供了肥沃的土壤。比如尼采就曾直言不讳地批评启蒙运动所标榜的理性和进步,并指出了欧洲文明的腐败和衰落。而两次世界大战再次揭露了现代科技的破坏性和欧洲文明的隐暗面,至此,现代性渐渐失去了乐观主义精神。随后,法兰克福学派更加激烈地批判了西方现代性和启蒙运动的遗产。马克思·霍克海默尔(Max Horkheimer)和西奥多·W.阿多诺(Theodor W. Adorno)在《启蒙辩证法》

① Mignolo, "Introduction:Coloniality of Power and De-colonial Thinking," p.155.
② Enrique Dussel, *The Invention of the Americas: Eclipse of the Other and the Myth of Modernity*. New York:Continuum,1995, p.50.

中试图解释为什么"人类没有进入真正的人性化状态,而是陷入了一种新的野蛮状态"[①]。他们发现,"启蒙,在最广泛的意义上可理解为思想的进步,一直旨在将人类从恐惧中解放出来,并使其成为主人。然而,完全被启蒙的地球却灾难重重"[②]。

尽管欧洲批评理论中不乏对现代性的批判,但西方主流历史叙事仍然倾向于将大屠杀这样的历史事件建构为违背西方文明和现代性"良善面孔"的例外事件,而不是将其归为现代性本身的失败。相比而言,20世纪50年代在世界反殖民主义运动中发挥重要作用的一批思想家,比如杜波依斯、泛非运动领袖 C. L. R. 詹姆斯(C. L. R. James)和乔治·帕德莫尔(George Padmore)、社会学家奥利弗·考克斯(Oliver Cox)、塞泽尔、法农等,则挑战了现代性的宏大叙事,将矛头直指西方现代性的殖民逻辑。其中,塞泽尔在反殖民主义宣言《殖民主义话语》中宣称大屠杀的野蛮行为与欧洲殖民主义的逻辑密不可分,即作为针对欧洲白人的种族犯罪,大屠杀与欧洲殖民者对欧洲外部有色人种实施的殖民行为遵循相同的逻辑,它们均为欧洲现代性的必然产物。[③] 而在《大地上的受苦者》一书中,法农指出了现代性的"反常逻辑"(perverted logic)[④],认为这种逻辑致力于贬低、扭曲、损毁殖民地自身的历史。

20世纪末,在后现代主义的理论背景下,针对现代性的批评越发丰富多元。后现代性是针对现代性的总体性所展开的批评,既是现代性的延续,也是与现代性的断裂。后现代思想中对现代性的批评也得到了解殖民研究者的认可。比如,基哈诺肯定了后现代性针对现代总体性所展开的批判。[⑤] 杜塞尔也认为:"原则上,后现代性也表达了对其他文化的不可通约性、差异性和自主性的尊重。"[⑥]然而,解殖民研究者发现这些后现代批评依然或多或少带有欧洲中心主义色彩,因为它们依旧聚焦"欧洲历史和欧洲思想史"[⑦]。米尼奥罗认为:"后现代主义沉溺在对现代世界历史的单边自我构想中,继续掩盖了殖民性,并维系着普遍和单一的逻辑……从欧洲(或北大西洋)出发向外延伸。"[⑧]同时,米尼奥罗也关注到后现代性的衍生物——后结构主义和后殖民主义——对现代性的反思。他认为,后结构主义虽然旨在扭转或打破等级制度,但同时也意味着继续使用主流话语体制(discursive regime)所规定的范畴,包括二元对立等术语。因此,它依旧停留在它所批评的体系中,属于体系内的批判,并未为批判话语提供外部视角。不仅如此,格罗斯福格尔认为:"作为认识论的后现代主义和后结构主义依旧被困在西方经典中,在其思想和实践领域中不断生产权力/知识的殖民性。"[⑨]也就是说,后现代主义和后结构主义不仅没有摧毁殖民性逻辑,还再生产或重组了权力/知识的殖民性。解殖民研究者认为后殖民主义具有相同的局限性,后殖民主义虽然注重历史的多元化,并试图挖掘殖民地人民被压抑的声音,但依旧"没有质疑欧洲中心主义的核心位置"[⑩],其批评仍未真正引入非西方的思维方式和认知方式。

---

① Max Horkheimer and Theodor W. Adorno. *Dialectic of Enlightenment*. Trans. Gunzelin Noeri. Stanford: Stanford University Press, 2002, p.xiv.
② Ibid., p.1.
③ Aimé Césaire, *Discourse on Colonialism*. Trans. Joan Pinkham. New York: Monthly Review Press, 2000. pp.35-36.
④ Fanon, *The Wretched of the Earth*, p.170.
⑤ Aníbal Quijano, "Coloniality and Modernity/Rationality," *Cultural Studies* 21.2-3 (2007), pp.176-177.
⑥ Enrique Dussel, "World-System and 'Trans'-Modernity," trans. Alessandro Fornazzari. *Nepantla: Views from South* 3.2 (2002), p.233.
⑦ Mignolo, "Delinking: The Rhetoric of Modernity, the Logic of Coloniality and the Grammar of De-coloniality," p.451.
⑧ Walter Mignolo, "Coloniality at Large: The Western Hemisphere in the Colonial Horizon of Modernity," trans. Michael Ennis. *CR: The New Centennial Review* 1.2 (2001), p.24.
⑨ Ramón Grosfoguel, "The Epistemic Decolonial Turn: Beyond Political-economy Paradigms," *Cultural Studies* 21.2-3 (2007), p.212.
⑩ Dussel, "World-System and 'Trans'-Modernity," p.233.

解殖民性"既是与以欧洲为中心的后现代性的断裂,也是与严重依赖后结构主义的后殖民项目的断裂,因为福柯、拉康和德里达为后殖民经典理论家(如萨义德、斯皮瓦克和巴巴)提供了理论基础。而解殖民性源自他处"①。解殖民研究致力于寻求批判现代性的另类他路。其中,杜塞尔聚焦"现代性的非理性迷思",认为正是这种非理性迷思"为种族灭绝的暴力提供了合法性"②。也就是说,种族灭绝等暴力事件根植于现代性自身的结构特征,而不是其他外部因素。在杜塞尔基础之上,米尼奥罗聚焦现代性话术。他发现:"现代性的话术是通过强化'拯救'而奏效的,无论是基督教、西方文明、二战之后的现代化进程和发展模式,还是苏联解体后的市场民主,均带有很强的救赎色彩。"③根据这套现代性的救赎话语,西方价值观和世界观被放置于"救世主"的位置,属于绝对真理,应当在全球被广泛传播。也就是说,非西方国家应当积极推进西方化。显然,现代性的救赎话术"隐藏了殖民性,即压迫和剥削的逻辑"④。因此,解殖民研究者认为,不仅需要从后现代性的角度,也需要从殖民性的角度对现代性展开批判,以便"将知识生产、反思及交流从欧洲现代性/理性的陷阱中解放出来"⑤。

三、现代性的隐暗面:殖民性

21世纪初学界出现的"解殖民转向"聚焦现代性的隐暗面——殖民性,认为殖民性"揭示了自16世纪以来西方文明的形成及其星际扩张的基本逻辑"⑥,并探究了去殖民化的可能路径。马尔多纳多-托里斯曾这样描述"解殖民转向":"解殖民转向并不是一个单独的理论流派,其包括多重理论方法,这些不同的理论方法均认为:在现代、后现代及信息时代,殖民性是最根本的问题,去殖民化或解殖民性的任务依旧未完成。"⑦也就是说,"解殖民转向"并不是一个同质的理论体系,它没有一个权威的主导理论,而是包括多种理论方法,其核心议题是如何消解殖民性,从而实现更加彻底的去殖民化。目前"解殖民转向"已发展为颇具规模的现代性/殖民性/解殖民性研究网络。该学术研究网络的核心人物有人类学家、批评理论家、文化研究者、女权主义者、哲学家、社会学家、教育学研究者、博物馆学研究者、时尚学研究者等。对他们来说,殖民性既是现代性的构成要素,也是"西方现代性在世界范围内传播的主要形式"⑧,"没有殖民性,现代性是不可能成为一种话语和一种实践的"⑨。因此,他们主张从世界各个领域的各个方面探讨现代性的殖民逻辑。

虽然殖民性得名于殖民主义,但对解殖民研究者来说,殖民性与殖民主义的区别很大。殖民主义"表示一种政治和经济关系,其中一个国家或一个民族的主权受制于另一个国家的权力",而殖民性"是

① Mignolo, "Delinking: The Rhetoric of Modernity, the Logic of Coloniality and the Grammar of De-coloniality," p.452.
② Enrique Dussel, "Eurocentrism and Modernity (Introduction to the Frankfurt Lectures)," *boundary 2*, 20.3 (1993), p.66.
③ Mignolo, "Delinking: The Rhetoric of Modernity, the Logic of Coloniality and the Grammar of De-coloniality," p.450.
④ Mignolo, "Introduction: Coloniality of Power and De-colonial Thinking," p.162.
⑤ Quijano, "Coloniality and Modernity/Rationality," p.177.
⑥ Walter Mignolo and Catherine Walsh, *On Decoloniality: Concepts, Analytics, Praxis*. Durham: Duke University Press, 2018, p.225.
⑦ Maldonado-Torres, "Thinking through the Decolonial Turn: Post-continental Interventions in Theory, Philosophy, and Critique—An Introduction," p.2.
⑧ Nelson Maldonado-Torres, "Race, Religion, and Ethics in the Modern/Colonial World," *Journal of Religious Ethics* 42.4 (2014), p.695.
⑨ Nelson Maldonado-Torres, "On the Coloniality of Being: Contributions to the Development of a Concept," *Cultural Studies* 21.2-3 (2007), p.244.

指由于殖民主义而产生的长期权力模式,它定义了文化、劳动力、主体间关系和知识生产,远远超出了殖民管理的严格限制"①。即殖民主义是指由殖民政府维持的一种政治和经济统治形式,而殖民性则代表了殖民帝国崩溃后持续存在的一种权力模式,主要发生在认知层面。也就是说,殖民主义可能有多重历史形态,如果维持它的政治和经济关系不复存在,它就会被摧毁,但被当作理解知识和创造知识的唯一原则,殖民性则很难根除。以冷战期间的去殖民化运动为例,米尼奥罗指出,"冷战期间的去殖民化活动旨在将殖民者赶出殖民地,因此原住民可以实现自治,但其形式依旧是民族国家"②。即这种去殖民化运动依旧没有摆脱殖民者留下的治理结构。事实上,虽然获得独立后的殖民地可以暂时免受持续、系统的殖民行动的干扰,但西方现代性迷思依旧深刻影响着原住民。被西方现代性所吸引的原住民不但深深认同着现代性自我塑造的叙事,即西方文化是理性的、进步的和高级的,而且也相信一旦实现西化,他们就会像殖民者一样,获取丰厚的物质财富,并占据主导地位。至此,殖民者的知识生产模式和意义生产模式依旧是控制原住民的有效方式。这也正是马尔多纳多-托里斯曾经说的"我们无时无刻不在呼吸殖民性"③,即当下殖民性仍然主宰着我们的世界。

针对殖民性的具体形式,马尔多纳多-托里斯曾谈过三种具体的殖民性:"权力的殖民性(coloniality of power)指的是现代剥削形式和统治(权力)形式之间的相互关系,知识的殖民性(coloniality of knowledge)与殖民对不同领域知识生产的影响有关,而存在的殖民性(coloniality of being)主要指殖民的生活经验及其对语言的影响。"④同时,埃斯科瓦尔也提出"自然的殖民性"(coloniality of nature)来批评西方常将自然作为理性、文明、先进等的对立面的观念。⑤ 值得注意的是,这些针对殖民性各个方面的探讨并不是截然分开的,而是相互交错的。人们也常将权力的殖民性放置于一个更宽的范畴中,认为权力的殖民性以殖民权力矩阵的方式渗透到全球社会生活的各个方面。作为一种复杂的管理和控制结构,殖民权力矩阵一方面阻碍了非西方文化的生产进程,另一方面也促使帝国资本主义渗透到全球各个角落,世界各个领域的游戏规则也由此建立起来。在当下世界秩序中,殖民权力矩阵已经成为强有力的社会文化管控工具,任何不遵守或违背矩阵规则的人都会在不同程度上被否定、被边缘化、被妖魔化。

四、认知脱钩与跨现代性

如何将世界从殖民权力矩阵中解放出来成为解殖民研究的重要议题。为了突破殖民权力矩阵,解殖民研究者认为应当重新审视、批判西方认识论和审美方式。他们认为,西方认识论通过宣传、推广知识生产的普遍假设——知识是透明的、客观的,并且独立于任何特定的地理历史语境——来将其他认识论边缘化,进而稳固了其自身的霸权主导地位。"为了建立一个总体的知识观,西方认识论(从基督教神学到世俗哲学和科学)假装知识独立于它产生的地理历史环境(基督教欧洲)和生命地理条件(基督教白人生活在基督教欧洲)。结果,欧洲成为认知表达的场所,世界其他地区成为从欧洲(以及后来的美

①　Maldonado-Torres,"On the Coloniality of Being: Contributions to the Development of a Concept," p.243.
②　Walter Mignolo, *The Politics of Decolonial Investigations*. Durham: Duke University Press, 2021, p.14.
③　Maldonado-Torres,"On the Coloniality of Being: Contributions to the Development of a Concept," p.243.
④　Ibid., p.242.
⑤　Arturo Escobar, *Territories of Difference: Place, Movements, Life, Redes*. Durham: Duke University Press, 2008, pp. 120−121.

国)角度描述和研究的对象。"①解殖民研究质疑这种西方中心的认知方式,并主张挖掘殖民地本土知识财富。同时,感觉和知觉本应是宇宙中生命体的普遍现象,每个民族国家都拥有属于本民族国家的独特审美方式。但文艺复兴以来,欧洲审美被贴上了"唯一""高级""正确"等标签,并随着殖民活动向世界各地"兜售",现已成为西方控制、管理主体的重要方式之一。因此,解殖民研究者强调为了建立更加公正、更加可持续的世界秩序,必须在各个层面,尤其是认知层面和审美层面,与西方现代性脱钩。

与西方主流的现代性批评范式不同,解殖民研究者强调从"思想"②和"想象"③方面与现代性/殖民性脱钩,即实现知识和审美的彻底去殖民化。"认知脱钩"这一概念来自基哈诺"认知重组"④的观点。他认为不应在西方宇宙观的范畴内建立新的思潮,而是应从那些常被污名化为迷信、野蛮的原住民文化中寻求不同的认识世界和理解世界的方式。在此基础之上,米尼奥罗提出了"认知不服从"⑤(epistemic disobedience)的观点,认为当务之急是对被西方文明和现代性所忽视的思维模式和生活实践进行认知重构,从而实现认知脱钩。用他的话来说,解殖民研究的"脱钩"旨在实现的是一种"认知转变"⑥。米尼奥罗发现,16世纪以来,随着殖民活动的开展,西方认识论开始向世界散播,并逐渐占据了主导位置。与此同时,欧洲现代性所体现的"帝国总体性观念"压制、排斥了西方以外的"其他总体性的可能性"⑦。因此,解殖民研究应致力于对西方认识论和总体性进行"祛魅",引入非西方的认识论和世界观,使之成为"游戏中的平等参与者"⑧。为实现认知转变,杜塞尔提出应立足"外部"⑨(exteriority)来打破现代性迷思,推进去殖民化进程。同样,借助格洛丽亚·E.安扎尔杜(Gloria E. Anzaldúa)的边界(borderlands)隐喻,米尼奥罗再次强调了"边界思维"(border thinking)的重要性。边界思维立足中间地带,旨在"超越西方认识论强加的范畴",不仅呼吁改变世界秩序参与者的"对话内容"——被阐明之物(the said, the enunciated),而且强调改变"对话语汇"——阐述过程(the saying, the enunciation)⑩,从而最终实现"政治和伦理转变"⑪。也就是说,为了实现真正的多元认知论,与注重改变对话内容的去西方化(dewesternization)不同,解殖民性意味着改变知识生产和传播的原则和前提。因此,解殖民视角下的跨文化交流将赋予"所有民族单独或集体选择的自由:在各种文化取向之间进行选择的自由,最重要的是,生产、批评、转化和传播社会文化的自由"⑫。即解殖民性会将跨文化交流从殖民权力矩阵中解放出来,指向更加自由、平等、包容的世界。

在《美洲的发明:他者的消失和现代性迷思》(*The Invention of the Americas: Eclipse of the Other*

---

① 转引自 Walter Mignolo, "Modernity and Decoloniality," *Oxford Bibliographies*. [2017 - 05 - 05].
② Ngugi wa Thiong'o, *Decolonising the Mind: The Politics of Language in African Literature*. Oxford: James Currey, 1986.
③ Serge Gruzinski, *La colonisation de l'imaginaire: Sociétés indigènes et occidentalisation dans le Mexique espagnol, XVI - XVIII*. Paris: Gallimard, 1988.
④ Quijano, "Coloniality and Modernity/Rationality," pp.176 - 178.
⑤ Walter Mignolo, *The Darker Side of Western Modernity: Global Futures, Decolonial Options*. Durham: Duke University Press, 2011, pp.118 - 145.
⑥ Mignolo, "Delinking: The Rhetoric of Modernity, the Logic of Coloniality and the Grammar of De-coloniality," p.453.
⑦ Ibid., p.451.
⑧ Ibid.
⑨ Enrique Dussel, *The Underside of Modernity: Apel, Ricoeur, Rorty, Taylor, and the Philosophy of Liberation*. Trans. & eds. Eduardo Mendieta. Atlantic Highlands: Humanities Press, 1996.
⑩ Mignolo, *The Darker Side of Western Modernity: Global Futures, Decolonial Options*, p.122.
⑪ L. Elena Delgado, Rolando J. Romero and Walter Mignolo, "Local Histories and Global Designs: An Interview with Walter Mignolo," *Discourse* 22.3 (2000), p.11.
⑫ Quijano, "Coloniality and Modernity/Rationality," p.178.

and the Myth of Modernity）一书中，杜塞尔提出了"跨现代性"[①]这一概念来进一步描述解殖民性所指向的全球世界秩序。他认为，与"后"不同，"这个'超越'（'trans-'）表明了一个起点……或从被现代性排除、否认或忽视为'无足轻重''毫无意义''野蛮'之中，或从'非文化'之中，或从'未知的模糊他物'之中出发"[②]。跨现代性"表达了对现代性的解殖民态度，向多种语言开放哲学，并除去现代性的殖民元素和偏见"[③]。跨现代性引入了不同的知识概念、不同的语言和声音，从而打破了它们之间的等级关系。杜塞尔认为跨现代性的未来指涉"多元文化、多才多艺、混合杂糅、后殖民、多元、宽容和民主"[④]。解殖民研究者认为跨现代性将会带领我们进入一个真正多元、多中心的世界。

自 2005 年"解殖民转向"这一概念正式进入学术界，"解殖民性"得到了越来越多学者的关注，相关研究成果颇丰。当然，解殖民研究也遇到了许多质疑声音。乔治·赫尔（George Hull）曾质疑解殖民性过于抽象和哲学化。[⑤] 在 2020 年《后殖民研究》（*Postcolonial Studies*）第 4 期的文章中，中国学者顾明栋认为米尼奥罗和沃尔什在其合著的《论解殖民性：概念、分析及实践》（*On Decoloniality: Concepts，Analytics，Praxis*）中对解殖民性的定义过于模糊空洞，他写道："如果解殖民性代表着一种思维方式和生活方式，那么殖民性也是一种思维方式和生活方式。同样，殖民化、去殖民化、殖民主义、后殖民主义及其他人类活动亦是如此。因此，（米尼奥罗和沃尔什）对解殖民性的定义并没有明确告诉我们解殖民性到底是什么。"[⑥]面对诸如此类的批评，米尼奥罗进行了回应，并在其同期文章中重新阐释了解殖民性。[⑦] 他认为，解殖民性不应该被概念化，或者将其与具体的概念框架捆绑在一起。解殖民性远非一种新的思想批判范式，因为它一旦成为一个范式，也就不再是解殖民性了。同时，解殖民性也不是一个行之有效、放之四海而皆准的方法，它更多的是一个出发点，一种欢迎多种可能性的开放话题。在 2021 年年底由英国研究方法中心（National Center for Research Methods，NCRM）组织的题为"解殖民研究方法：抵抗学界知识生产的殖民性"线上论坛[⑧]中，米尼奥罗发表了题为《解殖民研究方法：北大西洋以外的星际对话（全球东部和全球南部）》的讲演，再次坦言自己无法回答解殖民研究所使用的具体研究方法，解殖民研究的重点在于对具体问题展开解殖民思考。[⑨] 因此，作为一个星际批评意识，解殖民性的"适用对象是无限的"[⑩]，它既没有具体的概念体系，也无法形成统一的、权威的结论，但也正是这种开放性使其生命力不断。目前解殖民性不断生成，不断被阐释，在学界和社会公共领域继续上演着不同"剧本"。

解殖民研究的主要贡献在于揭露了知识的现代/殖民结构，提供了一种重新思考事件的视角，指明了新的生活实践方向。在 2021 年的著作《解殖民调研的策略》（*The Politics of Decolonial Investigations*）中，米尼奥罗全面考察了从 16 世纪到 20 世纪殖民性在世界各地的运作方式，揭示了西方文明自我塑造的

① Dussel, *The Invention of the Americas: Eclipse of the Other and the Myth of Modernity*，p.66.
② Dussel, "World-System and 'Trans'-Modernity," p.234.
③ Maldonado-Torres, "Thinking through the Decolonial Turn: Post-continental Interventions in Theory, Philosophy, and Critique—An Introduction," p.7.
④ Dussel, "World-System and 'Trans'-Modernity," p.236.
⑤ George Hull, "Some Pitfalls of Decoloniality Theory," *The Thinker* 89.4 (2021)，p.63.
⑥ Mingdong Gu, "What Is 'Decoloniality'? A Postcolonial Critique," *Postcolonial Studies* 23.4 (2020)，pp.596 - 600.
⑦ Walter Mignolo, "On Decoloniality: Second Thoughts," *Postcolonial Studies* 23.4 (2020)，pp.612 - 618.
⑧ 这次线上论坛邀请了 6 位不同领域的学者从不同的维度对解殖民研究方法进行了阐述。
⑨ 参见网址：https://www.ncrm.ac.uk/resources/video/? id=4558.
⑩ Mignolo, "On Decoloniality: Second Thoughts," p.615.

叙事与欧洲思想霸权位置的勾连,并提出了在知识/理解、统治、经济和人文这四个范畴内进行认知重组和审美重组的可能性。[①] 米尼奥罗再次强调了在学院内外实施解殖民策略的重要性,呼吁将人们从经典化与西方化的知识体系、认知方式和生活习惯中解放出来,从而建立多极化、多中心的世界秩序。米尼奥罗等解殖民研究者的呼吁可谓是应对当下岌岌可危的全球世界秩序的及时雨。当下全球世界秩序再次陷入困境,比如资源分配不均问题加剧、气候变暖问题越发严峻等。全球世界秩序危机再次暴露了殖民性逻辑,也再次将现代性批评推到聚光灯之下。如何建立真正多元、有序、可持续的全球世界秩序成为亟待解决的核心问题。为了维系其在世界秩序中的霸权地位,欧美等西方国家仍寄希望于改良现代性,企图通过再西方化来修复现代/殖民世界体系。显然,历史已经多次证实再西方化并不可能挽救当前的世界局势,而解殖民研究探究殖民权力矩阵运行机制的尝试及其所呼吁的另类他路则给人们带来了新的曙光。

第二节　经典文献选读

本章共有三篇选文,选文都是解殖民研究领域的重要文献。第一篇节选自阿尼巴尔·基哈诺发表在《文化研究》上的文章《殖民性与现代性/理性》("Coloniality and Modernity/Rationality")。他指出现代性与殖民性勾连,并主张通过"认知重组"来实现去殖民化。第二篇选文出自纳尔逊·马尔多纳多-托里斯发表在《跨现代性:葡语-西语世界的周边文化生产》(*TRANSMODERNITY: Journal of Peripheral Cultural Production of the Luso-Hispanic World*)上的专刊文章《解殖民转向的思考:后大陆理论、哲学和批评简介》("Thinking Through the Decolonial Turn:Post-continental Interventions in Theory,Philosophy,and Critique—An Introduction")。他详细梳理了解殖民转向的缘起及其核心观点。第三篇节选自瓦尔特·米尼奥罗的专著《解殖民调研的策略》,他在书中再次重申了解殖民研究所关注的核心问题及研究策略。

一、《殖民性与现代性/理性》选读[②]

[...]

Eurocentrism, cultural coloniality and modernity/rationality

During the same period as European colonial domination was consolidating itself, the cultural complex known as European modernity/rationality was being constituted. The intersubjective universe produced by the entire Eurocentered capitalist colonial power was elaborated and formalized by the Europeans and established in the world as an exclusively European product and as a universal paradigm of knowledge and of the relation between humanity and the rest of the

---

① Mignolo, *The Politics of Decolonial Investigations*,2021.
② Quijano, "Coloniality and Modernity/Rationality," pp.168-178.

world. Such confluence between coloniality and the elaboration of rationality/modernity was not in anyway accidental, as is shown by the very manner in which the European paradigm of rational knowledge was elaborated. In fact, the coloniality of power had decisive implications in the constitution of the paradigm, associated with the emergence of urban and capitalist social relations, which in their turn could not be fully explained outside colonialism and coloniality particularly not as far as Latin America is concerned. The decisive weight of coloniality in the constitution of the European paradigm of modernity/rationality is clearly revealed in the actual crisis of that cultural complex. Examining some of the basic questions of that crisis will help to illuminate the problem.

[...]

The epistemological reconstitution: de-colonization

The idea of totality in general is today questioned and denied in Europe, not only by the perennial empiricists, but also by an entire intellectual community that calls itself postmodernist. In fact, in Europe, the idea of totality is a product of colonial/modernity. And it is demonstrable, as we have seen above, that the European ideas of totality led to theoretical reductionism and to the metaphysics of a macro-historical subject. Moreover, such ideas have been associated with undesirable political practices, behind a dream of the total rationalization of society.

It is not necessary, however, to reject the whole idea of totality in order to divest oneself of the ideas and images with which it was elaborated within European colonial/modernity. What is to be done is something very different: to liberate the production of knowledge, reflection, and communication from the pitfalls of European rationality/modernity.

Outside the "West", virtually in all known cultures, every cosmic vision, every image, all systematic production of knowledge is associated with a perspective of totality. But in those cultures, the perspective of totality in knowledge includes the acknowledgement of the heterogeneity of all reality; of the irreducible, contradictory character of the latter; of the legitimacy, i.e., the desirability, of the diverse character of the components of all reality—and therefore, of the social. The idea of social totality, then, not only does not deny, but depends on the historical diversity and heterogeneity of society, of every society. In other words, it not only does not deny, but it requires the idea of an "other"—diverse, different. That difference does not necessarily imply the unequal nature of the "other" and therefore the absolute externality of relations, nor the hierarchical inequality nor the social inferiority of the other. The differences are not necessarily the basis of domination. At the same time—and because of that—historical-cultural heterogeneity implies the co-presence and the articulation of diverse historical "logic" around one of them, which is hegemonic but in no way unique. In this way, the road is closed to all reductionism, as well as to the metaphysics of an historical macro-subject capable of its own rationality and of historical teleology, of which individuals and specific groups, classes for instance, would hardly be carriers or missionaries.

The critique of the European paradigm of rationality/modernity is indispensable—even more, urgent. But it is doubtful if the criticism consists of a simple negation of all its categories; of the dissolution of reality in discourse; of the pure negation of the idea and the perspective of totality in cognition. It is necessary to extricate oneself from the linkages between rationality/modernity and coloniality, first of all, and definitely from all power which is not constituted by free decisions made by free people. It is the instrumentalisation of the reasons for power, of colonial power in the first place, which produced distorted paradigms of knowledge and spoiled the liberating promises of modernity. The alternative, then, is clear: the destruction of the coloniality of world power. [...]

The liberation of intercultural relations from the prison of coloniality also implies the freedom of all peoples to choose, individually or collectively, such relations: a freedom to choose between various cultural orientations, and, above all, the freedom to produce, criticize, change, and exchange culture and society. This liberation is, part of the process of social liberation from all power organized as inequality, discrimination, exploitation, and as domination.

二、《解殖民转向的思考：后大陆理论、哲学和批评简介》选读[①]

[...]

The Decolonial Turn

[...]

Decolonial thinking has existed since the very inception of modern forms of colonization—that is, since at least the late fifteenth and early sixteenth centuries—and, to that extent, a certain decolonial turn has existed as well, but the more massive and possibly more profound shift away from modernization towards decoloniality as an unfinished project took place in the twentieth century and is still unfolding now. This more substantial decolonial turn was announced by W.E. B. Du Bois in the early twentieth century and made explicit in a line of figures that goes from Aimé Césaire and Frantz Fanon in the mid-twentieth century, to Sylvia Wynter, Enrique Dussel, Gloria Anzaldúa, Lewis Gordon, Chela Sandoval, and Linda Tuhiwai Smith, among others, throughout the second half of the twentieth to the beginning of the twenty-first century. The events that led to its solidification include the collapse of the European Age in the first two World Wars, and the second wave of decolonization in Africa, Asia, the Caribbean, and other territories across the globe, including the Bandung Conference. Moments and movements that played a role in it and that are constitutive of it include the heightened perception of the linkages between colonialism, racism, and other forms of dehumanization in the twentieth-century, the formation of ethnic movements of

---

① Maldonado-Torres, "Thinking through the Decolonial Turn: Post-continental Interventions in Theory, Philosophy, and Critique—An Introduction," pp.1 - 15.

empowerment and feminisms of color, and the appearance of queer decolonial theorizing. Anti-colonial and decolonial political, intellectual, and artistic expressions existed before, but not necessarily in the same amount, or with the same degree of self-awareness and regional and global exchanges as in the twentieth-century, when one can refer to an increasingly self-conscious and coalitional effort to understanding decolonization, and not simply modernity, as an unfinished project.

There have been and there are differences and tensions among figures and movements that advance the decolonial turn. The decolonial turn does not refer to a single theoretical school, but rather points to a family of diverse positions that share a view of coloniality as a fundamental problem in the modern (as well as postmodern and information) age, and of decolonization or decoloniality as a necessary task that remains unfinished. These pair of special issues on "Thinking through the Decolonial Turn" aim to contribute to this turn not only by further clarifying its definition, depth, and scope, but also by doing so in dialogical manner. The articles provide analyses infused by a wide variety of decolonial discourses, including Africana and Caribbean philosophy, African American theology, feminism, Latina/o epistemology, Latin American liberation philosophy and theology, and modernity/coloniality/decoloniality. The contributors work in one or more of these areas, and a number of them have been aware or in dialogue with the work of at least some of the others. But, in addition to that, they read or heard a version of each other's contributions before submitting the final versions of their essays for review, and in some cases, before they wrote the first draft of their papers. This makes these two special issues particularly strong in intergenerational, interethnic, and interspatial exchanges as well as in intertextuality.

Departing from the intersection of the main theoretical currents present in these two special issues, one can also see the twentieth century as the moment when the decolonial skepticism, and the creative thought of figures such as the Caribbean-Algerian Frantz Fanon and the Chicana Gloria Anzaldúa—skepticism towards dehumanizing forms of thinking that present themselves as natural or divine—animate new forms of theorizing based on the scandal in face of the continuity of dehumanizing practices and ideas. These dehumanizing forces, logics, and discourses hardly seem to find an end in the current neoconservative and neoliberal moment, or in the liberal and Eurocentric radical responses that it sometimes generates. Continued Manichean polarities between sectors considered more human than others, the accelerated rhythm of capitalist exploitation of land and human labor—sometimes facilitated, as Fanon well put it, by neocolonial elites among the groups of the oppressed themselves—, as well as anxieties created by migration and rights claims by populations considered pathological, undesirable, or abnormal—to name only a few of the most common issues found today—, make clear that decolonization will remain unfinished for some time. Likewise, decolonial movements of racialized populations in as varied places as the United States, Mexico, Brazil, Bolivia, Europe, Australia, and New Zealand, to name only a few, make clear that decolonization is relevant in the present and will continue to be doing so in the considerable future.

[...]

Thinking through the Decolonial Turn

This is the first of two special issues in *Transmodernity* that are dedicated to stage a conversation among a number of Latin American, Latina/o, Caribbean, and African American voices around, through, and on the basis of the idea of a decolonial turn in theory, philosophy, and critique. The conversation seeks to deepen the understanding of the genealogy and at least some fundamental conceptual components of this turn. Reference to this turn already appears in the first issue of this journal, and there are already several publications that refer to or draw from it. What is unique about these articles is that all of them emerged in the effort to spell out the contours of decolonial theorizing and that all the authors were aware of each other's ideas before submitting or writing the articles. This means that there is a high degree of intertextuality, showing the movement of ideas, and the intersections and collaborations across what are sometimes taken as distinct areas or genealogies of thought: in this case, African American, Latina/o, Latin American, and Caribbean. The efforts here offer a sense of particularly critical and decolonial forms of each of these knowledge formations, and of a rich, ample, and complex body of thought that could be referred to as the thought of the decolonial turn.

The concept of the "decolonial turn" first came to light in a conference at the University of California, Berkeley in 2005. I was the main organizer and the concept reflected a long interest of mine in finding a way of articulating the massive theoretical and epistemological breakthroughs in the works of Third World figures, such as, for instance, Frantz Fanon, Enrique Dussel, Aníbal Quijano, and Sylvia Wynter. It was the kind of breakthrough that I also identified in the works of a younger but not less illustrious generation of scholars, including Linda Martin Alcoff, Lewis Gordon, María Lugones, Walter Mignolo, Chela Sandoval, and Catherine Walsh, and in collectives such as the modernity/coloniality/decoloniality network, the Caribbean Philosophical Association, and in a varied group of Latina/o philosophers and critics. And so, the idea was to bring together a number of scholars from these groups, and a number of others with similar theoretical approaches in the effort of fomenting further intersections in their work. Conference presenters received a selection of each other's writings before the conference, including essays by keynote speakers Enrique Dussel and Sylvia Wynter.

The conference "Mapping the Decolonial Turn: Trans/Post Continental Interventions in Philosophy, Theory, and Critique" took place one year after the first annual conference of the Caribbean Philosophical Association in Barbados, one year after Arturo Escobar and Walter Mignolo organized a meeting of the modernity/coloniality network at Duke University and the University of North Carolina, Chapel Hill, and right after the compilation of the essays that came out in the dossier on "post-continental philosophy" in *Worlds and Knowledges Otherwise*. The idea for a conference that brought together African American and Caribbean, as well as Latina/o and Latin American figures working on questions of liberation and decolonization came up even before these meetings, since the exchanges between the philosophers and theoreticians working on these areas was taking place since at least the late 1990s. I brought this idea when I joined the Ethnic Studies faculty at the University of California, Berkeley, where two of my colleagues not only supported me but also joined the conference as co-organizers. They were Ramón Grosfoguel and José David Saldívar. I thank both of them for their support and collegiality, as well as for enchanting moments, such as when envisioning the rebirth of the *Revista Chicano-riqueña*, even as the dream did not get to materialize.

When the conference "Mapping the Decolonial Turn" took place, both José David Saldívar and myself were part of a selected group of faculty participating in a working group on Critical Theory led by then UC Berkeley colleagues Judith Butler and Martin Jay. A few of the participants in the working group attended the conference, and Martin Jay served as respondent in a panel on Latina/o philosophy with Gertrude Gonzalez de Allen, María Lugones, Eduardo Mendieta, and Paula Moya. I thank Martin Jay for joining us in the conference and serving as respondent. Judith Butler also attended the event, and remained one of the most open, honest, and supportive colleagues in face of this theorizing that, different from mainstream critical theory, it does not seek its ground in a genealogy of European intellectuals. I thank her for her openness and support.

Even though it has been six years since the conference at Berkeley took place, the essays in these two issues are more recent. Also more recent is the avid use of the concept of decolonial turn, based not only in the introduction to the conference, which served as the point of departure for this introduction, but also by a number of publications in the last few years. They include several of my publications cited already, an edited project published in 2007 by Santiago Castro-Gómez and Ramón Grosfoguel, which used the concept of the "giro decolonial" [decolonial turn] as an organizing category. The concept was more recently highlighted by publications from the Unidad de Apoyo a Comunidades Indígenas en Guadalajara, México, by the Universidad de la Tierra in Chiapas, México, and by Ramón Grosfoguel's essay in the anthology *Globalization and the Decolonial Option*, edited by Walter Mignolo and Arturo Escobar. There are also multiple publications on decoloniality in the last few years, including works by Walter Mignolo and Catherine Walsh, as well as projects such as the Decolonial Feminism collective with María Lugones, Sylvia Marcos, Laura Pérez, and myself, when I was teaching at UC Berkeley, along with a number of former and current doctoral students such as Dalida María Benfield, Tara Daly, Marcelle Maese-Cohen, at Berkeley and Gabriela Veronelli, among others, at Binghamton University, New York. It is also important to mention a number of graduate students and former graduate students who have recently finished or are about to finish doctoral dissertations that contribute to the understanding of coloniality and decoloniality, including Daphne Taylor García, George Ciccariello-Maher, Jorge González, Leece

Lee, and Samuel Bañales, among others. Also of note is that the concept of coloniality of power has attracted the attention of mainstream leftist theorists Michael Hardt and Antonio Negri, causing, however, a debate about the extent to which they appropriate the concept without giving due recognition to its author—or, by extension, much reference to its already common usage among a number of southern intellectuals and scholars of color. And so, the moment is right for the publication of these essays that aim to elucidate and further contribute to the decolonial turn.

The original plan was to publish all the essays in a book, but it became increasingly clear that coloniality and decoloniality literature is being engaged by multiple constituencies in a wide diversity of countries and contexts, which makes the medium of an online open peer-reviewed journal the best option. Considering options for publication account for a good amount of the time between the submission of the final essays and this release. The emergence of *Transmodernity*, a peer-reviewed journal particularly focused on cultural and theoretical investigations from the Luso-Hispanic world, presented the perfect occasion for the publication of the essays.

The concept of transmodernity has been part and parcel of discussions among a number of authors in this volume. Particularly important in this has been the work of Enrique Dussel, the major Latin American philosopher who formulated one of the most powerful conceptualizations beginning more than ten years ago. As I argue in my essay on Dussel and the decolonial turn that appears in the first issue of *Transmodernity*, from a Dusselian perspective, transmodernity represents the horizon of a possible decolonized world. The Dusselian conception of transmodernity is about the transgression and transcendence of modernity, understood as a system premised on colonizing ideas, institutions, and practices. The concept invites critical and creative appropriations of selected modern ideas, along with multiple other conceptual frameworks that can contribute to forge a less oppressive future. It recognizes that liberation and decolonization can be told in multiple languages, with unique and rich meanings and conceptual bases, and therefore values south-south encounters and dialogues. Transmodernity, at least the Dusselian version of it, is one way of expressing a decolonial attitude with regards to modernity, opening philosophy to multiple languages and stripping modernity of its colonizing elements and biases.

三、《解殖民调研的策略》选读[①]

Introduction

[...]

---

① Mignolo, *The Politics of Decolonial Investigations*, pp.3 - 9.

I Prolegomenon

The Politics of Decolonial Investigations aims at healing colonial wounds and shrinking the wide spectrum of Western overconfidence to its own size. Colonial wounds are inflicted in all areas of lived experience，human and nonhuman，physical and mental，by the recursive enactment of the "arrogance of power". No living organism at this point in time is immune to coloniality，no less the changing cast of actors running the institutions that maintain coloniality under the rhetoric of modernity celebrating change，development，the cybernetic revolution，AI，and democracy as unquestionable victories. [...] These investigations shall contribute to rebuilding and reenacting our parameters of knowing and sensing and to the restitution of our love and mutual respect; it aims to restore the *communal*，encompassing the relationality of the human species with/in all the living universe，which has been destituted by the *social*，severing the human species from the cosmic planetary energy and the will to live for far too long.

[...]

In both crises，two levels of knowledge have been at work: the *doxa* (common belief，popular opinion) on the one hand，and the *episteme* (knowledge，logical and scientific understanding) on the other. Mainstream political economy and political theory have provided the epistemic foundation transmitted within the public sphere. In this book，I try to show how and why the politics of decolonial inquiry and analysis must be oriented toward changing the assumptions and presuppositions—not just the contents—that currently validate Western political economy，political theory，and the opinions transmitted by the corporate media to the public at large. Following Aníbal Quijano I call this reorientation *epistemic reconstitution*.

In his groundbreaking short essay，published in 1992，Quijano reoriented the task of decolonization vis-à-vis what decolonization meant during the Cold War: to expel the settlers so the natives could govern themselves. The governing institution was the nation-state without questioning the political theory and political economy upon which nation-states came into being. In view of the failure of the nation-state as a means to decolonization，Quijano turned to confront the hegemonic totality of knowledge that constituted the idea of Western modernity and to conceive the task of decolonization as epistemological reconstitution. He wrote:

The critique of *the European paradigm of rationality/modernity* is indispensable，even more，urgent. But it is doubtful if the criticism consists of a simple negation of all its categories; of the dissolution of reality in discourse; of the pure negation of the idea and the perspective of totality in cognition. It is necessary to extricate oneself from the linkages between rationality/modernity and coloniality，first of all，and definitely from all power which is not constituted by free decisions made by free people. It is the instrumentalization of the reasons for power，of colonial power in the first place, which produced distorted paradigms of knowledge and spoiled the liberating promises of modernity [...].

Although Quijano's expression is "epistemological reconstitution", the overwhelming attention he has paid since then to subjectivity and the control of the senses, rendered by Nelson Maldonado-Torres as "coloniality of being", suggests that the reconstitution shall be both epistemological and ontological, which is a claim in this book. Furthermore, as ontology cannot be reduced to pure materiality, coloniality of being in the world involves and presupposes coloniality of the senses. In the European paradigm of modernity/rationality, the coloniality of the senses has been enacted by modern and Western aesthetics: the entire field of philosophical aesthetics has been, since the late eighteenth century, an effective instrument to colonize aesthesis. Because knowledge (both epistemic and doxastic) controls and manages the subjectivity (aesthesis) of the population affected by it, decolonial reconstitution needs to be both epistemic and doxastic (which carries the weight of sensing and believing). My goal for this book is to help change the terms of the conversations (the presuppositions, assumptions, and enunciations), sustaining the "European paradigm of modernity/rationality" and hiding its darker side, coloniality. I will return to this point in section III. 3.

This is a book about "coloniality of power" and its consequences, topics on which I have spent virtually the last twenty-five years of my life, researching, teaching, writing, thinking, and working with other people in the same path. Quijano's concepts of "coloniality" and "coloniality of power" have revealed to us the darker side of modernity. They have uncovered the reality that there cannot be "power" without a modifier. [...] What options are left for decoloniality as epistemic reconstitution after the closing of the Third World and the demise of the socialist bloc in a world order reshaped by, on the one hand, the projects of de-Westernization and multipolarity and, on the other hand, the efforts to maintain the privileges of five hundred years of Westernization, by engaging in a renewed effort of re-Westernization to maintain the privileges of unipolarity? Yet in the turmoil of everyday life, the attention of millions of people across the planet is sucked into the increasing flow of traffic on the information highway, to the extent that no time or energy is left for thinking beyond the demands of the iPhone to which our eyes are glued like magnets. The magnitude of the geopolitical sphere, including the mass and social media that manipulate sensing and emotioning, is such that no future can be glimpsed beyond the offices of the current managers of global designs. [...]

The arguments that I unfold in this book are the results of two decades of sustained investigation into questions outlined in the previous paragraphs: our global order, daily life, and the intersection between them. All are embedded in the overall frame of modernity/coloniality, and they both encompass the international, the domestic, and the private and public spheres. All the chapters in this book deal with diverse aspects of the historical foundation, transformation, management of, and consequences to the rhetoric of modernity and the logic of coloniality, as well as dissent thereof, and the praxes of reconstitution and restitution, all of which I address in more detail in section III of this introduction. The basic presuppositions guiding these investigations are as follows. By "coloniality of power" I mean the energy driving the beliefs, attitudes, and desires of actors that built an apparatus of management as well as the colonial matrix of power（CMP）sustaining them. Coloniality of power is the *technics* of domination and CMP the instrument. I am building here on Oswald Spengler: "*Technics is the tactics of life*. It is the inner form of the *process* utilized in that struggle which is identical with life itself...*Technics is not to be understood in terms of tools*. What matters is not how one fashions things, *but the process of using them*" (emphasis in the original).

I will use in this book the term "praxis/es of living" instead of "tactics of life". The change of vocabulary is made, simply, to reflect Spengler's life experience and disciplinary training on the one hand and my own grounded praxis of living on the other. At stake here is the geopolitics of knowing, sensing, and believing. Both coloniality of power and CMP are disguised by the rhetoric of modernity: an overwhelming set of discourses, oral and written, write this script. Both fixed and moving images accompanied by soundtrack wind round and round the reel, projecting an image of the world, natural and cultural, upon the mind of the people as if it were the world itself. The rhetoric of modernity settled and maintains the "European paradigm of modernity/rationality", in Quijano's words. Apart from modernity, which is a concept that emerged in Europe, the rest are decolonial concepts that emerged in and from the South American Andes: Third World concepts in a way. You won't find them either in the social sciences and the humanities or in their North Atlantic hub; neither in western Europe nor in the US. Modernity is a European concept of which the Renaissance and the Enlightenment are two historical pillars. Modernity/coloniality is a decolonial concept, and though some distinguish between modernity and coloniality, I never do because coloniality is constitutive of modernity. This is a basic premise of the collective whole known by the compound modernity/coloniality/decoloniality. Coloniality and modernity/coloniality did not emerge in academe either and are unrelated to any specific discipline. Both concepts became prominent in public sphere debates in the early 1990s as an outcome of previous conversations about economic dependency in South America in which Quijano was heavily involved. Consequently, the sustained decolonial investigations I submit to the reader of this book are grounded in the genealogy of thoughts inherited from the 1960s by debates on economic dependency. At the time, economic and political dependency was the main concern. But Quijano expanded it to all domains of life （culture, subjectivity, everyday life） and explored the historic-structural dependency managed by the European paradigm of modernity/coloniality. In other words, he broadened the scope by the coloniality of power technics and its instrument, the CMP. However, this book intends to continue the energies of dissent that the rhetoric of modernity and the logic of coloniality provoked:

decoloniality both in its variegated manifestations in the political society and in the domain of decolonial investigations, epistemological (knowing) and ontological (being, sensing, emotioning—aesthesis) reconstitutions.

Although Quijano was trained in sociology, coloniality—short for the coloniality of power (*colonialidad del poder*)—was not introduced as a sociological concept but as a decolonial one. This means that coloniality of power and decoloniality, in this specific sense, were mutually created. Coloniality was a decolonial concept, and decoloniality, in this local configuration and not as a universal concept, acquired its meaning by bringing coloniality of power to light. There are many other meanings and uses of "decolonization", either in a strong political sense or sometimes as a metaphor, that are based on different presuppositions and do not necessarily take coloniality of power (and CMP) as the basic frame of analysis and as the prison house that decolonial doing and thinking aim to delink. My own work is limited to and grounded on the indissociable foundation of the decolonial analytics of the coloniality of power on the one hand and its political, ethical, and epistemic/philosophical consequences on the other.

The correlations between coloniality of power and decoloniality can be illustrated by analogy to the correlations between the unconscious and psychoanalysis. In Freud's work, the unconscious is a psychoanalytic concept, regardless of whether the word existed before his coinage of it and regardless of the fact that human beings (and animals too) have had dreams since the beginning of time: dreams aren't exclusive to the end of the nineteenth century, nor is their analysis. People have been analyzing their dreams from the moment they began to dream. But thanks to Freud, psychoanalytic analysis is credited to him and catalogued to that time. Freud created an indissociable bond between the analysis of the unconscious and the human mind itself to the extent that psychoanalysis and our unconscious workings became mutually constitutive and remain so to this day. Following this analogy, in the same way that psychoanalysis reveals hidden dimensions of the mind inaccessible to our conscious thought, decolonial thinking and decolonial analytics reveal the work of the colonial matrix of power, the hidden structure of Western civilization. This book is about the coloniality of power and its world-making instrumentalization, the CMP. The colonial matrix of power is—allow me to repeat—the instrumental and conceptual structure (which I will analyze in section III of this introduction) that the coloniality of power creates to enforce its regime of domination, management, and control. Going a step further with my analogy to Freud, I would add that while psychoanalytic investigations foster a therapeutic cure, decolonial investigations invite decolonial healing. Psychoanalysis deals with traumas, decoloniality with colonial wounds. This book is about understanding how the CMP governs us, and, in its boomerang effect, governs the actors implementing control and domination in the name of progress, development, and democracy. Such understanding is of the essence to know when, where, and how to delink and engage in communal praxis of decolonial healing through epistemic (of knowledge and ways of knowing) and aesthesic（being，sensing，and believing）reconstitution，which was the task Quijano as signed to decolonial thinking and doing at the end of the Cold War. This book，thirty years later，offers a decolonial praxis of Quijano's concept for our time.

四、思考与讨论

1. 基哈诺为何主张应继续推动去殖民化进程？我们如何理解他提出的通过"认知重组"（epistemological reconstitution）来实现彻底的去殖民化？它与传统的后殖民批评之间有哪些区别？

2."解殖民"转向是如何产生的？能否在当代世界文学作品中找出一些文化实践的实例来说明解殖民思维（decolonial thinking）的具体体现方式？

3. 米尼奥罗为何倡导改变"对话语汇"（the terms of the conversations）？在他看来，现代性话术存在哪些问题？这与传统的现代性批判范式有哪些不同？

本章推荐阅读文献：

［1］Ada María Isasi-Díaz and Eduardo Mendieta（eds.）. *Decolonizing Epistemologies: Latina/o Theology and Philosophy*. New York：Fordham University Press，2012.

［2］Aimé Césaire. *Discourse on Colonialism*. Trans. Joan Pinkham. New York：Monthly Review Press，2000.

［3］Aníbal Quijano. "Coloniality of Power，Eurocentrism and Latin America," *Nepantla: Views from South* 1.3（2000），pp.533 - 280.

［4］Arturo Escobar. *Territories of Difference: Place，Movements，Life，Redes*. Durham：Duke University Press，2008.

［5］Enrique Dussel. *The Invention of the Americas: Eclipse of the Other and the Myth of Modernity*. New York：Continuum，1995.

［6］Federico Luisetti，John Pickles and Wilson Kayer（eds.）. *The Anomie of the Earth: Philosophy，Politics，and Autonomy of the Earth in Europe and Latin America*. Durham：Duke University Press，2015.

［7］Freya Schiwy. "Decolonization and the Question of Subjectivity：Gender，Race，and Binary Thinking," *Cultural Studies* 21.2 - 3（2007），pp.271 - 294.

［8］Gloria Anzaldúa. *Borderlands/La Frontera: The New Mestiza*. San Francisco：Aunt Lute Books，2007.

［9］Linda Tuhiwai Smith. *Decolonizing Methodologies: Research and Indigenous People*. London：Zed Books，1999.

［10］María Lugones. "Heterosexualism and the Colonial/Modern Gender System," *Hypatia* 22.1（2007），pp.186 - 209.

[11] Nelson Maldonado-Torres. "Colonialism, Neocolonial, Internal Colonialism, the Postcolonial, Coloniality, and Decoloniality," *Critical Terms in Caribbean and Latin American Thought: Historical and Institutional Trajectories*. Eds. Yolanda Martínez-San Miguel, Ben. Sifuentes-Jáuregui and Marisa Belausteguigoitia. Hampshire: Palgrave Macmillan, 2016, pp.67 - 86.

[12] Nelson Maldonado-Torres. "On the Coloniality of Being: Contributions to the Development of a Concept," *Cultural Studies* 21.2 - 3 (2007), pp.240 - 270.

[13] Ngugi wa Thiong'o. *Decolonising the Mind: The Politics of Language in African Literature*. Oxford: James Currey, 1986.

[14] Ramón Grosfoguel. *Colonial Subjects: Puerto Ricans in a Global Perspective*. Berkeley: University of California Press, 2003.

[15] Sabelo J. Ndlovu-Gatsheni. *Epistemic Freedom in Africa: Deprovincialization and Decolonization*. London: Routledge, 2018.

[16] Santiago Castro-Gómez. "The Missing Chapter of Empire," *Cultural Studies* 21.2 - 3 (2007), pp.428 - 448.

[17] Sylvia Wynter. "Unsettling the Coloniality of Being/Power/Truth/Freedom: Towards the Human, After Man, Its Overrepresentation: An Argument," *New Centennial Review* 3.3 (2003), pp.257 - 337.

[18] Walter Mignolo. "Delinking: The Rhetoric of Modernity, the Logic of Coloniality and the Grammar of De-coloniality," *Cultural Studies* 21.2 - 3 (2007), pp.449 - 514.

[19] Walter Mignolo. "Modernity and Decoloniality," *Oxford Bibliographies*. [2017 - 05 - 05].

[20] Walter Mignolo. *The Politics of Decolonial Investigations*. Durham: Duke University Press, 2021.

第四章
生态批评

第一节　概　　论

20世纪60年代,以雷切尔·卡森(Rachel Carson)的《寂静的春天》(*Silent Spring*)的出版为标志,美国环境运动开始兴起。此后,生态批评逐步升温。1974年,美国学者约瑟夫·W.米克(Joseph W. Meeker)在其专著《生存的喜剧:文学的生态学研究》(*The Comedy of Survival: Studies in Literary Ecology*)中提出了"文学的生态学研究"(literary ecology)这一术语。米克认为,文学的生态学研究应当关注文学如何展现出人类与其他物种之间的关系,尤其是"细致而真诚地审视与发掘文学对人类行为和自然环境的影响"[①]。同年,美国学者卡尔·克罗伯(Karl Kroeber)发表文章,主张将"生态学"(ecology)和"生态"(ecological)两个概念共同纳入文学批评的视域。[②]

"生态批评"(ecocriticism)一词于1978年在学界出现,威廉·吕克特(William Rueckert)在发表的《文学与生态学:一次生态批评实验》("Literature and Ecology: An Experiment in Ecocriticism")一文中,首次明确地使用了"生态批评"这一说法,并提出将文学研究与生态学研究相结合,将生态学及其相关概念运用到文学研究中,建构一个生态诗学的研究体系。[③] "生态批评"的说法在提出后得到了学界广泛的认可,虽然之后也有学者提出诸如"环境批评"(environmental criticism)、"绿色研究"(green studies)、"绿色文化研究"(green cultural studies)等其他术语,但大多数学者依然倾向于使用"生态批评"这一术语。20世纪90年代起,随着环境问题日益严峻,学界刊发了诸多与生态批评理论相关的文章。1992年,文学与环境研究协会(Association for the Study of Literature and Environment, ASLE)正式成立,"生态批评的文学研究……开始成为一个受到认可的研究领域"[④]。

自诞生伊始,生态批评即是一门跨学科研究,涉及自然科学、文学、文学批评、人类学、历史学等诸多

---

① Joseph W. Meeker, *The Comedy of Survival: Studies in Literary Ecology*. New York: Charles Scribner's Sons, 1974, pp.3 - 4.
② Karl Kroeber, "Home at Grasmere: Ecological Holiness," *PMLA* 89 (1974), pp.132 - 141.
③ William Rueckert, "Literature and Ecology: An Experiment in Ecocriticism," *Iowa Review* 9.1 (1978), pp.71 - 86.
④ Cheryll Glotfelty, "Introduction," *The Ecocriticism Reader: Landmarks in Literary Ecology*. Eds. Cheryll Glotfelty and Harold Fromm. Athens: University of Georgia Press, 1996, p.xviii.

学科。正如生态批评家劳伦斯·布依尔（Lawrence Buell）所言，生态批评是一场"越来越异质化的运动"①。生态批评包含多种研究方法，因此生态批评概念本身是一个难以定义的术语，最简单明了的定义是由谢里尔·格洛特费尔蒂（Cheryll Glotfelty）给出的。1996 年，她在学界第一部生态批评论文集《生态批评读本：文学生态学的里程碑》（*The Ecocriticism Reader: Landmarks in Literary Ecology*）中将生态批评定义为"一门研究文学与物理环境之间关系的学科"②。1999 年，迈克尔·贝内特（Michael Bennett）和大卫·W. 蒂格（David W. Teague）则将生态批评定义为"对文化与环境之间的相互作用进行研究的学科"③。20 余年里，生态批评作为一门新兴学科取得了蓬勃的发展，批评方法越来越多种多样，大量研究著作涌现出来。目前，生态批评在西方学界已经大致经历了四次发展浪潮。④

一、20 世纪 80 年代：生态批评的第一次浪潮

生态批评的第一次浪潮兴起于 20 世纪 80 年代，其主要代表人物是英美两国的批评学者，他们强调将传统的自然书写（即"荒野"）作为解读对象。与当今的生态批评学者相同，在这次浪潮中，生态批评学者关注环境危机，认为人文科学与自然科学有义务唤起人们的环境意识，在文化与社会现实层面积极探寻解决环境问题的良方。因此，生态批评的第一次浪潮主要是"为自然言说"⑤，体现的是"一种政治分析方法"⑥。在这次浪潮中，生态批评学者认为人类与自然之间存在着文化上的差异，他们更加推崇自然的价值。

在生态批评的第一次浪潮中，批评学者的解读对象主要是非小说类的自然书写（non-fiction nature writing），这也与环境文学刚刚出现时作家的创作倾向相吻合。这一类研究的代表成果有乔纳森·贝特（Jonathan Bate）的《浪漫主义生态学：华兹华斯和环境传统》（*Romantic Ecology: Wordsworth and the Environmental Tradition*）、劳伦斯·库普（Laurence Coupe）主编的《绿色研究读本：从浪漫主义到生态批评》（*The Green Studies Reader: From Romanticism to Ecocriticism*）等。在生态批评的第一次浪潮中，学者们非常重视非人自然，或曰"荒野自然"，这种关注倾向也一直延续至今日。这种对"荒野自然"的重视具有非常重要的启示性意义，它使得人们开始意识到自然环境并不仅仅是被剥削的对象，也是需要被珍爱和保护的对象。

此外，值得注意的是，生态批评的第一次浪潮中出现了生态女性主义（eco-feminism）的旁支流派，主要代表人物包括卡伦·J. 沃伦（Karen J. Warren）、查伦·斯普瑞特奈克（Charlene Spretnak）、卡罗琳·麦钱特（Carolyn Merchant）、瓦耳·普鲁姆伍德（Val Plumwood）、范达娜·希瓦（Vandana

---

① Lawrence Buell, *The Future of Environmental Criticism: Environmental Crisis and Literary Imagination*. Malden：Blackwell，2005，p.1.
② Glotfelty, "Introduction," p.xviii.
③ Michael Bennett and David W. Teague, "Urban Ecocriticism：An Introduction," *The Nature of Cities: Ecocriticism and Urban Environments*. Eds. Michael Bennett and David W. Teague. Tucson：University of Arizona Press，1999，p.3.
④ 值得注意的是，本章针对生态批评研究发展所做的四次浪潮的分类并非绝对的，而且这几次浪潮的研究内容并非互相取代的，而是同时共存的，许多学者目前的研究内容仍然是被划入前两次浪潮的。也就是说，生态批评的四次浪潮研究内容各有侧重，并无优劣之分。
⑤ Lawrence Buell, *The Environmental Imagination: Thoreau，Nature Writing，and the Formation of American Culture*. Cambridge：Harvard University Press，1995，p.11.
⑥ Greg Garrard, *Ecocriticism*. New York：Routledge，2004，p.3.

Shiva)、玛丽亚·米斯(Maria Mies)、阿里尔·萨伦(Ariel Sallen)、罗斯玛丽·鲁瑟(Rosemary Reuther)等。20世纪70年代,在《寂静的春天》引起的生态风暴席卷全球时,欧美大陆也正处于女性主义运动的第二次浪潮之中。女性主义者认为,女性在父权社会中经历的不公正待遇恰如自然在人类社会中的遭遇一样,这种惺惺相惜之情将女权运动和环境保护运动联系在一起。换言之,生态女性主义是西方女权运动和环境保护运动共同催生的产物。

一般认为,"生态女性主义"这一术语最早出现于1974年,由法国女性主义学者弗朗索瓦·德·埃奥博尼(Françoise d'Eaubonne)在《女性主义的毁灭》(Le Féminisme ou La Mort)一书中提出。生态女性主义思想认为,自然的形象和女性的形象十分类似,"妇女与自然的联系有着悠久的历史,这个联盟通过文化、语言和历史而顽固地持续下来"[1]。自然和女性都是生命的孕育者,然而在现实社会中,二者又皆处于被控制和被征服的状态。这种自然和女性之间的天然联系,使生态女性主义在生态批评学界与女权主义运动阵营中都获得了很多的支持。生态女性主义者致力于消除人类对自然的主宰和性别歧视,尊重和维护所有生物的平等性和文化多元性,倡导建立一种人类与自然、男性与女性之间的和谐关系。生态女性主义者主张对逻各斯中心主义进行双重解构,既反对人类中心主义对自然环境的压迫,也反对男性中心主义对女性群体的压迫。正如查伦·斯普瑞特奈克指出的,生态女权主义者从传统关注性别歧视发展到关注人类全部的压迫制度(如种族主义、等级主义、歧视老人、歧视同性恋等),最终认识到"自然主义"(即对自然的穷竭)也是统治逻辑的结果。[2] 生态女性主义寻求普遍存在于男权社会中的边缘化自然与边缘化女性之间的某种特殊关系,将女性的解放和自然的解放统一为一体,试图建构一种不同于人类/自然二元对立的新型的文化形式。

生态女性主义在被提出后,魅力经久不衰,即使在生态批评流派十分多元化的今天,依然吸引了许多学者从事生态女性主义方面的研究,可见其哲学内涵之经典,引起的受众共鸣之广泛。生态女性主义针对的是男性中心主义文化语境中自然和女性的双重边缘化问题,其所主张的消除西方文明中的"人类中心主义"和"男性中心主义"的思想,对后世的许多生态批评流派都具有启发意义,其批评维度也决定了生态女性主义比较容易与其他研究方向进行交叉,如城市中的生态女性主义研究、后殖民视角下的第三世界的生态女性主义等都是非常值得生态批评研究者探讨的话题。

二、1995年前后：生态批评的第二次浪潮

生态批评的第二次浪潮出现在1995年前后。在这次浪潮中,除了英美两国学者之外,更多国家的批评家开始加入生态批评的阵营,研究对象也从非小说类的自然书写扩展至各种文学体裁。此外,少数族裔、日本环境文学作家的自然书写也开始进入人们的视野,生态批评的研究角度变得更加具有文化多元性。

生态批评的第二次浪潮在研究方向上也具有一定的现代革新性,尤其是本次浪潮中的生态批评学者开始质疑长久以来人类与非人类、自然与非自然之间的界限[3],认为这些界限是人为建构且造成生态

---

① ［美］卡洛琳·麦茜特：《自然之死：妇女、生态和科学革命》,吴国盛等译,长春：吉林人民出版社,1999年,第2页。
② ［美］C.斯普瑞特奈克：《生态女权主义建设性的重大贡献》,秦喜清译,载《国外社会科学》1997年第6期,第63—66页。
③ Garrard, *Ecocriticism*, p.5.

危机的原因。值得注意的是,在这次浪潮中,"环境"这一概念被重新定义,自然环境与城市环境被纳入研究范畴。① 实际上,在人类历史的发展过程中,自然的概念不断被重新塑造。尤其自工业革命后,城市空间和人造环境都被看作生态批评研究的沃土②,这些讨论为"城市生态批评"(urban ecocriticism)的诞生提供了理论土壤。1999 年,贝内特和蒂格在主编的《城市的自然:生态批评与城市环境》(The Nature of Cities: Ecocriticism and Urban Environments)一书中首次提出了"城市生态批评"的概念。城市生态批评关注人类的日常栖居地,注重从文化的角度看待城市化进程造成的环境影响。在生态批评的第二次浪潮中,虽然早期的城市生态批评研究更侧重社会学和政治学角度,但城市环境首次出现在生态批评的视野之内,依然具有重要的里程碑意义。③

生态批评第二次浪潮的另一个亮点是,生态批评研究衍生出更加具有政治性的生态正义运动。生态正义运动致力于从生态批评的角度阅读文学文本,以唤醒人们关于阶级、种族与性别的意识。生态正义运动关注贫穷地区人口的窘迫生活,指出这些人作为环境污染的受害者,比起其他人拥有更少的与自然环境接触的机会。例如,出身于乌克兰犹太家庭的美国作家伦纳德·杜步金(Leonard Dubkin)曾经提及,自己两岁那年随父母移民至芝加哥,他们同其他常见的新移民阶层一样,由于家境清贫而搬到城市西部的贫民窟居住。杜步金一家住在一栋人口密度极大的小公寓中,公寓周围完全没有绿化,以至于他直至十岁左右才第一次见到树木。④

生态正义研究的独特之处在于,它成功地将环境问题建构为一种社会问题,同时也重塑了西方环境运动的走向。生态批评作为一种人文类的哲学思考方式,往往被认为关注的是抽象的理论与思辨问题,而生态正义研究的出现使人们意识到,生态批评实际上具有很强的现实与实践指向,它所关注的不仅是文学作品中作家想象出来的人与自然的关系,也是现实社会中人与自然的关系。换言之,生态正义研究的最终目的是将生态哲学引向现实的生活世界,构建一种新的社会发展格局,改变目前损害生态正义的社会生产、生活方式以及价值结构。

三、2009 年之后:生态批评的第三次浪潮

2009 年,美国著名生态批评家乔尼·亚当森(Joni Adamson)和斯科特·斯洛维克(Scott Slovic)首次使用了"生态批评的第三次浪潮"这一表述。⑤ 斯洛维克认为,美国生态批评家帕特里克·D. 墨菲(Patrick D. Murphy)的《自然文学研究的广阔视野》(Farther Afield in the Study of Nature-Oriented Literature)一书从全球化与比较研究的角度重思生态批评研究,主张跨越不同种族与文化之间的界限,是生态批评第三次浪潮兴起的标志。生态批评的第三次浪潮的主要特色是以全球化作为研究框架,将更广阔的"地球"本身纳入宏观视野,重视不同文化之间的比较与分析。相比于此前的两次浪潮,生态批

---

① Buell, *The Environmental Imagination: Thoreau, Nature Writing, and the Formation of American Culture*, p.11.
② Lawrence Buell, "Ecocriticism: Some Emerging Trends," *Qui Parle: Critical Humanities and Social Sciences* 19.2 (2011), pp.87-115.
③ 此后的多年里,城市生态批评继续发展壮大,尤其在 2011 年以后,学界出现了许多高质量的文学批评研究成果。
④ Colin Fisher, *Urban Green: Nature, Recreation, and the Working Class in Industrial Chicago*. Chapel Hill: University of North Carolina Press, 2015, p.8.
⑤ Joni Adamson and Scott Slovic, "The Shoulders We Stand On: An Introduction to Ethnicity and Ecocriticism," *MELUS* 34.2 (2009), pp.5-24.

评的第三次浪潮在研究角度、研究对象、研究参与者等方面都显得更加成熟且多样化,将生态批评研究带向了一个高峰。

在生态批评的前两次浪潮中,学者们的研究非常注重"地方"(place)和"区域"(region)的概念,强调要建构一种对地方的认同感,即地方意识(sense of place),并且倡导重视地方或当地具有的生物学特征,以"生物区域"(bioregion)来划分地方,从而更深入地理解大地母亲,了解自己所居住的身边环境,培养对地方的归属感。与之相对,在生态批评的第三波浪潮中,学者们开始呼吁培养一种更加重视整体的地域观念,既要重视特定的地域,又要超越地域所带来的局限性。其中,2008 年厄休拉·K. 海斯(Ursula K. Heise)出版了专著《地方意识与星球意识:环境想象中的全球》(*Sense of Place and Sense of Planet: The Environmental Imagination of the Global*)[①],她在书中以 20 世纪 60 年代以来德美两国的环境文学为例,探讨了环境保护主义、生态批评和全球化、跨国主义以及世界主义之间的关系。海斯认为,这种关系可以用她所发明的"生态世界主义"(eco-cosmopolitanism)一词来表述。海斯试图通过"生态世界主义"的概念来传达她对全球性想象的重视,呼吁人们走出地方和区域的局限,在重视本地生态环境的同时,形成新型的区域主义观念,在全球环境的视野中综合衡量跨文化意识和跨文化共同体的建构,形成一种全球性的生态、政治及审美想象。

生态批评的第三次浪潮的另一亮点是开始出现针对学科内部建设的反思,也就是针对生态批评本身的批评,即生态批评批判研究,这也是生态批评研究逐渐走向成熟的标志。在这类研究中,蒂莫西·莫顿(Timothy Morton)的《没有自然的生态学:环境美学再思考》(*Ecology Without Nature: Rethinking Environmental Aesthetics*)[②]一书非常著名。莫顿从生态批评的根源术语"自然"入手,认为目前关于"自然"概念的解读实际上暗含了一种将人类与自然二元对立的思想,因此人们应当摒弃"自然"的概念,采用新的术语以推进研究。莫顿发明了"暗生态学"(dark ecology)的概念并提出了一系列相关术语来代替当前的生态批评术语,在学界影响深远。

除了以上两个重要的研究方向之外,生态批评的第三次浪潮还出现了比较式生态批评、生态性属研究、动物研究等研究角度。其中,比较式生态批评强调引入后殖民语境,在进行生态批评时从不同种族、不同文化乃至不同学科的维度切入,在比较的框架下讨论人类经验和非人类世界之间的联系。例如,加拿大学者萨拉·P. 卡斯蒂尔(Sarah P. Casteel)的《后来者:当代美洲文学的风景与归属》(*Second Arrivals: Landscape and Belonging in Contemporary Writings of The Americas*)涵盖加勒比文学研究、流散研究与后殖民研究,关注加勒比海裔作家所书写的新大陆的自然想象,探讨其中的历史内涵与地方诗学。卡斯蒂尔指出,当代美洲文学中的流散书写具有的一大特色是"关注文化异位(displacement)与地理异位经验所感知的景观"[③],并且通过重新审视有关起源和族裔的神话,展现出各种各样的归位(emplacement)形式,重点突出地方(place)与存在(being)之间的辩证关系。

生态性属研究中比较有特色的是关于男性气概建构的研究,例如马克·艾里斯特(Mark

① Ursula K. Heise, *Sense of Place and Sense of Planet: The Environmental Imagination of the Global*. Oxford: Oxford University Press, 2008.
② Timothy Morton, *Ecology Without Nature: Rethinking Environmental Aesthetics*. Cambridge: Harvard University Press, 2007.
③ Sarah P. Casteel, *Second Arrivals: Landscape and Belonging in Contemporary Writings of the Americas*. Charlottesville: University of Virginia Press, 2007, p.3.

Allister)主编的文集《生态男性：男性气概与自然新论》（*Eco-Man: New Perspectives on Masculinity and Nature*）①把时下大热的男性研究（尤其是男性气概研究）和生态批评相结合，指出自然在美国神话和历史中扮演了颇具矛盾性的角色，这实际上与男性对荒野的迷恋及其意图主宰自然的欲望有着一定的关系。文集探讨了自然对男性的塑造，以及男性对自然的多种影响模式。艾里斯特指出，生态批评中的性别研究一直为女性研究所主导，而男性研究也大多忽视了男性与自然之间的关系。生态批评中男性研究的介入打破了生态女性主义研究的单一局面，使生态批评的第三次浪潮中出现了生态男性研究（ecomasculine）的新视角。

动物研究是一个热度持续至今的研究方向。动物研究学者认为，很多人不是将动物看作一种复杂的生物，而是将其客体化为一种"宠物"。动物研究学者主张，动物并非被边缘化的"他者"，而是与人一样具有主体性的独立个体。例如，新西兰学者温迪·伍德沃德（Wendy Woodward）的《动物的凝视：南非叙事中的动物主体性》（*The Animal Gaze: Animal Subjectivities in Southern African Narratives*）②选取了一些南非作家的叙述性作品进行解读，包括奥利芙·施赖纳（Olive Schreiner）、扎克斯·米达（Zakes Mda）、尤金·N. 马雷（Eugene N. Marais）等人的作品。伍德沃德认为，这些作品中的动物都是具有较高的独立性的主体，可以感受复杂的情感并拥有能动性和意图性。当动物的主体性得到认可时，动物的凝视和人类的回应便形成一种跨物种的密切交流。换言之，动物研究理论认为，动物和人类之间的关系并非后者对前者的俯视，而是一种相互的、平等的"凝视"，人类的眼光并不带有任何优越感。

总体而言，生态批评的第三次浪潮跨越了种族、民族与国家的界限，将全球生态环境纳入视野，并且开始对生态批评研究的理论性和系统性进行反思，更加注重理论自身在实践层面的意义，促使研究者以革新的角度思考生态批评的基本术语和研究角度。

四、2012 年至今：生态批评的第四次浪潮

2012 年年末，斯洛维克撰文指出，随着生态批评研究中"物质转向"（material turn）的不断扩展，生态批评正在迎来以"物质主义生态批评"（Material Ecocriticism）为代表的"第四次浪潮"③。总体而言，生态批评的第四次浪潮在延续前几次思潮——如多元文化主义——的同时，以物质主义生态批评作为主要的分支研究流派，开始对非人或非活跃物质所具有的能动性展开研究。

物质主义生态批评的出现与新物质主义思潮的兴起有着直接的关联。21 世纪以来，受新物质主义理论（New Materialism）影响，越来越多的人文学术研究转而关注环境、场所、过程、力量与经验中蕴含的基本的物质性。其中，卡伦·巴拉德（Karen Barad）的《与宇宙相遇》（*Meeting the Universe Halfway*）、斯泰西·阿莱莫（Stacy Alaimo）和苏珊·赫克曼（Susan Hekman）主编的《物质女性主义》（*Material Feminism*）、简·贝内特（Jane Bennett）的《活力之物：一部物质的政治生态学》（*Vibrant Matter: A Political Ecology of Things*）、斯泰西·阿莱莫的《身体自然：科学、环境与物质自我》（*Bodily*

---

① Mark Allister, ed., *Eco-Man: New Perspectives on Masculinity and Nature*. Charlottesville: University of Virginia Press, 2004.
② Wendy Woodward, *The Animal Gaze: Animal Subjectivities in Southern African Narratives*. Johannesburg: Wits University Press, 2008.
③ Scott Slovic, "Editor's Note," *ISLE* 19.4 (2012), pp.619-621.

Natures: Science，Environment，and the Material Self）等学术著述为物质主义生态批评奠定了重要的理论基础，再次对新物质主义理论做出了积极的回应。这些著述指出，物质不仅仅是一种"工具化"的存在，还是本身拥有内在活力和能动性的存在。物质主义生态批评关注物质具有的"叙述"力所创造的意义是如何与人类的日常生活进行互动的，并将物质看作"叙述的场所"①。这些动态的能动性（agency）可以"形成叙事与故事，是可以被阅读和解读的"②。

物质主义生态批评不仅提供了针对话语和物质的新的认知方法，也促使人们从新的角度审视人类与非人存在之间的关系。2012 年，塞雷内拉·约维诺（Serenella Iovino）与赛尔皮尔·奥珀曼（Serpil Oppermann）在《物质主义生态批评的理论化：双联画视角》（"Theorizing Material Ecocriticism：A Diptych"）一文中指出，一些社会科学研究者、哲学家和女性主义思想家——尤其是女性主义科学家与身体女性主义理论家——更加推崇身体维度的存在经验和非二元主客体对立的现象学结构，而不是此前占据主导地位的语言学建构体系。③ 在这里，物质主义生态批评展现出与后现代主义理论之间的紧密联系：二者都认为语言和现实之间、自然和文化之间、话语实践和物质世界之间都以复杂的形式彼此交织。在此基础之上，物质主义生态批评提出，在自然与文化的生成过程中，物质活力始终存在；自然环境作为一种非人世界，其内部的各元素是彼此交织和互动的。物质主义生态批评试图赋予现实世界以活力，主张所有的物质实体都是具有活力和能动性的，甚至原子、金属、矿物质等也不例外。

为何物质主义生态批评格外强调非人物质所具有的活力呢？ 在《活力之物：一部物质的政治生态学》中，政治理论学家出身的简·贝内特指出，是否具有"活力"或能动性已经成为人类中心主义区分人类与物质的根据之一，换言之，人类认为物质不具有活力和能动性，因此将之视为一种低等于人类的存在形式，还狂妄地试图征服所有的非人物质，却忽略了自己周边或身体内部的各种非人物质具有的重要力量。④ 面对这种情况，物质主义生态批评试图通过指出非人物质具有固有的活力，证明人类存在和非人物质之间并无孰优孰劣之分，进而推进一种更加绿色的人类文化形式，促使人们更加关注人类与物质之间的相遇及其带来的各种影响。

在"物质"转向的这一背景下，生态批评的研究包括了从气候变化文学到生态诗学语言的研究，生态批评实践的实用主义倾向逐渐增强。在"学术型的生态批评"研究中，一种新型的"应用型生态批评"研究正在兴起，该研究涵盖了对包括衣食住行在内的基本人类行为与生活方式的研究。例如，贝内特在《活力之物：一部物质的政治生态学》中便关注了日常生活中的普通物质，如鱼油、金属、污染物、化学物质、干细胞、科研设备、垃圾等。她指出，这些看似平常的非人物质实际上具有固有的活力，对人类生活产生了重要的影响，比如垃圾等物质实际上会生成各种化学气体，脂肪酸等物质也会改变人类大脑的化学成分并影响人类日常的情绪。物质主义生态批评将人类的日常生活语境与生态批评对非人世界的关注联系在一起，促使生态批评的关注对象从动植物扩大至所有的非人物质，其还指出石头和金属也像动植物一样具有活力与生命力，都可以在非人环境和人造空间中叙述属于自己的故事。

①　Serenella Iovino and Serpil Oppermann，"Material Ecocriticism：Materiality，Agency，and Models of Narrativity," *Ecozon@* 3.1 (2012)，pp.75 - 91.

②　Serenella Iovino and Serpil Oppermann，"Stories Come to Matter," *Material Ecocriticism*. Eds. Serenella Iovino and Serpil Oppermann. Bloomington：Indiana University Press，2014，p.1.

③　Serenella Iovino and Serpil Oppermann，"Theorizing Material Ecocriticism：A Diptych," *Interdisciplinary Studies in Literature and Environment* 19.3 (2012)，pp.448 - 475.

④　Jane Bennett，*Vibrant Matter: A Political Ecology of Things*. Durham：Duke University Press，2010，p.ix.

总之,通过对生态批评发展脉络的回顾,我们可以看到自生态批评的概念形成以来,生态批评研究一直在不断发展,其研究方向和基本主张已经过多次变化。生态批评的多次浪潮发展也显示出生态批评具有很强的活力与演变能力。作为一种与现实世界联系紧密的文学批评范式,生态批评在未来依然会有很大的发展潜力。

第二节　经典文献选读

本章共有三篇选文。第一篇选自谢里尔·格洛特费尔蒂为学界首部生态批评论文集《生态批评读本:文学生态学的里程碑》所作的序言,序言对生态批评的诞生背景、概念界定、历史意义和未来发展做了提纲挈领的论述。第二篇选自厄休拉·K. 海斯为其专著《地方意识与星球意识:环境想象中的全球》所作的序言,文章梳理并探讨了全球化对文学与文化研究领域产生的影响,为生态批评如何超越"区域"概念的局限做了坚实的理论铺垫。第三篇选自近年物质主义生态批评领域的新锐塞雷内拉·约维诺与赛尔皮尔·奥珀曼于 2012 年发表于欧洲生态批评重要期刊 Ecozon@ 上的文章《物质主义生态批评:物质性、能动性和叙事模型》("Material Ecocriticism:Materiality,Agency,and Models of Narrativity"),该文章深入探讨了新物质主义思潮对生态批评的影响,以及物质主义转向下生态批评范式的新发展。

一、《生态批评读本:文学生态学的里程碑》选读[①]

Literary Studies in an Age of Environmental Crisis

In the mid-eighties, as scholars began to undertake collaborative projects, the field of environmental literary studies was planted, and in the early nineties it grew. In 1985 Frederick O. Waage edited *Teaching Environmental Literature: Materials*,*Methods*,*Resources*,which included course descriptions from nineteen different scholars and sought to foster "a greater presence of environmental concern and awareness in literary disciplines". In 1989 Alicia Nitecki founded *The American Nature Writing Newsletter*,whose purpose was to publish brief essays,book reviews,classroom notes,and information pertaining to the study of writing on nature and the environment. Others have been responsible for special environmental issues of established literary journals. Some universities began to include literature courses in their environmental studies curricula,a few inaugurated new institutes or programs in nature and culture,and some English departments began to offer a minor in environmental literature. In 1990 the University of Nevada,

---

① Cheryll Glotfelty and Harold Fromm,eds.,*The Ecocriticism Reader: Landmarks in Literary Ecology*. Athens:University of Georgia Press,1996,pp.XVII-XXV.

Reno, created the first academic position in Literature and the Environment.

Also during these years several special sessions on nature writing or environmental literature began to appear on the programs of annual literary conferences, perhaps most notably the 1991 MLA special session organized by Harold Fromm, entitled "Ecocriticism: The Greening of Literary Studies", and the 1992 American Literature Association symposium chaired by Glen Love, entitled "American Nature Writing: New Contexts, New Approaches". In 1992, at the annual meeting of the Western Literature Association, a new Association for the Study of Literature and Environment (ASLE) was formed, with Scott Slovic elected first president. ASLE's mission: "to promote the exchange of ideas and information pertaining to literature that considers the relationship between human beings and the natural world" and to encourage "new nature writing, traditional and innovative scholarly approaches to environmental literature, and interdisciplinary environmental research". In its first year, ASLE's membership swelled to more than 300; in its second year that number doubled, and the group created an electronic-mail computer network to facilitate communication among members; In its third year, 1995, ASLE's membership had topped 750 and the group hosted its first conference, in Fort Collins, Colorado. In 1993 Patrick Murphy established a new journal, *ISLE: Interdisciplinary Studies in Literature and Environment*, to "provide a forum for critical studies of the literary and performing arts proceeding from or addressing environmental considerations. These would include ecological theory, environmentalism, conceptions of nature and their depictions, the human/nature dichotomy and related concerns".

By 1993, then, ecological literary study had emerged as a recognizable critical school. The formerly disconnected scattering of lone scholars had joined forces with younger scholars and graduate students to become a strong interest group with aspirations to change the profession. The origin of ecocriticism as a critical approach thus predates its recent consolidation by more than twenty years.

What then *is* ecocriticism? Simply put, ecocriticism is the study of the relationship between literature and the physical environment. Just as feminist criticism examines language and literature from a gender-conscious perspective, and Marxist criticism brings an awareness of modes of production and economic class to its reading of texts, ecocriticism takes an earth-centered approach to literary studies.

Ecocritics and theorists ask questions like the following: How is nature represented in this sonnet? What role does the physical setting play in the plot of this novel? Are the values expressed in this play consistent with ecological wisdom? How do our metaphors of the land influence the way we treat it? How can we characterize nature writing as a genre? In addition to race, class, and gender, should *place* become a new critical category? Do men write about nature differently than women do? In what ways has literacy itself affected humankind's relationship to the natural world? How has the concept of wilderness changed over time? In what ways and to what effect is the environmental crisis seeping into contemporary literature and popular culture? What view of nature informs U.S. Government reports, corporate advertising, and televised nature documentaries, and to what rhetorical effect? What bearing might the science of ecology have on literary studies? How is science itself open to literary analysis? What cross-fertilization is possible between literary studies and environmental discourse in related disciplines such as history, philosophy, psychology, art history, and ethics?

Despite the broad scope of inquiry and disparate levels of sophistication, all ecological criticism shares the fundamental premise that human culture is connected to the physical world, affecting it and affected by it. Ecocriticism takes as its subject the interconnections between nature and culture, specifically the cultural artifacts of language and literature. As a critical stance, it has one foot in literature and the other on land; as a theoretical discourse, it negotiates between the human and the nonhuman.

Ecocriticism can be further characterized by distinguishing it from other critical approaches. Literary theory, in general, examines the relations between writers, texts, and the world. In most literary theory "the world" is synonymous with society—the social sphere. Ecocriticism expands the notion of "the world" to include the entire ecosphere. If we agree with Barry Commoner's first law of ecology, "Everything is connected to everything else", we must conclude that literature does not float above the material world in some aesthetic ether, but, rather, plays a part in an immensely complex global system, in which energy, matter, *and ideas* interact.

But the taxonomic name of this green branch of literary study is still being negotiated. In *The Comedy of Survival: Studies in Literary Ecology* (1972) Joseph W. Meeker introduced the term *literary ecology* to refer to "the study of biological themes and relationships which appear in literary works. It is simultaneously an attempt to discover what roles have been played by literature in the ecology of the human species". The term ecocriticism was possibly first coined in 1978 by William Rueckert in his essay "Literature and Ecology: An Experiment in Ecocriticism" (reprinted in this anthology). By ecocriticism Rueckert meant "the application of ecology and ecological concepts to the study of literature". Rueckert's definition, concerned specifically with the science of ecology, is thus more restrictive than the one proposed in this anthology, which includes all possible relations between literature and the physical world. Other terms currently in circulation include *ecopoetics*, *environmental literary criticism*, and *green cultural studies*.

Many critics write environmentally conscious criticism without needing or wanting a specific name for it. Others argue that a name is important. It was precisely because the early studies lacked a common subject heading that they were dispersed so widely, failed to build on one another, and became both difficult to access and negligible in their impact on the profession. Some scholars like the term *ecocriticism* because it is short and can easily be made into other forms like *ecocritical* and *ecocritic*. Additionally, they favor *eco-* over *enviro-* because, analogous to the science of ecology, ecocriticism studies relationships between things, in this case, between human culture and the physical world. Furthermore, in its connotations, *enviro-* is anthropocentric and dualistic, implying that we humans are at the center, surrounded by everything that is not us, the environment. *Eco-*, in contrast, implies interdependent communities, integrated systems, and strong connections among constituent parts. Ultimately, of course, usage will dictate which term or whether any term is adopted. But think of how convenient it would be to sit down at a computerized database and have a single term to enter for your subject search.

[…]

An ecologically focused criticism is a worthy enterprise primarily because it directs our attention to matters about which we need to be thinking. Consciousness raising is its most important task. For how can we solve environmental problems unless we start thinking about them?

I noted above that ecocritics have aspirations to change the profession. Perhaps I should have written that I have such aspirations for ecocriticism. I would like to see ecocriticism become a chapter of the next book that redraws the boundaries of literary studies. I would like to see a position in every literature department for a specialist in literature and the environment. I would like to see candidates running on a green platform elected to the highest offices in our professional organizations. We have witnessed the feminist and multi-ethnic critical movements radically transform the profession, the job market, and the canon. And because they have transformed the profession, they are helping to transform the world.

A strong voice in the profession will enable ecocritics to be influential in mandating important changes in the canon, the curriculum, and university policy. We will see books like Aldo Leopold's *A Sand County Almanac* and Edward Abbey's *Desert Solitaire* become standard texts for courses in American literature. Students taking literature and composition courses will be encouraged to think seriously about the relationship of humans to nature, about the ethical and aesthetic dilemmas posed by the environmental crisis, and about how language and literature transmit values with profound ecological implications. Colleges and universities of the twenty-first century will require that all students complete at least one interdisciplinary course in environmental studies. Institutions of higher learning will one day do business on recycled-content paper—some institutions already do.

In the future we can expect to see ecocritical scholarship becoming ever more interdisciplinary, multicultural, and international. The interdisciplinary work is well underway and could be further facilitated by inviting experts from a wide range of disciplines to be guest speakers at literary conferences and by hosting more interdisciplinary conferences on environmental topics. Ecocriticism has been predominantly a white movement. It will become a multi-ethnic movement when stronger connections are made between the environment and issues of social justice, and when a diversity of voices are encouraged to contribute to the discussion. This volume focuses on ecocritical work in the United States. The next collection may well be an international one, for environmental problems are now global in scale and their solutions will require worldwide collaboration.

二、《地方意识与星球意识：环境想象中的全球》选读[①]

Over the last decade and a half, the concept of "globalization" has emerged as the central term around which theories of current politics, society, and culture in the humanities and social sciences are organized. In literary and cultural studies, it is gradually replacing earlier key concepts in theories of the contemporary such as "postmodernism" and "postcolonialism". While studies of globalization tend to shift away from the aesthetic and cultural focus that dominated many analyses of postmodernism to a more economic and geopolitical emphasis, many of them nevertheless continue to be centrally concerned with the development of modernity in the late twentieth and early twenty-first centuries. Like other concepts that describe the most recent evolution of the modern—such as "late modernity" or "postmodernity"—globalization has elicited a spectrum of competing analyses and evaluations. While some sociologists (Anthony Giddens, for example) see it as a consequence of modernization processes as they have unfolded over approximately the last two centuries, others, for example Ulrich Beck, describe it as a departure into a different kind of modernity, and yet others (for instance, Martin Albrow) define it as a development that leaves the boundaries of the modern behind. Concurrently, some theorists (for example Immanuel Wallerstein, David Harvey, and Leslie Sklair) see globalization principally as an economic process and as the most recent form of capitalist expansion, whereas others emphasize its political and cultural dimensions, or characterize it as a heterogeneous and uneven process whose various components— economic, technological, political, cultural—do not unfold according to the same logic and at the same pace, an argument that has been proposed in different guises by Arjun Appadurai, James Clifford, and Néstor García Canclini. All theorists of globalization would agree that even as the processes this concept describes affect a multitude of regions and nations the world over, they transform them in fundamentally different ways; opinions diverge, however, on whether this unevenness should be described as yet another dimension of the capitalist North's persistent attempts to dominate and exploit the South, or whether the power and interest structures it results from are more dispersed and complex.

"Globalization" "globalism" and "globality", then, have evolved into complex theoretical notions that refer to a wide range of different phenomena and have been approached from a variety of analytical perspectives. In this multidisciplinary debate, the question of what cultural and political role attachments to different kinds of space might play, from the local and regional level all the way to the national and global, has assumed central importance. Literary and cultural critics as

---

① Heise, *Sense of Place and Sense of Planet: The Environmental Imagination of the Global*, pp.4 - 8.

well as anthropologists, sociologists, historians, philosophers and political scientists have investigated the imaginative strategies and devices that allow individuals and communities to form attachments to these different types of spaces and to maintain them over time as an integral part of their identities, and have explored what overarching cultural and ideological purposes such commitments have been made to serve in different communities. These analyses began before globalization rose to prominence as an organizing intellectual term; from the early 1980s to the mid-1990s, they were centrally shaped by various poststructuralist philosophies and their shared resistance to what were perceived to be "essentialist" concepts of identity, that is, assumptions about the inherent characteristics of individuals and groups deriving from specific categories of nationality, ethnicity, race, gender, or sexual orientation. The thrust of the intellectual effort undertaken in those years was to show that such categories, which had earlier been assumed to be self-evident, natural, and sometimes biologically grounded, were in fact highly artificial and historically contingent, and were maintained and legitimated by specific practices, discourses, and institutions. Discourses about the nation and national identity, among others, were criticized as establishing "imagined communities", in Benedict Anderson's influential term, that often led to the denial and oppression of differences within the nation and aggression or imperialism between nations.

In search of countermodels to such nation-based concepts of identity, a wide range of theorists instead presented identities shaped by hybridity, creolization, mestizaje, migration, borderlands, diaspora, nomadism, exile, and deterritorialization not only as more politically progressive but also as potential grounds for resistance to national hegemonies. The abundance of studies focusing on such forms of identity often emphasized their marginal status in the mainstream culture and polity, a marginality that was viewed as both disabling and potentially empowering, insofar as it provided a view of the dominant culture from outside. Inevitably, a certain theoretical ambiguity accompanied the development of this line of argument, as hybridity, diaspora, and marginality sometimes turned into quasi-essentialist categories themselves, especially in some of the more emphatic validations of ethnicity, local identity, and "situated knowledge"; concurrently, other analyses emphasized the continued necessity of questioning essentialisms even in discourses that understood themselves as oppositional. The most important dimension of this phase of theoretical development for the purposes of the argument I will develop here is the fact that it produced an abundance of cultural studies that were skeptical vis-à-vis local rootedness and instead validated individual and collective forms of identity that define themselves in relation to a multiplicity of places and place experiences. Anthropologist James Clifford's influential work *Routes*—with its pun on the phonetic homonymy of "roots" and "routes"—proposed one of the most pointed formulations of this line of analysis by describing even the premodern and "locally rooted" communities that often form the anthropologist's object of study as "traveling cultures" associated with a wide range of places.

Migration, in his work as well as that of other theorists, moved from the margins to the core of cultural identity—not only that of individuals but of entire societies.

In the later 1990s, as discussions of globalization spread from the social sciences to the humanities, studies of the relationship of identity to various kinds of space also shifted in emphasis to concepts such as "transnationalism" or "critical internationalism". Theorists from a variety of fields, at the same time, began to recuperate the term "cosmopolitanism" as a way of imagining forms of belonging beyond the local and the national. Philosophers Anthony Appiah and Martha Nussbaum, anthropologists James Clifford and Aihwa Ong, sociologists Ulrich Beck, Anthony Giddens, Ulf Hannerz, and John Tomlinson, political scientists Patrick Hayden, David Held, and Anthony McGrew, as well as literary critics such as Homi Bhabha, Pheng Cheah, Walter Mignolo, and Bruce Robbins, among others, have all engaged with this notion in the attempt to free it from the connotations of social privilege and leisure travel that accompanied it in earlier periods. While there are considerable differences in the way these theorists rethink cosmopolitanism, they share with earlier theorists of hybridity and diaspora the assumption that there is nothing natural or self-evident about attachments to the nation, which are on the contrary established, legitimized, and maintained by complex cultural practices and institutions. But rather than seeking the grounds of resistance to nationalisms and nation-based identities in local communities or groups whose mobility places them at the borders of national identity, these theorists strive to model forms of cultural imagination and understanding that reach beyond the nation and around the globe. In one way or another, all of them are concerned with the question of how we might be able to develop cultural forms of identity and belonging that are commensurate with the rapid growth in political, economic, and social interconnectedness that has characterized the last few decades.

Cogent as this reasoning is in its search for new forms of transnational cultural identity, it has not gone unchallenged. Historian Arif Dirlik, literary critic Timothy Brennan, and other theorists have recently reemphasized the value of local and national identities as forms of resistance to some dimensions of globalization. Critiques of the "essentialism" of local identities and of national belonging, Dirlik and Brennan argue, omit consideration of the ways localism and nationalism can serve progressive political objectives and legitimate emancipatory projects, especially in the developing world and in a context of rapid economic globalization. Several recent anthologies—Prazniak and Dirlik's *Places and Politics in the Age of Globalization*, Mirsepassi, Basu, and Weaver's *Localizing Knowledge in a Globalizing World*, or Jasanoff and Martello's *Earthly Politics*, for example—all seek to revalidate local and national foundations of identity as a means of resisting the imperialist dimensions of globalization.

With this wave of countercritiques, the theoretical debate has arrived at a conceptual impasse: while some theorists criticize nationally based forms of identity and hold out cosmopolitan identifications as a plausible and politically preferable alternative, other scholars emphasize the importance of holding on to national and local modes of belonging as a way of resisting the imperialism of some forms of globalization. Fredric Jameson sums up this quandary when he highlights how local and regional identities used to be pitched against the homogenizing force of the nation, only to point out that

> when one positions the threats of Identity at a higher level globally, then everything changes: at this upper range, it is not national state power that is the enemy of difference, but rather the transnational system itself, Americanization and the standardized products of a henceforth uniform and standardized ideology and practice of consumption. At this point, nation-states and their national cultures are suddenly called upon to play the positive role hitherto assigned—against them—to regions and local practices...And as opposed to the multiplicity of local and regional markets, minority arts and languages, whose vitality can certainly be acknowledged all over the world uneasily coexisting with the vision...of their universal extinction, it is striking to witness the resurgence—in an atmosphere in which the nation-state as such, let alone "nationalism", is a much maligned entity and value—of defenses of national culture on the part of those who affirm the powers of resistance of a national literature and a national art.

This conflict between a conceptualization of national identity as either an oppressive hegemonic discourse or a tool for resistance to global imperialism, and of local identity as either an essentialist myth or a promising site of struggle against both national and global domination, leads Arif Dirlik even more pointedly to declare a theoretical stalemate. He acknowledges the

> intractability of the problem...with existing discussions of place/space in which the defense and the repudiation of place both carry considerable theoretical plausibility and for that same reason seem in their opposition to be confined within a theoretical world of their own out of which there is no exit that is to be revealed by theory.

If Dirlik falls prey to a rather comical non sequitur by following up this categorical rejection of a theoretical solution with a sustained theoretical defense of place—against his own suggestion that the entire discussion should be shifted to the level of specific case studies—he and Jameson nevertheless accurately pinpoint the conceptual contradictions in many current discourses about place. It might be more useful to think of such contradictions as a starting point for reflecting on the kinds of categories and abstractions that are commonly used in cultural theory than to reject them wholesale, since such rejection would presumably lead back to the theory resistance and hyperspecific analyses of detail that were already rehearsed (and later abandoned) in cultural studies in the early 1990s.

三、《物质主义生态批评：物质性、能动性和叙事模型》选读①

The idea that matter possesses agency is of central significance in the new materialisms. Against the visions that associate agency with intentionality and therefore with human intelligence, the claim for material objects to act with effectivity is a way to "[absolve] matter from its long history of attachment to automatism or mechanism". Accordingly, the true dimension of matter is not that of a static and passive substance or being, but of a generative becoming. This is evident for instance in the theory of "agential realism", developed by the feminist thinker and quantum physicist Karen Barad—one of the key-figures of the new materialisms—in her groundbreaking work *Meeting the Universe Halfway* (2007). Reality, Barad maintains, is a symmetric entanglement of material and discursive processes. Here the word "'matter' does not refer to an inherent, fixed property of independently existing objects"; rather, Barad concedes, "'matter' refers to phenomena in their ongoing materialization". In other words, matter "is not a blank slate", or "immutable or passive", but *"a doing, a congealing of agency"*; and Barad calls it *"a stabilizing and destabilizing process of iterative intra-activity"*. She further proclaims that "[m]atter is neither fixed and given nor the mere end result of different processes. Matter is produced and productive, generated and generative. Matter is agentive, not a fixed essence or property of things". On the premise of an intrinsically "agentive" matter, Barad proposes a theory of agential realism—an onto-epistemological vision of reality—as a continuous process that involves simultaneously ("intra-actively", in Barad's terminology) matter and meanings, and where embodiments and forms co-emerge into a unitary field of existence.

[...]

The agency of matter, the interplay between the human and the nonhuman in a field of distributed effectuality and of inbuilt material-discursive dynamics, are concepts that influence deeply the ideas of narrativity and text. If matter is agentic, and capable of producing its own meanings, every material configuration, from bodies to their contexts of living, is "telling", and therefore can be the object of a critical analysis aimed at discovering its stories, its material and discursive interplays, its place in a "choreography of becoming". Material ecocriticism proposes basically two ways of interpreting the agency of matter. The first one focuses on the way matter's (or nature's) nonhuman agentic capacities are described and represented in narrative texts (literary, cultural, visual); the second way focuses on matter's "narrative" power of creating configurations of meanings and substances, which enter with human lives into a field of co-emerging interactions. In this latter case, matter itself becomes a text where dynamics of "diffuse" agency and non-linear

---

① Iovino and Oppermann, "Material Ecocriticism: Materiality, Agency, and Models of Narrativity," pp.75 – 91.

causality are inscribed and produced.

[...]

Taking matter "as a text" means questioning the very idea of text. The text, for material ecocriticism, encompasses both human material-discursive constructions and nonhuman things: water, soil, stones, metals, minerals, bacteria, toxins, food, electricity, cells, atoms, all cultural objects and places. The characteristic feature of these material configurations is that they are not made of single elements, isolated from each other. Rather, they form complexes both natural and cultural, and in many cases human agency and meanings are deeply interlaced with the emerging agency and meaning of these nonhuman beings. Similar to Deleuze and Guattari, Latour calls these material and discursive intersections "assemblages" or "collectives". In their agentic capacity they are inextricably connected to our lives, and in most cases (as atoms, molecules, bacteria, toxins, etc.) they are part of our bodies, of our "material self". Heeding the continuity (the intra-action, Barad would say) of human and nonhuman in these open and evolving dynamics, material ecocriticism attends to the stories and the narrative potentialities that develop from matter's process of becoming.

The borders of this discourse are open to fathom a vast array of nature's constituents as well as culture's trash and garbage, which are manifestly "vibrant" and have "trajectories, propensities, or tendencies of their own". These "things" are, as the "Thing Theory" exponent Bill Brown claims, semantically irreducible to objects. They "speak" in a world of multiple interacting processes, such as climate change or the systems of production and consumption of global capitalism, entailing geopolitical and economic practices and thus reminding us of the fact that "the linguistic, social, political and biological are inseparable". In other words, the corporeal dimensions of human and nonhuman agencies, their literary and cultural representations, are inseparable from the very material world within which they intra-act. In some profound sense, matter's configurations always display "an enactive dance" indicating that our knowledge practices, our stories and narratives are part of "natural processes of engagement and...part of the world". This means a substantial co-implication of knowing and being. As Barad explains: "We do not obtain knowledge by standing outside of the world; we know because 'we' are of the world. We are part of the world in its differential becoming." In this understanding, regardless of how great the difference between the human self and the material agency may be, the world comes to be constituted by multiple intra-actions of this "differential becoming". This is a model of unavoidable partnership between different agents in creating reality.

Material ecocriticism, in our view, traces the artistic and cultural expression of these views, opening up textual possibilities of the materiality created in art, culture, and literature. In its transversal analysis of materiality and of material "ongoing stories", it considers the cultural and literary potentials emerging from a natural environment in which the human agents co-exist and co-act with biological organisms that exhibit agentic capacities. But not only that: going beyond the domain of the "biological", it relocates the human species in broader natural-cultural environments of inorganic material forces such as electricity, electro-magnetic fields, metals, stones, plastic, and garbage.

This leads us to a further consideration. If embodiment is the site where a "vibrant matter" performs its narratives, and if human embodiment is a problematic entanglement of agencies, the body is a privileged subject for material ecocriticism. As the debate on material feminisms has convincingly highlighted it, corporeal matter opens the patterns of agency to the structural interplay between the human and the nonhuman, being therefore crucial to overcome the idea of an "inert" matter positioned as antithetical to free human agency. It also shows how the material self is not an independent, "encapsulated" and circumscribed reality. The material self lives instead in "a world sustained by queer confederacies" in which the human is always intermingled with alien presences. As Jane Bennett perceptively remarks:

One can invoke bacteria colonies in human elbows to show how human subjects are themselves nonhuman, alien, outside vital materiality. One can note that the human immune system depends on parasitic helminth worms for its proper functioning or cite other instances of our cyborgization to show how human agency is always an assemblage of microbes, animals, plants, metals, chemicals, word-sounds, and the like.

In a more specific eco-narrative sense, the body reveals the reciprocal interferences of organisms, ecosystems, and humanly made substances (those that Alaimo calls "xenobiotics"). It is, therefore, a "collective" of agencies and a material palimpsest in which ecological and existential relationships are inscribed "in terms of flourishing or...illness". This becomes strikingly evident when "individuals and collectives must contend not only with the materiality of their very selves, but with the often invisibly hazardous landscapes of risk society". Alaimo's concept of "trans-corporeality" is highly significant here. Trans-corporeality—a "movement across bodies" as Alaimo defines it—is a model of dynamic concurrence, permeability, and "interconnected agencies" of material substances and discursive practices. Highlighting the role of the often-undetectable material forces, or "flows of substances...between people, places, and economic/political systems", trans-corporeality complements the conventional ecological vision according to which everything is connected with everything else. Alaimo's concept provides a more complete interpretive insight not only into the narratives of environmental health and risk, but also into every dynamic that takes place in what Nancy Tuana has called "an interactionist ontology", namely, "an ontology that *rematerializes the social and takes seriously the agency of the natural*".

Matter's "active, self-creative, productive", and "unpredictable" dimension is of crucial importance for material ecocriticism. Clearly，the supposed determinate boundaries of things，objects，human agents，concepts，and texts become more fluid and permeable. All these human and nonhuman agents enact the materiality of meaning through specific combinations of material and discursive practices. This is an interplay of life and its expressions as articulated emphatically by the arch-postmodern author Raymond Federman，who always underlined the crucial aspect of the fictional narratives of his own life by stating："My body is，I hope，in the text too […]. I am very tired when I am finished writing because I have used my body." Examples like these shed light on biological and textual entanglements in terms of their efficacy in encoding and producing meanings. This perspective sees material reality，or all objects，forces，things，natural and cultural systems，and processes as players in co-creating social and cultural meanings.

四、思考与讨论

1. 在谢里尔·格洛特费尔蒂看来，生态批评是在怎样的历史语境中诞生的？生态批评的研究动机、研究对象、核心诉求是什么？

2. 厄休拉·K. 海斯为什么倡导人们从"世界主义"的角度重新阐释生态批评？全球化对生态批评产生了怎样的影响？在全球环境的视野中，该如何看待地方与全球之间的关系？

3. 新物质主义思潮如何引起生态批评的"物质转向"？塞雷内拉·约维诺与赛尔皮尔·奥珀曼是如何看待物质的能动性的？将物质视作一种文本的观点，使生态批评的研究对象产生了哪些变化？

本章推荐阅读文献：

［1］Cheryll Glotfelty and Harold Fromm（eds.）. *The Ecocriticism Reader: Landmarks in Literary Ecology*. Athens：University of Georgia Press，1996.

［2］Christopher Schliephake. *Urban Ecologies: City Space，Material Agency，and Environmental Politics in Contemporary Culture*. Lanham：Lexington，2014.

［3］David Abram. *Becoming Animal: An Earthly Cosmology*. New York：Pantheon Books，2010.

［4］Greg Garrard. *Ecocriticism*. New York：Routledge，2004.

［5］Jane Bennett. *Vibrant Matter: A Political Ecology of Things*. Durham：Duke University Press，2010.

［6］Karen Thornber. *Ecoambiguity: Environmental Crises and East Asian Literatures*. Ann Arbor：University of Michigan Press，2012.

［7］Lawrence Buell. *The Future of Environmental Criticism: Environmental Crisis and Literary Imagination*. Malden：Blackwell，2005.

［8］Lawrence Buell. *Writing for an Endangered World: Literature，Culture，and Environment in the U.S. and Beyond*. Cambridge：Harvard University Press，2001.

［9］Patrick D. Murphy. *Farther Afield in the Study of Nature-oriented Literature*. Charlattesville：University of Virgina Press，2000.

［10］Roderick Frazier Nash. *Wilderness and the American Mind：Fifth Edition*. New Haven：Yale University Press，2014.

［11］Scott Slovic. "Ecocriticism：Containing Multitudes，Practicing Doctrine，" *ASLE News* 11.1（1999）.

［12］Serenella Iovino and Serpil Oppermann（eds.）. *Material Ecocriticism*. Bloomington：Indiana University Press，2014.

［13］Timothy Morton. *Ecology Without Nature: Rethinking Environmental Aesthetics*. Cambridge：Harvard University Press，2007.

［14］Ursula K. Heise. *Sense of Place and Sense of Planet: The Environmental Imagination of the Global*. Oxford：Oxford University Press，2008.

［15］程虹：《寻归荒野》，北京：生活·读书·新知三联书店，2011 年。

［16］胡志红：《西方生态批评史》，北京：人民出版社，2015 年。

［17］王诺：《欧美生态文学》，北京：北京大学出版社，2003 年。

第五章
性别研究

第一节　概　　论

　　"性别"（gender）是作为个体的人被社会与文化赋予的身份和角色，是用来分析两性差异的一种身份概念。性别是建立在生理性属基础之上的一种社会性属，因此也叫社会性别。"性别"的概念通常与"性"（sex）的概念相对。如果说建立在雌性和雄性差异基础上的"性"是一个生理概念，那么建立在女性和男性差异基础上的"性别"则是一个文化概念。就此而言，"性别这一概念可以用来指后天习得的（而不是由生理决定的）举止和行为"①，也就是说，"sex 是与生俱来的生理特性，而 gender 则是社会建构的产物"②。换言之，性是性别的基础，"性是身体的，本原性的；而性别则是一种身份，是由性而生的社会身份"③。因此性别研究应当既包含对 sex 的研究，也包含对 gender 的研究，不能把两者截然分开。作为一个学术概念，我们现在使用的"性别"一词主要从 20 世纪 70 年代初开始流行；作为一个分析范畴，"性别"一词用来分析"生物学意义上的性差异和这些性差异如何被用来在行为特性和能力素质之间划定界限，即一部分行为特性和能力素质被认定为'具有男性特征'，另一部分行为特性和能力素质被认定为'具有女性特征'"④。

　　性别是社会个体的一大身份，也是与个体生命关系最为紧密的一种身份，是个体"最基本、最具实体意义的身份本源"⑤。正如玛莉安·苏兹曼（Marian Salzman）、艾拉·塔西亚（Ira Matathia）和安·奥瑞里（Ann O'Reilly）所言："尽管全世界，尤其是西方世界已经发生了翻天覆地的变化，性别仍然是确定一个人身份最重要的方面……与一个人身份的其他方面相比——种族、国籍、社会阶层、性取向等等——性别仍然是我们身份的最基本内容。"⑥与种族、阶级等其他身份相比，性别与个体生命体验之间的联系更为紧密，一个人"出生的第一刻被告知于世的第一个身份就是性别"⑦。性别意识是社会个体

---

① Andrew Edgar and Peter Sedgwick, eds., *Key Concepts in Cultural Theory*. London: Routledge, 1999, p.106.
② 刘岩等：《性别》，北京：外语教学与研究出版社，2019 年，第 4 页。
③ 李小江：《女性/性别的学术问题》，济南：山东人民出版社，2005 年，第 162 页。
④ Jane Pilcher and Imelda Whelehan, *Fifty Key Concepts in Gender Studies*. London: SAGE Publications Ltd, 2004, p.56.
⑤ Jennifer M. Jeffers, *Beckett's Masculinity*. New York: Palgrave Macmillan, 2009, p.4.
⑥ ［美］玛莉安·苏兹曼、［美］艾拉·塔西亚、［美］安·奥瑞里：《未来男性世界》，康赟等译，北京：首都师范大学出版社，2006 年，第 228 页。
⑦ 李小江：《女性/性别的学术问题》，第 177 页。

永远无法摆脱和消除的一种身份意识,对个体的思想行为和身心健康有着深远的影响,对性别身份的认知、建构与实践伴随着个体的成长,贯穿个体生命始终。性别也是参悟人性的一个重要维度,是"思考我们人性的一种主要方式"①,是深入理解诸多社会问题的一个重要切入点和突破口。可以说,当今世界上诸多问题其实都可以从男女两性的关系上找到问题的源头。② 性别渗透于个体生命和生活的方方面面,对性别问题的认知和解决不仅关系到个体健康人格的建构,而且也关系到两性关系的和谐,以及婚姻和家庭的美满。

古今中外,漫长的人类历史文化所积淀的性别规范和准则,也为社会个体的成长与人格完善提供了参照和依据,具有很强的道德约束力。从宏观角度讲,性别关系到人类的生存和繁衍,性别文明素养关系到一个国家或民族的国际形象。由此可见,性别是人类的一个基本命题,坦诚地面对和研究性别问题,客观公正地看待两性问题,是社会进步的标识,也是人文关怀的重要体现。对于人文学者而言,关注性别问题,至少不轻视和排斥性别问题,是其社会责任感和现实关怀的一大体现。正如著名男性气质研究学者 R.W. 康奈尔(R.W. Connell)所强调的那样:"如果没有对性别不断深入的理解,我们也不能理解阶级、种族和全球性的不平等。性别关系是整体社会结构的一个主要组成部分,性别政治则是我们集体命运的主要决定力量之一。"③在文学研究领域,性别更是一个不可或缺的研究视角,它"不仅丰富了文学书写与文学解读,而且使文学特有的人文精神有更加具体的表达"④。与其他学科相比,文学中的性别专题研究还相对比较薄弱,还有很大的学术空间。

一、传统女性主义研究的局限性与性别研究的兴起

人类对性别问题的关注由来已久,但鉴于女性长期受男权思想体制的束缚和压迫,以往的性别研究经常以女权或女性主义研究的形式出现,更多地关注女性议题,因而在很多时候是女性研究的代名词,男性和男性气质的问题迟迟没有成为研究对象。既然性别包括男性和女性,那么无论男性问题还是女性问题,都应当得到重视和关注。在这种情况下,如果学者仅仅将注意力集中在女性一方身上,其研究必然不能真实、全面地反映整个男女权力关系的图景。⑤ 对女性问题过于关注,而忽略男性及整个人类群体,研究结论就会缺乏普适性。⑥ 这是因为:第一,女性的生活状况绝对不简单是她们个人的事,两性的社会生活是必不可分的;第二,父权制产生的压迫既是对女性的也是对男性的;第三,妇女解放不是妇女个人的解放,而是人的解放,是男女共同的解放。⑦ 就此而言,主要以女性为关注对象的女性主义显然存在一定的局限性,在研究内容和研究范围方面存在着丰富和拓展的内在需求。

在这样的学术认知驱动下,西方高校或研究机构之前开展的"妇女研究"(women's studies)或"女性主义研究"(feminist studies)逐渐变成"性别研究"(gender studies)。相比之前的女性或女性主义研究,

① [英]苏珊·弗兰克·帕森斯:《性别伦理学》,史军译,北京:北京大学出版社,2009年,第17页。
② 刘永杰:《性别理论视阈下尤金·奥尼尔剧作研究》,北京:中国社会科学出版社,2014年,第19页。
③ [美]R.W. 康奈尔:《男性气质》,柳莉等译,北京:社会科学文献出版社,2003年,第104页。
④ 刘岩:《从性别政治到生命政治:21世纪西方性别研究热点探微》,载《社会科学研究》2019年第2期,第157页。
⑤ 龚静:《销售边缘男性气质:彼得·凯里小说性别与民族身份研究》,成都:四川大学出版社,2015年,第67页。
⑥ 祝平燕、夏玉珍:《性别社会学》,武汉:华中师范大学出版社,2007年,第29页。
⑦ 佟新:《社会性别研究导论》(第二版),北京:北京大学出版社,2011年,第12页。

性别研究视两性为研究对象,既关注女性经验,也关注男性经验,特别讨论导致两性不平等的社会机制。① 在各种因素的促进下,性别研究正式兴起,并且逐渐由边缘进入主流,成为 20 世纪下半叶西方人文社会科学中出现的重要研究领域。② 在研究路径和运思方式方面,性别研究摆脱了二元对立思维模式,没有在男权或女权、男性中心或女性中心等问题上过多纠结,"从代表部分群体利益的政治运动走向具有普适意义的学术研究"③。经过半个多世纪的探索,性别研究在合理继承和吸纳女性主义优秀研究成果和学术思想的同时,在研究内容、研究范式等方面不断拓展、深化和突破。到目前为止,性别研究已经成为一个由社会学、心理学、人类学、哲学、文化学、历史学、文学等诸多学科和学者参与的跨学科或多学科研究领域,并取得了丰硕的研究成果,为人类性别文明的进步做出了卓越贡献。

二、性别研究的基本内容和核心概念

在诸多学科和学者的共同努力下,性别研究在研究范围和研究内容方面不断拓展和丰富,在研究方法和研究范式方面不断更新,逐渐形成一套比较完整的概念体系。其中,性别角色、性别认同、性别差异、性别平等、性别刻板印象等概念构成了性别议题分析和理论建构的重要学术话语和理论工具。

在性别研究领域,性别角色(gender roles)是一个必须首先面对的核心概念,在整个概念体系中居于主导地位。可以说,性别认同、劳动性别分工、性别气质等其他概念都是围绕它展开的。从这一概念的基本内涵上看,性别角色是指社会依照人们的生理性别将某些社会责任和权利交付给男性和女性,从而形成一系列的制度安排,如家庭制度中的两性劳动分工,母亲角色与父亲角色分别承担不同的社会责任和权利。④ 性别角色既包含个体在家庭和社会中所扮演的角色和责任,也涉及个体的人格特性和行为模式,正如祝平燕和夏玉珍所定义的那样,性别角色是由于人们性别不同而产生的符合一定社会期望的品质特征,包括男女两性所持的不同态度、人格特征和社会行为模式。⑤ 性别角色具有典型的社会建构性,是建立在个体生理属性和性别气质基础上的一种功能划分。性别角色理论主张,作为一个男人或一个女人就需要满足人们对某一性别的一整套期望,这就是性别角色。任何文化背景下都有两种性别角色:男性角色和女性角色。性别角色理论区分了男性气质与女性气质的不同,与男性气质联系在一起的是技术熟练、进取心、主动、竞争力、抽象认知等等;而与女性气质联系在一起的是自然感情、亲和力、被动等等。男性气质和女性气质很容易被解释为内化的性别角色,它们是社会习得或社会化的产物。⑥ 可以说,合理的性别角色的划分有利于两性在家庭和社会中优势互补与协作,让两性各自的性别优势得到充分发挥,对两性家庭和社会责任的担当也具有一定的规范性。同时我们也必须注意到,性别角色这种群体性划分有可能会强化两性差异,会使某些陈旧性别观念得到固化,因此要与时俱进,有继承,也要有更新和改造。

性别角色为男性和女性划定了各自的行为规范和责任,但要落实到实践上则需要性别认同(gender

---

① 佟新:《社会性别研究导论》(第二版),第 13 页。
② 刘岩等:《性别》,第 2 页。
③ 李小江:《女性/性别的学术问题》,第 179 页。
④ 佟新:《社会性别研究导论》(第二版),第 29 页。
⑤ 祝平燕、夏玉珍:《性别社会学》,第 98 页。
⑥ 方刚、罗蔚:《社会性别与生态研究》,北京:中央编译出版社,2009 年,第 183 页。

identity)的参与。性别认同也被称为"性别身份"或"性别同一性",是指性别气质与第一性征的一致性状况,是个人对所属性别群体相对稳定的理解和认知,人们在认识自己生理性别的同时也理解和认识了他(她)们的社会性别角色和性别规范,是人们对于自身作为某一性别存在的确认。① 性别认同主要包括社会的性别认同和自我的性别认同。社会的性别认同是社会赋予性别的属性,是判断一个人是男人还是女人的标志。"性别认同将个人与具有相同属性的其他人联系起来,并发生关系,组织其生活中的意义和经验。"②自我的性别认同是"自我发展的过程,它将人们分为不同的个体"③。总体来看,在大多数历史阶段和大多数主流文化中,异性恋(heterosexuality)是性别认同的基础,主要体现为对男性或女性身份和角色的认同,其他性别认同则经常处于被排斥和被歧视的状态。但随着时代的发展和人类性别文明的进步,人们对同性恋、双性恋、跨性别等其他性别认同变得越来越包容,体现出相当的人文关怀。

与性别角色相关的另一个概念是性别差异(gender difference)。与性别角色一样,性别差异也是一个颇具争议的概念,争论主要在性别本质论(essentialism)和社会建构论(constructionalism)两大思想阵营之间展开。在性别本质论看来,男女生理差异是一种本质存在,这种差异跨越了文化和历史,且可能产生不平等,因生理产生的性别不平等可能难以改变,这种认识论被简称为"性别本质主义"或"性别本质论",有时也被称为"生物决定论"。④ 在学界,这种性别本质论饱受质疑和诟病,其中最旗帜鲜明地与之抗衡的就是社会建构论。在社会建构论看来,两性生理上的差异不是造成性别不平等的原因,不平等是社会有目的地建构两性差异的后果,社会定义了两性行为的差异具有不同的社会价值,这种认识论被称为"社会建构主义"或"社会建构论"。⑤ 在社会建构论者看来,性别不是个体的固有本质,个体的性别角色、性别气质、性别认同更多的是后天社会文化建构的产物。总体来看,性别本质论和社会建构论都对我们深入认识人类性别属性做出了突出的贡献,但同时也各有偏颇。其实,性别本质论和社会建构论是不可分割的"一体两面",因为人类性别身份就是在先天生理属性和后天社会文化属性的相互作用下建构而成的。对于两性的性别差异,我们不能进行等级或优劣的划分,而是要给予尊重,因为"对于性别差异的尊重就是对每一个生命个体的尊重"⑥。

与性别差异紧密相关的一个概念是性别平等(gender equality),性别平等同样是一个颇具争议的概念。可以说,性别平等是性别研究的一大宗旨和学术使命。在佟新看来,性别研究的核心是"揭示社会性别体制的状况,分析导致其产生和再生产的社会机制,以最终实现两性平等"⑦。而性别研究的基本内容则是揭示两性不平等的现状,分析性别不平等产生和再生产的社会机制,寻找人之解放的道路和实践两性平等的方法。⑧ 毋庸置疑,这一研究宗旨的学术定位有一定的确当性,因为性别平等有利于两性的身心健康和社会价值的实现,是人类和谐社会建构的组成部分和标志。在什么是真正意义上的性别平等方面,佟新强调的"有差异的平等"观念对于我们正确认识性别平等问题具有一定的借鉴意义。

---

① 佟新:《社会性别研究导论》(第二版),第 30 页。
② 同上书,第 68 页。
③ 同上书,第 69 页。
④ 同上书,第 78 页。
⑤ 同上。
⑥ 刘岩:《从性别政治到生命政治:21 世纪西方性别研究热点探微》,第 160 页。
⑦ 佟新:《社会性别研究导论》(第二版),第 8 页。
⑧ 同上书,第 8 - 12 页。

祝平燕、夏玉珍认为，"我们要求性别平等，并不是要彻底消除男女之间的差异，而是在承认男女差异的基础上实现平等"①，"性别平等是承认差异的平等，承认多种类型的人格、性格、性别气质的价值，性别平等就是要为人们创造条件，让人自由地、自然地自我发展"②。可以说，以上几位学者的论断还是比较中肯的，切中了现实生活中性别实践的复杂性，有利于避免性别平等表象下的不平等。另外，从审美的角度讲，不顾男女性别气质差异的平等也会让人类世界变得单调和乏味，正如祝平燕和夏玉珍所说的那样，"要求女人像男人一样，以及要求只有一种类型的男人，就是'硬汉男人'，这样的社会决不会美好，因为丧失了多元与丰富，只剩下单调与乏味。在这样的社会中，人的发展是不均衡的畸形发展，因为每个人都要压抑自己的本性去争取达到不符合本性的目标"③。

　　最后一个值得我们仔细考量的概念是性别刻板印象（gender stereotypes）。这个概念之所以重要，是因为在很多情况下诸多性别观念和意识形态主要是以性别刻板印象的形式传播、建构和运作的，而且在一个人的成长过程中，性别刻板印象潜移默化地影响着个体的发展，一点一点地塑造着个体的行为。④ 如果说"刻板印象是人们对某个社会群体形成的过分简单化的、滞后于现实变化的以及概括性的看法"⑤，那么"性别刻板印象即性别定型观念，是关于男女应具备的心理特征和所从事活动的相对固定的看法。它是对两性的一种信念和态度。当人们以性别为基础，赋予男女两性以不同的特征框架时，性别刻板印象就产生了"⑥。性别刻板印象有两个潜在缺陷：其一，作为一种惰性的认知方法或过程，它把复杂的问题简单化，并且抹杀了个体差异，"没有把人当作个体来看待，而是把他们当成人工制品，当成我们所建构类别的延伸物"⑦；其二，虽然性别刻板印象当中有许多正面积极的常识或判断，但其也潜藏着一定的贬损意味和歧视性。后一点从学者的定义就可看出："性别刻板印象可以被定义为根据个体的性别而对其持有的一种标准化的并且通常带有轻蔑贬损意味的观念或印象。"⑧这也提醒人们对性别刻板印象保持必要的批判距离，对于其中包含的诸多陈规陋俗和错误观念，不能盲目认同和遵从。总之，性别刻板印象概念的提出旨在提醒人们对诸多性别流俗保持一种思辨的态度，而不是一味随波逐流、盲从盲信，这一点在讨论男性气质和女性气质话题时尤为重要。

三、性别研究的两大分支：男性气质与女性气质

　　与传统女性主义相比，性别研究在两性的关注度方面开始趋于平衡，不仅关注女性问题，也关注男性问题，研究者的态度和立场也更为客观公正，他们能够以伦理关怀的眼光审视种种性别问题。到目前为止，由男性气质（masculinity）、女性气质（femininity）、父性（fatherhood）、母性（motherhood）、酷儿理论（queer theory）等研究分支构成的学术体系已经形成。这些研究分支既可以看作性别研究的有机组成部分，也自成一体，具有相当的独立性和体系性。下面我们将主要对男性气质和女性气质这两大研

---

① 祝平燕、夏玉珍：《性别社会学》，第 131 页。
② 同上。
③ 同上。
④ 同上书，第 107 页。
⑤ 同上。
⑥ 同上。
⑦ Pilcher and Whelehan，*Fifty Key Concepts in Gender Studies*，p.167.
⑧ Ibid.

究分支进行简要概述。

如果单纯从字面意义或常识的角度看,男性气质无非是男人之为男人的特性。然而作为一个学术概念和研究领域,男性气质有着无比丰富和复杂的内涵和外延,既可以指男性的性别气质,也可以指男性的性别角色和性别规范。这一点从学界对男性气质的定义就可看出。根据简·皮尔彻(Jane Pilcher)和伊梅尔达·威尔汉(Imelda Whelehan)的定义,男性气质"是与成为一个男人(being a man)相关的一种社会实践和文化表征"[①]。但从这一简单的定义来看,男性气质的内涵远远超出了人们对性别气质的惯常理解,已经指向社会实践和文化表征层面。祝平燕和夏玉珍认为男性气质固化和稳定的内容至少包括三个成分:地位、坚强和非女性化。[②] 地位代表功成名就和受人尊重,是社会成就取向;坚强是力量和自信的表现;非女性化是指避免女性类型的活动。在性别气质的刻板印象中,男性不能依赖、软弱、温柔等。男性气质总是与雄心勃勃、大胆、争强好斗和具有竞争力联系在一起。可见,男性气质不仅涉及男性勇敢、坚强等性别气质,而且还涉及男性的社会地位、阶级身份、社会成就、兴趣爱好等诸多社会文化要素。除此之外,男性气质还包括男性的情感表达、道德素养、身体、性能力等方面的内容。

男性气质同时也是一个动态的、多元的文化概念,不同的时代或者同一时代不同的文化,甚至同一文化中的不同群体,对男性气质的认知和实践也不尽相同。为了显示男性气质的这种复杂性和多元性,西方学界经常用英文单词 masculinity 的复数形式 masculinities 来表示男性气质,正如皮尔彻和威尔汉所言:"'男性气质'复数形式的使用承认了成为一个男人的方式以及有关男人的文化表征并非一成不变的,它们不仅随着历史的变化而变化,而且也会因文化的不同而不同。这种差异不仅体现在不同的社会之间,而且也体现在同一社会的不同男性群体之间。"[③]著名的男性气质研究学者 R. W. 康奈尔更是按照权力等级秩序把男性气质分成霸权性男性气质(hegemonic masculinity)、从属性男性气质(subordinate masculinity)、共谋性男性气质(complicit masculinity)和边缘性男性气质(marginal masculinity)四种类型,以此展示同一社会和文化中男性气质的多种样态。

作为性别研究领域的一大分支,男性气质研究在 20 世纪 70 年代兴起,经过众多学科的优秀学者的共同努力,在研究内容、研究方法、概念体系等方面不断拓展和深化,如今已经成为一个世人瞩目的学术研究领域,有关男性气质的论文和著作也如雨后春笋般涌现出来。在国外学界,以 masculinity、manliness 和 manhood 为主题词的著作层出不穷,相关的论文更是难以胜数。在国内学界,男性气质研究虽然起步较晚,仅仅有十几年的学术史,但无论从研究文献的发表数量上看,还是从研究内容的广度和深度上看,都呈现出良好的发展势头。到目前为止,作为性别研究领域中的核心概念和话题,男性气质已经成为社会学、人类学、心理学、历史学、文学、影视文化、新闻传播等学科或领域中的重要研究视角。

与男性气质关联的另一概念是女性气质(femininity)。与男性气质一样,女性气质同样是一个复杂多元的概念,不同阶级、民族、性取向、年龄的女性对女性气质的认知和实践也不尽相同。尽管如此,大家在女性气质的文化内涵方面还是有些大致相同的看法。在诸多女性气质刻板印象中,女人味总是与

---

① Pilcher and Whelehan, *Fifty Key Concepts in Gender Studies*, p.82.
② 祝平燕、夏玉珍:《性别社会学》,第 38 页。
③ Pilcher and Whelehan, *Fifty Key Concepts in Gender Studies*, pp.82 - 83.

羞涩、腼腆、胆小、多愁善感、温柔以及在性生活中的被动相联系。[①] 根据祝平燕和夏玉珍的定义,女性气质是指女性应当具有同情心、令人感到亲切、对他人关心等,其成分主要包括与家庭关系相关的一切和与男性气质相对立的一切特征,如温柔、爱整洁、依赖男性等。[②] 除此之外,女性气质还包括喜欢聊天、做事得体、分寸感强、善良、虔诚笃信、陶醉于自己的容貌、文静、对安全有强烈的需要、欣赏艺术和文学、善于表达等特点。[③]

以上定义包含了许多诸如温柔、爱整洁、体贴、细心、做事得体、善良、文静等中性和美好的品质修养和行为方式,而有些定义或刻板印象则是非常负面和消极的。根据达妮察·斯卡拉(Danica Skara)的考察,与女性相关的概念经常是黑暗的、被遗弃的、差等的、非理性的、被动的,这些关联在西方语言和文化中大量存在。[④] 有鉴于此,对于社会流俗和大众文化中的诸多女性气质定义和刻板印象,人们需要保持一种思辨的态度:对于女性气质文化内涵中的优良传统和美德要肯定、继承和发扬,对于那些落后、消极和反动的女性气质刻板成见则不能盲目认同和遵从,而是要对之进行批判、抵制和改造。

从学术史的角度来看,学界对女性气质的关注由来已久,而且女性气质也一直是女性主义学术体系的一个焦点问题,对女性气质的定义和态度构成了不同时期女性主义思潮的风向标。然而在悠久的女性主义研究史中,女性气质更多的是作为一个问题性(problematic)概念而存在的,其为女性主义思潮的不同立场和观点提供了一个舆论场。随着性别研究的兴起,女性气质作为一个学术概念的合法性逐渐获得学术界的认可,女性气质研究作为性别研究的一个重要分支逐渐走向独立,关于女性气质的专著和论文也不断涌现。但与蓬勃发展的男性气质研究相比,女性气质研究在成果数量和质量方面都还有待提升,在学术话语、研究体系等方面还有待完善和深化。

第二节　经典文献选读

本章共有三篇选文。第一篇节选自简·皮尔彻和伊梅尔达·威尔汉合著的《性别研究的 50 个关键概念》(*Fifty Key Concepts in Gender Studies*)中的"性别"(Gender)词条,该词条对性别概念的整体状貌进行了简要的概述。第二篇节选自迈克尔·基梅尔(Michael Kimmel)和埃米·阿伦森(Amy Aronson)合编的《男性和男性气质:社会、文化和历史百科全书》(*Men and Masculinities: A Social*, *Cultural*, *and Historical Encyclopedia*)中的"男性气质"(Masculinities)词条,该词条由主编基梅尔亲自撰写,对男性气质的定义和文化特性进行了深入探讨。第三篇节选自萨曼莎·霍兰(Samantha Holland)的女性气质研究专著《另类的女性气质:身体、年龄和身份》(*Alternative Femininities: Body*, *Age and Identity*)中的"女性气质"(Femininity)一节,该节对女性气质的思想内涵和相关要素进行了多角度分析。所选的这三篇文章对于我们从总体上把握性别、男性气质和女性气质的思想内涵与文化特

---

① 祝平燕、夏玉珍:《性别社会学》,第 39 页。
② 同上。
③ 同上书,第 39 页。
④ Danica Skara, "Body, Depictions and Metaphors," *Encyclopedia of Sex and Gender*. Ed. Fedwa Malti-Douglas. Detroit: Thomson Gale, 2007, p.167.

性具有一定的指导意义。

一、《性别研究的 50 个关键概念》选读①

Gender

The concept of gender, as we now use it came into common parlance during the early 1970s. It was used as an analytical category to draw a line of demarcation between biological sex differences and the way these are used to inform behaviours and competencies, which are then assigned as either "masculine" or "feminine". The purpose of affirming a sex/gender distinction was to argue that the actual physical or mental effects of biological difference had been exaggerated to maintain a patriarchal system of power and to create a consciousness among women that they were naturally better suited to "domestic" roles. In a post-industrial society those physiological sex differences which do exist become arguably even less significant, and the handicap to women of childbirth is substantially lessened by the existence of effective contraception and pain relief in labour. Moreover, women are generally long outliving their reproductive functions, and so a much smaller proportion of their life is defined by this. Ann Oakley's pathfinding text, *Sex, Gender and Society* (1972) lays the ground for further exploration of the construction of gender. She notes how Western cultures seem most prone to exaggeration of gender differences and argues that "the 'social efficiency' of our present gender roles centres round women's role as housewife and mother. There is also the more vaguely conceived belief that any tampering with these roles would diminish happiness, but this type of argument has a blatantly disreputable history and should have been discarded long ago".

This was not the first time that such distinctions had been made—indeed they were very much the stuff of anthropology, psychoanalysis and medical research; significantly for feminism, Simone de Beauvoir had explored this distinction in *The Second Sex* two decades previously with her statement that "One is not born, but rather becomes, a woman". De Beauvoir's discussion makes clear the ways in which gender differences are set in hierarchical opposition, where the masculine principle is always the favoured "norm" and the feminine one becomes positioned as "Other". For de Beauvoir femininity can only be defined as lack—"between male and eunuch", so that civilisation was masculine to its very depths, and women the continual outsiders.

The majority of feminists in the 1970s seemed to embrace the notion of gender as "construct" and popular youth culture seemed to endorse this in the 1970s' passion for "unisex" clothing. However, Shulamith Firestone is one exception who suggested in *The Dialectic of Sex* (1970) that patriarchy exploits women's biological capacity to reproduce as their essential weakness. The only

---

① Pilcher and Whelehan, *Fifty Key Concepts in Gender Studies*, pp.56 – 59.

way for women to break away from the oppression, she argues, is to use technological advances to free themselves from the burden of childbirth. Moreover, she advocates breaking down the biological bond between mothers and children and establishing communes where monogamy and the nuclear family are things of the past.

Few feminists were ultimately sympathetic to Firestone's view of childbirth and the mother—child bond—not least because technology and its uses were and still are firmly in the hands of men. Those feminists, such as cultural feminists, who questioned whether all key differences are an effect of culture rather than biology, preferred to value and celebrate the mothering role as evidence of women's "natural" disposition towards nurturance and pacifism, and would be loath to relinquish it even if they could.

As feminism matures, "gender slips uneasily between being merely another word for sex and being a contested political term". Oakley argues that backlash writings return gender to a close association with the biological or natural, in order to suggest that much of feminist discourse was straining against forces that were, after all, ineluctable. For her the conceptualisation of gender is the key cornerstone of second wave feminism and its major strength—attempts to discredit it are at the heart of backlash agendas precisely *because* of its success as an analytical term. In colloquial usage, however, there is a constant slippage between sex and gender so that, for example, people are generally asked to declare their "gender" instead of sex on an application form.

Recent writings on sex and gender suggest that feminism has relied upon too great a polarisation of the sex/gender distinctions, observing that the meanings attached to sex differences are themselves socially constructed and changeable, in that we understand them and attach different consequences to these biological "facts" within our own cultural historical contexts. More recent gene research also attempts to argue that biology does contribute to some behavioural characteristics and the example of research on transgendered individuals reinforces this (given that many transgendered people characterise their sense of something being wrong with them as being trapped in the wrong body).

Moira Gatens makes the point that evidence "that the male body and the female body have quite different social value and significance cannot help but have a marked effect on male and female consciousness". Certain bodily events, she argues, are likely to take on huge significance, and particularly so if they only occur to one sex: she cites the example of menstruation. She also makes the point that masculinity is not valued *per se* unless being "performed" by a biological male: hence the male body itself is imbued in our culture with the mythology of supremacy, of being the human "norm". Judith Butler's theorisation about gender introduces this notion of performativity—the idea that gender is involuntarily "performed" within the dominant discourses of heteroreality, which only deliberately subversive performances like drag can successfully undermine. Butler's conception of gender is perhaps the most radical of all, taking as she does a Foucauldian model, and asserting that all identity categories "are in fact the *effects* of institutions, practices, discourses with multiple and diffuse points of origin". She argues further that "the sex/gender distinction suggests a radical discontinuity between sexed bodies and culturally constructed genders. Assuming for the moment the stability of binary sex, it does not follow that the construction of 'men' will accrue exclusively to the bodies of males or that 'women' will interpret only female bodies".

This approach questions the whole way we make appeals to identity. The concept of gender as performance suggests a level of free play with gender categories that we enter into socially. The result is that individuals have the potential to create "gender trouble" and challenge the way discourse establishes and reinforces certain meanings and "institutions", such as that of "compulsory heterosexuality". Butler's most radical deconstruction of the sex/gender distinction has been embraced in particular by queer theorists and third wave feminists. However, Butler has more recently denied that performativity allows the degree of "free play" with gender that some of these theorists have suggested. In the wider world, there remain constant shifts between conceptualisations of the human being as controlled by either predominantly biological or social forces. This is most marked by a return of popular science tracts which, using a quasi-Darwinian logic, suggest powerfully that our biology is once again our destiny. The substantial shifts in women's lives and expectations since the 1960s show just how malleable the category of femininity is; whether masculinity has shown itself to be quite so elastic, is open to question.

二、《男性和男性气质：社会、文化和历史百科全书》选读①

Masculinities

Masculinities refers to the social roles, behaviors, and meanings prescribed for men in any given society at any one time. As such, the term emphasizes gender, not biological sex, and the diversity of identities among different groups of men. Although we experience gender to be an internal facet of identity, masculinities are produced within the institutions of society and through our daily interactions.

Much popular discourse assumes that biological sex determines one's gender identity, the experience and expression of masculinity and femininity. Instead of focusing on biological universals, social and behavioral scientists are concerned with the different ways in which biological sex comes to mean different things in different contexts. "Sex" refers to the biological apparatus, the male and the female—our chromosomal, chemical, anatomical organization. "Gender" refers to the meanings that are attached to those differences within a culture. "Sex" is male and female;

---

① Michael Kimmel and Amy Aronson, eds., *Men and Masculinities: A Social, Cultural, and Historical Encyclopedia*. Santa Barbara: ABC‑CLIO, Inc., 2004, pp.503‑507.

"gender" is masculinity and femininity—what it means to be a man or a woman. Although biological sex varies very little, gender varies enormously. Sex is biological; gender is socially constructed. Gender takes shape only within specific social and cultural contexts.

The use of the plural—masculinities—recognizes the dramatic variation in how different groups define masculinity, even in the same society at the same time, as well as individual differences. Although social forces operate to create systematic differences between men and women, on average on some dimensions, even these differences *between* women and men are not as great as the differences *among* men or *among* women.

The meanings of masculinity vary over four different dimensions; thus four different disciplines are involved in understanding gender:

First, masculinity varies across cultures. Anthropologists have documented the ways that gender varies cross-culturally. Some cultures encourage men to be stoic and to prove masculinity, especially by sexual conquest. Other cultures prescribe a more relaxed definition of masculinity, based on civic participation, emotional responsiveness, and collective provision for the community's needs. What it means to be a man in France or among Aboriginal peoples in the Australian outback are so far apart that it belies any notion that gender identity is determined mostly by biological sex differences. The differences between two cultures' version of masculinity is often greater than the differences between the two genders.

Second, definitions of masculinity vary considerably in any one country over time. Historians have explored how these definitions have shifted, in response to changes in levels of industrialization and urbanization, position in the larger world's geopolitical and economic context, and with the development of new technologies. What it meant to be a man in colonial America is quite different from what it meant in 1900 or what it might mean to be a man in America today.

Third, definitions of masculinity change over the course of a person's life. Developmental psychologists have examined how a set of developmental milestones lead to difference in our experience and our expression of gender identity. Both chronological age and life-stage require different enactments of gender. In the West, the issues confronting a man about proving himself and feeling successful change as he ages, as do the social institutions in which he attempts to enact those experiences. A young, single man defines masculinity differently from a mid dle-aged father and an elderly grandfather.

Finally, the meanings of masculinity vary considerably within any given society at any one time. At any given moment, several meanings of masculinity coexist. Simply put, not all American or Brazilian or Senegalese men are the same. Sociologists have explored the ways in which class, race, ethnicity, age, sexuality, and region all shape gender identity. Each of these axes modifies the others. Imagine, for example, two "American" men: one, an older, black, gay man in Chicago; the other, a young, white, heterosexual farm boy in Iowa. Wouldn't they have different definitions of masculinity? Each is deeply affected by the gender norms and power arrangements of his society.

If gender varies so significantly—across cultures, over historical time, among men and women within any one culture, and over the life course—we cannot speak of masculinity as though it were a constant, universal essence, common to all men. Thus, gender must be seen as an ever-changing fluid assemblage of meanings and behaviors and we must speak of *masculinities*. By pluralizing the terms, we acknowledge that masculinity means different things to different groups of people at different times.

Recognizing diversity ought not obscure the ways in which gender definitions are constructed in a field of power. Simply put, all masculinities are not created equal. In every culture, men contend with a definition that is held up as the model against which all are expected to measure themselves. This "hegemonic" definition of masculinity is "constructed in relation to various subordinated masculinities as well as in relation to women," writes sociologist R.W. Connell. As Goffman once described it: "In an important sense there is only one complete unblushing male in America: a young, married, white, urban, northern, heterosexual, Protestant, father, of college education, fully employed, of good complexion, weight, and height, and a recent record in sports...Any male who fails to qualify in any one of these ways is likely to view himself—during moments at least—as unworthy, incomplete, and inferior."

Definitions of masculinity are not simply constructed in relation to the hegemonic ideals of that gender, but also in constant reference to each other. Gender is not only plural; it is also relational. Surveys in Western countries indicate that men construct their ideas of what it means to be men *in constant reference* to definitions of femininity. What it means to be a man is to be unlike a woman; indeed, social psychologists have emphasized that while different groups of men may disagree about other traits and their significance in gender definitions, the "antifemininity" component of masculinity is perhaps the single dominant and universal characteristic.

Gender difference and gender inequality are both produced through our relationships. Chodorow argued that the structural arrangements by which women are primarily responsible for raising children creates unconscious, internalized desires in both boys and girls that reproduce male dominance and female mothering. For boys, gender identity requires emotional detachment from the mother, a process of individuation through separation. The boy comes to define himself as a boy by rejecting whatever he sees as female, by devaluing the feminine in himself (separation) and in others (male superiority). Girls, by contrast, are bound to a pre-Oedipal experience of connection to the same-sex parent; they develop a sense of themselves through their ability to connect, which leads to a desire to become mothers themselves. This cycle of men defining themselves through their distance from, and devaluation of, femininity can end, Chodorow argues, only when parents participate equally in child rearing.

Although recognizing gender diversity, we still may conceive masculinities as attributes of identity only. We think of gendered individuals who bring with them all the attributes and behavioral characteristics of their gendered identity into gender-neutral institutional arenas. But because gender is plural and relational, it is also situational. What it means to be a man or a woman varies in different institutional contexts. Those different institutional contexts demand and produce different forms of masculinity. "Boys may be boys," cleverly comments feminist legal theorist Deborah Rhode, "but they express that identity differently in fraternity parties than in job interviews with a female manager." Gender is thus not only a property of individuals, some "thing" one has, but a specific set of behaviors that are produced in specific social situations. And thus gender changes as the situation changes.

Institutions are themselves gendered. Institutions create gendered normative standards, express a gendered institutional logic, and are major factors in the reproduction of gender inequality. The gendered identity of individuals shapes those gendered institutions, and the gendered institutions express and reproduce the inequalities that compose gender identity. Institutions themselves express a logic—a dynamic—that reproduces gender relations between women and men and the gender order of hierarchy and power.

Not only do gendered individuals negotiate their identities within gendered institutions, but also those institutions produce the very differences we assume are the properties of individuals. Thus, "the extent to which women and men do different tasks, play widely disparate concrete social roles, strongly influences the extent to which the two sexes develop and/or are expected to manifest widely disparate personal behaviors and characteristics". Different structured experiences produce the gender differences that we often attribute to people.

For example, take the workplace. In her now-classic work, *Men and Women of the Corporation* (1977), Rosebeth Moss Kanter argued that the differences in men's and women's behaviors in organizations had far less to do with their characteristics as individuals than it had to do with the structure of the organization and the different jobs men and women held. Organizational positions "carry characteristic images of the kinds of people that should occupy them," she argued, and those who do occupy them, whether women or men, exhibited those necessary behaviors. Though the criteria for evaluation of job performance, promotion, and effectiveness seem to be gender neutral, they are, in fact, deeply gendered. "While organizations were being defined as sex-neutral machines," she writes, "masculine principles were dominating their authority structures." Once again, masculinity—the norm—was invisible. For example, secretaries seemed to stress personal loyalty to their bosses more than did other workers, which led some observers to attribute this to women's greater level of personalism. But Kanter pointed out that the best way for a secretary—of either sex—to get promoted was for the boss to decide to take the secretary with him to the higher job. Thus the structure of the women's jobs, not the gender of the job holder, dictated their responses.

Sociologist Joan Acker has expanded on Kanter's early insights and specified the interplay of structure and gender. It is through our experiences in the workplace, Acker maintains, that the differences between women and men are reproduced and by which the inequality between women and men is legitimated. Institutions are like factories, and one of the things that they produce is gender difference. The overall effect of this is the reproduction of the gender order as a whole.

Institutions accomplish the creation of gender difference and the reproduction of the gender order through several gendered processes. Thus, "advantage and disadvantage, exploitation and control, action and emotion, meaning and identity, are patterned through and in terms of a distinction between male and female, masculine and feminine". We would err to assume that gendered individuals enter gender-neutral sites, thus maintaining the invisibility of gender-as-hierarchy, and specifically the invisible masculine organizational logic. On the other hand, we would be just as incorrect to assume that genderless "people" occupy those gender-neutral sites. The problem is that such genderless people are assumed to be able to devote themselves single-mindedly to their jobs, to act as though the only responsibility they have toward their families is financial, and may even have familial supports for such single-minded workplace devotion. Thus, the genderless job holder turns out to be gendered as a man.

Take, for example, the field of education. The differences we assume are the properties of boys and girls are often subtly—or not so subtly—produced by the educational institutions in which we find ourselves. This takes place in the structure of the institution itself: by having boys and girls form separate lines to enter the school through different entrances; separating boys and girls during recess and encouraging them to play at different activities; tracking boys into shop and girls into home economics (as if boys would naturally want to repair cars and girls would naturally want to learn how to cook). It also takes place in the informal social interactions with teachers who allow boys to disrupt or interrupt classes more easily than girls or who discourage girls from excelling in science or math classes. And it takes place in the dynamics of the interactions among boys and girls as well, both in the classroom and outside.

Embedded in organizational structures that are gendered, subject to gendered organizational processes, and evaluated by gendered criteria, then, the differences between women and men appear to be the differences solely between gendered individuals. When gender boundaries seem permeable, other dynamics and processes can reproduce the gender order. When women do not meet these criteria (or, perhaps more accurately, when the criteria do not meet women's specific needs), we see a gender-segregated workforce and wage, hiring, and promotional disparities as the "natural" outcomes of already-present differences between women and men. It is in this way that those differences are generated and the inequalities between women and men are legitimated and reproduced.

There remains one more element in our exploration of masculinities. Some psychologists and sociologists believe that early childhood gender socialization leads to gender identities that become fixed, permanent, and inherent in our personalities. However, many sociologists disagree with this notion today. As they see it, gender is less a component of identity—fixed and static—that we take with us into our interactions than it is a product *of* those interactions. In an important article, West and Zimmerman argued that "a person's gender is not simply an aspect of what one is, but, more fundamentally, it is something that one *does*, and does recurrently, in interaction with others". We are constantly "doing" gender, performing the activities and exhibiting the traits that are prescribed for us.

Doing gender is a lifelong process of performances. As we interact with others, we are held accountable to display behavior that is consistent with gender norms—at least for that situation. Thus, consistent gender behavior is less a response to deeply internalized norms or personality characteristics and more a negotiated response to the consistency with which others demand that we act in a recognizable masculine or feminine way. Gender is less an emanation of identity that bubbles up from below in concrete expression; rather, it is an emergent property of interactions, coerced from us by others.

Understanding how we "do" masculinities, then, requires that we make visible the performative elements of identity, and also the audience for those performances. It also opens up unimaginable possibilities for social change; as Suzanne Kessler points out in her study of "intersexed" people (hermaphrodites, those born with anatomical characteristics of both sexes, or with ambiguous genitalia): "If authenticity for gender rests not in a discoverable nature but in someone else's proclamation, then the power to proclaim something else is available. If physicians recognized that implicit in their management of gender is the notion that finally, and always, people construct gender as well as the social systems that are grounded in gender-based concepts, the possibilities for real societal transformations would be unlimited." Kessler's gender utopianism raises an important issue. In saying they we "do" gender, we are saying that gender is not only something that is done to us. We create and re-create our own gendered identities within the contexts of our interactions with others and within the institutions we inhabit.

三、《另类的女性气质：身体、年龄和身份》选读[①]

Femininity

Since the key overall theme of the research is femininity (how it is rendered, played out, resisted and understood), here I review ideas about and definitions of femininity and how these

---

① Samantha Holland, *Alternative Femininities: Body, Age and Identity*. Oxford: Berg, 2004, pp.7 - 14.

definitions do (or do not) link to the research. "What is femininity?" is a question which has exercised feminist writers for decades and many feminist writers have attempted to pin down the elusive concept of femininity. For example, Brownmiller asserts that "femininity, in essence, is a romantic sentiment, a nostalgic tradition of imposed limitations"; Wolf argues that "femininity is code for femaleness plus whatever a society happens to be selling. If 'femininity' means female sexuality...women never lost it and do not need to buy it back"; and Smith comments that "the notion of femininity does not define a determinate and unitary phenomenon". Early accounts, such as Millett appear to skate close to placing sex and gender as the equivalent categories to nature and culture, which created difficulties as women were already aligned closely to nature (thus actually concurring with essentialist notions of women being emotional and unpredictable). A consensus was reached on the difference between sex and gender which helpfully repositioned gender as a general category which applied equally to men or women: for example, Scott provides an explanation that gender (that is, femininities and masculinities) is a "social category imposed upon a sexed body" and Furman explains that her "assumption is that a woman's sex—her femaleness—is biologically based, whereas her gender—her femininity—is socially constructed". However, pithy definitions aside, femininity often continues to elude analysis. "Femininity increasingly became an exasperation, a brilliant, subtle aesthetic that was bafflingly inconsistent at the same time it was minutely, demandingly concrete, a rigid code of appearance and behaviour defined by do's and don't-do's".

The difficulties lie primarily in the fact that the term "femininity" is a concept which refers to a set of gendered behaviours and practices, and yet which is fluid and not fixed, and can mean as many different things as there are women (just as there are as many "masculinities" as there are men). As Butler argues, it is "a stylized repetition of acts" and is fragile, shifting, contextual and never complete. Glover and Kaplan concur with the idea of masculinity and femininity as contextual and unfinished, referring to historical differences in gender ideals and especially when "one considers the range of competing definitions of what it has meant to be a man or a woman". For these reasons, there are a variety of accounts of what femininity is and how is it "done": for example, femininity has been seen variously as a normative order, that is, a set of psychological traits (such as that women are considered to be more nurturing than men, be less aggressive and have fewer spatial skills); it has been seen as a performance; and it has been seen as a process of interaction. [...] Mirza argues that "post-modernism has allowed the celebration of difference, the recognition of otherness, the presence of multiple and changeable subjectivities". Some feminist theorists have challenged the idea of sex and gender as definite categories as unworkable (as not all sex/gender categories necessarily work: for example, not all women are able to become pregnant). "Post-modernist arguments...suggest not only that gender identity is commonly much more fluid than commonly supposed, but also that the sex/gender distinction is untenable, because biological differences are not significant in themselves, but only if society makes them so". The main problem is avoiding notions of essentialism: ideas that femininity equates with young, white, slim, heterosexual, able-bodied women have been refuted by a number of theorists who point out that femininity should never be simply a singular descriptive term, but instead should always be femininities and genders. Therefore, because of these pluralities, theorists need to always take account of the differences between women, differences of ethnicities, class, age, body size, as well as celebrate and challenge (rather than bemoan) the differences between men and women.

A central question to this research is how the interviewees understand traditional femininities and, as a result, place themselves in opposition to them. Smith argues that femininity involves "assembling a miscellaneous collection of instances apparently lacking coherence...Its descriptive use relies on our background and ordinary knowledge of everyday practices, which are the source and origin of these instances"; so, in other words, we "just know" what femininity means, what it is and how it is done—except, when asked to explain it, it becomes much more difficult. Smith criticises Brownmiller for collecting (into topics), but not analysing, the phenomena of femininity, "thus enacting the indeterminacy of the concept". As Smith explains, "we can produce examples" but they will not have a pattern or even rationality so "inquiry...has to begin with the ordinary and unanalysed ways in which we know what we are talking about when we use the concept", which is exactly what my own research sets out to do. One of the key ways that femininity has come to be understood and learnt is through what Furman calls "the traditional practices of femininity and beautification", the "actual practices, actual activities", which construct the phenomena. The way that we learn the current practices is, to a large part, through the visual images of mass media. The rules for femininity have come to be culturally transmitted more and more through the deployment of what Bordo calls "standardized visual images". As a result, femininity itself has come to be largely a matter of constructing, in the manner described by Erving Goffman, the appropriate surface presentation of the self. We no longer are told what "a lady" is or of what femininity consists. Rather, we learn the rules directly through bodily discourse: through images which tell us what clothes, body shape, facial expression, movements and behavior is required.

Smith notes that femininity is created as a "distinctively textual phenomenon". By this she means,

to address femininity is to address a textual discourse vested in women's magazines and television, advertisements, the appearance of cosmetic counters, fashion displays, and to a lesser extent, books...Discourse also involves the talk women do in relation to such texts, the work of producing oneself to realise the textual images, the skills involved in going shopping, making and choosing clothes, making decisions about colours, styles, make-up.

This relation to the texts of femininity is particularly relevant to this research (and the gaps it seeks to fill) as the women involved both do and do not join in the sort of talk Smith describes, and both do and do not engage with many of the textual elements of femininity. For example, of course they do watch television but they criticise fashion magazines and, while they do wear make-up and buy or make clothes, they seek to exist outside the "fashion displays". Craik calls these textual activities a "recipe for femininity", which implies that all of the ingredients must be included in a particular way to guarantee success. She argues, quoting Walkerdine, that

> the assumption of femininity is "at best shaky and partial". The ideals and fantasies offered to women are points of orientation for the realisation of a gendered self...To this end, the media have provided the means for promoting desirable images and icons of femininity, because they can be endlessly reproduced and widely consumed.

This type of analysis (rules, requirements, orientation) seems to place women as mindless consumers, in thrall to the power of media images. However, Smith refutes the idea of femininity as only an effect of patriarchy or that women are merely the passive dupes of either mass media or male power. She argues that it is important to avoid the "treatment of women as passive victims...to recognise women's active and creative part in its social organisation...They are active, they create themselves". This statement echoes many of the findings of this research in that many of the interviewees were concerned with the creation and maintenance of themselves as "alternative" women. At the same time they challenge Smith's assertion that "a woman active in the discourse works within its interpretive circles, attempting to create in her own body the displays which appeal to the public textual images as their authority and depend upon the doctrines of femininity for their interpretation". They consume only some of the discourses of femininity so are able to move away from them, in a limited way. Additionally, they cannot be said to be entirely active in the discourse: although they count themselves as "feminine", their appearance critiques the "public textual images" and does not look to the "doctrines" of traditional femininity for their interpretation.

Girls learn early the standardised images through a variety of texts, for example, from magazines. Other studies highlight how fairy tales create doctrines of femininity or how play creates powerful images which remain one of our "yardsticks" for femininity as adults. Both Lees and Sharpe have studied how femininity is learnt, rendered and resisted by girls and young women at school and home. As Gaines argues, "from the mid-teens...[there is] a close link between dressing the part and playing the part", the part being to fulfil the requirements of modern femininity. This is a difficult task for, as Wolf argues, "young women have been doubly weakened: raised to compete like men in rigid male-model institutions, they must also maintain to the last detail an impeccable femininity". Wolf's polemic focuses on what Smith later called the textual discourse of femininity, including women's magazines, beauty culture and dieting and eating disorders, highlighting how a range of institutions (from work practices to religion and media images) serve to perpetuate the ideologies about femininity and how women suffer through them. These negative associations of inferiority and worse, which so stubbornly cling to the subjective and objective representations of woman, have been one of feminism's strongest *raisons d'être* and continue to divide feminist theorists about what is "natural" and what is cultural. To describe the negative feelings which women still feel and witness about themselves as women, some feminists have adopted the term "abjection", its usual meaning being to feel inferior, to attempt to theorise "the interaction between the ways in which societies and women themselves too often conceive of femininity". Abjection, although not a term used in the empirical chapters, is a relevant concept in that many of my interviewees were indeed negative about femininity.

There are other, more positive ways to resist the negative connotations of femininity. Glover and Kaplan outline an important concept for this research, the concept of the paradox. They argue that "the mix of abjection and euphoria that is the psychic condition of modern femininity...can be thought of as a creative paradox rather than as pure contradiction or simple complement, for the tension between these opposed psychic states has been productive rather than otherwise". They draw on the work of Scott, who explains that a paradox can be both true and false at the same time, as well as something which is resistant to dominant ideas. Therefore the term is "an immensely suggestive way of posing the 'riddle' or the 'problem' of femininity" and is of particular use to this research as many of the accounts of my interviewees are contradictory (for example, placing themselves in relation to, and yet simultaneously resistant to, the idea of femininity) and therefore paradoxical in nature. However, girls (and women) often find ways to resist the restrictions of femininity, which were echoed by many of the accounts of my interviewees. As McRobbie found, girls used fashion as a counter-discourse to resist the anti-feminine doctrines of school, and Blackman, similarly, found that a group of "New Wave" girls made themselves highly visible through their appearance. This type of resistance, which subverts feminine qualities while working within a general framework of femininity (for example, using fashion as the tool to resist other doctrines), is relevant to this research in that my interviewees exhibited a very similar attitude to resistance.

Ussher discusses the difference between women who were apparently traditionally (and knowingly) feminine and those who resist many aspects of traditional femininity. Although both categories entail some elements of resistance or subversion, Ussher draws a distinction between the former ("doing girl") and the latter ("resisting girl"). The former is when a woman uses feminine masquerade (using all the trappings of traditional femininity). The latter is when "that which is traditionally signified by 'femininity' is invariably ignored or denied (often derided)—the necessity for body discipline, the inevitability of the adoption of the mask of beauty and the adoption of coquettish feminine wiles". This type of resistance highlights the elements of masquerade present in femininity. "Feminists have more recently turned to masquerade as a theoretical paradigm, as a supplement to, as well as a reaction against, theories of voyeurism and fetishism which posit a generic male spectator". This works (not necessarily consciously) by distancing the woman from her rendition of femininity—Barbara Cartland was a good example. Studlar notes that masquerade often involves a type of "excess femininity" in which (as Doane argues) to "construct a distance between the woman and her public assumption of excessive feminine accoutrements". Tseëlon's account of masquerade was most helpful in that I was able to draw a parallel between her definition of masquerade and the actions of some of my interviewees:

> Some professional women...flash their femininity to signal that they are not really so threatening, and to reassure that their power is just a charade. Femininity is thus a disarming disguise: it is donned, like masquerade, to disguise the female's desire...[for] power...The woman deflects attention from her desire for power through its opposite: constructing a very feminine, non-threatening image of herself.

In this way masquerade relies entirely on an oppositional masculinity against which to define itself. Tseëlon argues that, from a feminist perspective, the "concept of masquerade is double-edged. It implies the instability of the feminine position" defining subjectivity through distance, denial and defence. However, it can also be empowering: it "simultaneously disguises and calls attention to what it tries to hide, in the process of hiding it".

Yet still sexualised femininity becomes less associated with women as they age, making clear the link between femininity as a cultural phenomenon inscribed upon the bodies of young women. There is a difference between "popular" and academic constructions of age in that cultural representations offer more polarised, and not necessarily more positive, images whereas academic constructions tend to concentrate on the reality for "real" women. For example, Bordo argues that actresses for whom

> face-lifts are virtually routine...are changing cultural expectations of what a woman "should" look like at forty-five and fifty. This is touted in popular culture as a liberating development for older women...[where] fifty is still sexy. But in fact...[they] have not made the aging female body sexually more acceptable. They have established a new norm—achievable only through continual cosmetic surgery—in which the surface of the female body ceases to age physically as the body grows chronologically older.

There is nothing liberating about not being able to age; Wolf calls it "the cult of the fear of age". To scratch the surface of this ostensibly liberating development reveals stereotypes and unpalatable truths about the longevity of femininity having nothing to do with the lifespan of the woman associated with it，evading the truth of academic accounts which reveal facts such as，"Because women form the largest proportion of the very old，where the most severe problems of care are concentrated，the notion of elderly women as problematic becomes even more pronounced and generalised".

四、思考与讨论

1. 在两性性别差异方面存在两种针锋相对的观点，一种是本质主义，一种是建构主义，如何看待这两种观点？关于女性的生育功能，女性主义者当中存在怎样的分歧，其分歧的缘由是什么？

2. 什么是男性气质(masculinity)？根据迈克尔·基梅尔的观点，男性气质的定义和文化内涵会随着哪些因素的变化而变化？

3. 什么是女性气质(femininity)？为什么说女性气质是流动的(fluid)而不是一成不变的？如何辩证地看待传统女性气质(traditional femininity)？

本章推荐阅读文献：

[1] Betty Friedan. *The Feminine Mystique* . New York：Dell，1974.

[2] David D. Gilmore. *Manhood in the Making: Cultural Concepts of Masculinity* . New Haven：Yale University Press，1990.

[3] David Glover and Cora Kaplan. *Genders* . London：Routledge，2000.

[4] Elaine Showalter. *A Literature of Their Own: British Women Novelists from Brontë to Lessing* . Princeton：Princeton University Press，1977.

[5] Erving Goffman. *Stigma: Notes on the Management of Spoiled Identity* . Englewood Cliffs：Prentice-Hall，1963.

[6] Fedwa Malti-Douglas（ed.）. *Encyclopedia of Sex and Gender* . Detroit：Thomson Gale，2007.

[7] Gail Bederman. *Manliness & Civilization: A Cultural History of Gender and Race in the United States* , *1880 - 1917* . Chicago：The University of Chicago Press，1995.

[8] Harriet Bradley. *Gender* . Cambridge：Polity Press，2013.

[9] Harvey C. Mansfield. *Manliness* . New Haven：Yale University Press，2006.

[10] Jane Pilcher and Imelda Whelehan. *Fifty Key Concepts in Gender Studies* . London：SAGE Publications Ltd，2004.

[11] John Archer and Barbara Lloyd. *Sex and Gender* . Cambridge：Cambridge University Press，2002.

[12] Kate Millett. *Sexual Politics* . London：Virago，1977.

［13］Michael Kimmel and Amy Aronson（eds.）. *Men and Masculinities: A Social，Cultural，and Historical Encyclopedia*. Santa Barbara：ABC-CLIO，Inc.，2004.

［14］Michael S. Kimmel. *Manhood in America: A Cultural History*. New York：Oxford University Press，2006.

［15］R. W. Connell. *Gender and Power: Society，the Person and Sexual Politics*. Stanford：Stanford University Press，1987.

［16］R. W. Connell. *Masculinities*. Berkeley：University of California Press，2005.

［17］Samantha Holland. *Alternative Femininities: Body，Age and Identity*. Oxford：Berg，2004.

［18］Simone de Beauvoir. *The Second Sex*. London：Vintage，1997.

［19］Todd W. Reeser. *Masculinities in Theory: An Introduction*. Chichester：Wiley-Blackwell，2010.

［20］Victor J. Seidler. *Transforming Masculinities，Men，Cultures，Bodies，Power，Sex and Love*. London：Routledge，2006.

第六章
白人性研究

第一节　概　　论

20世纪90年代以来，一股被称为"白人性研究"（Whiteness Studies）或"批判性白人研究"（Critical White Studies）的新思潮在美国学界快速兴起，并席卷哲学、政治学、人类学、文学、社会学、历史学、法学等几乎所有人文领域，成为令人瞩目的学术热点之一。简单来说，白人性研究就是对处于种族权力制度中心的"白人性"进行批判性审视的一场理论思潮和文化实践。"白人性"并不等同于长着白皮肤的人，而是以肤色为基础所建构起来的一套种族制度神话。众所周知，种族主义是美国长期存在的社会问题，也是一切人文研究无法回避的根本性问题。但到底什么才是美国种族问题的症结所在？诚如N.佩因特（N. Painter）所指出的，以往人们（尤其是白人学者）总是倾向于"聚焦种族主义的受害方"[1]，把黑人视作有问题的一方，把白人假定为分析和解决问题的一方。于是黑人的民族问题、家庭问题、心理问题、道德问题、犯罪问题、经济问题等都成了"问题"。然而现在人们却要把视线倒过来，对准自认为没有问题的白人一方，去反思和批判以白色为象征的白人特权身份。南希·麦克休（Nancy McHugh）曾自问："在我们（白人）所建构的世界里，我们总习以为常地把其他种族的人们看作问题，并有权对自己的问题保持无知。"[2]从现在开始，白人以及他们身上的白色将被视为"问题"，因为一些学者相信"要想理解少数族裔的状况，就必须先弄清楚白人被赋予的文化特权"[3]。

白人性研究与20世纪60年代的种族和权力批判有密切关联，几乎所有的白人性研究者都在某种程度上认同政治左派。后结构主义、女权主义、性别研究、后殖民主义等各种文化理论有关主体、权力、性别、种族和身份的批判研究为它提供了基本的理论资源。虽然不同学科领域的白人性研究不尽相同，但其共有特征是它们都在"探究权力和压迫是如何通过各种奉行白人优先的政治话语和文化实践被表达、重新界定和确认的"[4]。白人性研究的最终目的则是"让白人性显形，以便打破由白人主

---

① 转引自 Barbara Applebaum, "Critical Whiteness Studies," *Oxford Research Encyclopedias*. [2016-06-02].

② Nancy McHugh, "Keeping the Strange Unfamiliar: The Racial Privilege of Dismantling Whiteness," *White Self-Criticality Beyond Anti-racism: How Does It Feel to Be a White Problem?* Ed. George Yancy. New York: Lexington Books, 2015, p.148.

③ Roberto Rodriguez, "The Study of Whiteness (Caucasians)," *Black Issues in Higher Education* 16 (1999), p.20.

④ France Twine and Charles Gallagher, "The Future of Whiteness: A Map of the 'Third Wave'," *Ethnic and Racial Studies* 31.1 (2008), p.7.

导的权力制度"[1]。需要指出的是,白人性研究并非黑人和其他少数族裔学者的专利,也有非常多的白人知识分子参与其中。下面我们就从它的缘起以及它的几个主要议题——白人性的建构性、白人特权或霸权、白人的"无知"或"色盲"等——为切入点展开介绍。

一、"白人性"研究的缘起

和大部分理论思潮一样,虽然白人性研究是在20世纪90年代出现并发展为热点的,但人们总可以在更久远的过去找到它的思想先驱,其中最常被提起的人物便是杜波依斯,其20世纪30年代之后的著作几乎涉及所有白人性研究的重要议题。香农·沙利文(Shannon Sullivan)发现,早期的杜波依斯曾认为种族歧视和迫害的根源在于白人对黑人真实状况的无知,大部分白人都是好的,只有少数白人才是种族主义分子,只要纠正他们对黑人历史和现状的误解,种族主义自然就会终结。但他在后期逐渐认识到,种族主义的存在是确保所有白人永远获得经济和社会优势的秘诀,为了长期确保这一优势,白人往往在无意识中紧握特权不放,因此反种族主义斗争的焦点就应该是那些隐蔽在白人无意识中的东西,而不仅是日常生活中那些显而易见的歧视。[2] 弗朗斯·特瓦恩(France Twine)等人也发现杜波依斯早在1936年出版的《美国的黑色重构:1860—1880》(*Black Reconstruction in America 1860 - 1880*)一书中便已关注到种族身份与经济利益之间的密切关联。白人底层工人更愿意强调自己的白人种族身份而不是作为穷人的阶级身份,因为这种身份认同可以在心理和物质上带来额外好处。由此,杜波依斯便被公认为白人性研究的理论先驱,他的后期著作"为白人性研究提供了理论基础"[3]。

托妮·莫里森(Toni Morrison)于1992年出版的《在黑暗中游戏:白人性与文学想象》(*Playing in the Dark: Whiteness and the Literary Imagination*)被公认为白人性研究兴起的标志性著作。她在该书中主要挑战了有关美国主流白人文学的一个基本假定,即它的发生与发展均与黑人无关,或者说黑人至多只是在白人文学中扮演无关紧要的角色。莫里森分析马克·吐温、福克纳、海明威等不同阶段的白人作家的作品后指出,非裔文化对白人文学乃至整个美国文化都有重要影响。即便那些看上去与种族问题无甚相关的白人文学,其中也有受黑人影响的内容,"这是一种黑色的、执着的在场,或隐或现,为文学想象发挥中介作用"[4]。实际上,莫里森这部著作的重要性并不仅在于她发掘出黑人对美国文学的贡献,更在于她所倡导的研究种族问题的新思路:"把批判的眼光从种族主义的受害方转向加害方,从被描述和被想象的一方转向主动描述和想象的一方,从服务方转向被服务方。"[5]莫里森可谓是吹响了白人性研究的进攻号角,由此人们才突然意识到:"白人自身的种族主体性,或他们的'族裔性'(racialness),从未像少数族裔那样得到同等关注。"[6]白人性研究向种族问题中久被忽视的关键一方——白人,或者

---

① Applebaum, "Critical Whiteness Studies".
② Shannon Sullivan, "Remembering the Gift: W. E. B. Du Bois on the Unconscious and Economic Operations of Racism," *Transactions of the Charles S. Peirce Society* 2 (2003), pp.205 - 225.
③ Twine and Gallagher, "The Future of Whiteness: A Map of the 'Third Wave'," p.7.
④ Toni Morrison, *Playing in the Dark: Whiteness and the Literary Imagination*. Cambridge: Harvard University Press, 1992, p.46.
⑤ Ibid., p.90.
⑥ Amanda Lewis, "'What Group?' Studying Whites and Whiteness in the Era of 'Color-Blindness'," *Sociological Theory* 4 (2004), p.624.

白人性——发起持续挑战，"让白人性显形"就成为其斗争口号。

二、"白人性"的社会建构性

白人性并非与生俱来的，而是一个被建构出来的种族身份——这被视为白人性研究的一个基本立场。白人性研究者把后结构主义和女性主义对人的主体、性别和身份的解构方法运用于白人性研究中，认为白人的种族身份和社会性别一样，并非与生俱来的一种生物学事实，而是一种社会历史建构。传统上，人们把种族视为某种本质化的遗传属性，肤色、毛发和眼睛的色彩等就是进行人种划分的基本依据。这种看法受到白人性研究者的根本质疑。玛丽莲·弗赖伊(Marilyn Frye)借鉴女性主义理论提出："我建议用'白人的'(whitely)和'白人性'(whiteliness 或 whiteness)这一对术语对应女性研究中的'男性气概的'(masculine)和'男性气概'(masculinity)。生有白皮肤(就像生为男性一样)被认为是一种生物决定的生理特征，但作为白人(就像作为男人一样)却是一种根深蒂固的存在方式。"[1]波伏娃的经典理论认为，女人并非生来就是女人，只是后来才"成为女人"。同样，人也并非生来就是白人或黑人，而是后天"变成/被区分为"白人和黑人。由此，人的种族身份也就不是静态的"存在"(being)，而是一个动态的"生成"(becoming)或建构过程。正如对男性身份的关注晚于对女性身份的研究一样，以往人们也只是关注黑人种族身份的被建构性，忽视对白人性建构的认识。因此，"白人性研究的目的就是揭露一个似乎仍未被探究的社会现象，即白人性的社会建构，并把有关它的新知识传播开来"[2]。

既然白人性也是一种社会建构，那么这种建构就是一个历史的过程。由此，"通过研究在不同地域和时代的那些被视为白人的人在身份上的流动性和延展性来关注白人性的偶然性"[3]，并还原欧洲移民在美国逐渐"变白"的历史过程，自然就成为白人性研究的一个重点话题。瓦莱丽·巴布(Valerie Babb)系统考察了"白人性"在美国几个世纪以来的生成过程。[4] 她分析早期欧洲移民留下的各种文字材料后发现，白人在当时并不被视为一个优越种群，来自欧洲不同国家的移民也并未把他们想象成一个共同的白人种族。他们更看重自己在国别和宗教信仰上与别人的差异而非种族差异。白人之间也存在普遍的地位差别，尤其是爱尔兰人、意大利人、犹太人等更受盎格鲁-撒克逊人歧视。奴隶也并非专指黑人，白人契约奴的法律地位和现实处境与黑人几乎没有差别。谢里尔·哈里斯(Cheryl Harris)也指出17世纪末是种族主义制度在美国确立的关键时期。在烟草种植等殖民地经济利益的驱使下，蓄奴制正式被确立，黑人在法律上被固定为奴隶，定性为财产，从此种族身份建构完成关键一步。白色不再仅仅是肤色，而且意味着附加给那些长着白皮肤的人的各种特权和自由。由于金发、碧眼、白皮肤这些无甚特别的生物属性成为特权的标志，它们也就变成"白人性神话"。基督徒/异教徒、文明/野蛮、高贵/低贱、纯洁/堕落、自由/奴隶、主人/财产全都被整合成新的种族二元对立：白人/黑人。[5]

种族身份建构的参与要素不仅是法律，还有在人类学、医学、生物学等方面持续数百年的各种伪科

---

① Marilyn Frye, *Willful Virgin: Essays in Feminism*, *1976-1992*. Freedom, CA: Crossing Press, 1992, p.151.
② Teresa Guess, "The Social Construction of Whiteness: Racism by Intent, Racism by Consequence," *Critical Sociology* 4 (2006), p.653.
③ Applebaum, "Critical Whiteness Studies".
④ Valerie Babb, *Whiteness Visible: The Meaning of Whiteness in American Literature and Culture*. New York: New York University Press, 1998, pp.10-35.
⑤ 参见 Cheryl Harris, "Whiteness as Property," *Harvard Law Review* 8 (1993), pp.1720-1724.

学话语，以及在文学、哲学、艺术学等方面的文化政治实践，它们最终的共同目的就是在科学和道德上证明白人天生的内在优越性和种族制度存在的合法性。同时，这种建构也没有仅停留在话语层面，还借助政治、经济、法律、甚至皮鞭、枷锁等暴力手段延伸至黑人的日常生活中。也就是说，白人性的建构实际上是通过暴力规训手段"把黑人变为他者"来实现的，白人的存在离不开对其他有色人种的界定，没有黑人就没有白人。"白人性观念的基础是排斥和种族征服"①，黑人被降格为"下等人"（subperson），白人便升格为上等人、正常人、标准人。白人有关自我的一切良好感觉都基于这个二元化的身份建构。

对白人性研究者来说，揭露白人性的建构本质只是批判的第一步，但也是理解种族主义全部奥秘的关键一步。只有先否定白人性是一种固定不变的生物属性，把它从一个貌似正常、普通的身份还原为特权身份，我们才有可能识破附着在它身上的神秘色彩和各种隐形的种族特权，进而才有可能从根本上找到解决种族主义的途径。

三、白人特权与霸权

一提到种族主义，可能很多人想到的是美国历史上的蓄奴制、种族隔离、种族歧视等。这种看法实际上比较肤浅，它容易带来的误解就是：随着后民权运动时代的美国在政治、经济、教育、法律等各个层面不断改进，日常生活中的种族隔离和歧视已经看不见了，奥巴马当选为第一任黑人总统似乎更说明黑人政治地位的根本改变，于是很多人便认为种族主义在美国已不复存在，至多只是残留在少数顽固的白人种族主义分子头脑中。这就造成美国社会存在一个十分矛盾的现象：人们在政治、经济和文化生活的方方面面都可以感受到巨大的种族差异和矛盾，却又几乎看不到明显的歧视性种族政策。在白人性研究者看来，要想解决这一矛盾，就必须从根本上改变对种族主义的理解。种族主义不仅仅是出现在社会表面和个体身上的歧视性言行，更是"社会构建出来的一套态度、观念和实践体系，它拒绝给予黑人和其他有色人种那些白人享有的机遇、尊严、自由和回报"②。经过精心打扮，种族主义如今已经不再那么面目狰狞，而是变得更加隐蔽，藏匿在社会深层次结构中，化身为"在文化、制度、个人等层面上的特权网"③。

白人性研究者认为，"白人特权"（white privilege）要比"种族歧视"更能揭示种族主义的深层秘密，而且这种特权并非指在法律和道德上明确规定的各种特殊待遇，而是指所有白人——不管他是否在表面上支持种族主义——仅凭自己的白人性便可确保的"本不应该获得的利益和优势"④。对此，佩吉·麦金托什（Peggy McIntosh）曾给出一个非常经典的"背包隐喻"。他说："我发现白人特权就好比一个隐形背包，里面装满了不劳而获的物品，我每天都可以拿它们兑换现金，但我自己却被要求对此佯装无知。白人特权就像一只隐形的、没有重量的背包，里面装满了特殊的装备、保险单、工具、地图、各种指南、密码本、护照、信用卡、衣物、指南针、应急设备、支票等。"⑤有了这个万能的特权包，白人便可以轻松自在

---

① Sarah Hoagland, "Denying Relationality: Epistemology and Ethics and Ignorance," *Race and Epistemologies of Ignorance*. Eds. Shannon Sullivan and Nancy Tuana. New York: State University of New York Press, 2007, p.99.

② Joe Feagin and Hernan Vera, *White Racism*. New York: Routledge, 1995, p.7.

③ Applebaum, "Critical Whiteness Studies".

④ Ibid.

⑤ Peggy McIntosh, "White Privilege and Male Privilege: A Personal Account of Coming to See Correspondences between Work and Women's Studies," *Critical White Studies: Looking Behind the Mirror*. Eds. R. Delgado and J. Stefancic. Philadelphia: Temple University Press, 1997, p.291.

地生活在美国社会。虽然白人无时无刻不在依赖它，却像鱼儿感受不到水一样忽视它的存在。但对没有特权包的黑人来说，生活中却处处都是种族主义的壁垒，它们就像透明玻璃一样，看不见却摸得着，阻碍黑人在精神和物质上实现法律允诺他们的各种经济和文化权益。白人性研究强调，这种制度性的种族主义远比暴力性的种族主义更隐蔽，也更难根除。它实际上在后民权运动时代完成了被法律明令禁止的种族主义行径。

尽管"白人特权说"有助于我们更好地理解种族主义的制度化特征，但它也存在诸多不足。在芭芭拉·阿普勒鲍姆（Barbara Applebaum）看来，白人特权说只关注个体层面上的白人特权，它充其量只能引导白人意识到特权包的存在，却对其背后的一整套特权制度缺乏批判。况且把特权比作背包还容易让人误以为它是某种可以被轻易自愿放弃的东西。[1] 其实真正的白人特权都属于"无意识习惯"[2]。最典型的一个例子是，大部分白人可以在商场里闲逛却不必担心被保安当作窃贼防范，而即便是穿着体面的黑人却随时有可能被保安视为心怀不轨的坏人。因此，查尔斯·米尔斯（Charles Mills）提出应该用"白人霸权"（white supremacy）来代替"白人特权"，因为"霸权"一词能更清楚地显示作为一种制度存在的种族主义。在他看来，白人霸权就是一种未明说的政治制度，"一种由各种正式和非正式的规则、社会经济特权和规范组成的特定权力结构"[3]。白人霸权之于种族主义社会就像男性霸权之于父权社会，它由白人主导，服务于白人利益，并不断在重复性的日常实践中得到再生和巩固。正是由于它的存在，形形色色的白人特权才会衍生出来。反过来说，只要它的存在和再生机制未受挑战，那么即便清除日常生活中看得见的白人特权，结构性的种族差异也依然无法改变，也不可能从根本上铲除种族主义。

四、特权俱乐部与种族契约论

玛丽莲·弗赖伊曾把白人群体比作一个排他性的"特权俱乐部"，她说：

> 身为白人并非一种生物学状态，而是代表着成为一个特殊社会政治团体中的成员，这个团体始终由那些在自己和他人眼中拥有最无可争议的会员身份的人所维系。［……］它通过一些接纳同仁和排斥异己的仪式凝聚自身，并在成员之间培养一种可被用来剥削他人的行事风格和态度，同时要求成员对它效忠以换取回报。它把自身界定为人类的模范，并通过有关血统和皮肤的神话把自身的存在合理化或自然化，并在实践中排除异己、殖民他者，推行奴隶制度。[4]

对白人来说，白皮肤就是与生俱来的"会员通行证"，他们无须提交任何申请便已被接纳为成员。而那些没有这张"通行证"的人永远也不可能被接纳，充其量只能根据自身被"白化"的程度而享受少部分会员权益。比如大部分黑人中产阶级都必须严格遵守白人价值观念，服从白人的工作和生活方式。即便如此，他们仍有可能被白人俱乐部的任何一位成员歧视。

① Applebaum，"Critical Whiteness Studies".
② Shannon Sullivan，*Revealing Whiteness: The Unconscious Habits of Racial Privilege*. Bloomington：Indiana University Press，2006，p.6.
③ Charles Mills，*The Racial Contract*. Ithaca：Cornell University Press，1997，p.3.
④ Frye，*Willful Virgin: Essays in Feminism*，1976－1992，pp.149－150.

相比于弗莱伊的"特权俱乐部"概念，米尔斯提出的"种族契约论"也有异曲同工之妙，且影响更大。米尔斯借用经典社会契约论的基本理念和范畴来构建种族分析框架，这对我们理解种族主义的深层运作机制很有启发。他说：

> 所谓种族契约就是在人类的一部分成员——根据种族、血统、谱系、文化等标准被界定为白人，同时也是完整人的人——之间签订的正式或非正式协议或元协议，他们据此把剩余部分人类归为"非白人"，在早已由白人定居或建立的、由白人主导的政府中，后者是被区别对待的、道德地位低等的"下等人"……或者只被当作外人对待。白人之间奉行的道德和司法上的规则在他们与非白人交往时通常不起作用，或者只以修改后的形式被运用，但无论怎样，这一契约的总体意图总是给予白人群体优势地位，剥削非白人群体的身体、土地、资源，拒绝给他们平等的社会经济机会。①

米尔斯认为自己提出的种族契约论与霍布斯、洛克、卢梭等人的经典社会契约论在意图上更接近，即不是为了用它判断当前社会制度是否合法，而是用它去描述和解释现有社会和政府的起源。他尤其从卢梭那里得到启发，他认为，我们与其探讨如何构建一个理想化的社会契约，不如反思一个欺骗性的现实契约是如何实现并被普遍接受的。比如美国《独立宣言》明确宣布人人平等，却仍旧允许蓄奴制存在数百年，同时对至今仍顽固存在的种族不平等视而不见。

当然，无论"社会契约"还是"种族契约"，都不是真正存在的一纸协定，而是研究者用来解释人如何从某种自然状态进入国家和社会状态的理论假定。我们知道，社会契约论的隐含前提是，所有人平等制定并遵守契约，共同让渡权利，一起享受由此带来的各种权益。但种族契约与它有根本不同。它不是由白人和黑人共同达成的约定，而是由白人秘密制定并强加给黑人的不平等契约。白人是真正的缔约方，黑人则是被约束、被剥夺的对象，他们在不知情、被蒙蔽和欺骗的情况下沦为下等人，"被指定为生而不平等、不自由的人"②。社会契约一旦确立，就意味着所有人都从自然人变成文明社会的平等公民；而种族契约却意味着人从此被划分为上等人和下等人。按照种族契约建立的政府也只是为了永远维系上等人（白人）的优势地位。

米尔斯指出，虽然种族契约的首要目的是"确保白人（对黑人）的经济剥削并把它合法化"③，但它同时还在道德层面发挥重要作用。它不仅规定了不同种族的人在政治、经济和法律方面的区别待遇，更默许白人在道德上向黑人行不义之事，并视其为合理合法。白人之间被禁止的不道德行为，在白人与黑人之间就变成正常之举。比如白人奴隶主会随意拆散奴隶家庭、售卖他们的子女，男奴隶主与女黑奴所生的孩子也会被当作奴隶对待。即便在今天，白人在道德上享有的特权地位依旧存在，只是更隐蔽。比如他们可以想当然地把大部分黑人想象成坏人并避免与之接触。

米尔斯的种族契约论已被白人性研究者广泛接受，成为揭示种族主义深层机制的理论假说。实际上，不管是"特权俱乐部"还是"种族契约论"，两种说法都有一层不容忽视的意蕴，那就是对白人来说，他们虽然生来就可以享受特权，但同时也需要履行一定的"会员义务"或"契约"。比如在马克·吐温的经

---

① Mills, *The Racial Contract*, p.11.
② Ibid.
③ Ibid., p.32.

典小说《哈克贝利·费恩历险记》中就有一个情节,哈克在试图帮助黑奴吉姆逃脱的过程中曾深感自责,感到自己背叛了白人社会,成为"罪人":"人家既然都知道我哈克·费恩帮过一个黑人去寻找自由,所以,我要是再见到那个小镇上的人,谅我随时都要汗颜,无地自容,只好趴下来苦苦求饶了……反正越是琢磨这件事,我的良心就越受折磨,我也越发觉得自己心眼儿坏,下流,没出息。"①弗雷德里克·道格拉斯(Frederick Douglass)在其著名的《弗雷德里克·道格拉斯——一个美国奴隶的生平自述》(*Narrative of the Life of Frederick Douglass，on American Slave，Written by Himself*)中也写道:"在当时,对黑人表现出一丝人性都会被指责为废奴主义者,而被这么称呼的人要承担可怕的后果。"②而在托妮·莫里森的小说《秀拉》中,一群刚搬到梅德林镇的爱尔兰移民为了缓解本地白人对他们的歧视和抵制,便开始主动伤害对他们并无恶意的本地黑人老居民。"事实上,故意招惹和欺负黑人倒成了那些白人新教徒的共同爱好。在某种意义上,只有迎合了老居民们对待黑人的态度,他们在这个世界里的地位才能得到保障。"③也就是说,身为白人,他们感到自己有"义务"遵照"白人的方式行动"(to act whitely)④,或者"操演白人性"(to perform whiteness)⑤,因为只有"通过操演按照特定白人种族主义认识导向建构的、表现为白人性的身体和主体性"⑥,他们才能不断"拷贝"和维持自己身上的白人性。也就是说,他们需要把种族主义当成一种自然的、正常的、合理的社会制度,心安理得地接受它带来的好处,并以统一的方式对待"非俱乐部成员",或者至少默许同伴们的行为,无视发生在身边的不义之举。而这正是我们将在下一节讨论的重要议题。

五、种族无知与肤色盲视

所谓的白人种族无知有两层意思。首先是指白人对黑人真实状况的无知。他们出于种族偏见,并受历史上那些伪科学话语误导,往往认为黑人都是进化不完整的野蛮人。在他们眼里,黑人智力低下、感情麻木、肌肉发达,只适宜被当作牛马对待,并为白人服务。如前文所述,杜波依斯曾把这种无知视为种族主义产生的根源,认为只要消除了这种无知,种族主义自然就会瓦解。这显然是把复杂问题简单化了。此种无知主要出现在历史上,但也不能说它在今天已经消失。它是因知识的匮乏或误解而导致的无知,或者说是一种被动产生的无知,它可以通过普及正确知识进行弥补,虽然这未必有助于从根本上消除种族主义。

还有一种无知则完全不同。它不是一般意义上的误解或盲视,而是对真实状况的有意回避,"是他们刻意培养出来的无知"⑦。米尔斯认为这种无知与马克思所说的"意识形态"、福柯所说的"话语"、布迪厄所说的"习性"意义相近,可以理解为一种用于感知和阐释的特殊光学棱镜,一种世界观,一种对世

---

① 马克·吐温:《哈克贝利·费恩历险记》,潘庆舲译,杭州:浙江文艺出版社,2016年,第263页。
② Frederick Douglass，*Narrative of the Life of Frederick Douglass，an American Slave，Written by Himself*. New York：W. W. Norton & Co.，1997，p.128.
③ [美]托妮·莫里森:《秀拉》,胡允桓译,海口:南海出版公司,2014年,第57页。
④ George Yancy，*Black Bodies，White Gazes: The Continuing Significance of Race*. New York：Rowman & Littlefield Publishers，Inc.，2008，p.24.
⑤ George Yancy，"Whiteness and the Return of the Black Body," *Journal of Speculative Philosophy* 4（2005），p.224.
⑥ Yancy，*Black Bodies，White Gazes: The Continuing Significance of Race*，p.48.
⑦ Shannon Sullivan and Nancy Tuana，eds.，*Race and Epistemologies of Ignorance*. New York：State University of New York Press，2007，p.3.

界的特定认知倾向,或"一种获得某些错误知识的先验倾向"①。按照上一节我们谈到的说法,白人身为特权俱乐部成员,他们有义务按照种族契约规定好的方式去认识现实,同时对不正义的结构和现象保持无知,这样他们才能够确保自身和群体利益。也正因为如此,沙利文才提出一个看似矛盾却非常有洞察力的概念——无知认识论(epistemology of ignorance)。他说:"无知认识论是对复杂的无知现象的探究,其目的是区别不同的无知形式,揭示它们被生产和维系的原因,以及它们在知识实践中发挥的作用。"②他强调的是,这种无知绝非真正的、无意为之的无知,而是"出于控制和剥削意图而主动生产出来的无知"③,是在刻意拒绝了解发生在过去和现在的真相。可以说,"无知"是白人成为种族主义同谋者和受益者的前提。

很多人认为种族特权不过是白人在政治、经济和社会生活各方面获得的优势和好处,但在阿普勒鲍姆看来,保持无知其实也属于种族特权范畴。他说:"白人的无知本身不但是一种特权,而且它的作用恰恰就是保护(其他)特权。"④因为白人对种族剥削保持无知,也就可以保护不公正的种族制度免受质疑,同时心安理得地获得好处。这种状况在当今美国更为常见。绝大部分白人都会认为种族主义已经消失,今天的种族不平等状况已经有了根本改善。他们不认为现在还存在任何所谓的种族分界线。白人在经济、教育等领域占据的主导地位不过是他们更努力付出的结果。现在甚至已有不少白人开始抱怨对黑人及其他非白人族裔的过度偏袒反倒使白人成为弱势群体。这就是阿普勒鲍姆所说的一种典型的无知,又被称作"肤色盲视"(colorblindness),即否认种族肤色还在发挥作用。但对黑人来说,感受却完全不同。他们无时无刻不感受到肤色带给他们的各种阻碍。恰如皮埃尔·奥雷勒斯(Pierre Orelus)所说:"只有那些长有特权皮肤的人才敢说看不到肤色差异,才敢说肤色无关紧要。"⑤实际上,保持无知既是当前白人从种族主义获益的前提,又是他们保护和维护种族主义的主要方式。

沙利文认为:"当与白人种族主义做斗争时,一个主要问题就是很多白人往往不认为它是个问题。"⑥阿普勒鲍姆更是一针见血地指出:"当前开展持续性反种族主义斗争的最潜在阻力是,白人非但拒绝承认种族主义仍是问题,还想当然地认为自己是'好人',置身于种族结构之外。"⑦这种自我感觉良好的"好白人"恰恰是不公正的种族结构的最隐蔽、最顽固的支持者。比如著名黑人作家理查德·赖特(Richard Wright)在《土生子》(Native Son)中所描写的道尔顿先生,他一边给黑人捐款做慈善,一边却经营房地产公司对黑人租客进行剥削。拉尔夫·埃利森(Ralph Ellison)的名著《看不见的人》(Invisible Man)中的校董诺顿先生亦属同类角色。在当代美国黑人作家查尔斯·约翰逊(Charles Johnson)的作品中,这种"好白人"也屡见不鲜,比如《牧牛传说》(Oxherding Tale)中的乔纳桑,《中间航道》(Middle Passage)中的钱德勒,《明戈的教育》(The Education of Mingo)中的摩西等。他们全都把自己视为黑人的监护人,收养黑奴做义子。只要奴隶们乖乖听话为其服务,这些"好白人"就会以"仁慈"的

① Charles Mills, "Global White Ignorance," *Routledge International Handbook of Ignorance Studies*. Eds. M. Gross & L. McGoey. London: Routledge, 2015, p.218.
② Sullivan and Tuana, *Race and Epistemologies of Ignorance*, p.1.
③ Ibid.
④ Applebaum, "Critical Whiteness Studies".
⑤ Pierre Orelus. "Unpacking the Race Talk," *Journal of Black Studies* 6 (2013), p.583.
⑥ Sullivan, "Remembering the Gift: W. E. B. Du Bois on the Unconscious and Economic Operations of Racism," p.205.
⑦ Barbara Applebaum, "Flipping the Script...and Still a Problem: Staying in the Anxiety of Being a Problem," *White Self-Criticality Beyond Anti-racism: How Does It Feel to Be a White Problem?* Ed. George Yancy. New York: Lexington Books, 2015, p.1.

手段对待他们,教他们识字,甚至把财产分给他们。但只要黑奴稍有忤逆,"好白人"就会立即露出残酷的本性。这种"好白人"在如今的美国社会更多见。在他们看来,种族主义就是对非白人进行身体迫害和经济剥削,但这都是那些"坏白人"干的错事,与自己无关。或者说即便有关系,至多也就是在过去有关系,因为那都是发生在过去的事情,他们现在早已为此感到内疚和忏悔,并愿意在实践当中通过做善事来弥补过失。但当他们把种族主义归咎于少数人的时候,那种制度性的白人霸权便得到忽略和开脱,也就得以延续下去。而且在白人性研究者眼中,愧疚、自责、忏悔和做善事,都不过是白人借以否认自己是种族主义同谋的心理防御机制,他们只是想在道德上为自己寻找舒适安全的避难所。所以阿普勒鲍姆提醒人们:"白人必须警惕自己想做好人的愿望,这样才能在挑战不公正的种族制度的过程中和有色人种结成同盟。"①在白人性研究者看来,比日常生活中的这些好白人更隐蔽的种族主义同谋者就是躲在白人性研究者内部、自诩为坚定的反种族主义者的白人知识分子。他们通过手中的思想武器,向种族主义的理论基础发起猛烈批判,以证明种族主义的荒谬,实际上却同时也为自己赢得一个最无懈可击的道德制高点。对一个学院派白人反种族主义者来说,他的批判声音越高,自己看上去就越清白,但同时也丝毫不影响他居住在半隔离状态的白人中产社区,舒服地享受现有的一切便利,即"在反对白人霸权的同时又能获得白人性带来的物质利益"②。对于这种理论上的反种族主义者,乔治·扬希(George Yancy)曾进行过辛辣嘲讽,认为他们批判种族主义不过是"为事业考虑"而摆出的"学术姿态"③。谈论反种族主义话语反倒悖论性地变成他们与种族主义同谋的"策略工具"④。

自20世纪90年代初发轫以来,白人性研究在不到30年的时间里产生广泛影响,取得不俗成就,其快速发展势头仍未有减弱之势。回望20世纪后半期的理论热潮,还没有哪个流派或学说的热度能够持续如此之久。于是就有人提出,白人性研究不过是理论终结之后,趁着"尸骨未寒"所迸发出的最后全部力量。当主体、上帝、性别、作者、文本、阶级等都被解构完成之后,白人主体便成为最后剩下的需被攻克的堡垒。因此,它终将"不过是一阵快速驶过的学术潮流",是被后结构主义思潮遗弃的学术孤儿们为了获得"一种新的自命不凡的合法性"⑤而兴起的纯粹学术活动。

这种看法当然失之偏颇。它忘记了杜波依斯早在1903年就为后人发出的预言:"20世纪的问题将是种族分界线(color line)问题。"⑥如今历史的脚步早已进入21世纪,但无论在美国还是欧洲,种族问题非但没有解决,反倒有愈演愈烈之势。多元文化主义和自由主义政策在西方频频遭遇危机,保守主义、民族主义右翼势力重新抬头,所有这些都说明,种族问题仍是人类在未来很长时间内面临的主要问题之一。因此,虽不排除有少数人可能是为了学术投机,但更多的人却是为了回应时代关切,才从事白人性研究工作。通过揭示白人性的建构性、白人霸权的运作机制、无知作为种族主义同谋的方式,白人性研究并不是要让白人为这一切感到内疚和忏悔,更不是为了颠倒种族结构,让黑人享有特权。它的最终目的和女权主义、性别研究、后殖民主义、马克思主义等批评理论一样,是揭示不公正的等级制度被制

---

① Applebaum, "Flipping the Script...and Still a Problem: Staying in the Anxiety of Being a Problem," p.16.
② George Yancy, "Introduction," *What White Looks Like: African American Philosophers on the Whiteness Question*. New York: Routledge, 2004, p.17.
③ George Yancy, *Look, a White: Philosophical Essays on Whiteness*. Philadelphia: Temple University Press, 2012, p.27.
④ Alison Bailey, "Strategic Ignorance," *Race and Epistemologies of Ignorance*. Eds. Shannon Sullivan and Nancy Tuana. New York: State University of New York Press, 2007, p.87.
⑤ Twine and Gallagher, "The Future of Whiteness: A Map of the 'Third Wave'," p.4.
⑥ W. E. B. Du Bois. *The Souls of Black Folk*. New York: Bantam Books, 1989, p.1.

造、维系和再生的秘密机制,揭露那些隐蔽的权力和话语,为实现真正的正义和平等创造条件。同时,白人性研究所提出的新概念、新理论也为文学和文化研究提供了极富启发的、可操作性强的新方法和新视角。在过去 30 年间,在文学研究领域运用白人性研究的批评实践已非常普遍,并取得显著成果。

当然,白人性研究在发展过程中也暴露出一些问题,或者说像它的后结构主义先驱一样陷入类似的困境。首先,随着它对白人性建构的批判越深入彻底,它给人的感觉反倒是越把白人性本质化了。如果说白人特权真的是"白人想去挑战但却仍在维护的东西"[1],他们充其量只能成为"反种族主义的白人种族主义者"[2]的话,那白人种族主义身份似乎就是一个永远攻不克的堡垒。这实际上也是对"白人性"的一种本质化和妖魔化解读,即白人性研究非但没有解构白人性、破坏白人霸权,反倒更加强化了它们,这与白人性研究的初衷相违背。其次,也就是扬希所指出的,它也和之前的后现代主义、后结构主义一样,有越来越被"知识化和学术化"[3]的危险,从而失去批判性锋芒,并被资本主义社会和学术体制所吸纳,最终沦为它所批判的对象的一部分。如何解决这两个问题,的确是白人性研究首先要考虑的事。但无论如何,白人性研究所做出的贡献不容抹杀。经过它的持续质疑和挑战,白人性再想安全地处于那个隐形的、不被注意的特权位置上已经不可能了。

第二节　经典文献选读

以下两篇选读文章都是白人性研究方面的重要综述性文献。第一篇节选自芭芭拉·阿普勒鲍姆 2016 年 6 月为《牛津研究百科全书》(*Oxford Research Encyclopedias*)所撰写的词条"批判性白人研究"。她在文中较为全面地介绍了批判性白人研究理论的几个核心议题。第二篇选文出自弗朗斯·特瓦恩和查尔斯·加拉格尔(Charles Gallagher)为《民族与种族研究》(*Ethnic and Racial Studies*)2008 年第 1 期"白人性与白人身份"(Whiteness and White Identities)专刊所合作撰写的导言《白人性研究的未来:图绘"第三次浪潮"》("The Future of Whiteness:A Map of the 'Third Wave'"),他们在文中详细梳理了白人性研究在过去 30 年所经历的 3 次浪潮,同时对未来发展趋势做出了展望。

一、《批判性白人研究》选读[4]

Whiteness, Racism, and White Supremacy

CWS is a growing body of scholarship whose aim is to reveal the invisible structures that produce and reproduce white supremacy and privilege. Some of the foundational research in CWS

---

[1] Applebaum, "Flipping the Script... and Still a Problem:Staying in the Anxiety of Being a Problem," p.6.
[2] Yancy, *Look*, *a White: Philosophical Essays on Whiteness*, p.175.
[3] Maria Davidson, "Thinking about Race, History, and Identity:An Interview with George Yancy," *The Western Journal of Black Studies* 1(2016), p.11.
[4] Applebaum, "Critical Whiteness Studies".

can be found in historical analyses that focused on the construction of whiteness and how some European-based groups "became white" (Italians, Irish, and Jews) in American society. This scholarship demonstrated the contingent nature of whiteness by studying the fluidity and malleability of who was considered white or not throughout different eras, regions, and along other social group intersections within the United States and globally.

An important objective of CWS is to make whiteness visible, in order to disrupt white dominated systems of power. White norms permeate white dominated society, yet these norms appear to be common and value-neutral to the social groups that benefit from them. These norms create the standards by which "difference" is constructed. Scholars in the field seek to make explicit the ways in which whiteness is a determinant of social power and to demonstrate how whiteness works through its invisibility. Whiteness often goes unnoticed for those who benefit from it, but, for those who don't, whiteness is often blatantly and painfully ubiquitous. Quoting from Hazel Carby, Richard Dyer argues that it is important to study whiteness, to "make visible what is rendered invisible when viewed as the normative state of existence" in order to dislodge whiteness from its position of dominance. It is impossible, then, to gain an understanding of systemic racism without understanding how whiteness works, and Dyer claims that whiteness, because it is presumed neutral and normal, can only be studied by making it "strange".

Whiteness is understood to be not just about a skin color, but intimately related to the construction of race. Whiteness is dependent for its meaning on the process of negation of what is outside its borders. For instance, whiteness means nothing without the existence of blackness. The center and periphery are mutually constituent. As Ruth Frankenberg puts it, "Whiteness comes to self-name...simply through a triumphant 'I am not that'." In this sense, CWS explores the practices and policies involved in the social construction of race.

While the definition of whiteness is difficult to pin down, there is widespread agreement that whiteness is a socially constructed category that is normalized within a system of privilege. Frankenberg defines whiteness as "a location of structural advantage, of race privilege. Second it is a 'standpoint', a place from which white people look at ourselves, at others, and at society. Third, 'whiteness' refers to a set of cultural practices that are usually unmarked and unnamed". Cheryl Harris suggests that whiteness is best understood as a form of property rights that is systemically protected by social institutions such as law. Thus whiteness involves a culturally, socially, politically, and institutionally produced and reproduced system of institutional processes and individual practices that benefit white people while simultaneously marginalizing others. The reference to property rights highlights that white people have an investment in whiteness, which can obscure how white people, even with the best of intentions, are complicit in sustaining a racially unjust system.

By focusing on making whiteness visible, however, CWS risks the danger of recentering whiteness. Sara Ahmed argues that "any project that aims to dismantle or challenge the categories that are made invisible through privilege is bound to participate in the object of its critique". This is not to imply that the project of critical whiteness studies should be suspended but rather that we must be vigilant about the ways in which projects of critique can be complicit with what they attempt to disrupt. This critical vigilance, I contend, is prominent in much of the CWS scholarship, as will become evident. Yet understanding the dangers of making whiteness visible does not lead to hopelessness. Instead, the significance of CWS is that the field has produced more nuanced and complex analyses of whiteness as a result of such vigilance. This type of critical self-reflection, I would argue, is one of the most important lessons to be learned from CWS, and I will frame this article with such vigilance in mind.

A key concept often referred to in CWS is "white supremacy". [...] Instead the term has been appropriated to refer to the continual pattern of widespread, everyday practices and policies that are made invisible through normalization and thus are often taken for granted as just what is.

Charles Mills points out that white supremacy is to race what patriarchy is to gender. White supremacy, as a form of oppression, is to be understood, following Iris Marion Young, as a structural concept that is reproduced by the everyday practices of a well-intentioned liberal society. The outcome of white supremacy has deleterious impact on the lives of the racially marginalized, while simultaneously affording benefits or privileges for white subjects as a collective. David Gillborn defines white supremacy as "a comprehensive condition whereby the interests and perceptions of white subjects are continually placed centre stage and assumed as 'normal'". White supremacy, therefore, presumes a conception of racism as a system of privilege that white people, often unwittingly, perpetuate in what seems to white people as common, unremarkable, and sometimes even seemingly "good" practices and in the implementation of what seems to be racially neutral policies.

[...]

The System of Oppression Behind Privilege

In his essay, "The Color of Supremacy: Beyond the Discourse of White Privilege", Zeus Leonardo acknowledges the importance of studying white privilege, but he insists that we must do so in ways that do not mask the system of oppression that creates and maintains privilege. White privilege must be studied not from a personal perspective, but from the perspective of white supremacy, because it is "the condition of white supremacy that makes white privilege possible".

Leonardo points out how white privilege pedagogy, with its emphasis on invisibility, often implies that privilege occurs without the participation of the subject of domination. It portrays an image in which domination occurs behind the backs of whites, instead of on the backs of people of color. Leonardo takes issue with the underlying passivity implied in the conceptualization of white privilege, and, pointing to McIntosh's essay, he shows how "white racist teachings, life lessons, and values are depicted as actions done or passed on to white subjects". Leonardo draws attention to the passivity assumed in white privilege pedagogy in his response to a seemingly innocent comment made by James Joseph Scheurich, a white educational researcher who has published many articles on whiteness and his own struggles to become aware of it. Scheurich equated white privilege to walking down the street and having money put in one's pocket without one's knowledge. Leonardo explains that this description of white privilege minimizes the active role that whites play in maintaining the system of racial oppression. "If money is being placed in white pockets," Leonardo wants to know, "who places it there?"

Leonardo concedes that the description of white privilege that Scheurich works with has been of some value, because it encapsulates unearned privilege and white people's obliviousness about it. He insists, however, that it is also dangerous because it "downplay(s) the active role of whites who take resources from people of color all over the world, appropriate their labor, and construct policies that deny minorities full participation in society". White people benefit not only from having money put in their pockets, Leonardo argues, they also take resources from people of color. Failing to pay attention these processes perpetuates white innocence. To be critical of white supremacy, as Leonardo contends, involves being less concerned about "the issue of unearned advantages, of the state of being dominant, and more around the direct processes that secure domination and the privileges associated with it".

It is not that privilege should not be addressed, but we must do so with the type of complexity that highlights how people who benefit from privilege are accountable for the reproduction of racial injustice. One of the ways that whites actively perpetuate systemic injustice is when they are privileged in ways that give them permission to be ignorant, oblivious, arrogant, and destructive. Such negative white privilege is often manifested in discursive practices that deny complicity and that profess white innocence. To ignore such privilege is to disregard the injustice that good white people are perpetrating now, in the present, and continually. White privilege pedagogy, which focuses more on positive white privilege, ironically works to protect white innocence rather than challenge white supremacy. In the next section, I will focus on the ways in which dominance is sustained through negative white privilege or the practices of "average, tolerant people, of lovers of diversity, and of believers in justice".

Negative White Privilege and Complicity

Privilege, as Sonia Kruks explains, is "a benefit that redounds to the members of one group through the oppression of those of another". We must begin to focus on the discursive strategies that secure systemic dominance, because dominance is not maintained without agents.

White students who read McIntosh's article often come away understanding privilege as a sort of material gain and even psychological advantage. The term "privilege", which has a positive connotation, invites this impression. But what white students often fail to comprehend, although McIntosh clearly mentions this in her essay, is how white privilege also involves protecting a type of ignorance, arrogance, and denial. To explicate how white people are conferred dominance, McIntosh introduces two different manifestations of white privilege, which she refers to as positive and negative privileges. Positive forms of privilege are benefits that all should share. For example, neighbors should be decent toward one another. Negative forms of privilege, however, are benefits that no one should have because they reinforce dominant/subordinate power differences. McIntosh offers the privilege to be arrogant, ignorant, and dismissive of others, as illustrations of negative privilege. About one type of negative white privilege she explains, "We were given the cultural permission not to hear voices of people of other races, or to tepid cultural tolerance for hearing or acting on such voices..."

Understanding negative privilege underscores that privilege is not only a matter of passively receiving benefits but also consists in ways of being in the world. Sara Ahmed discusses the phenomenology of whiteness, which she illustrates by pointing to the tendency of white people to always be the center often without realizing it. Adrienne Rich makes a similar observation when she describes what she calls "white solipsism" or the penchant of whites "to speak, imagine, and think as if whiteness described the world". Shannon Sullivan exemplifies white privilege as unconscious habits of whiteness when she highlights "white ontological expansiveness" or the tendency for white people "to act and think as if all spaces—whether geographical, psychical, linguistic, economic, spiritual, bodily, or otherwise—are or should be available to them to move in and out of as they wish". These are all systemically privileged ways of being in the world that sustain dominance and are alluded to by McIntosh when she introduces the notion of negative privileges that none should have. Negative white privilege functions to authorize white people to be ignorant, oblivious, and arrogant, often without realizing that that is what they are doing. In what follows, I summarize the scholarship on systemic white ignorance and white denials of complicity. Both are forms of negative, white privilege that work hand-in-hand to protect the system of white supremacy from contestation.

Systemic White Ignorance as Meta-Ignorance

Privilege...gives whites a way to not know that does not even fully recognize the extent to which they do not know that race matters or that their agency is closely connected with their status.

Cris Mayo's provocative but discerning quote highlights the connection between privilege and ignorance. White ignorance is systemic—there exists an epistemology of ignorance that functions to keep privilege invisible to those who benefit from it. Charles Mills draws on the concept of an epistemology of ignorance to investigate the question: "How are white people able to consistently do the wrong thing while thinking that they are doing the right thing?" White ignorance, Mills contends, is part of an epistemology of ignorance, "a particular pattern of localized and global cognitive dysfunctions (which are psychologically and socially functional), producing the ironic outcome that whites will, in general, be unable to understand the world they themselves have made". Similarly, Linda Alcoff cautions that we should not perceive white ignorance as merely an individual's bad epistemic practice, but rather as "a substantive epistemic practice itself".

In his oft-cited book, *The Racial Contract*, Mills argues that a Racial Contract underwrites the modern Social Contract. The Racial Contract is a covert agreement or set of meta-agreements between white people to create and maintain a subperson class of non-whites that solidifies the boundaries of white and personhood. The purpose of the Racial Contract is to "secur[e] the privileges and advantages of the full white citizens and maint[ain] the subordination of nonwhites". To achieve this purpose, there is a need to perpetuate ignorance and to misinterpret the world as it really is. *The Racial Contract* is an agreement to not know and an assurance that this will count as a true version of reality by those who benefit from the account. That such ignorance is socially sanctioned is of extreme importance. Not only is such a lack of knowledge an inverted epistemology that misinterprets the social world, but it is also officially sanctioned. White ignorance, thus, will feel like knowledge to those who benefit from the system because it is supported by the social system as knowledge.

Eve Sedgwick expands our understanding of systemic ignorance by pointing out that ignorance is not a passive lacking, as the term "ignorance" implies. Ignorance is actively maintained. Building on Sedgwick's insight and applying it to color ignorance (or an unwillingness to notice race), Cris Mayo contends that such ignoring is not a "lack of knowledge" but "a particular kind of knowledge" that does things, that promotes white innocence while conserving non-white marginality. We get a better sense of what Mayo means when Mills notes that such ignorance affects not only what one believes. It also influences the questions one believes are important to ask and the problems one believes are valuable to pursue. Mills points to the privilege of not having to ask certain questions when he notes that the Racial Contract involves

> ...simply a failure to ask certain questions, taking for granted as a status quo and baseline the existing color-coded configurations of wealth, poverty, property, and opportunities, the pretense that formal, juridical equality is sufficient to remedy inequities created on a foundation of several hundred years of racial privilege, and that foundation is a transgression of the terms of the social contract.

Therefore, white ignorance not only influences how one understands the social world but also is a type of knowledge that actively protects systemic racial injustice from challenge.

White ignorance itself not only is a type of white privilege (who has the privilege to be ignorant?) but also works to safeguard privilege. Mills underscores that it is white group interest that is a "central causal factor in generating and sustaining white ignorance". Such ignorance functions to mystify the consequences of such unjust systems, so that those who benefit from the system do not have to consider their complicity in perpetuating it. Members of the dominant group, for instance, have a vested interest in not knowing. Linda Alcoff emphasizes not only that white people have less interest in understanding social injustice than those who are victimized by such systems, but also that white people have a positive interest in remaining ignorant. One of the types of vested interests that such ignorance serves is the sustaining of one's moral self-image.

Inconclusion

Throughout this article, I hope it has become evident that CWS has developed under the belief that we must be continually vigilant about the ways that progressive projects, even the progressive project of CWS, can be complicit with what they attempt to disrupt. Even good intentions must be interrogated for their implications in the maintenance of white supremacy. This means that CWS will continue to evolve, and that is why this section is titled "inconclusion".

Vigilance has been advanced by many scholars who study systemic racial injustice. Mayo promotes "perpetual vigilance" as a "necessary way to live one's life". George Yancy advocates vigilance for the white anti-racist because whiteness "is deferred by the sheer complexity of the fact that one is never self-transparent, that one is ensconced within structural and material power racial hierarchies". Whiteness continuously "ensnares" and "ambushes" white people so that whiteness finds ways to hide "even as one attempts honest efforts to resist it". Being an anti-racist white, therefore, is a project that always requires another step and does not end in a white person's having "'arrived' in the form of an idyllic anti-racist". This should not lead to hopelessness, Yancy insists, but rather "one ought to exercise vigilance". Vigilance, according to Yancy, involves the "continuous effort on the part of whites to forge new ways of seeing, knowing, and being".

二、《白人性研究的未来：图绘"第三次浪潮"》选读①

The Future of Whiteness: A Map of the "Third Wave"

[...]

First wave whiteness

The critical treatment of whiteness owes its greatest intellectual debt to the work of W.E.B. Du Bois. Three observations that Du Bois made about race and whiteness provide the theoretical

---

① Twine and Gallagher, "The Future of whiteness: A Map of the 'Third Wave'," pp.4 – 24.

foundation for critical white studies. In *Black Reconstruction in America 1860 - 1880* (1936) Du Bois argued that white labourers in the United States came to embrace the racial identity of the dominant group, rather than adopt an identity framed around a class solidarity with recently freed slaves, because white workers received a "public and psychological wage" by joining or at least queuing themselves up for admission into the white race. Membership in the dominant group provided labourers on the margins of whiteness an extensive and heady mix of social and material privileges. On the material level white labourers could monopolize economic, social and state resources. At the social psychological level all white workers, but particularly those white workers on the economic or social margins, were provided with an inexhaustible "wage" in the form of social status, symbolic capital and deference from blacks that embracing white supremacy provided. By adopting the racist beliefs and practices of the dominant group, labourers from southern and eastern Europe were able to eventually shed the stigma of occupying a middling racial identity between whites and blacks. The material rewards of whiteness were substantial for immigrant labourers. Whiteness granted workers racially exclusive footing on the first rung of America's expanding industrial mobility ladder, provided an inherited racialized social status to future generations who would come to see themselves as unambiguously white and created the ability to accumulate and transfer intergenerational wealth.

In *The Philadelphia Negro* (1899) Du Bois provides a scathing critique of "color prejudice" that he chronicled in his groundbreaking study of Philadelphia's Seventh Ward. The ideological import, cultural meaning and how the relative invisibility of whiteness by whites maintains white supremacy was observed by Du Bois over one hundred years ago. The larger problem combating the issue of racial prejudice, Du Bois argued, was that "most white people are unconscious of any such powerful and vindictive feeling; they regard color prejudice as the easily explicable feeling that intimate social intercourse with a lower race is not only undesirable but impractical if our present standards of culture are to be maintained". Du Bois explains that for whites colour prejudice "is not to-day responsible for all or perhaps the greatest part of the N* gro[①] problems; or of the disabilities under which the race labors...they cannot see how such a feeling has much influence on the real situation or alters the social condition of the mass of N* groes". What follows in the next thirty-five pages in *The Philadelphia Negro* is Du Bois chronicling the ways white supremacy results in discrimination, institutional racism, prejudice and the material deprivation of blacks, a situation a majority of whites are "unconscious" of, or do not care to "see". This blind spot to racial inequality remains in large part unchanged. In the United States a majority of whites (71 percent) believe blacks have "more" or "about the same opportunities" as whites even though every quality of life indicator tells a story of continued and in many cases growing racial inequality.

---

① 原文为对有色人种的蔑称，下文蔑称处理方式相同。

White supremacy, in concert with early modern capitalism, cemented in place a two-tiered, mutually reinforcing system of material and psychological oppression that is painfully evident throughout the globe. Unlike the rather obvious patterns of discrimination and legally sanctioned state sponsored terror that characterized much of US history, contemporary discursive accounts of race and whiteness serve to make the material benefits of whiteness appear normal, natural and unremarkable. Third wave whiteness is an attempt to make the privileges associated with whiteness "conscious" by illustrating how white advantage are maintained through various ideological narratives. These accounts include how colour blindness as a political ideology is increasingly used to negate institutional racism or state reforms, the use of cultural deficit arguments to explain away racial inequality and demonize racial minorities and how appeals to nationalism are employed to mask the extent to which racism motivates reactionary politics. These accounts of inequality also serve to deflect attention away from the critiques of white racial dominance and towards other ostensibly non-racial social concerns like immigration, class inequality, post 9/11 geo-politics and cultural nationalism.

Du Bois details, and critical white studies expounds upon, how whiteness operates as the normative cultural center that is for many whites an invisible identity. Du Bois understood that whiteness is not monolithic nor is it a uniform category of social identification. As Du Bois phrased it in *The Souls of Black Folk* whites in the South were not of a "solid" or uniform opinion concerning racial matters. He explains that "To-day even the attitude of the Southern whites towards blacks is not, as so many assume, in all cases the same". While acknowledging that racial prejudice, institutional racism and white supremacy are core features of US society, Du Bois nonetheless discerned that there was no single white experience concerning race that all whites universally shared. Du Bois's framing of whiteness as a host of competing, situational, mutating and at time warring ethnic identities is a point of inquiry of third wave whiteness.

Finally, Du Bois's observation that "the problem of the twentieth century is the color line" has been used as prophetic judgement of the struggles the United States would be forced to confront. However the rest of this oft-quoted line demonstrates Du Bois's keen understanding that white supremacy's hegemony was global in scope. The entire line in the opening second chapter of *Souls* reads "The problem of the twentieth century in the problem of the color-line—the relation of the darker to the lighter races of men in Asia and Africa, in America and in the islands of the sea".

Whiteness as a form of privilege and power "travels" from western countries to colonies throughout the world. As whiteness travels the globe it reinvents itself locally upon arrival. As Raka Shome points out "whether it was the physical travel of white bodies colonizing 'other worlds' or today's neocolonial travel of white cultural products—media, music, television products, academic texts, and Anglo fashions" white hegemony continues to shape the colour line. [...] Bleaching salons and "Fair and Lovely" lightening soaps are part of the 250 million dollar "fairness-cosmetics market" in India. After controlling for all the relevant variables (English proficiency, education, work experience) researchers in the United States found that immigrants with lighter skin earned up to 15 percent more compared to immigrants with darker skin. Not only does whiteness travel the globe but it also reinvents within locally upon arrival.

Second wave whiteness: black theorists, feminist theorists and critical legal theorists

Second wave whiteness includes a host of critical race scholars, many of them US blacks who continued on in the DuBoisian tradition of challenging and making white supremacy and institutional racism visible. The seminal works of E. Franklin Frazier, St. Clair Drake, Horace Cayton, James Baldwin and Ralph Ellson (to name just a few) presented unflinching empirical accounts of racism and its root causes. These scholars were the Cassandras of their time; providing detailed, accurate accounts of racial inequality that would went unheeded, disregarded or ignored.

Throughout much of the twentieth-century mainstream, white social scientists did not focus on the institutions that created, reproduced and normalized white supremacy. The focus that guided whites in the academy primarily concerned itself with the pathology of racist individuals rather than the structural forces that produced racist social systems. The question that guided a majority of race research after the Second World War in the United States was framed by Gunnar Myrdal's *An American Dilemma: The Negro Problem and Modern Democracy* (1944). As Myrdal saw it, the dilemma the United States found itself in was the need to reconcile the deeply held belief of equal opportunity for all and profound racism that structured every facet of American society. It was Myrdal's contention that:

> even a poor and uneducated white person in some isolated and backward rural region in the Deep South, who is violently prejudiced against the N*gro and intent upon depriving him of civil rights and human independence, has also a whole compartment of in his valuation sphere housing the entire American Creed of liberty, equality, justice and fair opportunity for everybody.

The cognitive dissonance was defined as the tension guilt-wracked whites experienced trying to negotiate the ideal of equal opportunity and the Jim Crow racism in which they were embedded. America's racial dilemma was not the depths of which white supremacy organized every social, economic and cultural aspect of society; nor was it the material or symbolic rewards racism delivered to whites. The problem occurring to Myrdal was to be found in "what goes on in the minds of white Americans". As a matter of sociological research the material and psychological advantages normalized through white supremacy that Du Bois outlined were rejected in favour of an approach that focused on the individual afflictions of the "white mind", rather than the structures that reproduce racism and inequality from one generation to the next.

Toni Morrison, a Pulitzer Prize winning novelist and US black literary theorist, helped usher in scholarship that would shift attention away from psychologistic accounts of racial inequality to ones that examined the discursive practices that render whiteness invisible. In *Playing in the Dark* (1992), a critical interpretation of US fiction, Morrison reveals how whiteness operates as a cultural referent and normative identity through literacy tropes that frame all races but whiteness as marked categories. Through this act of racial negation immigrant populations could both come to understand their own "Americanness as an opposition to the resident black population" and frame American as a racial signifier that would come to "mean" only white.

Critical legal theory has also made significant contributions to second wave whiteness by linking how legal institutions define who is white and consequently which groups are entitled to the material and social advantages whiteness confers. Using Du Bois's notion that whiteness operates as a "wage" Cheryl Harris, a US black legal theorist, argues that being defined by the courts as white granted rights to groups who were then able to lay claim to the resources (land, jobs, contracts, schools) that only whites could enjoy. She argues that whiteness, like land or buildings, operates as a form of "property", one that needs to be policed, guarded and regulated. Ian Haney Lopez examines how the law came to define non-white and white status and the implications this definition had for citizenship. Being unfit for naturalization became synonymous with being non-white which also became shorthand for "degeneracy of intellect morals, self restraint" while being white signified "moral maturity self-assurance, personal independence and political sophistication". The state did of course maintain white privilege in these court cases, but Lopez argues the parameters of whiteness were altered through this process and the nation itself was permanently remade as racially categories were redefined. This nation building through racial exclusion for some and inclusion for others has been the focus of similar works done on Brazil and South Africa.

How racial minorities have been written out of history, the lack of attention to the way immigrants on the racial margins were whitened and the means by which culture and ideology work to constantly re-cloak whiteness as a normative identity have been a central focus of white studies' second wave. Historians such as David Roediger, Theodore Allen and Matthew Jacobson have retold the story of race and ethnic identity in the United States by examining how changes in American labour practices, the racial ambiguity of European immigrants and the tangible rewards groups received for aligning themselves with the dominant group all conspired to reframe race, rework whiteness and maintain white supremacy.

Third wave whiteness

The articles in this special issue provide a preliminary map of what we provisionally term the "third wave" of whiteness studies. This "wave" can be distinguished from earlier waves in several ways. First, third wave whiteness employs a range of innovative and renovative research methodologies including the use of internet sites, racial consciousness biographies, music and photo-elicitation interviews. The increasing use of what Twine terms "racial consciousness biographies" has enabled sociologists, particularly ethnographers, to carefully explore how whites produce, translate, and negotiate whiteness in their everyday private and public lives. This wave of research builds upon earlier work in critical race studies by scholars who have examined how people learn race and racism. One example of this type of innovative use of racial biographies is the work of Karyn McKinney who collected racial biographies of two hundred university students in two regions in the United States. In this same tradition, this special issue includes an example of this type of research by Philomena Essed and Sandra Trienekens. Drawing on two separate research studies, they strategically employ similar innovative research methodologies to explore the meaning and cultural translation of whiteness as a Dutch cultural expression of everyday racism. Essed and Trienekens draw on student essays and analyses of newspaper discussions of multiculturalism to demonstrate how the meaning of whiteness is translated and managed in a European nation in which it is taboo to systemically collect date by race or ethnicity.

Second, the third wave of whiteness studies is characterized, by an interest in the cultural practices and discursive strategies employed by whites as they struggle to recuperate, reconstitute and restore white identities and the supremacy of whiteness in post-apartheid, post-industrial, post-imperial, post-Civil Rights. Troy Duster uses the term "neo-apartheid" to describe these contexts. This reconstitution of white identities, recuperation of white privilege, and less often resistance to racism, has been a central focus of third wave whiteness studies. Some of this work owes a significant debt to feminist scholarship on race, intimacy and the gendered labour of carework that women in heterosexual families are required to provide. This research examines the quotidian production of white identities "on the ground" as people move across public, private, urban, rural spaces. In this special issue, Melissa Steyn and Donald Foster contribute an article that belongs to this genre of third wave whiteness studies. Drawing on discourses that they call "white talk" in two mainstream newspaper columns from the largest daily circulation in South Africa, Steyn and Foster analyse discursive moves that attempt to defend ongoing racial inequality and buttress white supremacy in post-apartheid South Africa.

Third, whiteness studies scholars, based in the United States, are also shifting their analytical lens away from European immigrants and their descendants towards an analysis of white identity formations among immigrant and post-migration communities whose national origins are in the Caribbean, Latin America, Mexico and other nations outside of Europe. Since 1965 the vast majority of immigrants to the United States are coming from Mexico, the Caribbean, Central and South America and only a minority from Europe. In the United States, the addition of the "Hispanic" category to the 1970 census and the subsequent classification of individuals with Spanish surnames as "Hispanic" or Latino has generated new identities and political constituencies at the federal and national level. This community has diverse origins and, rather than being a monolithic group, is fractured not only along lines of class, education and region but between those who self-identify as "white" and those who embrace a "brown", black or multiracial identity. Sociological analyses of the recruitment of ethnic minorities to "whiteness" and the strategic deployment of whiteness by groups currently at its margins are needed to better understand the production of whiteness and the achievement of "white" identities by members of ethnic minorities. The complicated meaning of whiteness and white identities to the Hispanic/Latino populations, has been undertheorized by whiteness studies scholars, particularly as it intersects with age, class, skin colour, tenure and region in the United States.

In "White Americans, the new minority?: Non-blacks and the ever-expanding boundaries of whiteness", Jonathan Warren and France Winddance Twine argued that the white category has expanded in the United States to include groups previously excluded and that it will continue to expand, with blacks continuing symbolically and politically to represent the most significant racially defining other at the national level. Thus, there exists a space for non-black immigrants and their children to position themselves as "white". The evidence that whiteness is continuing to expand in the United States, and that it continues to incorporate ethnics of multiracial, Asian, Mexicans and other Latinos of non-European heritage, is evident among some segments of the US born Asian American population. For Asian Americans whose parents were born in the United States, particularly where one parent is white, the assertion that Asians will remain or be viewed as "forever foreign" does not necessarily reflect the ways in which the white race has historically incorporated groups who have been on the racial margins. A 2000 National Health Interview Survey of multiracial offspring found that among those who self-identify as being both Asian and white, close to half of the respondents marked white as their "main race" in follow-up interviews. In interracial relationships where the father was white about two-thirds of multiracial Japanese and Chinese families defined their offspring as white. These families are more likely to live in white suburbs and tend to have attitudes on race relations, and more specifically negative attitudes concerning blacks, that are similar to whites. Light skinned, middle-class Latinos, many who self-define as white already, are marrying non-Hispanic whites. It is likely the children of these unions will self-identify and be viewed as members of the white race. The "racial redistricting" or redrawing of the colour line that is taking place in the US points to an expansion of the white population over the next fifty years.

三、思考与讨论

1. 如何理解阿普勒鲍姆所说的"白人性的偶然性"(the contingent nature of whiteness)? 它与传统上的本质主义种族身份观有哪些区别?

2. 香农·沙利文所提出的"无知认识论"(epistemology of ignorance)对我们研究文学中的种族问题有哪些重要启示? 能否在美国经典文学作品中找出一些例子来说明这种悖谬的认识论现象?

3.第三次白人性研究浪潮与前两次浪潮有哪些区别？能否在当代美国文学作品中找出一些文化实践和话语策略的实例来说明白人在后民权运动时代是如何恢复和重建白人身份霸权的？

本章推荐阅读文献：

〔1〕Annlouise Keating. "Interrogating 'Whiteness,' (De) Constructing 'Race'," *College English* 8 (1995)，pp.901 - 918.

〔2〕Barbara Applebaum. "Critical Whiteness Studies," *Oxford Research Encyclopedias*. 〔2016 - 06 - 02〕.

〔3〕Charles Mills. *The Racial Contract*. Ithaca：Cornell University Press，1997.

〔4〕Cheryl Harris. "Whiteness as Property," *Harvard Law Review* 8 (1993)，pp.1707 - 1791.

〔5〕France Twine and Charles Gallagher. "The Future of Whiteness：A Map of the 'Third Wave'," *Ethnic and Racial Studies* 31.1 (2008)，pp.4 - 24.

〔6〕George Yancy. *Black Bodies，White Gazes: The Continuing Significance of Race*. New York：Rowman & Littlefield Publishers，Inc.，2008.

〔7〕George Yancy (ed.). *White Self-Criticality Beyond Anti-racism: How Does It Feel to Be a White Problem?* New York：Lexington Books，2015.

〔8〕George Yancy. *Look，a White: Philosophical Essays on Whiteness*. Philadelphia：Temple University Press，2012.

〔9〕Joe Feagin and Hernan Vera. *White Racism*. New York：Routledge，1995.

〔10〕John Warren. "Whiteness and Cultural Theory：Perspectives on Research and Education," *The Urban Review* 2 (1999)，pp.185 - 203.

〔11〕Peter Kolchin. "Whiteness Studies：The New History of Race in America," *The Journal of American History* 1 (2002)，pp.154 - 173.

〔12〕R. Delgado and J. Stefancic (eds.). *Critical White Studies: Looking Behind the Mirror*. Philadelphia：Temple University Press，1997.

〔13〕Robyn Wiegman. "Whiteness Studies and the Paradox of Particularity," *boundary 2* 3 (1999)，pp.115 - 150.

〔14〕Shannon Sullivan and Nancy Tuana (eds.). *Race and Epistemologies of Ignorance*. New York：State University of New York Press，2007.

〔15〕Shannon Sullivan. *Revealing Whiteness: The Unconscious Habits of Racial Privilege*. Bloomington：Indiana University Press，2006.

〔16〕Shelly Fishkin. "Interrogating 'Whiteness'，Complicating 'Blackness'：Remapping American Culture," *American Quarterly* 3 (1995)，pp.428 - 466.

〔17〕Teresa Guess. "The Social Construction of Whiteness：Racism by Intent，Racism by Consequence," *Critical Sociology* 4 (2006)，pp.649 - 673.

［18］Timothy Barnett. "Rereading 'Whiteness' in English Studies," *College English* 1（2000），pp.9 - 37.

［19］Toni Morrison. *Playing in the Dark: Whiteness and the Literary Imagination*. Cambridge：Harvard University Press，1992.

［20］Valerie Babb. *Whiteness Visible: The Meaning of Whiteness in American Literature and Culture*. New York：New York University Press，1998.

［21］W. E. B. Du Bois. *The Souls of Black Folk*. New York：Bantam Books，1989.

第七章
情动理论

第一节　概　　论

　　近 20 年来,"情动"理论(affect theory)日益成为中西方关注的焦点。无论在人文科学还是社会科学领域,都有很多学者开始探索情动理论,他们将之作为理解经验领域(包括身体的经验)的一条道路,或者超越当下基于修辞学和符号学主导范式的另一种范式。自 21 世纪以降,一些消极的形容词在学术研究领域频繁出现,比如"创伤""忧郁""无常""残酷"等等,这些词汇作为一种新的文化现象,体现出西方社会的一种普遍忧患意识。它延伸出一种疑惑甚至是质问,其矛头是新自由主义下的当代秩序。在这样的背景下,当代性正脱离现代性的话语范式,进入一种更加短暂、临时和模棱两可的状态。"情动"理论正是在这样一种质问式的写作背景下展开的。

　　"情动"(affect)作为一个哲学概念始于贝内迪克特·德·斯宾诺莎(Benedict de Spinoza),后由德勒兹和费利克斯·瓜塔里(Félix Guattari)将其发展成有关主体性生成的重要概念。在《伦理学》(*Ethics*)中,斯宾诺莎将"情动"视为主动或被动的身体感触,即身体之间的互动过程,这种互动会增进或减退身体活动的力量,亦对情感的变化产生作用。斯宾诺莎不是要测度事物的各种状态,也不是去给出好坏、高低、强弱的标准,他感兴趣的是由一种状态到另一状态的运动和转化,即由强到弱或反之的动态过程,并根据所能受到的影响与所能改变的幅度来定义身体是什么,这就是他所谓的"情动"。德勒兹在其关于斯宾诺莎的著作中,着重阐释了这个概念,并在《千高原:资本主义与精神分裂》(*A Thousand Plateaus: Capitalism and Schizophrenia*)中对其进行了创造性的解释。受德勒兹的启发,当今一大批理论家对此概念进行研究,并借助它解释一些文化现象,以至于当代的文化、艺术、思想、政治等领域出现了所谓的"情动转向"(affective turn),这成为很重要的理论现象,也是一种新的理论上的景观。

　　在欧美和澳洲的思想界,对于情动理论的研究大致可以分成哲学本体论意义上的情动理论和女性主义情动理论两条脉络。前者以斯宾诺莎、德勒兹和布赖恩·马苏米(Brian Massumi)为代表,后者以西尔万·汤姆金斯(Silvan Tomkins)、伊芙·科索夫斯基·塞奇威克(Eve Kosofsky Sedgwick)、劳伦·贝兰特(Lauren Berlant)等人为代表。这两条脉络以马苏米为节点,常常相互交织。其间还伴随着一个非常重要的枢纽人物,即斯图尔特·霍尔(Stuart Hall)曾经的学生和助手、美国文化研究界最具影响力的学者之一劳伦斯·格罗斯伯格(Lawrence Grossberg),他带动了学界对情动理论的研究。

一、斯宾诺莎的先驱意义：情动的起源和性质

"情动"研究是从荷兰哲学家斯宾诺莎开始的，他的思想是当代大多数学者研究这一领域的源头。"情动"是斯宾诺莎哲学体系里的一个概念，正如斯宾诺莎在他的《伦理学》第二部分和第三部分里讨论的那样，"情动"是一种身体与感觉、情绪相关联的状态。

那么，"情动"何以作为一个问题在斯宾诺莎那里被谈论？在《伦理学》中，斯宾诺莎提出他之所以进行情动研究是因为他认为，情动来自不适当的观念，是人生软弱无能和变化无常的原因，但它不应该被归结为人性的缺陷，因为这些情绪和自然万物一样，都出于自然的力量，因此情动也有其确切原因和性质，并且可以被理解且值得我们去重视。与笛卡尔试图通过提出一些伦理原则来改良这些缺陷不同，在斯宾诺莎看来，没有任何东西是源于自然和人的缺陷的，也没有一个人真正了解情动的性质、分类以及应对它的方法。因此，他决定借用笛卡尔的几何学研究法来考察情动的本性和力量，以及心灵如何克制情感，这是斯宾诺莎在《伦理学》中的任务。

在《伦理学》第三部分"论情动的起源和性质"中，斯宾诺莎首先区分了何为"整全原因"（adequate cause）和"部分原因"（partial cause）、何为"主动"和"被动"这两个概念。"心灵具有整全的观念时便主动，具有不整全的观念时就被动，心灵拥有越多不整全的观念，就越容易陷入激情（passion），反之，越能自主。"①在他看来，如果我们是事情的整全原因，即如果发生在我们身上和身边的事情都是因为我们自身的本性，只借助我们自己就能明晰地了解此物，那么我们可以称之为"主动"；如果我们是事情的非整全原因，即如果发生在我们身上或身边的事不全是因为我们自身的本性，我们只是部分的原因，我们则称之为"被动"。在第三部分，斯宾诺莎首次对情动进行了界定："我将情动理解为身体的应变，它会使身体活动的力量增强或减弱，同时也可将情动理解为这些应变的观念。"②在斯宾诺莎这里，情动首先是一种身体的状态，再是其观念。"观念"在这里强调的是，身体的行动经过心灵的确认，才成为"情动"，心灵的确认是前提之一，情动仅指人类的情动。也正是在此意义上，斯宾诺莎开始了对于人类的 48 种情动的考察和探讨。

斯宾诺莎对于情动的探讨，主要分为三种基本类型：快乐（joy）、痛苦（sorrow）和欲望（desire）。这是三种基本情动。其他情动，诸如惊异、轻蔑、爱、恨、偏好、厌恶、敬爱、嘲笑、希望、恐惧、信心、失望等，皆源于这三者。在斯宾诺莎看来，这三种基本的情动类型都是在人作为被动者的情境下产生的。其中，当心灵由较小完满的情感过渡到较大完满的情感时，就称之为"快乐"；而当心灵由较大完满的情感过渡到较小完满的情感时，则称之为"痛苦"。他把"欲望"肯定为人的本质，因为在他看来，人的本质是会因为任何应变而注定去做某些能促进自我保护的事，欲望就是意识到偏好本身的偏好，所以说，偏好，或者说"欲望"，就是人的本质。③ 而"快乐"和"痛苦"则是所有情动的基础，因为所有的情动都以快乐和痛苦为条件，所有的情动中都包含着快乐或不快乐。斯宾诺莎以几何学的方式将这些"情动"推衍而出，却不对它们的伦理价值做出评判。他对人类的三种基本情动和由此而来的诸种重要情动给予详细的列举和

---

① Benedict Spinoza，*Ethics*. Trans. W. H. White. Hertfords：Wordsworth Editions，2001，p.100.
② Ibid.，p.98.
③ Ibid.，p.146.

考察。在他看来,所有的情动都没有善恶之分,虽然我们在很多情况下会被外物所扰、徘徊动摇、担心自己的前途命运,但每个人的一切都由情动所掌控,不受任何情动影响的人则更容易处处摇摆。[①] 斯宾诺莎在这里论述的是主要的心灵矛盾,而非一切心灵矛盾。一切情动都是不完美的,但不能因此说它们都是坏的。

在此基础上,斯宾诺莎提出了他的"心物平行说",并以此来观照情动。迈克尔·哈德(Michael Hardt)曾说:"斯宾诺莎使得我们每次考量心灵思考的力量的时候,必须同时尝试着去辨识身体行动的力量是如何与心灵思考的力量对应的……这一点很重要,就其同时标示着心灵与身体的当下状态而言,情动横跨于这一关系之上……这就使得我们不断提出身心关系的问题。"[②]在斯宾诺莎看来,心灵思考的力量平行于身体行动的力量,然而心灵不能决定身体,身体也不能决定心灵,两者是两个封闭的系统,彼此不相往来,是平行的对应关系。所以,笛卡尔是把身与心作为两个分离的实体,而到了斯宾诺莎这里,他认为只有"神"这一个唯一且无限的实体,身和心不过是一个实体的不同表现模式,前者遵循物理性的因果律,后者遵循的是感觉、记忆和概念的法则。而两者之所以看似有关联和一致性,是因为两者都被一个实体所影响着。在《伦理学》里,斯宾诺莎将身和心的关系问题提了出来,但并没有完全解决这个问题。关于斯宾诺莎的身和心的关系问题的探讨一直持续到了当代学术界。他用一种科学理性的几何学方式对人类的诸种情动做了严密的考察和分析,洞悉它们的永恒状况和性质,这在思想史和学术史上都是第一次。

二、德勒兹的遗产:情动与观念的生成

"情动"(affect)和"情状"(affection)正是在德勒兹和费利克斯·瓜塔里合写的《千高原:资本主义与精神分裂》出版之后才变得引人注目的。在一篇名为《德勒兹在万塞讷的斯宾诺莎课程(1978—1981)记录——1978 年 1 月 24 日 情动与观念》("Gilles Deleuze on Spinoza's Concept of 'Affect' Cours Vincennes")的授课稿中,以及在他 1993 年出版的《批评与临床》(*Critique et Clinique*)中,德勒兹先后重点谈论了有关"情动"的概念评述。在"情动"的谱系上,德勒兹的贡献主要有三个。首先,他明确区分了"情动"和"情状",以"强度"(intensity)的概念取消了斯宾诺莎有关身体/心灵二分的观念;其次,他在斯宾诺莎专指人类的情动的基础上增加了非人的维度,使情动开始脱离"经过心灵确认"这一前提;最后,他还将"情动"的概念拉入他的"流变—生成"理论体系里,重点阐发了他有关"积极情动"的理解。

德勒兹首先批评了斯宾诺莎《伦理学》的诸多法文译本中的错误译法,即在斯宾诺莎用拉丁文写成的《伦理学》原著里,affectio 和 affectus 是有区别的,但译者没有对 affectio 和 affectus 做出区分,而是将其都翻译成了 affection。德勒兹明确指出,斯宾诺莎在他的原文中使用这两个不同的拉丁词是基于一定的理据的,在法文中,这两个拉丁词有明确的对应词,应该用 affection 译 affectio,用 affect 译 affectus,前者是"情状",后者是"情动"。为了探讨情动,德勒兹先从对于"何为一个观念"的界定说起,他认为,观念是一种表象某物的思想样式,究其表象某物而言,观念具有一种客观现实,比如三角形的观

---

① Spinoza, *Ethics*, p.103.
② Antonio Negri and Michael Hardt, "Value and Affect," *boundary 2* 26.2 (1999), pp.77 - 88.

念就是对三角形进行表象的思想样式。这是区分"观念"和"情动"的出发点。比如希望和爱属于不表象任何对象的思想样式，它们是"情动"，观念总是先于情动的，所以要先存在一个被希望者的观念、被爱者的观念。这是德勒兹对于观念和情动做出的区分，也是他对于情动的第一次界定。同时他指出，这种观念除具有一种客观现实以外，还拥有一种形式现实，这个形式现实就是"它自身就是某物"。在"所有观念都是某物"的基础上，他再现了斯宾诺莎关于"观念总是彼此相继的"的观点，即一个观念总是接续着另一个观念，与其说我们拥有观念，不如说观念在我们之中显示自身。这里出现了德勒兹增加的另一维度，斯宾诺莎强调的是观念本身的相互接续，而德勒兹强调的是这种相互接续本身对"我"的影响，也就是说，在"我"之中不断变化的某种机制，与观念自身的接续不同，这是一种"存在之力"（force of existing），或者"行动之力"（the power of acting）。这种"存在之力"会因为某物给予"我"的观念的"某种等级的现实性或完备性"[①]的不同而增强或减弱。在德勒兹看来，这样一种力的增强或减弱就是"情动"，"affectus 就是存在之力的连续变化，而此种变化为某人所拥有的观念所界定"[②]。后来在他的《批评与临床》里，德勒兹再次强调了"情状是一个物体（body）对我的身体所起的即刻影响，而且对我自己的绵延（duration）——快乐或痛苦，高兴或悲伤——也产生着作用。从一个状态转化到另一个状态的，是过渡，是生成，是上升，是降落，是力量（power）的连续不断的变化"[③]。因此，我们将之称为"情动"更为确切，而不是"情状"。这样，他就把"情动"与"情状"区分开了，前者指身体的存在之力的增强或减弱，或者经过内心确认了的身体的变化，后者指与实体相对、不能独立存在、要依靠另一个东西才能存在的状态。所谓情动，德勒兹更强调的是介于两种状态之间的差异性绵延，或者一种状态到另一种状态的持续变化，而非某一种单一的状态。由此，情动表现的不是被影响、被改变与被触动之后的身体，影响、改变、触动本身就成为身体，身体就是能影响与被影响的行动力与存在力，通过情动，身体成为差异的保证，"我"有一具差异于他人的身体，因为"我"有独特的动静快慢改变，而情动就是这个独特改变的表现。[④]

还有一点需要提及的是，在斯宾诺莎的概念里，"情状"是指"存在于他物之中，并借由他物而能被设想的事物"[⑤]；而在德勒兹的语境下，"情状"却增生了另一种不同的含义，它是"一个物体在承受另外一个物体作用时的状态，是一个效果"[⑥]。德勒兹不断地强调物体间的"相遇"、物体间的混合与相互作用，以及身体相遇之后产生的或愉快或不愉快的情动转变，从而为他重点引申的两个观点做准备：第一，"我们只能认识自身，我们只能经由外部物体/身体在我们自己身上所施加的情状来认识它们"[⑦]，因此"情状—观念"是一个不充分的观念，因为它们对相互作用或混合的原因一无所知，人又如何能脱离由我们的行动能力的增强或减弱所构成的被动情动呢？第二，既然每一个人都具有承受情动的力量，那么一个身体能做什么？"我不停地穿越在这些行动能力之流变中，通过我所拥有的情状—观念，我不停地追随着情动的连续流变之线，以至于在每个时刻，我的承受情动的力量都得以完全发挥出来"[⑧]。在这里，

---

① 在斯宾诺莎和德勒兹看来，观念不仅具有一种客观现实，同时还具有一种形式现实。观念现实是指一种表象性的思想样式，形式现实是指观念自身就是某物，比如三角形的客观现实是表象三角形的观念，而三角形观念自身就是某物。斯宾诺莎通常将观念的此种形式现实界定为观念自身所具有的某种等级（degree）的现实性或完备性。

② Gilles Deleuze, "Lecture Transcripts on Spinoza's Concept of Affect (1978—1981)," *Les Cours de Gilles Deleuze*, 2017, p.3.

③ Gilles Deleuze, *Essays Critical and Clinical*. Trans. Daniel W. Smith and Michael A. Greco. London: Verso, 1998, p.139.

④ 杨凯麟：《分裂分析德勒兹》，郑州：河南大学出版社，2017 年，第 138 页。

⑤ Spinoza, *Ethics*, p.3.

⑥ Deleuze, "Lecture Transcripts on Spinoza's Concept of Affect (1978—1981)," p.4.

⑦ Ibid., p.5.

⑧ Ibid., p.8.

一种承受情动的力量,成为一种强度或是一种强度的阈限。德勒兹以强度的方式来界定人的本质,即一个人在生活中承受情动能力的极限。

德勒兹将情动置于整个哲学史中来思考,也正是在此意义上,他开始了对于积极情动的思考。德勒兹明确区分了悲苦情动和令人愉悦的积极情动。在他看来,悲苦情动会削弱一个人的行动能力,同时意味着个体处于一种有害的关系中。在这种关系里,人认识不到"共同概念"(common notions),即个人无法对两个身体或两个灵魂所共享之物形成一个共同概念。而"一个小愉悦顿时使我们进入一个具体的观念世界,它肃清了悲苦情动或那些处于挣扎之中的事物,所有这些都是连续流变的一部分。但同时,这个愉悦还推动我们进一步超越连续流变,使我们至少拥有一种掌握共同概念的潜能"①。也就是说,令人愉悦的积极情动使得我们形成对于施加与被施加情动的身体所共有之物的概念,这种认识有可能失败,但当成功之时,我们会变得明智。情动在这里不仅是一种非常积极且极具潜能的存在,更被德勒兹视为"生命的劳作",并上升到人生的本体论的高度。他不止一次提道:"我们如果知道整个宇宙的所有关系处于何种秩序中,就能够界定整个宇宙承受情动的能力。"②

德勒兹对于情动的讨论是他从对斯宾诺莎伦理学的阐释中自然引申出来的。他之所以如此重视解释这个概念,是因为情动本身在斯宾诺莎的研究中就是一个既重要又困难的问题。之所以说它重要,是因为这关系到如何真正从斯宾诺莎的形而上学的研究——包括对实体一元论、实体的属性关系等的研究——过渡到本身理应也是斯宾诺莎本人旨归的实践哲学维度。而说它困难,是因为这一过渡并不那么容易,症结在于斯宾诺莎的《伦理学》第三部分讨论了作为身体情状的情动,并引向人的奴役与自由的主题,还开始集中使用"情动"概念,这引起了诸如"被动情动向主动情动如何过渡"以及内部细分和向外延伸的一系列问题。实际上,在这个环节,主动情动的获得与真观念的获得最终变成一体两面的问题。因而也可以说,斯宾诺莎所谓的"三种知识"之间如何过渡也相应地会在这个"情动"的问题结构上得到解释,甚至不是简单地解释澄清,而是一种"再问题化"。

三、《情动的自治》与情动理论的纽结点

在德勒兹之后,《千高原:资本主义与精神分裂》在英语学界的翻译者马苏米在他使用的术语笔记里,给予"情动"如下的定义:

> 情动(affect)/情状(affection),这些词都不能代表一个人的感觉(在德勒兹和瓜塔里那里是"情绪")。L'affect (affectus)是一种能够影响和受到影响的能力(ability),这是和身体的一种体验状态到另一种状态相对应的一种非个人的强度(prepersonal intensity),意味着身体的行动能力的增强或减少。L'affection (affectio)视每一个这样的状态是被影响的身体和发挥影响功能的身体之间的相遇,这里的身体在最广泛的意义上包括心灵或理想的身体。③

---

① Deleuze, "Lecture Transcripts on Spinoza's Concept of Affect (1978—1981)," p.10.
② Ibid., p.11.
③ Brian Massumi, "Foreword," *A Thousand Plateaus: Capitalism and Schizophrenia*. Gilles Deleuze and Félix Guattari. Trans. Brian Massumi. Minneapolis: University of Minnesota Press, 1987, p.xvi.

马苏米强调"情动"是一种能够产生影响、也能接受影响的能力，是一种中间状态，是一种"力"或"强度"。在著名的《情动的自治》（"The Autonomy of Affect"）一文以及其随后出版的著作《虚拟的寓言》（*Parables for the Virtual*）里，马苏米对"强度"做了进一步的延伸，他对于"情动"的理解是同另一个常用的术语相关联的，即"虚拟"（virtual）。具体而言，他认为情动是"实际中的虚拟与虚拟中的实际同时互相参与，一方从另一方中出现，又回到另一方中"①。在马苏米的理论体系里，"情动的自治"和对虚拟的理解息息相关，而虚拟与人类感知到的外部刺激相连。为了更好地引入虚拟的概念，马苏米描述了一个实验研究的例子，这个研究检测的是儿童对同一部影片的三个版本的不同感知和反应。例子讲的是德国电视台拍过一个短片故事作为实验，短片讲的是一个人在屋顶花园上堆了一个雪人，午后阳光里的雪人开始融化，他看着不忍心，把雪人移到了山间阴凉处然后与之告别的故事。有研究小组把这个片子制作成三个版本：无声版、增加了事实说明的事实版、在关键转折点上加了表达场景情绪的情绪版。然后这三个版本被拿去给一组九岁的孩子看，让他们回忆看到了什么，并根据"愉快"的程度打分。结果最愉快的版本是无声版，排名在中间的是情绪版，得分最低的是事实版。但当这些孩子被要求按照"高兴—悲伤"（happy-sad）和"快乐—不悦"（pleasant-unpleasant）来评价影片里的一个个单独场景的时候，更奇怪的事情发生了，悲伤（sad）的场景被认为最有快感（pleasant），即越悲伤，越快乐。马苏米评价道，这个实验强调了在人类感知外部刺激的过程中引发感情的东西的首要性。马苏米认为人类感知外部刺激至少发生在两个层面：形式/内容层面，效果/强度层面。形式/内容与象征秩序有关，因此人们能通过自己的体验去理解他们在这个层面上的感知。相反，在效果/强度这个层面，身体对外部刺激的感知是"一个非意识的且永不会成为意识的自主残留"②，它与任何可以变成叙事的可能性不再相关，马苏米把它解释为"叙事的非定域化"（narratively delocalized）。形式/内容和效果/强度之间的关系是被修改和修改者的关系，后者是隐形的；只有通过考察效果/强度在形式/内容层面上留下的痕迹，我们才能感受到它的存在。强度不产生意义，但是可以改变意义，它是一种悬置状态，存在中断和瓦解的潜能。它在我们试图锁定或描述它的时候消失，但是改变了我们生产出来的叙述。对于马苏米来说，这种对"强度"的强调，其实是对"情动"的强调。他以强度来界定情动，实际上是对情动和情绪（emotion）进行了根本性的区分。在他看来，情绪是个人的，属于自我的领域；而情动是在外部的或超出自我的，是在主体间发生的一个现象。这意味着一个人可以是情绪的，但一个东西不能是情绪的；同时一个东西可以被表达情动，如礼物等，但是一个人很难这样，除非她/他变成一种对象化的存在，最极端的形式便是视觉图像——被物质化。

将强度作为界定情动的本质界定，这是马苏米对于德勒兹理论的继承，同时他走得更远。如果说在斯宾诺莎那里，情动只发生在有心灵的主体之间、要经过心灵的确认，那么到了马苏米这里，他对之进行了一种"物质化"的强调和处理。对于情动的理解使得马苏米采取了一种相当激进的反人文主义的写作立场。他认为，为了准确地描述和阐释情动在社会中的结构，学者们应该彻底放弃以人类为中心的对社会现实的理解。这个社会现实是一个复杂的集合，而这个集合不仅包括人类，还包括非人类。就马苏米而言，这些可以产生情动、压制人类意识理性、塑造人类身体和心灵的多种可能性的东西，是社会进程的复杂性得以概念化的关键，这个复杂的社会进程包含着各种无法解释的以主体和意识形态为中心的理

---

① Brian Massumi，"The Autonomy of Affect，" *Cultural Critique* 31. 2 (1995)，p.96.
② Ibid.，p.85.

性主义理论。

马苏米从情动的定义、情动之于感觉和情绪的不同入手,用了大量的笔墨细致地剥开了生命体在萌芽状态时内含的诸多形式,讲述了情动发展的前阶段以及它的亚稳定性和非地方性关联。他认为情动像硬币的两面,它同时参与现实和虚拟,并在感知和认知中显示出来。正因为对情动在虚拟中的参与的强调,马苏米越来越关注情动在政治文化里的运用,比如他写诞生于未来的情动现实,分析美国对于诸多尚未发生且没有足够真实依据的事件的政治和军事行动,探讨关于威胁的政治本体论等等。与此同时,他对情动的研究日益走向一种对于情动政治的探讨。在马苏米看来,意识无法理解身体对于外界刺激的情动反应,这种"无能"在后现代时代变成了一种政治资源。

四、塞奇威克与女性主义情动批判

在马苏米的理论开始产生影响力的同时,塞奇威克和亚当·弗兰克(Adam Frank)在1995年发表了一篇影响深远的文章《控制论世界的羞耻:阅读西尔万·汤姆金斯》(Shame in the Cybernetic Fold: Reading Silvan Tomkins),从此在西方打开了持续至今的"情动转向"风潮。女性主义情动理论肇始于塞奇威克,从某种意义上来说,它深受德勒兹的影响。同时还要提及的是,在女性主义情动理论发展变化的过程中,有不少学者,如塞奇威克、劳伦·贝兰特等,已经开辟出了一条和德勒兹不同的对于情动研究的路径。

塞奇威克是女性主义情动理论的先驱和代表,她是在美国和朱迪思·巴特勒(Judith Butler)齐名的性和性别研究专家。她早期致力于性别研究和对酷儿理论的开拓性研究,其突破性的代表作为《男人之间》(Between Men)和《密柜认识论》(Epistemology of the Closet)。性和性别是塞奇威克早期研究的重点,1991年,她患上乳腺癌,以此为转折点,加之对于青少年同性恋者的关注,她以自身的经历和身体经验开始转向对"情动"领域的研究,并在同一个时期对心理学家汤姆金斯的思想进行挖掘,将对"羞耻"(shame)等情动的研究当作她后期的有关酷儿、身体等学术研究的重心。

塞奇威克认为"羞耻"有两个方面非常引人注目而且让人深受启发。一方面,她试图讲出羞耻和主客体的关系;另一方面,她试图阐述羞耻和身份认同的关系。在羞耻和主客体的关系方面,塞奇威克举了一个操演的例子,她用了一个和奥斯汀在婚礼上的"我愿意"类似的词——"(你)不要脸!"(Shame on you!)。但是和奥斯汀第一人称的叙述不同,塞奇威克一直强调要脱离以第一人称为中心的知识论框架并转向情动研究,因此她在这里的主语是第二人称。在这句话中,"我"是被隐藏的,是随着这句话的说出才被召唤出来的,即在赋予别人羞耻感的过程中隐藏了自己的主体能动性,是借着说明它的操演意图来获得自己的操演力的,也就是赋予别人羞耻。[1] 同时,因为缺少明确的动词,第一人称在这里便处于一种不确定的、延宕的状态,因为不知道这个主体究竟是一个单数还是复数,是过去、现在还是将来的状态,是能动性还是被动性,所以这些都可能被质疑,而不能被相信。在羞耻和身份认同的关系方面,塞奇威克谈及社会的医疗体系、教育体系以及公共体系对于青少年同性恋在精神和肉体上的压制,以及主流女同性恋和男同性恋对于青少年同性恋的忽视。"羞耻"是塞奇威克提出来的用来对应"酷儿"的历史内

---

① [美]塞奇威克:《情感与酷儿操演》,金宜蓁、涂懿美合译,载《性/别研究》1998年第3-4期(合刊),第100页。

涵的词汇，"羞耻"的污名和绝望的无力感相伴而生。假如"酷儿"是个在政治上有力的名词——实际上它就是——那绝不是因为它可以挣脱童年时的羞耻场景，而是因为它把那种羞耻的场景当作一种近乎取之不尽的能量转换来源。[①] 但塞奇威克认为，羞耻不仅在干扰着身份认同，同时还在建构着身份认同，它不是一个孤立的和内在的心理结构，而是与其他情动一样，是一种存在于不同人身上或不同文化当中的自由元素，它附着于身体的某个区域、某类感官系统或某种行为举止上，并持续不断地强化或改变几乎所有事情的意义。[②] 塞奇威克在这里富有启发性的做法是她的思考面从同性恋群体、酷儿群体扩展到整个因种族、性别、亚文化等受到权力压迫的群体，她举例说，那些想要解决或消除个人或群体羞耻的策略和口号都将失败，这些口号并不能让这个个体和群体心理上的羞耻感有所减少，因为这种羞耻感不是简单地被附加到身体本身，而是参与了身份的建构和认同。

从塞奇威克在生前出的最后一本书《触摸感受：情动、教学和操演》(*Touching Feeling：Affect，Pedagogy，Performativity*)中可以看出，汤姆金斯的情动理论对于她后期的转型产生了重要影响，使她开始远离早年迷恋的有关"衣橱"或"密柜"的认识论危机，转向研究身体体验、感情和亲密关系。在塞奇威克看来，情动理论提供了一个描述人类多样性体验的非常有用的词汇。她和汤姆金斯都赞同理解是一种扩展的可能性，而不是一种消灭可能性的方式。在《触摸感受：情动、教学和操演》中，塞奇威克首先要阐述清楚的问题便是：什么是"感受"(feeling)？它如何被触摸到？但是在某种意义上，这个"什么"是超出可以清晰表达的范畴的。可是有一件事情塞奇威克知道，尽管这个"什么"很难被清晰表达，但是它有"纹理"(texture)和"似乎存在于纹理和情感之间的一种亲密"[③]。从该书中的理论观点来看，这个时期塞奇威克对于情动理论的思考已经相当成熟。在弗洛伊德、拉康、福柯、德里达之后，在后结构主义和女权主义之后，她思考的是理论该如何发展的问题。她不仅重新探索了感觉、情绪、情动的重要性，同时认为汤姆金斯开辟了一条理论的科学主义道路，使得理论变得不那么铁板一块，并同时开启了女性主义"情动"理论研究。

第二节　经典文献选读

本章共有两篇选文。第一篇节选自德勒兹的一份课程讲稿《德勒兹在万塞讷的斯宾诺莎课程(1978—1981)记录——1978 年 1 月 24 日 情动与观念》。在文中他对斯宾诺莎的"情动"概念进行了全面而又深刻的阐释和解读。该文章不啻为学术史上的典范之作，亦是情动理论中基础且非常重要的文献之一。第二篇节选自塞奇威克《触摸感受：情动、教学和操演》一书中的《偏执性阅读和修复性阅读，或者，你太偏执了，你可能认为这篇文章是关于你的》("Paranoid Reading and Reparative Reading，or，You're So Paranoid，You Probably Think This Essay Is About You")，该文章是塞奇威克将精神分析学家梅兰妮·克莱因(Melanie Klein)和心理学家汤姆金斯的理论运用到情动与文学批评上的成功实践。

---

① ［美］塞奇威克：《情感与酷儿操演》，第 101 页。
② 杨洁：《那一个文学理论家"酷儿"：管窥伊芙·科索夫斯基·塞芝维克》，载《时代文学》(下半月)2010 年第 9 期，第 153 页。
③ Eve Kosofsky Sedgwick，*Touching Feeling：Affect，Pedagogy，Performativity*. Durham：Duke University Press，2003，p.17.

一、《德勒兹在万塞讷的斯宾诺莎课程(1978—1981)记录——1978 年 1 月 24 日情动与观念》选读[①]

Today we pause in our work on continuous variation to return temporarily, for one session, to the history of philosophy, on a very precise point. It's like a break, at the request of some of you. This very precise point concerns the following: what is an idea and what is an affect in Spinoza? Idea and affect in Spinoza. During March, at the request of some of you, we will also take a break to consider the problem of synthesis and the problem of time in Kant.

For me, this produces a curious effect of returning to history. I would almost like for you to take this bit of history of philosophy as a history tout court. After all, a philosopher is not only someone who invents notions, he also perhaps invents ways of perceiving. I will proceed largely by enumeration. I will begin chiefly with terminological remarks. I assume that the room is relatively mixed. I believe that, of all the philosophers of whom the history of philosophy speaks to us, Spinoza is in a quite exceptional situation: the way he touches those who enter into his books has no equivalent.

It matters little whether you've read him or not, for I'm telling a story. I begin with some terminological cautions. In Spinoza's principal book, which is called the Ethics and which is written in Latin, one finds two words: AFFECTIO and AFFECTUS. Some translators, quite strangely, translate both in the same way. This is a disaster. They translate both terms, affectio and affectus, by "affection". I call this a disaster because when a philosopher employs two words, it's because in principle he has reason to, especially when French easily gives us two words which correspond rigorously to affectio and affectus, that is "affection" for affectio and "affect" for affectus. Some translators translate affectio as "affection" and affectus as "feeling" [sentiment], which is better than translating both by the same word, but I don't see the necessity of having recourse to the word "feeling" since French offers the word "affect".

Thus when I use the word "affect" it refers to Spinoza's affectus, and when I say the word "affection", it refers to affectio.

First point: what is an idea? What must an idea be, in order for us to comprehend even Spinoza's simplest propositions? On this point Spinoza is not original, he is going to take the word "idea" in the sense in which everyone has always taken it. What is called an idea, in the sense in which everyone has always taken it in the history of philosophy, is a mode of thought which represents something. A representational mode of thought. For example, the idea of a triangle is the mode of thought which represents the triangle. Still from the terminological point of view, it's quite

---

[①] Gilles Deleuze, "Spinoza: The Velocities of Thought: Gilles Deleuze on Spinoza's Concept of "Affect" Cours Vincennes. Lecture 00, 24 January 1978: Affect and Idea". Trans. Timothy S. Murphy. https://deleuze.cla.purdue.edu/lecture/lecture-00/. [2023 – 12 – 25].

useful to know that since the Middle Ages this aspect of the idea has been termed its "objective reality". In texts from the 17th century and earlier, when you encounter the objective reality of the idea this always means the idea envisioned as representation of something. The idea, insofar as it represents something, is said to have an objective reality. It is the relation of the idea to the object that it represents.

Thus we start from a quite simple thing: the idea is a mode of thought defined by its representational character. This already gives us a first point of departure for distinguishing idea and affect (affectus) because we call affect any mode of thought which doesn't represent anything. So what does that mean? Take at random what anybody would call affect or feeling, a hope for example, a pain, a love, this is not representational. There is an idea of the loved thing, to be sure, there is an idea of something hoped for, but hope as such or love as such represents nothing, strictly nothing.

Every mode of thought insofar as it is non-representational will be termed affect. A volition, a will implies, in all rigor, that I will something, and what I will is an object of representation, what I will is given in an idea, but the fact of willing is not an idea, it is an affect because it is a non-representational mode of thought. That works, it's not complicated.

He thereby immediately infers a primacy of the idea over the affect, and this is common to the whole 17th century, so we have not yet entered into what is specific to Spinoza. There is a primacy of the idea over the affect for the very simple reason that in order to love it's necessary to have an idea, however confused it may be, however indeterminate it may be, of what is loved.

In order to will it's necessary to have an idea, however confused or indeterminate it may be, of what is willed. Even when one says "I don't know what I feel", there is a representation, confused though it may be, of the object. There is a confused idea. There is thus a primacy, which is chronological and logical at the same time, of the idea over the affect, which is to say a primacy of representational modes of thought over non-representational modes. It would be a completely disastrous reversal of meaning if the reader were to transform this logical primacy through reduction. That the affect presupposes the idea above all does not mean that it is reduced to the idea or to a combination of ideas. We must proceed from the following point, that idea and affect are two kinds of modes of thought which differ in nature, which are irreducible to one another but simply taken up in a relation such that affect presupposes an idea, however confused it may be. This is the first point.

Now a second, less superficial way of presenting the idea-affect relation. You will recall that we started from a very simple characteristic of the idea. The idea is a thought insofar as it is representational, a mode of thought insofar as it is representational, and in this sense we will speak of the objective reality of an idea. Yet an idea not only has an objective reality but, following the hallowed terminology, it also has a formal reality. What is the formal reality of the idea? Once we say that the objective reality is the reality of the idea insofar as it represents something, the formal reality of the idea, shall we say, is—but then in one blow it becomes much more complicated and much more interesting—the reality of the idea insofar as it is itself something.

The objective reality of the idea of the triangle is the idea of the triangle insofar as it represents the triangle as thing, but the idea of the triangle is itself something; moreover, insofar as it is something, I can form an idea of this thing, I can always form an idea of the idea. I would say therefore that not only is every idea something—to say that every idea is the idea of something is to say that every idea has an objective reality, it represents something—but I would also say that the idea has a formal reality since it is itself something insofar as it is an idea.

What does this mean, the formal reality of the idea? We will not be able to continue very much further at this level, we are going to have to put this aside. It's necessary just to add that this formal reality of the idea will be what Spinoza very often terms a certain degree of reality or of perfection that the idea has as such. As such, every idea has a certain degree of reality or perfection. Undoubtedly this degree of reality or perfection is connected to the object that it represents, but it is not to be confused with the object: that is, the formal reality of the idea, the thing the idea is or the degree of reality or perfection it possesses in itself, is its intrinsic character. The objective reality of the idea, that is the relation of the idea to the object it represents, is its extrinsic character; the extrinsic character and the intrinsic character may be fundamentally connected, but they are not the same thing. The idea of God and the idea of a frog have different objective realities, that is they do not represent the same thing, but at the same time they do not have the same intrinsic reality, they do not have the same formal reality, that is one of them—you sense this quite well—has a degree of reality infinitely greater than the other's. The idea of God has a formal reality, a degree of reality or intrinsic perfection infinitely greater than the idea of a frog, which is the idea of a finite thing.

If you understood that, you've understood almost everything. There is thus a formal reality of the idea, which is to say the idea is something in itself; this formal reality is its intrinsic character and is the degree of reality or perfection that it envelopes in itself.

Just now, when I defined the idea by its objective reality or its representational character, I opposed the idea immediately to the affect by saying that affect is precisely a mode of thought which has no representational character. Now I come to define the idea by the following: every idea is something, not only is it the idea of something but it is something, that is to say it has a degree of reality which is proper to it. Thus at this second level I must discover a fundamental difference between idea and affect. What happens concretely in life? Two things happen...And here, it's curious how Spinoza employs a geometrical method, you know that the Ethics is presented in the form of propositions, demonstrations, etc....and yet at the same time, the more mathematical it is, the more extraordinarily concrete.

Everything I am saying and all these commentaries on the idea and the affect refer to books two and three of the Ethics. In books two and three, he makes for us a kind of geometrical portrait of our life which, it seems to me, is very very convincing. This geometrical portrait consists largely in telling us that our ideas succeed each other constantly: one idea chases another, one idea replaces another idea for example, in an instant. A perception is a certain type of idea, we will see why shortly. Just now I had my head turned there, I saw that corner of the room, I turn...it's another idea; I walk down a street where I know people, I say "Hello Pierre" and then I turn and say "Hello Paul". Or else things change: I look at the sun, and the sun little by little disappears and I find myself in the dark of night; it is thus a series of successions, of coexistences of ideas, successions of ideas. But what also happens? Our everyday life is not made up solely of ideas which succeed each other. Spinoza employs the term "automaton": we are, he says, spiritual automata, that is to say it is less we who have the ideas than the ideas which are affirmed in us. What also happens, apart from this succession of ideas? There is something else, that is, something in me never ceases to vary. There is a regime of variation which is not the same thing as the succession of ideas themselves. "Variations" must serve us for what we want to do, the trouble is that he doesn't employ the word...What is this variation? I take up my example again: in the street I run into Pierre, for whom I feel hostility, I pass by and say hello to Pierre, or perhaps I am afraid of him, and then I suddenly see Paul who is very very charming, and I say hello to Paul reassuredly and contentedly. Well. What is it? In part, succession of two ideas, the idea of Pierre and the idea of Paul; but there is something else: a variation also operates in me—on this point, Spinoza's words are very precise and I cite them: (variation) of my force of existing, or another word he employs as a synonym: vis existendi, the force of existing, or potentia agendi, the power [puissance] of acting, and these variations are perpetual.

I would say that for Spinoza there is a continuous variation—and this is what it means to exist—of the force of existing or of the power of acting.

How is this linked to my stupid example, which comes, however, from Spinoza, "Hello Pierre, hello Paul"? When I see Pierre who displeases me, an idea, the idea of Pierre, is given to me; when I see Paul who pleases me, the idea of Paul is given to me. Each one of these ideas in relation to me has a certain degree of reality or perfection. I would say that the idea of Paul, in relation to me, has more intrinsic perfection than the idea of Pierre since the idea of Paul contents me and the idea of Pierre upsets me. When the idea of Paul succeeds the idea of Pierre, it is agreeable to say that my force of existing or my power of acting is increased or improved; when, on the contrary, the situation is reversed, when after having seen someone who made me joyful I then see someone who makes me sad, I say that my power of acting is inhibited or obstructed. At this level we don't even know anymore if we are still working within terminological conventions or if we are already moving into something much more concrete.

I would say that, to the extent that ideas succeed each other in us, each one having its own degree of perfection, its degree of reality or intrinsic perfection, the one who has these ideas, in this case me, never stops passing from one degree of perfection to another. In other words there is a continuous variation in the form of an increase-diminution-increase-diminution of the power of acting or the force of existing of someone according to the ideas which s/he has. Feel how beauty shines through this difficult exercise. This representation of existence already isn't bad, it really is existence in the street, it's necessary to imagine Spinoza strolling about, and he truly lives existence as this kind of continuous variation: to the extent that an idea replaces another, I never cease to pass from one degree of perfection to another, however miniscule the difference, and this kind of melodic line of continuous variation will define affect (affectus) in its correlation with ideas and at the same time in its difference in nature from ideas. We account for this difference in nature and this correlation. It's up to you to say whether it agrees with you or not. We have got an entirely more solid definition of affectus; affectus in Spinoza is variation (he is speaking through my mouth; he didn't say it this way because he died too young...), continuous variation of the force of existing, insofar as this variation is determined by the ideas one has.

Consequently, in a very important text at the end of book three, which bears the title "general definition of affectus", Spinoza tells us: above all do not believe that affectus as I conceive it depends upon a comparison of ideas. He means that the idea indeed has to be primary in relation to the affect, the idea and the affect are two things which differ in nature, the affect is not reducible to an intellectual comparison of ideas, affect is constituted by the lived transition or lived passage from one degree of perfection to another, insofar as this passage is determined by ideas; but in itself it does not consist in an idea, but rather constitutes affect.

When I pass from the idea of Pierre to the idea of Paul, I say that my power of acting is increased; when I pass from the idea of Paul to the idea of Pierre, I say that my power of acting is diminished. Which comes down to saying that when I see Pierre, I am affected with sadness; when I see Paul, I am affected with joy. And on this melodic line of continuous variation constituted by the affect, Spinoza will assign two poles: joy-sadness, which for him will be the fundamental passions. Sadness will be any passion whatsoever which involves a diminution of my power of acting, and joy will be any passion involving an increase in my power of acting. This conception will allow Spinoza to become aware, for example, of a quite fundamental moral and political problem which will be his way of posing the political problem to himself: how does it happen that people who have power [pouvoir], in whatever domain, need to affect us in a sad way? The sad passions as necessary. Inspiring sad passions is necessary for the exercise of power. And Spinoza says, in the Theological-Political Treatise, that this is a profound point of connection between the despot and the priest—they both need the sadness of their subjects. Here you understand well that he does not take sadness in a vague sense, he takes sadness in the rigorous sense he knew to give it: sadness is the affect insofar as it involves the diminution of my power of acting.

When I said, in my first attempt to differentiate idea and affect (that the idea is the mode of thought which represents nothing [?]), that the affect is the mode of thought which represents nothing, I said in technical terms that this is not only a simple nominal definition, nor, if you prefer, only an external or extrinsic one.

In the second attempt, when I say on the other hand that the idea is that which has in itself an intrinsic reality, and the affect is the continuous variation or passage from one degree of reality to another or from one degree of perfection to another, we are no longer in the domain of so-called nominal definitions, here we already acquire a real definition, that is a definition which, at the same time as it defines the thing, also shows the very possibility of this thing.

What is important is that you see how, according to Spinoza, we are fabricated as such spiritual automata. As such spiritual automata, within us there is the whole time of ideas which succeed one another, and in according with this succession of ideas, our power of acting or force of existing is increased or diminished in a continuous manner, on a continuous line, and this is what we call affectus, it's what we call existing.

Affectus is thus the continuous variation of someone's force of existing, insofar as this variation is determined by the ideas that s/he has. But once again, "determined" does not mean that the variation is reducible to the ideas that one has, since the idea that I have does not account for its consequence, that is the fact that it increases my power of acting or on the contrary diminishes it in relation to the idea that I had at the time, and it's not a question of comparison, it's a question of a kind of slide, a fall or rise in the power of acting.

No problem, no question.

二、《偏执性阅读和修复性阅读，或者，你太偏执了，你可能认为这篇文章是关于你的》选读①

How are we to understand paranoia in such a way as to situate it as one kind of epistemological practice among other, alternative ones? Besides Freud's, the most usable formulations for this purpose would seem to be those of Melanie Klein and (to the extent that paranoia represents an affective as well as cognitive mode) Silvan Tomkins. In Klein, I find particularly congenial her use of the concept of positions—the schizoid/paranoid position, the depressive position—as opposed to, for example, normatively ordered stages, stable structures, or diagnostic personality types. As Hinshelwood writes in his *Dictionary of Kleinian Thought*, "The term 'position' describes the characteristic posture that the ego takes up with respect to its objects...[Klein] wanted to convey,

---

① Eve Kosofsky Sedgwick, "Paranoid Reading and Reparative Reading, or, You're So Paranoid, You Probably Think This Essay Is About You," *Touching Feeling: Affect, Pedagogy, Performativity*. Ed. Eve Kosofsky Sedgwick. Durham: Duke University Press, 2003, pp.128 - 130.

with the idea of position, a much more flexible to-and-fro process between one and the other than is normally meant by regression to fixation points in the developmental phases". The flexible to-and-fro movement implicit in Kleinian positions will be useful for my discussion of paranoid and reparative critical practices, not as theoretical ideologies (and certainly not as stable personality types of critics), but as changing and heterogeneous relational stances.

The greatest interest of Klein's concept lies, it seems to me, in her seeing the paranoid position always in the oscillatory context of a very different possible one: the depressive position. For Klein's infant or adult, the paranoid position—understandably marked by hatred, envy, and anxiety—is a position of terrible alertness to the dangers posed by the hateful and envious part-objects that one defensively projects into, carves out of, and ingests from the world around one. By contrast, the depressive position is an anxiety-mitigating achievement that the infant or adult only sometimes, and often only briefly, succeeds in inhabiting: this is the position from which it is possible in turn to use one's own resources to assemble or "repair" the murderous part-objects into something like a whole—though, I would emphasize, not necessarily like any preexisting whole. Once assembled to one's own specifications, the more satisfying object is available both to be identified with and to offer one nourishment and comfort in turn. Among Klein's names for the reparative process is love.

Given the instability and mutual inscription built into the Kleinian notion of positions, I am also, in the present project, interested in doing justice to the powerful reparative practices that, I am convinced, infuse self-avowedly paranoid critical projects, as well as in the paranoid exigencies that are often necessary for nonparanoid knowing and utterance. For example, Patton's calm response to me about the origins of HIV drew on a lot of research, her own and other people's, much of which required being paranoiacally structured.

For convenience's sake, I borrow my critical examples as I proceed from two influential studies of the past decade, one roughly psychoanalytic and the other roughly New Historicist—but I do so for more than the sake of convenience, as both are books (Judith Butler's *Gender Trouble* and D. A. Miller's *The Novel and the Police*) whose centrality to the development of my own thought, and that of the critical movements that most interest me, are examples of their remarkable force and exemplarity. Each, as well, is interestingly located in a tacit or ostensibly marginal, but in hindsight originary and authorizing relation to different strains of queer theory. Finally, I draw a sense of permission from the fact that neither book is any longer very representative of the most recent work of either author, so that observations about the reading practices of either book may, I hope, escape being glued as if allegorically to the name of the author.

I would like to begin by setting outside the scope of this discussion any overlap between paranoia per se on the one hand, and on the other hand the states variously called dementia praecox (by Kraepelin), schizophrenia (by Bleuler), or, more generally, delusionality or psychosis. As

Laplanche and Pontalis note，the history of psychiatry has attempted various mappings of this overlap："Kraepelin differentiates clearly between paranoia on the one hand and the paranoid form of dementia praecox on the other；Bleuler treats paranoia as a sub-category of dementia praecox，or the group of schizophrenias；as for Freud，he is quite prepared to see certain so-called paranoid forms of dementia praecox brought under the head of paranoia…[For example，Schreber's] case of 'paranoid dementia' is essentially a paranoia proper [and therefore not a form of schizophrenia] in Freud's eyes". In Klein's later writings，meanwhile，the occurrence of psychoticlike mental events is seen as universal in both children and adults，so that mechanisms such as paranoia have a clear ontological priority over diagnostic categories such as dementia. The reason I want to insist in advance on this move is，once again，to try to hypothetically disentangle the question of truth value from the question of performative effect.

I am saying that the main reasons for questioning paranoid practices are other than the possibility that their suspicions can be delusional or simply wrong. Concomitantly，some of the main reasons for practicing paranoid strategies may be other than the possibility that they offer unique access to true knowledge. They represent a way，among other ways，of seeking，finding，and organizing knowledge. Paranoia knows some things well and others poorly.

I'd like to undertake now something like a composite sketch of what I mean by paranoia in this connection—not as a tool of differential diagnosis，but as a tool for better seeing differentials of practice. My main headings are：

> Paranoia is anticipatory.
> Paranoia is reflexive and mimetic.
> Paranoia is a strong theory.
> Paranoia is a theory of negative affects.
> Paranoia places its faith in exposure.

三、思考与讨论

1. 斯宾诺莎为什么要提出"情动"这个概念？德勒兹对于斯宾诺莎的"情动理论"有怎样的继承和开拓？何为"情动转向"？

2. 怎样理解"情动"？它和"感受"(feeling)、"情绪"(emotion)有什么区别？怎样理解情动的本质？

3. 塞奇威克的"情动理论"和以往的性别理论有何区别？怎样理解"偏执性阅读"和"修复性阅读"？

本章推荐阅读文献

[1] Aaron D. Chandler. "Introduction to Focus：The Affective Turn，" *American Book Review*

29. 6（2008），pp.3 - 4.

［2］Alexander E. Chang. "Art and Negativity: Marxist Aesthetics after the Affective Turn," *Culture，Theory and Critique* 53. 3（2012），pp.235 - 247.

［3］Clara Fischer. "Feminist Philosophy, Pragmatism, and the 'Turn to Affect': A Genealogical Critique," *Hypatia* 10. 10（2016），pp.1 - 17.

［4］David Rogers. "Powerful Emotions," *American Book Review* 29. 6（2008），p.8.

［5］Debra B. Bergoffen and Gail Weiss. "Embodying the Ethical: Editor's Introduction," *Hypatia* 26. 3（2011），p.459.

［6］Elizabeth Duquette. "In Defense of the Affective Fallacy," *American Book Review* 29. 6（2008）: pp.7 - 8.

［7］Eve Kosofsky Sedgwick and Adam Frank. "Shame in the Cybernetic Fold: Reading Silvan Tomkins," *Touching Feeling: Affect，Pedagogy，Performativity*. Ed. Eve Kosofsky Sedgwick. Durham: Duke University Press，2003.

［8］Gilles Deleuze and Félix Guattari. *A Thousand Plateaus: Capitalism and Schizophrenia*. Trans. Brian Massumi. Minneapolis: University of Minnesota Press，1987.

［9］Linda M. G. Zerilli. "The Turn to Affect and the Problem of Judgment," *New Literary History* 46. 2（2015），pp.261 - 286.

［10］Marguerite La Caze and H. M. Lloyd. "Editor's Introduction: Philosophy and Affective turn," *Parrhesia* 13（2011），pp.1 - 13.

［11］Melissa Gregg and Gregory J. Seigworth（eds.）. *The Affect Theory Reader*. Durham: Duke University Press，2010.

［12］Paul Hoggett and Simon Thompson（eds.）. *Politics and the Emotions: The Affective Turn in Contemporary Political Studies*. New York: Continuum，2012.

［13］P. T. Clough（ed.）. *The Affective Turn: Theorizing the Social*. Durham: Duke University Press，2007

［14］R. C. Solomon. *The Passions: Emotions and the Meaning of Life*. Indianapolis: Hackett，1993.

［15］Ruth Leys. "Affect and Intention: A Reply to William E. Connolly," *Critical Inquiry* 37. 4（2011），pp.799 - 805.

［16］Ruth Leys. "The Turn to Affect: A Critique," *Critical Inquiry* 37. 3（2011），pp.434 - 472.

［17］Stephen Ahern（ed.）. *Affect Theory and Literary Critical Practice: A Feel for the Text*. Cham: Palgrave Macmillan，2019.

［18］William E. Connolly. *Neuropolitics: Thinking，Culture，Speed*. Minneapolis: University of Minnesota Press，2002.

［19］William Egginton. "Affective Disorder," *Diacritics* 40. 4（2012），pp.25 - 43.

第八章
数字人文研究

第一节　概　　论

毫无疑问，"大数据"已经成为当下人们谈论的焦点话题之一。虽然能够说清楚究竟什么是大数据的人并不多，但几乎所有人都能够感觉到，它正在深刻影响我们社会生活的方方面面，并将塑造我们未来的行为模式。对文学研究来说，它也带来了一个新的挑战。数字人文研究的代表人物之一马修·L. 乔克斯（Matthew L. Jockers）写道："对科学产生如此巨大影响的因素正在缓慢但确切无疑地彻底改变人文学科的研究方式。"①马修·K. 戈尔德（Matthew K. Gold）也在他主编的《数字人文纷争》（*Debates in the Digital Humanities*）中写道："数字人文工作的应用模式预示着人文学术性质的重大转变。"②随着数字人文热潮兴起，我们不禁要反思，大数据手段的运用对文学研究究竟意味着什么？文学问题能否通过数学运算的方式来解决？它给深陷困境的人文学科带来的到底是福音还是棺材上的另一颗钉子？

克里斯·安德森（Chris Anderson）于 2008 年 6 月在由他主编的在线杂志《连线》（*WIRED*）上发表的一篇富有挑衅意味的文章经常被人们提及。他在这篇题为《理论的终结：数字洪流让科学方法变得过时》（"The End of Theory：The Data Deluge Makes the Scientific Method Obsolete"）的文章中宣称："在这个世界上，大量的数据和应用数学取代了所有其他可能使用的工具：从语言学到社会学，再到关于人类行为的每一种理论。忘记分类法、本体论和心理学吧！谁知道人们为什么这么做？关键是他们做了，我们可以用前所未有的逼真程度来跟踪和测量它。只要有了足够的数据，这些数字就不言自明了。"③一般来说，无论在科学还是人文领域，理论常被视为一种高度精练的经验总结，能够对人们的行为进行有效的指导，对实践过程进行反思，并对可能的结果做出预测。但安德森认为大数据时代的数学工具将使得这一切显得落伍，鲍德里亚对消费社会的描述、布迪厄对阶级习性的分析，都远远赶不上谷歌和阿里云对人的行为数据的跟踪调查。维克托·迈耶-舍恩伯格（Viktor Mayer-Schönberger）和肯尼思·库克耶（Kenneth Cukier）也附和安德森的论点，认为基于大数据的统计学模型优于基于假设的

---

① Matthew L. Jockers, *Macroanalysis: Digital Methods and Literary History*. Chicago：University of Illinois Press, 2013, p.3.
② Matthew K. Gold, "Introduction：The Digital Humanities Moment," *Debates in the Digital Humanities*. Ed. Matthew K. Gold. Minneapolis：University of Minnesota Press, 2012, p.xi.
③ Chris Anderson, "The End of Theory：The Data Deluge Makes the Scientific Method Obsolete," *WIRED*. [2008 - 06 - 23].

传统科学模型,他们写道:"大数据只涉及'what',而不涉及'why'。我们并不总是需要知道现象的起因;相反,我们可以让数据自己说话。在大数据出现之前,我们的分析通常局限于测试我们在收集数据之前就被定义好的少量假设。当我们让数据说话时,我们可以构建我们从未想过的模型。"[1]因为理论无论多么精致或高深,总有很多假设、猜想和虚构的成分在里面,远不如数学计算更加精确客观。尤其是在云计算时代,我们现在拥有前所未有的收集和分析数据的能力,完全可以抛弃所有理论假设,用可靠的数学方法来解决一切问题。

众所周知,理论自 20 世纪 80 年代兴起以来,早已习惯了各种抵制,宣称要终结理论的各种声音也从未间断。但是这一次由大数据的支持者所制造的威胁似乎更加严峻。美国当代著名批评家杰弗里·R. 迪利奥(Jeffrey R. Di Leo)便认为,大数据在导致理论终结方面的作用应当尤其成为我们惧怕大数据的理由,他说:"尽管至少从 20 世纪 90 年代初以来,文学界和批评理论界一直在与这一世界末日故事的众多版本进行抗争,但最近由大数据推出的这一版本在这方面是一项全新的、更具雄心的努力。因此,理论在过去 25 年中所遭受的各种'死亡',与大数据一手制造的理论'死亡'相比,显得微不足道。"[2]我们需要思考的是,大数据的运用究竟对人文研究意味着什么?

一、什么是大数据?

英文中的"数据"(data)一词来源于拉丁语 dare,意为"给出、呈现"(to give)。这是一种比较朴素的现实主义观念,该观念认为事物之间的关系能够通过数字被直观呈现出来。在非洲乌干达地区,考古学家发现早在 18 000 年前的古人类就已经开始使用计数工具,这意味着人类很早就已学会通过数据来思考和把握世界。不过直到 17 世纪末,真正意义上的统计学才伴随工业革命的兴起在英国出现,数据计量也开始成为促进社会发展的有力工具。但毫无疑问,统计学意义上的数据在很长时间内都是十分有限的,通常都是来源于对样本的抽样调查。直到 20 世纪现代电子计算机出现并被大规模运用之后,人类收集和加工数据的能力才得以极大拓展,大数据的时代也逐渐开启。

迪利奥曾指出,虽然很少有人给出大数据的定义,但数据能否被可视化想象是一个很好的区分点。当我们收集和加工的数据规模大到难以被可视化想象时,就可称之为"大数据"了。他说:"大数据代表的是人类想象力的边界,而不是技术的前沿……当人类无法想象出对于存储数据量的图像,而只能用数学符号来表示时,这样的数据就成为大数据了。"[3]比如汉语中用来形容一个人学问高的成语——学富五车、汗牛充栋、才高八斗等——都是可以被具象化的描述,"五车""八斗""充栋"也就算不上"大数据",但如果说某人藏书 1TB,我们就很难做出具象化的想象了,因为这样的数据对应的是抽象的数学方程,而不是书架和文件柜。

需要指出的是,早期的大数据并不像今天这样被理解为有潜在价值的"矿藏",相反,它被视为"无法

---

[1] Viktor Mayer-Schönberger and Kenneth Cukier, *Big Data: A Revolution That Will Transform How We Live, Work and Think*. New York: Houghton Mifflin Harcourt Publishing Company, 2013, p.14.

[2] Jeffrey R. Di Leo, *Higher Education under Late Capitalism: Identity, Conduct, and the Neoliberal Condition*. New York: Palgrave MacMillan, 2017, p.78.

[3] Ibid., p.83.

管理的盈余"①,就像被开采处理后的尾矿渣一样,留着无用,弃之可惜。直到数据挖掘技术被广泛应用,大数据潜在的认知价值和商业价值才被人们充分认识到,貌似毫无价值的废物堆照样可以被大数据筛选出有价值的信息。特别是进入21世纪以后,随着互联网和云计算的飞速发展,大数据技术在很多应用领域大显神通,它的含义也在逐渐发生变化。就像20世纪80年代的theory被大写为Theory一样,英文中的big data也常被大写为Big Data,这个形容词"大"不再单单意味着体量庞大,更意味着一种超级能力,一种"新兴经济和文化秩序的护身符"②。在经济上,这个短语表示一种以数据为媒介的商业形式,以谷歌和支付宝对用户网上行为习惯的收集利用最为典型。在文化上,它代表一种新的知识生产形式甚至是文化意识形态。尼克·库尔德利(Nick Couldry)提醒人们注意"'大数据'这个词所做的意识形态工作"③,它不仅指计算方法和技术提供的庞大数据集,还指分析数据集以产生有用的见解或具有重大价值的商品和服务的效益,这就预先肯定了"大数据"处理结果的价值,并暗示人类获取知识的方式进入了一个全新阶段,大数据已经成为另一种知识秩序的源头。

应当承认,大数据方法让我们能够提出从未想到过的问题,看到从未被看到的模式。但这是否足以让人们像当年的阿基米德一样自信地宣称:只要有足够的数据,便可以撬动世界?安德森在他那篇颇有些哗众取宠的文章中表达的观点就是这样的。在他看来,以往的科学方法都建立在可测试的假设之上:科学家首先观察现象,然后在头脑中有一个假设,并构建理论模型,再通过实验证据对理论进行测试,继而找出事物和现象之间的因果联系,使理论得以确立,并使其进一步用于指导实践。但在当今大数据时代,这种方法已经太落伍了。大数据计算能够将海量因素纳入观测,不必假设事物现象之间的因果联系,只需要对它们之间的相关性进行考察就够了。谷歌技术是最典型的数据应用,它的创始理念是,我们不必关心为什么某些设计会比其他设计更受欢迎,只要数据分析证明有效就足够了。"它并没有假装对广告文化和惯例有任何了解——它只是假设更好的数据和更好的分析工具将使它成为赢家。"④这意味着我们有了一种全新的理解世界的方式:不需要任何理论的指引,只要有海量数据以及处理这些数据的统计工具,我们就能够得到知识。

二、大数据对人文研究意味着什么?

大数据在各个领域的普及应用也必然引发人文学科的广泛回应,兴奋者有之,激烈反对者也有之。最具争议的话题之一就是由安德森引发的讨论:大数据带来的新知识生产模式是否意味着理论的终结。富尔维奥·马佐基(Fulvio Mazzocchi)把安德森的观点做了进一步推演:"不需要更多的理论或假设,也不需要再讨论实验结果是反驳还是支持原来的假设。在这个新时代,真正有价值的是复杂的算法和统计工具,我们可以通过筛选大量的数据找出可以转化为知识的信息。"⑤在大数据的支持者看来,数

① Rafael Alvarado and Paul Humphreys, "Big Data, Thick Mediation, and Representational Opacity," *New Literary History* 48.4 (2017), p.730.
② Ibid., p.729.
③ Nick Couldry, "The Myth of Big Data," *The Datafied Society: Studying Culture through Data*. Eds. Mirko Tobias Schäfer and Karin van Es. Amsterdam: Amsterdam University Press, 2017, p.235.
④ Anderson, "The End of Theory: The Data Deluge Makes the Scientific Method Obsolete".
⑤ Fulvio Mazzocchi, "Could Big Data Be the End of Theory in Science? A Few Remarks on the Epistemology of Data-driven Science," *EMBO Reports* 16.10 (2015), p.1250.

据驱动的研究才是真正的知识生产模式。提出一个假设—用实验进行检验—分析结果—重新提出假设，这样一种已经沿用几个世纪的科学方法，在大数据时代将不再是最可靠的方法。数据驱动的研究将取代假设驱动的传统研究，前者只需分析大量的数据就可以产生新颖的知识模式和规则。任何天才的理论构想都不如直接从数据中诞生的知识可靠。社会学家和政治经济学家威廉·戴维斯（William Davies）悲观地写道："（如果大数据的梦想实现了）我们也许有一天将不再需要经济学、心理学、社会学、管理学等独立学科……数学家和物理学家会通过研究大数据集来发现一般行为规律。有关市场（经济学）、工作场所（管理学）、消费者选择（市场研究）以及组织与联想（社会学）的学问都将被大数据所取代，它将最终破解人类行为选择的奥秘。"[1]

如果说就连经济学、社会学和管理学这样具有巨大应用价值的学科都会被更有市场潜力的大数据所替代的话，那么像文学研究这样一般被视为"非功利、无目的"的自由探索就更无幸免可能了。不过也有不少人认为，大数据一方面为传统人文研究带来挑战——侧重细读、思辨和联想的传统方法在数学运算和数据实证面前被严重矮化——但另一方面也意味着新的发展机遇。自从现代文学研究作为一门学科被确立以来，它一直由于不够科学化而遭受批评，因为文学学者得出的结论很少像科学结论那样是可验证、可重复的，研究者无论怎样克制，仍会有无法抑制的个人偏见，他们得出的结论充其量也只能是"观点"（argument），而非客观知识。虽然瑞恰兹、弗莱和结构主义者都曾试图以科学的名义改造文学研究，但文学研究方法终究无法与真正意义上的科学方法相比。不过大数据技术让一些人看到了曙光。乔克斯倡导用基于信息技术的"宏观分析"来取代基于文本细读的"微观分析"，他说："不管你喜不喜欢，今天的文学史学者再也不能冒险做一个细读者了：现有数据的绝对数量使得传统细读作为一种详尽或确定的证据收集方法站不住脚了……文学研究者必须采用新的、主要是计算性的收集证据的方法。"[2]在他看来，基于数据统计的宏观分析方法才是文学研究的未来，它将为文学研究奠定真正的科学基础，我们在计算机的帮助下能够进行更有效的阅读实践，可以看到更多、更深层的东西，比如在大型文本语料库中查找单词使用频率，这将大大节省我们实际阅读整个作品的时间，从而超越我们作为单个读者所能阅读的东西。

虽然20世纪末理论热的兴起为文学研究注入了极大的活力，但对文化建构主义和意识形态批判的过分倾注导致相对主义盛行，好像一切都是文化建构之物，什么都不再具有本质主义意义上的确定性。在一些人看来，数字人文技术将为当代人文思想摆脱这种激进怀疑主义提供机会，因为计算机本身就是"一种完全不能容忍模棱两可和不确定性的装置"[3]，它必然能够将人文研究从相对主义的泥潭中解救出来，同时超越后现代话语中根深蒂固的唯我主义，朝着客观、科学的目的前进。让-加布里埃尔·加纳夏（Jean-Gabriel Ganascia）认为，通过使用大数据和计算机，我们可以把人文学科更新为一门理性地研究人类文化生产的学科，"这意味着数字人文学科正在将我们推向一个'后理论时代'，在这个时代，解释变得不如工具、档案或其他数字方法的制作重要"[4]。理论已经不能够继续激活文学研究，文化政治批判也不如扎实的知识生产更符合当下所需。一时之间，借助大数据技术来终结理论成为众多反理论者

① William Davies，*The Happiness Industry: How the Government and Big Business Sold Us Well-Being*. New York：Verso，2015，p.237.
② Jockers，*Macroanalysis: Digital Methods and Literary History*，p.9.
③ Stephen Ramsay，*Reading Machines: Toward an Algorithmic Criticism*. Chicago：University of Illinois Press，2011，p.ix.
④ Jean-Gabriel Ganascia，"The Logic of the Big Data Turn in Digital Literary Studies," *Front. Digit. Humanit* 2.7（2015）.

的高调呼声,随声附和者此起彼伏。赫尔曼·拉帕波特(Herman Rapaport)主张:"与其做批评家英雄,不如做擅长输入和检索数据的专家。"①伊恩·斯特德曼(Ian Steadman)也声称:"未来的学者们如果想把他们的研究提升到我们认为重要的水平,可能就必须学会编码……"②如果说在理论的时代,批评家更关心的是围绕"做什么"和"为什么"的问题进行意识形态批判的话,那么现在就应该更关注"如何做"的问题。大数据文学研究将帮助人们摆脱意识形态纷争,转向更客观、更科学的文学知识生产,它不仅会极大拓展研究者的研究效率和范围,也将对过去几十年来一直被坚持的一些根深蒂固的假设提出疑问。比如文学研究的对象究竟是什么?是少数被精挑细选出来的经典,还是全部已经出版过的作品?文学研究的目的是什么,是抱着怀疑的态度对其中隐含的意识形态进行批判,还是像经济学家处理统计学数据一样进行客观分析得出有利用价值的结论?批评家究竟有哪些社会职责?他们应该做人文价值的捍卫者和批判的监督者,还是在数字实验室里自顾忙碌的数据工作者?当大卫·布鲁克斯(David Brooks)宣称"数据是一个透明可靠的镜头,可以让我们过滤掉情绪主义和意识形态"③的时候,当人们普遍认为定量研究将比意识形态批判更有价值的时候,人文学者绝对不应该只是对新技术带来的机遇感到兴奋,更应该保持警惕。

三、对大数据方法的批判性思考

如上所述,大数据不仅为人文学科带来方法技术层面的转变,还有可能带来深层意识形态上的转型。虽然文学研究吸纳大数据科学的方法有一些明显好处,特别是能够使文学研究与时俱进,展现出一定的自我更新活力,但这些变化也可能会给这一学科的某些根本方面带来损害,特别是它过去多年来一直赖以存身的文本细读方法和政治批判功能。正因如此,马里奥·阿奎利纳(Mario Aquilina)才提醒人们:"在文学研究中需要对跨学科方法的含义保持批判意识。应该接受改变,但必须在一个批判性和反思性的框架内。"④渴望为文学研究提供一个数学方案,以避开研究者的主观偏见,实现科学的客观性,这种设想虽然能够暂时平息人们对文学研究可靠性的疑问,却也回避了它的根本责任,毕竟没有几个读者是为了寻求科学知识而去阅读文学的。像安德森那样急切地宣称大数据时代的来临将会彻底终结理论探索是一种很盲目的技术乐观主义。作为一种强大的知识生产新模式,大数据已成为一种新的"技术神话",需要批判性的拷问。

在中立的幌子下,大数据对客观性的标榜往往回避了数据在塑造研究结果方面的作用,似乎收集的数据只会以准确的方式来再现它,而不是积极地定义它的轮廓。人们常认为,大数据计算可以在没有先入为主想法的情况下进行,但这是不可能的,即使我们想这样做,也做不到,因为数据并非客观存在的,而是必须首先被视为数据。所以马佐基才认为:"更多的数据不一定产生更多的知识。数据本身是没有意义的。那种认为'只要有足够数据,数字就可以说明问题'的观点没什么意义。"⑤数据常被视为文本

---

① Herman Rapaport, "Big Data: Communicating Outside the Medium of Meaning," *Symploke* 24. 1-2 (2016), p.448.

② Ian Steadman, "Big Data and the Death of the Theorist," *WIRED*. [2013-01-25].

③ 转引自 Mario Aquilina, "The Work of the Literary Critic in the Age of Big Data," *Interdisciplinary Literary Studies* 19. 4 (2017), p.500.

④ Aquilina, "The Work of the Literary Critic in the Age of Big Data," p.500.

⑤ Mazzocchi, "Could Big Data Be the End of Theory in Science? A Few Remarks on the Epistemology of Data-driven Science," p.1253.

某一特定方面的直接反映,就好像是照片一样。但实际上文本中的数据并不是随机的,而是被"制造"出来的产物,理论假设在数字人文研究中起着至关重要的作用,因为它们事先决定了哪些数据会被寻找和收集。研究者的背景知识、兴趣和研究策略都会影响被检查和测量的内容,甚至实验设计也依赖于特定的理论、方法和技术。马佐基进一步抨击了大数据技术伪装的客观面貌:"大数据方法是一种倒退,它假定了一种'不带个人视角的'客观性模型。这样一种认为数据算法分析是真实和中立的保证的看法事实上反映了该领域在哲学上的不成熟。"①数据本身并不能为自己说话,而只能为它所包含的前提假设说话。假定数据是中立的,这本身就是一种非中立的立场。认为只要有了足够的数据,数字就能说明一切,这实际上是一个认识论陷阱,而事实恰恰相反,随着数据量的增加,理论在分析中扮演着越来越重要的角色。② 算法不仅仅是提取和加工信息的工具,它们会在深层次上影响和改变文学研究的性质和功能。因此我们绝不应毫无批判地接受大数据背后的算法文化,即使是非常有用的工具也有可能制造出我们并不想要的后果。

如果说过去数十年来由理论驱动的文学研究以意识形态批判为主要特征的话,那么随着 21 世纪以来新自由主义氛围的日渐浓厚和反理论运动的呼声再次高涨,不以批判为目的的实证主义研究找到了适宜的社会土壤。这也正是大数据或者说数字人文研究兴起的背景。批评理论是颠覆性的,即理论试图推翻或者颠覆现状,而包括数字人文研究在内的种种反理论的论调是为了维护现状,当前文学批评领域的后批评和反理论趋势不过是学者向高等教育界的新自由主义递交的一份更大投降书的表征。③

迪利奥也认为,以安德森为代表的大数据支持者想要用算法来终结理论的观点与倡导人文研究与市场功利主义结合的新自由主义论调之间"存在可怕共谋"④。理论常被反对者批判为太钟情于社会建构主义,理论对以种族、阶级和性别分析为批判焦点的多元文化主义的过分偏好导致文学经典被纷纷去神秘化为意识形态的伪装。相比之下,数据驱动的文学研究"缺乏对种族、阶级、性别和性问题的关注……更倾向于研究驱动的项目,缺乏政治承诺"⑤。美国数字人文研究的领军人物刘艾伦(Alan Liu)也对此做出反思,他指出:"数字人文学科在文化批判领域的作用明显缺失。因此,当数字人文主义者批判性地开发工具、数据和元数据时,他们很少将批判延伸到社会、经济、政治或文化的全部领域。"⑥作为人文学者,我们坚信人文研究最不可替代的价值就是以特殊视野实现对社会的批判性监督。无论是在文本中还是现实世界中,有关平等、权利、身份、正义、公平、共同体等重要问题的想象将会永远存在,而且永远不会仅仅靠大数据计算来得到答案,因此也永远需要持续的批判性探究。虽然计算机能够精确统计出作家对这些概念使用的频次和差异,但公平和正义比剥削和压迫更好的说法无须寻求大数据支持。所以正像约翰娜·德鲁克(Johanna Drucker)所反问的那样:"问题不在于数字人文是否需要理论,而在于如果没有它,数字学术还能否算是人文研究?"⑦

① Fulvio Mazzocchi, "On Big Data: How Should We Make Sense of Them?" *Mètode Science Studies Journal* 11 (2021), p.12.
② Alyssa Wise and David Shaffer, "Why Theory Matters More Than Ever in the Age of Big Data," *Journal of Learning Analytics* 2.2 (2015), p.5.
③ Robert T. Tally Jr., "Critique Unlimited," *What's Wrong with Antitheory?*. Ed. Jeffrey R. Di Leo. London: Bloomsbury Academic, 2020, p.116.
④ Di Leo, *Higher Education under Late Capitalism: Identity, Conduct, and the Neoliberal Condition*, p.88.
⑤ Gold, "Introduction: The Digital Humanities Moment," p.xii.
⑥ Alan Liu, "Where Is Cultural Criticism in the Digital Humanities?" *Debates in the Digital Humanities*. Ed. Matthew K. Gold. Minneapolis: University of Minnesota Press, 2012, p.491.
⑦ Johanna Drucker, "Humanistic Theory and Digital Scholarship," *Debates in the Digital Humanities*. Ed. Matthew K. Gold. Minneapolis: University of Minnesota Press, 2012, p.94.

大数据在文学研究中的使用只是一种手段,数字人文研究的中心应该是人文而非数字。借助计算机手段,人文学者能够以更大的规模、更快的速度做一些更精细的研究,比如统计单词出现频次、分析单个文本与复杂社会因素的关系等。数字技术是对人文学术或现有研究范式的补充,使用计算机进行更有效的文本分析不应破坏该领域的框架价值和理想。面对新技术条件的出现,文学研究既不能置之不理,也不能毫无质疑地迎接它们在人文领域中的实际应用,而应该在审慎接受的同时保持批判性反思。阿德琳·高(Adeline Koh)提醒我们:"人文学科如果持续关注计算和方法论,而没有对其社会影响进行深刻内省的反思,那就是对自我的贬低。"①

第二节　经典文献选读

下面两篇选文都出自数字人文研究领域的名篇。第一篇节选自马修·L.乔克斯的专著《宏观分析:数字方法与文学史》(*Macroanalysis: Digital Methods and Literary History*)。乔克斯和佛朗哥·莫雷蒂(Franco Moretti)是斯坦福大学文学实验室的同事。他在文中热情宣扬用"宏观分析"作为文学研究的基本方法,以替代以往的"文本细读",他认为数字技术手段可以有效排除文学研究者的主观偏见,能够使文学研究变得像科学实验一样客观。第二篇节选自戴夫·帕里(Dave Parry)的论文《数字人文研究还是数字人文主义》("The Digital Humanities or a Digital Humanism"),该文发表于马修·K.戈尔德主编的论文集《数字人文纷争》上。帕里在文中指出,数字技术能够提供全新的批判视角,让批评家完成很多以前无法完成的工作,继而弥补现有学术范式的不足,成为对传统人文研究的有益补充。

一、《宏观分析:数字方法与文学史》选读②

Literary studies should strive for a similar goal, even if we persist in a belief that literary interpretation is a matter of opinion. Frankly, some opinions are better than others: better informed, better derived, or just simply better for being more reasonable, more believable. Science has sought to derive conclusions based on evidence, and in the ideal, science is open to new methodologies. Moreover, to the extent possible, science attempts to be exhaustive in the gathering of the evidence and must therefore welcome new modes of exploration, discovery, and analysis. The same might be said of literary scholars, excepting, of course, that the methods employed for the evidence gathering, for the discovery, are rather different. Literary criticism relies heavily on associations as evidence. Even though the notions of evidence are different, it is reasonable to insist that some associations are better than others.

---

① Adeline Koh, "A Letter to the Humanities: DH Will Not Save You," *Disrupting the Digital Humanities*. Eds. Dorothy Kim and Jesse Stommel. Earth, Milky Way: Punctum Books, 2018, p.44.

② Jockers, *Macroanalysis: Digital Methods and Literary History*, pp.6-10.

The study of literature relies upon careful observation, the sustained, concentrated reading of text. This, our primary methodology, is "close reading". Science has a methodological advantage in the use of experimentation. Experimentation offers a method through which competing observations and conclusions may be tested and ruled out. With a few exceptions, there is no obvious corollary to scientific experimentation in literary studies. The conclusions we reach as literary scholars are rarely "testable" in the way that scientific conclusions are testable. And the conclusions we reach as literary scholars are rarely "repeatable" in the way that scientific experiments are repeatable. We are highly invested in interpretations, and it is very difficult to "rule out" an interpretation. That said, as a way of enriching a reader's experience of a given text, close reading is obviously fruitful; a scholar's interpretation of a text may help another reader to "see" or observe in the text elements that might have otherwise remained latent. Even a layman's interpretations may lead another reader to a more profound, more pleasurable understanding of a text. It would be wasteful and futile to debate the value of interpretation, but interpretation is fueled by observation, and as a method of evidence gathering, observation—both in the sciences and in the humanities—is flawed. Despite all their efforts to repress them, researchers will have irrepressible biases. Even scientists will "interpret" their evidence through a lens of subjectivity. Observation is flawed in the same way that generalization from the specific is flawed: the generalization may be good, it may even explain a total population, but the selection of the sample is always something less than perfect, and so the observed results are likewise imperfect. In the sciences, a great deal of time and energy goes into the proper construction of "representative samples", but even with good sampling techniques and careful statistical calculations, there remain problems: outliers, exceptions, and so on. Perfection in sampling is just not possible.

Today, however, the ubiquity of data, so-called big data, is changing the sampling game. Indeed, big data are fundamentally altering the way that much science and social science get done. The existence of huge data sets means that many areas of research are no longer dependent upon controlled, artificial experiments or upon observations derived from data sampling. Instead of conducting controlled experiments on samples and then extrapolating from the specific to the general or from the close to the distant, these massive data sets are allowing for investigations at a scale that reaches or approaches a point of being comprehensive. The once inaccessible "population" has become accessible and is fast replacing the random and representative sample.

In literary studies, we have the equivalent of this big data in the form of big libraries. These massive digital-text collections—from vendors such as ChadwyckHealey, from grassroots organizations such as Project Gutenberg, from nonprofit groups such as the Internet Archive and HathiTrust, and from the elephants in Mountain View, California, and Seattle, Washington—are changing how literary studies get done. Science has welcomed big data and scaled its methods accordingly. With a huge amount of digital-textual data, we must do the same. Close reading is not only impractical as a means of evidence gathering in the digital library, but big data render it totally inappropriate as a method of studying literary history. This is not to imply that scholars have been wholly unsuccessful in employing close reading to the study of literary history. A careful reader, such as Ian Watt, argues that elements leading to the rise of the novel could be detected and teased out of the writings of Defoe, Richardson, and Fielding. Watt's study is magnificent; his many observations are reasonable, and there is soundness about them. He appears correct on a number of points, but he has observed only a small space. What are we to do with the other three to five thousand works of fiction published in the eighteenth century? What of the works that Watt did not observe and account for with his methodology, and how are we to now account for the works not penned by Defoe, by Richardson, or by Fielding? Might other novelists tell a different story? Can we, in good conscience, even believe that Defoe, Richardson, and Fielding are representative writers? Watt's sampling was not random; it was quite the opposite. But perhaps we only need to believe that these three (male) authors are representative of the trend toward "realism" that flourished in the nineteenth century. Accepting this premise makes Watt's magnificent synthesis into no more than a self-fulfilling project, a project in which the books are stacked in advance. No matter what we think of the sample, we must question whether in fact realism really did flourish. Even before that, we really ought to define what it means "to flourish" in the first place. Flourishing certainly seems to be the sort of thing that could, and ought, to be measured. Watt had no such yardstick against which to make a measurement. He had only a few hundred texts that he had read. Today, things are different. The larger literary record can no longer be ignored: it is here, and much of it is now accessible.

At the time of my Thanksgiving dinner back in the 1990s, gathering literary evidence meant reading books, noting "things" (a phallic symbol here, a biblical reference there, a stylistic flourish, an allusion, and so on) and then interpreting: making sense and arguments out of those observations. Today, in the age of digital libraries and large-scale book-digitization projects, the nature of the "evidence" available to us has changed, radically. Which is not to say that we should no longer read books looking for, or noting, random "things", but rather to emphasize that massive digital corpora offer us unprecedented access to the literary record and invite, even demand, a new type of evidence gathering and meaning making. The literary scholar of the twenty-first century can no longer be content with anecdotal evidence, with random "things" gathered from a few, even "representative" texts. We must strive to understand these things we find interesting in the context of everything else, including a mass of possibly "uninteresting" texts.

"Strictly speaking," wrote Russian formalist Juri Tynjanov in 1927, "one cannot study literary phenomena outside of their interrelationships." Unfortunately for Tynjanov, the multitude of interrelationships far exceeded his ability to study them, especially with close and careful reading as his primary tools. Like it or not, today's literary-historical scholar can no longer risk being just a close reader: the sheer quantity of available data makes the traditional practice of close reading untenable as an exhaustive or definitive method of evidence gathering. Something important will inevitably be missed. The same argument, however, may be leveled against the macroscale; from thirty thousand feet, something important will inevitably be missed. The two scales of analysis, therefore, should and need to coexist. For this to happen, the literary researcher must embrace new, and largely computational, ways of gathering evidence. Just as we would not expect an economist to generate sound theories about the economy by studying a few consumers or a few businesses, literary scholars cannot be content to read literary history from a canon of a few authors or even several hundred texts. Today's student of literature must be adept at reading and gathering evidence from individual texts and equally adept at accessing and mining digital-text repositories. And mining here really is the key word in context. Literary scholars must learn to go beyond search. In search we go after a single nugget, carefully panning in the river of prose. At the risk of giving offense to the environmentalists, what is needed now is the literary equivalent of open-pit mining or hydraulicking. We are proficient at electronic search and comfortable searching digital collections for some piece of evidence to support an argument, but the sheer amount of data now available makes search ineffectual as a means of evidence gathering. Close reading, digital searching, will continue to reveal nuggets, while the deeper veins lie buried beneath the mass of gravel layered above. What are required are methods for aggregating and making sense out of both the nuggets and the tailings. Take the case of a scholar conducting research for a hypothetical paper about Melville's metaphysics. A query for whale in the Google Books library produces 33,338 hits— way too broad. Narrowing the search by entering whale and god results in a more manageable 3,715 hits, including such promising titles as American Literature in Context and Melville's Quarrel with God. Even if the scholar could further narrow the list to 1,000 books, this is still far too many to read in any practical way. Unless one knows what to look for—say, a quotation only partially remembered—searching for research purposes, as a means of evidence gathering, is not terribly practical. More interesting, more exciting, than panning for nuggets in digital archives is the ability to go beyond the pan and exploit the trommel of computation to process, condense, deform, and analyze the deeper strata from which these nuggets were born, to unearth, for the first time, what these corpora really contain. In practical terms, this means that we must evolve to embrace new approaches and new methodologies designed for accessing and leveraging the electronic texts that make up the twenty-first-century digital library.

This is a book about evidence gathering. It is a book about how new methods of analysis allow us to extract new forms of evidence from the digital library. Nevertheless, this is also a book about literature. What matter the methods, so long as the results of employing them lead us to a deeper knowledge of our subject? A methodology is important and useful if it opens new doorways of discovery, if it teaches us something new about literary history, about individual creativity, and about the seeming inevitability of influence.

二、《数字人文研究还是数字人文主义》选读[①]

As the earlier introductory word-frequency analysis suggests, what digital humanists mean by "digital humanities" is not that they use computers to write or read humanities-based texts; rather, a digital humanities scholar uses digital devices to perform critical and theoretical observations that are not possible with traditional pencil or typewriter aided analysis. That is, computers and by extension the digital enable a new critical lens for understanding traditional humanistic subjects of inquiry, a lens not available prior to the invention of computing technologies. At this point we do not even have to distinguish between the people who make tools for this type of analysis and those who use these tools for analysis. The defining feature is the relation of a digital tool to the scholarship being performed.

In the same way that the Birmingham School or Yale deconstruction opened up new ways of critiquing texts not possible prior to their inception, computers inaugurate a school of critique, a new series of tools through which we can analyze texts. This is to say nothing of the relative significance of any of these movements but rather to point out that all of them see themselves as movements, as ways of critiquing and analyzing texts that illustrate or reveal textual meaning in a way previously unavailable prior to the invention of their particular methodologies. Simply using a computer does not make one a digital humanities scholar—typing your manuscript on a word processor does not let you in the club; your work needs to share an affinity with a certain method of approach to humanities scholarship. In this regard, the computer is a necessary, but not sufficient, factor in the digital humanities. One could certainly imagine the digital being incorporated in other ways, but certainly it is a primary enabling factor for the rise of digital humanities.

Perhaps the best way to explain this view of digital humanities is, as Alex Reid suggests, through a Venn diagram in which the humanities is one circle, the digital another, and their overlap constitutes the field of digital humanities. In many respects, this works to describe any one of a number of methodological approaches to the humanities. A Venn diagram with the feminism school as one circle, humanities another, and their overlap constitutes a humanities scholar who practices feminist humanism—or similarly Marxism as one circle, humanities as another, constitutes Marxist humanities scholarship. This is often how scholars describe their endeavors: "I work at the intersection of computing, feminism, and eighteenth-century writing."

On the whole, this version of the digital humanities treats the digital as an adjective, a word that modifies the unchanged notion of the humanities, leaving the core of what happens unaltered,

---

[①] Dave Parry, "The Digital Humanities or a Digital Humanism," *Debates in the Digital Humanities*. Ed. Matthew K. Gold. Minneapolis: University of Minnesota Press, 2012, pp.431 - 437.

instead updating the means by which it is done. It makes humanities relevant in the age of computing and demonstrates that humanists, too, can use computers to do better, more elaborate projects; deal with large data sets; count word occurrences; and produce interesting textual visualizations. In this sense, the rhetorical shift from humanities computing—humanities as the adjective that modifies computing, humanities as a way of computing—to digital humanities, the digital as a way of doing humanities, seems rather predictable. It is both more descriptive of actual practice and less threatening to traditional humanistic scholars. Using computers to engage in more efficient textual analysis does little to disrupt the framing values and ideals of the field; rather, it merely allows them to be accomplished on a larger scale and at a faster pace.

In this respect, digital humanists talk about the digital as something added to the humanities, a supplement to the existing scholarly paradigm. The question in this type of scholarship is how the digital can be used to enhance, reframe, or illuminate scholarship that is already done or, in some cases, how the digital can do it more efficiently. While texts become data and word frequency counts substitute for sentence-level analysis, the goal remains markedly the same: a hermeneutics of the text meant to discern what it is a text (or a large corpora of texts) means.

This all suggests that there is a nondigital humanities—a humanities unaffected by the digital. This comes to be a rather problematic claim when we realize that the digital has so altered the academic culture that there are relatively few scholarly activities that are not already significantly altered by the digital. Almost all scholars at this point use computers rather than typewriters and use e-mail to converse with colleagues dispersed around the globe. Library card catalogs have been replaced by computer searches, and journal articles are often available only by electronic means. The practice of the humanities, of the academy as a whole (certainly within the American and European contexts), is thoroughly integrated with the digital and is, at this point, impossible to separate from it.

But for the most part, epistemological claims of large data sets notwithstanding, the digital has done little to alter the structure of the humanities. Digital humanities now means that one can build tools to read texts and produce data—for instance, to design a tool as part of a project to study eighteenth-century manuscripts—but the work of the humanities scholar remains largely unchanged by the existence of the computational device. The digital is a means to do what has always been done, a means to do it more efficiently and better, but still to do what has always been done. To be sure, the incorporation of the digital has led to the emergence of more varied scholarly writing practices, such as the ability to have multimodal scholarly writing that incorporates images and sound within a work. However, I still see this work along a continuum of academic writing, rather than work that marks any sort of significant rupture: using the new to do more of the same. I think the speed at which the digital humanities have been so easily incorporated into humanities programs—Kirschenbaum notes that the transition from term of convenience to whole scale movement was less than five years—should give us pause. It certainly suggests that the digital humanities are not all that transformative and certainly not a threat to the business of humanities departments or the university as a whole.

This is not to suggest that there are not some significant and interesting projects being done under the banner of DH both within and outside of academia but rather that a great deal of what is being done, what is seen as central and representative of digital humanities scholarship, does little to question the founding principles of academic knowledge, again, especially within the humanities. A digital humanism that replaces an ivory tower of bricks and mortar with one of supercomputers and server farms crunching large amounts of textual data and producing more and more textual analysis simply replaces one form of isolationism with another, reinscribing and reenforcing a very conservative form of humanities-based scholarship.

[...]

And so, there are at least two digital humanisms: one that sees the digital as a set of tools to be applied to humanistic inquiry (design, project, tools, data) and another that sees the digital as an object of study (social media, digital games, mobile computing). As Kathleen Fitzpatrick observes, digital humanities can be defined as "a nexus of fields within which scholars use computing technologies to investigate the kinds of questions that are traditional to the humanities or, as is more true of my own work, who ask traditional kinds of humanities-oriented questions about computing technologies".

This definition would be more inclusive than the one derived from the word-frequency approach used at the beginning of this essay. Indeed, it is in the group that asks humanities-oriented questions about computing technologies, where Kathleen places her own work, that I would also include mine. And so here we have two versions (under one definition), sometimes in conflict, over what constitutes the digital humanities. The first is the sense that the digital is a direct, almost practical use of computational means for research in the humanities: computer-enabled reading. The second invokes scholars who study media or, more popularly, "new media" (a somewhat problematic term as "new media" is neither new nor media).

Given what the data reveals about how people who identify as digital humanists talk about their work, given what is included in journals and conferences under the rubric of "digital humanities", the first definition appears to be carrying the day—that is, that the digital humanities I have been discussing for the majority of this essay, the one that sees the computational as a tool for doing humanities-based research, is becoming the privileged term, with the media studies version of the digital humanities serving a marginal role. As much as the "big tent" definition and narrative is iterated, the practice of what actually occurs points to a different reality.

Now, I could argue that this type of polarity or conflict, between a digital humanism of computational technologies as adjectival modification of humanities research trumping a digital humanities of humanities-based research into the digital，is an unfortunate academic development. Indeed，it seems to me that the dominant type of digital humanism privileges the old at the expense of the new，even while it brings computational technologies into humanities buildings. And，personally，I find the first form of digital humanism，well，frankly，rather boring. I am not really interested in scholarship that counts word occurrence in Jane Austen texts，or even word occurrence across all the texts written in the same year as Austen's. While Ngram viewers might illuminate certain interesting，up until now unnoticed statistical trends regarding word usage and ultimately，perhaps，cultural meaning，if they become the paradigmatic example of what it means to perform a humanities reading，I fear not only for the future relevance of the humanities but also for our ability to resist being easily replaced by Watson-style computers. (There is nothing particularly new here. Italo Calvino imagined just such a computational reading practice in *If on a Winter's Night a Traveler* far before the instance of any humanities-based computing.) If using computational technologies to perform text analysis becomes just the latest way to make humanities exciting and relevant，to argue for funding，to beg not to be eliminated from the university，then DH will soon also go the way of any number of other textual reading schools：historically important，yes，culturally transformative，no. My hope is that DH can be something more than text analysis done more quickly.

三、思考与讨论

1. 在马修·L.乔克斯看来,文学研究与科学研究有哪些差别? 当下的文学研究为何要引入"宏观分析"的方法? 与传统的文本细读相比,它能带来哪些好处?

2. 在戴夫·帕里看来,当前的数字人文研究有哪些不足? 除了一些新的文本分析工具和手段,数字人文还给我们的文学研究带来哪些更深层次的改变?

3. 能否从总体上思考一下数字人文研究出现的社会语境? 与此前在20世纪的文学批评史上频繁出现的科学主义思潮相比,数字人文研究体现出怎样的科学化冲动? 它能在多大程度上改变人文研究与科学研究相比的弱势地位?

本章推荐阅读文献：

［1］Chris Anderson. "The End of Theory：The Data Deluge Makes the Scientific Method Obsolete," *WIRED*.［2008－06－23］.

［2］David M. Berry. *Critical Theory and the Digital*. New York：Bloomsbury，2014.

［3］David M. Berry（ed.）. *Understanding Digital Humanities*. Basingstoke：Palgrave Macmillan，2012.

［4］Dorothy Kim and Jesse Stommel. *Disrupting the Digital Humanities*. Earth，Milky Way：

Punctum Books，2018.

　　［5］Franco Moretti. *Distant Reading*. London：Verso，2013.

　　［6］Franco Moretti. *Graphs，Maps，Trees: Abstract Models for Literary History*. London：Verso，2007.

　　［7］Jean-Gabriel Ganascia. "The Logic of the Big Data Turn in Digital Literary Studies," *Front. Digit. Humanit* 2.7 (2015).

　　［8］Mario Aquilina. "The Work of the Literary Critic in the Age of Big Data," *Interdisciplinary Literary Studies* 19.4 (2017)，pp.493 – 516.

　　［9］Matthew L. Jockers. *Macroanalysis: Digital Methods and Literary History*. Chicago：University of Illinois Press，2013.

　　［10］Matthew K. Gold（ed.）. *Debates in the Digital Humanities*. Minneapolis：University of Minnesota Press，2012.

　　［11］Rafael Alvarado and Paul Humphreys. "Big Data，Thick Mediation，and Representational Opacity," *New Literary History* 48.4 (2017)，pp.729 – 749.

　　［12］Stephen Ramsay. *Reading Machines: Toward an Algorithmic Criticism*. Chicago：University of Illinois Press，2011.

　　［13］Viktor Mayer-Schönberger and Kenneth Cukier. *Big Data: A Revolution That Will Transform How We Live，Work and Think*. New York：Houghton Mifflin Harcourt Publishing Company，2013.

第九章
反理论

第一节　概　　论

　　以"语言学转向"为标志的各种批评理论不仅为人们提供了文学研究的新思路,更带来了一场学术范式的革命。就像乔纳森·卡勒所说,"理论"使文学研究的本质发生了根本变化。[①] 正因如此,理论的兴起必然会招来抵制。20 世纪 80 年代虽然是公认的"理论热"时期,但也是理论初次遭遇猛烈抵抗的时代。1982 年夏,两位来自加州大学伯克利分校的青年学者史蒂文·纳普(Steven Knapp)和沃尔特·迈克尔斯(Walter Michaels)在权威期刊《批评探索》(*Critical Inquiry*)上合作发表《反对理论》("Against Theory")一文,他们以一种确切的口吻宣称各种新兴理论都是误导性的,整个理论大厦貌似巍峨堂皇,但其实建立在虚空的基础之上,因而不堪一击。理论假定自己是一种凌驾于实践之上的元话语,但其实这完全是一种妄想姿态,它既不能提供可靠的文本阐释方法,也不能带来任何实践效果。所以纳普和迈克尔斯二人响亮地喊出了"反对理论"的口号:"整个批评理论事业就是被误导的,因此应该被抛弃。"[②]

　　这篇战斗檄文般的文章一经发表便立即在美国理论界引发巨大反响。在不到一个月的时间内,《批评探索》相继收到 7 篇回应文章,其中不乏像 E. D. 赫什(E. D. Hirsch)这样的理论大家写的文章。这些文章于 1983 年 6 月被集中发表在该刊上,促成理论与反理论两大阵营的第一次论战高潮。此后两年多时间内又有多位重量级理论家加入这场论战,于是《批评探索》又在 1985 年 3 月发表了由斯坦利·费什(Stanley Fish)、理查德·罗蒂(Richard Rorty)、纳普、迈克尔斯等人撰写的多篇论文,其他理论家也在各种刊物上发表文章,这场论战也因此被推向第二次高潮。此后,《批评探索》还在 1985 年专门把此前该刊发表过的 12 篇相关文章编纂成书再次出版,题为《反对理论:文学研究与新实用主义》(*Against Theory: Literary Studies and the New Pragmatism*),并由时任主编 W. J. T. 米切尔(W. J. T. Mitchell)撰写了导言。

　　虽然在 1985 年 3 月发表费什等人的文章时,米切尔便声称这是围绕"反理论"这一议题的"最后一轮讨论"[③],但事情到此还远未结束,人们继续争辩的热情依然不减。1987 年 7 月,纳普和迈克尔斯又在

---

① 乔纳森·卡勒:《文学理论入门》,李平译,南京:译林出版社,2008 年,第 1 页。
② Steven Knapp and Walter Michaels, "Against Theory," *Critical Inquiry* 8. 4 (1982), p.724.
③ W. J. T. Mitchell, "Editor's Preface," *Critical Inquiry* 3 (1985), p.432.

《批评探索》上发表《反对理论》的姊妹篇《反对理论续篇：诠释学与解构主义》（"Against Theory 2：Hermeneutics and Deconstruction"），对之前并未涉及的诠释学和解构主义进行批判，这场论战由此进入第三次高潮。在此后的 10 多年时间内，又有多位批评家撰文参与商榷，其中包括著名哲学家乔治·威尔逊（George Wilson）、语言学家约翰·瑟尔（John Searle）等人。

以纳普、迈克尔斯、费什等人为代表的反理论者的主张是：理论根本不能产生它所宣称的效果，它既不会改进文本批评实践，更不能带来社会变革。任何理论都不能保证其操作者按照设计好的方法得出预期效果。从表面上来看，文学理论似乎在促进文本解读方面卓有成效，比如女性主义让我们"发现"了很多经典文本中暗含的性别政治等，但这种"发现"也不过是一种主题先行的阐释，是用预先设定好的框架去嵌套文本的结果。真正影响批评实践的是批评者的信念（接近于一般所说的意识形态），而非什么理论方法。任何一种理论都不可能真正改变批评者的信念，是批评者的既有信念决定了他会选择何种理论。理论虽然表面上促进了文学研究的繁荣，但也导致文学学术变得高度学院化、制度化和精英化，使文学学术成为少数人的智力游戏，它本身也就越来越失去影响并改造社会现实的能力。

可以说，由纳普和迈克尔斯发起的这场论战的影响力之大、持续时间之久、参与人数之多在近几十年的美国学术界都实属罕见，因为这不仅仅是一场学术论争，也是一场有关文学研究的职业路线之争。正像米切尔所指出的："它挑战的不仅是一种思考和写作的方式，更是一种谋生的手段。如果纳普和迈克尔斯是对的，那么整整一代的学者们似乎就将失去工作了。"[1]

实际上，虽然反理论运动进行得如火如荼，但 20 世纪 80 年代的理论家们并不相信理论真的会就此终结。1982 年，就在反理论运动发起不久，解构大师保罗·德曼（Paul de Man）便在《理论的抵抗》（*The Resistance to Theory*）一书中乐观地宣称："文学理论不会有死亡的危险，它只会继续繁荣，而且越受抵制越繁荣。"[2]J. 希利斯·米勒（J. Hillis Miller）在 1986 年就任美国现代语言协会（MLA）主席时也以"理论的胜利"为题发表就职演讲，表达了对理论胜利的高度自信。在他看来，人们对理论的攻击越猛烈，反倒越是说明理论的胜利，"若不是因为它活跃且有威胁，它也就不会受到攻击了"[3]。他和德曼一样乐观，认为当时正在发生的根本不是理论的终结，而只不过是理论的转向，即从以语言学为导向的理论转向历史、文化、社会、政治、体制、阶级、性别，以及制度化意义上的物质基础、生产条件、技术、分配等等。[4] 这种转向的发生，正是得益于理论——米勒所指的主要是后结构主义——对人们的思想启蒙，即人们不再把意义视为内在于文本的固定之物，而是关注意义在世界"文本"中被建构、播撒和自我解构的方式与过程。

一、21 世纪以来的反理论运动

21 世纪以来，理论虽然并没有死亡，但它所招致的厌烦情绪确实越来越常见。正如杰弗里·R. 迪

---

[1] W. J. T. Mitchell, "Introduction," *Against Theory: Literary Studies and the New Pragmatism*. Ed. W. J. T. Mitchell. Chicago：The University of Chicago Press，1985，p.2.

[2] Paul de Man，*The Resistance to Theory*. Minneapolis：University of Minnesota Press，1986，p.19.

[3] J. Hillis Miller, "Presidential Address 1986. The Triumph of Theory, the Resistance to Reading, and the Question of the Material Base," *PMLA* 102. 3 (1987)，p.286.

[4] Ibid.，p.283.

利奥所说:"理论与反理论是在同一时间在学术界诞生的,它们的历史就像一枚硬币的两面。"①自现代批评理论出现的那一刻开始,对理论的抵制就已经开始,两者互相依存,也互相激发活力。当下反理论热也正是因为理论前所未有的"茁壮、强健"②才兴起的。只不过在过去的数十年间,理论始终能够在与反理论的对抗中占据上风,并在文学院系彻底站稳脚跟,仍然拒绝接受理论的研究者也不得不退至边缘。传统自由人文主义模式的研究虽然仍然存在,但已经不再是主流。然而近 20 多年来,随着人文学科陷入困境,理论热潮逐渐冷却,反对理论的声音骤然从四处响起。就像 20 世纪 80 年代曾经轰动一时的反理论运动一样,今天又有很多学者站出来表示反对理论,而且他们中的很多人还都是在理论的熏陶下成长起来的优秀学者。他们尤其反对用过度政治化的批评实践伤害人们对文学的热爱和欣赏,宣称反对理论就是拯救文学,还要"让文学批评回归理智和理性"③。在他们看来,只要能把破坏性的理论驱逐出去,就可以让文学研究摆脱目前的困境,恢复生机。

反理论阵营的立场尽管并不完全一致,但其共同特点是都主张抛弃政治先行的意识形态分析,回归对经典文学的文本细读。文森特·利奇(Vincent Leitch)戏称反理论者为"一群热爱文学的人"(I-love-literature crowd)④,他们全都厌恶批评理论对社会建构主义的执着,对以种族—阶级—性别分析为批判焦点的多元文化主义的偏执,以及对意识形态批判和解构经典的偏好。反理论者能够容忍理论的最大限度,就是像中世纪经院哲学家用信仰驯服理性一样去驯服理论,让理论充当文学文本欣赏的侍女,而不能容忍让理论反过来凌驾于文本欣赏之上。

20 世纪 80 年代的那次反理论运动与当时里根总统和撒切尔夫人上台后大力推行新自由主义政策有关,它对人文学科造成的巨大消极影响主要表现在人们对高等教育价值的理解越来越"粗俗、务实或职业化"⑤。而当前新一轮的反理论运动同样也是在新自由主义势力不断升级的背景下发生的。在奥巴马任美国总统期间,美国教育部开始以学生的学费投入和预期薪酬为基准来衡量大学价值,而在特朗普任美国总统期间,这种倾向更加明显,"所有层面的学校都推行以获利为目的的教育"⑥。在这种风气影响下,高等学校越来越被视为工厂,知识被想象为一种工业产品,需要被越来越高效地生产和传输,以供学生消费。教师的工作也被同样的逻辑衡量、考核和评估。趁着欧美国家新自由主义势力的猖獗蔓延,反理论者很好地利用了当前西方社会整体偏向保守主义的政治风向以及人们普遍对过分"政治正确"的厌恶,他们彼此呼应,从不同方向攻击理论,共同捍卫作为文化遗产的文学经典和学术传统,维护一种常识性的现实主义语言和再现理论,抨击具有许多当代理论特征的文学研究的政治化。"其总的观点是保守的,其特点是怀念更早和更好的时代和方法。"⑦

在利奇看来,当前的反理论者都是"毫无感恩之心的继承人"⑧,因为他们都是在理论热潮时期成长

---

① Jeffrey R. Di Leo, "Down with Theory!: Reflections on the Ends of Antitheory," *What's Wrong with Antitheory?*. Ed. Jeffrey R. Di Leo. London: Bloomsbury Academic, 2020, p.97.
② Jeffrey R. Di Leo, "Introduction: Antitheory and Its Discontents," *What's Wrong with Antitheory?*. Ed. Jeffrey R. Di Leo. London: Bloomsbury Academic, 2020, p.1.
③ Ibid., p.2.
④ Vincent Leitch, "Antitheory," *The Bloomsbury Handbook of Literary and Cultural Theory*. Ed. Jeffrey R. Di Leo. London: Bloomsbury Academic, 2019, p.343.
⑤ Tally Jr., "Critique Unlimited," p.122.
⑥ Kenneth J. Saltman, "Antitheory, Positivism, and Critical Pedagogy," *What's Wrong with Antitheory?*. Ed. Jeffrey R. Di Leo. London: Bloomsbury Academic, 2020, p.75.
⑦ Leitch, "Antitheory," p.343.
⑧ Ibid., p.344.

起来的一代,曾在多方面受惠于理论学术的启蒙,但在学科遭遇危机的时刻,为了急于摆脱困境,却毫不犹豫地选择背叛理论。汤姆·埃尔斯(Tom Eyers)也指出,后批评者对理论的描绘完全是"漫画式的"[①],理论绝非如他们所描绘的那样教条笨拙。拉康、德里达、福柯等人全都反对简单化的深度阅读模式,20 世纪后半期的绝大多数理论家在思想上要比反理论者复杂得多,前者的分析也更深入、更有独创性。反理论者之所以想要驱逐理论,是因为他们在政治和经济方面的考虑多于在学术上的考虑,其中最典型的代表就要数弗吉尼亚大学英文教授芮塔·菲尔斯基(Rita Felski)了。她长期担任理论批评的旗舰期刊《新文学史》(New Literary History)的主编,如今却成为反理论呼声最高的后批评转向倡导者。而且就在当前大部分人文学术都难以获得研究资助的情况下,菲尔斯基居然从丹麦政府获得一笔总额高达 420 万美元的巨额研究基金资助,这不免让人惊叹"反对批评(理论)特别有利可图"[②]。

思考反理论运动,必须把它置入新自由主义大学理念日渐强化这一语境中。利奇也在最近的文章中指出,当下反理论运动发生的语境正是"与极端自由放任的晚期资本主义主导经济模式相关的大学公司化"[③]。职业培训式的高等教育理念已被深深植入公众心中,它尤为强调学业效率和教育的工具性。由此导致的一个政治后果是"这个时代在政治上越来越玩世不恭、冷漠无情、麻木不仁"[④]。而批评理论的教育目标不是为社会培训更多"驯服的"、高效的劳动者,而是培养学生对资本主义体制的批判精神,并唤起他们改造现实的政治冲动。20 世纪 80 年代兴起的各种理论流派的共同点就是它们都致力于提出疑问,想要透过世界呈现在我们面前的样子将问题看得更深、更透彻,"批评理论是颠覆性的,与其说这体现在政治行动上,不如说这体现在更加字面或词源学的意义上,即理论试图推翻或者颠覆现状"[⑤]。然而近年来,由于人文学科危机等多种因素,理论批评的价值和功能正被日益质疑为一种缺少合法性的实践。它既不能为社会提供有效知识,又不能指导普通读者的阅读实践,还鼓动学生对社会现实不满,这对整个文学批评构成损害。在罗伯特·塔利(Robert T. Tally Jr.)看来,反理论的诸多论调就是为了维护晚期资本主义社会现状,放弃理论就意味着放弃对资本主义的社会批判,成为新自由主义学术生产体制的驯服主体。

二、反理论运动与人文学科危机

理论主要就是语言学转向之后的产物,而当前的反理论运动则主要就是"反语言学转向"[⑥]。向现实主义的语言观念回归,就是相信观念和世界之间存在确切的、稳定的、实在的联系,相信作者通过文本真诚地向读者传达了期待被认同的情感和意义,读者也应该出于合作原则而真诚地去接纳它们。有人宣称反对一切理论,而非某一种具体理论,但实际上这是不可能的。如迪利奥所说:"反理论不是拒绝理论,而是理论的增殖,是把理论的地盘往外围扩张,并突破语言学转向的局限,或者超越结构主义和后结

---

① Tom Eyers,"(Anti) Theory's Resistances," *What's Wrong with Antitheory?*. Ed. Jeffrey R. Di Leo. London:Bloomsbury Academic,2020,p.230.

② Tally Jr.,"Critique Unlimited," p.124.

③ Leitch,"Antitheory," p.349.

④ Robin Goodman,"How Not to Be Governed Like That:Theory Steams On," *What's Wrong with Antitheory?*. Ed. Jeffrey R. Di Leo. London:Bloomsbury Academic,2020,p.134.

⑤ Tally Jr.,"Critique Unlimited," p.116.

⑥ Jeffrey T. Nealon,"Antitheory 2.0:The Case of Derrida and the Question of Literature," *What's Wrong with Antitheory?*. Ed. Jeffrey R. Di Leo. London:Bloomsbury Academic,2020,p.27.

构主义的藩篱。从这一角度来看,反理论只是对一种理论形式不满,并提出其他形式的理论作为替代。"①反理论者并没有统一的核心主张,他们通常不过是试图把那些早已被理论去神秘化了的观念——比如透明的语言、稳定的文本、真诚的情感、实在的意义等——重新复活。理论最大的发现之一便是:完全没有理论的批评是不可能的,因为任何一种批评都必然意味着有一套概念、假定和思维框架。那些声称没有理论的人,只是没有对这些早已形成惯例的事物进行反思而已。正如苏格拉底之前并非没有哲学家,在索绪尔之前也并非没有理论家。迪利奥指出:"反理论有诸多谬误之处,但最大谬误之一就是它制造了一种假象,似乎人文学科可以离开理论来思考文学和文化。"②做一个反理论者并非意味着没有理论,而是意味着对传统和惯例不加质疑地接受。

从根本上来说,反理论者的不满与其说来自人文学科外部,不如说来自内部。理论与反理论之战则更像是围绕"制度性主导权所展开的理论内部斗争"③。趁着新自由主义和保守主义浪潮,此前数十年间被理论驱赶到文学院系边缘的传统主义者要发起一场反扑,夺回被理论长期占领的讲台和阵地,让文学研究重新回到理论热兴起之前的样子。在塔利看来,反理论者提出的拯救人文学科的方案完全是"滑稽可笑的"④,人文学科的敌人不会因为人们采取了反批评的阅读方式而改变他们的观念,因为他们想要的是更加有用的工具性学科,而非更加温顺、无能的文学研究。以工具使用价值来呈现人文工作,要么在原则上立刻失败,要么会让我们受制于更加严苛的"成果"考核,这将不可避免地证明文学评论家和学者缺乏他们所宣称的工具价值。新自由主义下的教育政策拒绝考虑学习和知识与世界有什么关系,也不鼓励培养学生批判性思考的能力和运用知识去改造世界的能力。通过诉诸一种与批评理论根本不符的公共话语,即一种完全致力于维持某种现状并限制对其进行批评和谋求变革的话语,后批评和反理论者将自己的阵地割让给了敌人,让那些怀有极端功利主义或实用主义兴趣的新自由主义者对人文学科提出非常苛刻的条件。塔利相信,只有坚持理论批判才能继续维护人文学科的尊严,"一种强有力的批判理论和实践对于 21 世纪抵抗向人文学科发起的攻击更有必要……(因为)这种批评理论和实践是人文学科存在的根本原因"⑤。

在克里斯蒂安·海恩斯(Christian Haines)看来,理论是有乌托邦冲动的,它通过启发人们批判性地思考有关身份、历史、经典和规范的社会建构和政治偶然性,使人能够想象另一个世界的可能性,"而反理论……则从根本上是反乌托邦的"⑥。当反理论者号召人们放弃批评理论时,他们也就是在劝人们安于现状,向新自由主义妥协投降。他们倡导的拯救人文学科的方案根本行不通,因为他们没有看到导致人文学科面临危机的真正根源是新自由主义和教育私有化,而不是理论。"批评理论解决不了危机,但后批判转向对批评理论的先发制人的打击,剥夺了学生和教师应对我们所面临的状况所需的设备。"⑦

毫无疑问,反理论者也都是密切关注人文学科前途命运的人,他们提出的各种主张也都是为了真诚地拯救人文学科,让它能够重新焕发生机,为年轻学者和学生的未来职业赢回价值和尊严,然而反理论

---

① Di Leo,"Introduction:Antitheory and Its Discontents,"p.3.
② Ibid.,p.6.
③ Ibid.,p.22.
④ Tally Jr.,"Critique Unlimited,"p.130.
⑤ Ibid.,p.117.
⑥ Christian Haines,"Eaten Alive,or,Why the Death of Theory Is Not Antitheory," *What's Wrong with Antitheory?*. Ed. Jeffrey R. Di Leo. London:Bloomsbury Academic,2020,p.176.
⑦ Ibid.,p.183.

者的策略能否从根本上拯救人文学科仍值得怀疑。利奇对此提出了疑问：

> 反理论者带给理论的信息是明确的：回归本位，即文学欣赏。做该做的事情。扭转悲惨的颓势。恢复正典。排队。宣布你对文学的热爱。我喜欢文学。大声说吧，我爱文学。一个很大的问题是，我自己——作为一个自称是理论家的人——毫无疑问地热爱文学，我代表大多数理论家这样说。但一个更大的问题是，我们这些理论家坚持要研究"我爱文学"这个主题是如何运作的，但谁来定义"文学"？某些批评性效忠誓言和相关谴责会以何种代价出现？为什么会出现？在何处出现？批判性探究会制造混乱。它可以被指控腐蚀社会，尤其是学生，正如我们所知道的，这正是反理论者的常见指责。归根结底，热爱文学的方式有很多。攻击理论都不了忙。[①]

反理论者把人文学科陷入危机的根源归咎于理论的批判性，认为是理论与资本主义体制的不合作态度让它成为不受欢迎的敌人，只要放弃批判，把文学研究恢复到理论兴起之前的样子，就能够让高等教育的投资者重新恢复兴趣。这种看法在罗宾·古德曼（Robin Goodman）看来是幼稚的。他指出："不管菲尔斯基如何说，对文本的细读、纯描述和不需要中介的体验并不能抵挡文学研究在市场文化面前的合法化危机。"[②]如果理论家宣布放弃批判，让人文研究重新变得温顺、服从，这或许会暂时缓解人文学科与商品逻辑主导的资本主义社会体制的矛盾关系，却几乎不可能从根本上让人文学科恢复繁荣。

最后需要指出的是，无论是理论热还是反理论热，从根本上来说都是应对文学批评合法化危机的产物。卡勒在其经典著作《结构主义诗学》的前言部分说，他在美国引入以结构主义为代表的法国理论，是"为了使批评重新活跃起来，使它从单一的阐释作用中解放出来，为了建立一个理论体系，以证明批评是一门学问，使我们对批评进行辩护时不再有那么多的保留"[③]。"文学批评学科处于一种永恒的危机状态"[④]，它自20世纪初诞生以来，就总是面临不同的危机考验，总是需要在不同的历史时刻根据社会语境的变化对自身的存在合理性做出不同的辩护。理论虽然不可能一劳永逸地解决文学学科的存在合法性问题，但的确在让这个学科变得更加活跃的方面做出了巨大贡献。文学研究究竟是应该继续坚持富含政治潜能的理论批判，还是收起批判的锋芒，回归一种更温和、更富有建设性的学术传统，抑或走向以数字人文研究为代表的更具科学化的跨学科实践，这应当是文学学科未来所面临的重大抉择。

第二节　经典文献选读

本章共有三篇选文。第一篇节选自《批评探索》前主编 W. J. T. 米切尔为他所编写的论文集《反对理论：文学研究与新实用主义》所撰写的导言。他在文中对1980年代围绕纳普和迈克尔斯的两篇反对理论的文章所引发的争论做了全面系统的介绍。第二篇节选自《新文学史》前主编、当代"后批判转向"

---

① Leitch, "Antitheory," p.351.
② Goodman, "How Not to Be Governed Like That: Theory Steams on," p.146.
③ 乔纳森·卡勒：《结构主义诗学》，盛宁译，北京：中国人民大学出版社，2018年，第2页。
④ Peter Uwe Hohendahl. *The Institution of Criticism*. Ithaca：Cornell University Press, 1982, p.44.

的代表人物芮塔・菲尔斯基发表于《美国书评》(*American Book Review*)2017 年第 5 期上的一篇短文。她在文中对她所倡导的"后批判式阅读"(postcritical reading)进行了较为集中的阐述和辩护。最后一篇节选自《美国书评》主编、休斯顿大学(维多利亚)的英文教授杰弗利・R. 迪利奥为他主编的论文集《反理论错在哪里?》(*What's Wrong with Antitheory?*)所撰写的导言。迪利奥在这篇导言中对 21 世纪以来反理论运动发生的根源及其与理论之间的辩证互动关系做了鞭辟入里的分析。

一、《反对理论：文学研究与新实用主义》选读①

Introduction：Pragmatic Theory

The following collection of essays might as well be entitled *A Defense of Theory* as *Against Theory*. Most of the contributors defend some version of literary theory，either as a mode of critical practice or as a body of thought which stands outside critical practice and provides it with basic principles，methods，and investigative problems. The reason for the potentially misleading title is that all these essays were written in response to Steven Knapp and Walter Benn Michaels' essay "Against Theory"，first published in *Critical Inquiry* in summer 1982. Seven responses，as well as Knapp and Michaels' rejoinder，appeared in the June 1983 issue of *Critical Inquiry*，and are all reprinted here，along with two new statements by Richard Rorty and Stanley Fish and a final reply by Knapp and Michaels. The controversy has drawn so much attention among literary critics that it seemed appropriate to collect it in a single volume where the course of the debate can be followed from start to finish.

As in most debates，part of the controversy is over the question of just what is at issue. What is theory，in the study of literature or in other disciplines? What is at stake in being "for" or "against" theory? What sorts of values and interests are being challenged（and endorsed）by the antitheoretical arguments of those who are sometimes called the "New Pragmatists"（Fish，Knapp，Michaels，and Rorty）in literary study? One thing that will quickly become apparent to the reader of this collection is that the sides in this debate do not settle into two clearly defined camps. Those who defend theory against Knapp and Michaels do so for all sorts of different reasons，and they represent a wide range of theoretical positions，from the interpretive realism and historicism of E. D. Hirsch，Jr.，to the textual objectivism of Hershel Parker，to the deconstructionist orientation of Jonathan Crewe. The pragmatic，antitheoretical camp is not completely unified either：Knapp and Michaels chide Fish for occasional lapses into the theoretical mode，and Rorty finds himself at odds with a movement that，some would say，he largely helped to create with his efforts to revive the American pragmatist tradition and ally it with certain antitheoretical tendencies in European

---

① W. J. T. Mitchell，ed.，*Against Theory: Literary Studies and the New Pragmatism*. Chicago：The University of Chicago Press，1985，pp.1 - 10.

philosophy.

What is the importance of all this fuss over theory in literary studies? A gross oversimplification of the controversy might go this way: in the last twenty years, theory has, for a variety of reasons, become one of the "glamour" fields in academic literary study. Structuralism, semiotics, hermeneutics, deconstruction, speech-act theory, reception theory, psychoanalytic theory, feminism, Marxism, and various philosophical "approaches" have become a familiar part of the professional structure of literary study. Any literature department that does not have a "theorist" of some sort on its faculty is clearly out of step. More important, any specialist trained in one of the traditional historical fields in literary history is likely to be asked what sort of theory he or she subscribes to. The general assumption is that everyone has a theory that governs his or her practice, and the only issue is whether one is self-conscious about that theory. Not to be aware of one's theoretical assumptions is to be a mere practitioner, slogging along in the routines of scholarship and interpretation.

Given the dominance of theory in contemporary literary study, it was inevitable that someone would issue a challenge to it. We might say, in fact, that the antitheoretical polemic is one of the characteristic genres of theoretical discourse: the philosophy of science has Paul Feyerabend's *Against Method*; Marxist criticism has E. P. Thompson's *Poverty of Theory*. And one of the most influential branches of modern theory in literature and philosophy is called "antifoundationalism", a thoroughgoing skepticism that calls into question all claims to ground discourse in fundamental principles, "facts", or logical procedures. From a very broad perspective, then, "Against Theory" may be seen as an inevitable dialectical moment within theoretical discourse, the moment when theory's constructive, positive tendency generates its own negation. From a narrower professional perspective, it should be clear why Knapp and Michaels' antitheoretical arguments, whatever their particular merits, strike many critics as scandalous. The challenge is not just to a way of thinking and writing but to a way of making a living. If Knapp and Michaels are right, then it looks as though a whole generation of scholars is out of work: "If accepted, our arguments would indeed eliminate the 'career option' of writing and teaching theory."

Not surprisingly, then, most of those who respond to "Against Theory" think Knapp and Michaels are wrong. Some (like Crewe and Daniel O'Hara) define their "error" in political and moral terms, characterizing the "New Pragmatism" as a "petty theodicy of the guild", a cynical nihilism that "comforts the champions of the status quo". Others (the majority) are more dispassionate. They find various particular problems in "Against Theory" that are more or less damaging to its argument, while acknowledging that the essay raises important questions. All would agree, I think, that "Against Theory" is a tour de force, whether for good or ill: it is absolutely sure of its position, rarely hedging or qualifying its attack on literary theory; it is disconcertingly ingenious in its rhetorical and argumentative strategies, an ingenuity that continues unabated in

Knapp and Michaels' replies to their critics; it is undeniably witty in its mustering of examples (Crewe notes, somewhat ruefully, that the example of the wave-poem is "destined no doubt to become famous"). Probably the most fascinating feature of the essay is its spare, laconic, almost enigmatic style. The crisp declarative sentences of "Against Theory" contain none of the notorious jargon of literary theory; no special expertise is needed to read it. But the clarity of Knapp and Michaels' argument against theory is accompanied by a studious reserve about motives. The essay gives the impression that its authors are in the grip of an insight that is quite indifferent to questions of value, interest, or power. They declare insouciantly that their argument has "no consequences" and that it is "indifferent" to the existence of professional literary study. It is hardly surprising that these tacit denials of political or self-interest have provoked charges that the essay is a sort of careerist exercise which promotes a reactionary politics. Perhaps the most paradoxical and intriguing feature of "Against Theory" is that an essay which argues that meaning and intention are essentially the same thing should be so clear about its meaning while remaining so inscrutable about its intentions.

The essential value of "Against Theory", then, aside from its merits as a piece of writing in itself, is its function as a catalyst, a provocation to dialogue. Even if Knapp and Michaels are wrong both in their general claims about the function of theory and in their specific argument about meaning and intention, their "error" has the sort of clarity and definition that encourages the articulation of unsuspected insights. "Against Theory" has provided an ideal test case for *Critical Inquiry*'s central editorial principle, the notion of what I have elsewhere called "dialectical pluralism". This principle suggests that certain kinds of "errors", ably and vigorously defended, are far more interesting than a host of truths universally acknowledged and (for that reason) left unexamined. Knapp and Michaels help us to see theory's need to defend, not merely assume, its value for critical practice, and they provide the occasion for this defense on a very broad front, one that does not (in the usual fashion) pit one theory against another but asks us to see the project of literary theory as a coherent whole, united by certain fundamental problems of common concern.

All the defenses of theory in this collection of essays would have to be called "pragmatic". O'Hara and Crewe suggest that theory is a goad to critical progress and reform, providing models for practice and for the evaluation of practice. Steven Mailloux proposes that theory be regarded as a distinct kind of rhetorical practice, one that has had far-reaching consequences for other modes of critical practice. Adena Rosmarin and Rorty see literary theory as a place for a fruitful conversation between literature and philosophy. Hirsch, Parker, and William Dowling use "Against Theory" as an occasion to clarify specific problems in the notion of textual meaning, particularly the relation between "authorial" meaning and "textual" or "formal" conditions of meaning—the choice between grounding a text's meaning in "its" author or "an" author.

[....]

Knapp and Michaels seem right, then, in pointing to these sorts of differentiations, the desynonymizing of terms that have the same reference, as one of the fundamental characteristics of theoretical discourse. Where they seem wrong is in their claim that these distinctions originate in theory and that their abolition would lead to the collapse of theory and a return to practice. Actually, the distinctions arise in practice, in ordinary usage, and are developed into theories that (like all theories) are doomed to "fail" at one point or another—"fail" in the sense of not achieving the goal of complete mastery that Fish attributes to theory in the strong, nontrivial sense.

By a curious route, then, Knapp and Michaels out-theorize the theorists. Only in theory would anyone want to deny that there is a difference between meaning and intention; in practice, we use the distinction all the time. Only in theory would we want (as Knapp and Michaels do) to collapse the distinction between "knowledge" and "true belief" (in practice, to say that I *believe* something to be the case is tantamount to saying that I do not *know* it for a fact). The only question is, as Rosmarin suggests, What sort of theory would want to suspend these distinctions—and what other sorts of commonsense distinctions does it retain as foundational assumptions? Where would such a theory lead us? The answer of Michaels, Knapp, and Fish is unequivocal: it leads nowhere. This is a theory that has no consequences in the sense that theories have always wanted to have consequences—that is, by suggesting methods, pedagogical routines, procedures of verification, and so forth. If we take them literally (or, should I say, if the authors mean what they say), this is a theory of pure self-negation, what O'Hara calls "revisionary madness", articulating what many will see as the ultimate nihilism of contemporary theory. But if it is nihilism, it is one that demands an answer, not easy polemical dismissal—one that calls for theory to clarify its claims, not to mystify them with the easy assurance of intellectual fashion and institutional authority. If this volume aids in that clarification, it will have served its purpose.

二、《后批判式阅读》选读①

Literary studies, in recent decades, have been overrun by forms of critique: styles of suspicious reading that take their bearings from Freud and Foucault, Marx, and Butler. Incoming students are confronted with a dizzying array of theories and frameworks: tying them together, however, is a shared stance of skepticism, knowingness, and detachment. The prevailing ethos is one of againstness. This does not mean that English professors loathe literature, as conservative scholars like to lament. On the contrary, they often prize literary works as vital allies in struggles against error and injustice: the writings of Joyce or Woolf are deciphered to show how they subvert social norms and pull the rug out from under commonsense beliefs. The language of literary studies is

---

① Rita Felski, "Postcritical Reading," *American Book Review* 38. 5 (2017), pp.4 - 5.

littered with *de* words：novels and poems are widely hailed for deconstructing and demystifying, defamiliarizing and destabilizing.

This line of thought is not mistaken or misguided as far as it goes—few people would deny that literature can cast a critical light on social reality. And yet it is also notably one-sided. What about *re* words? How does literature replenish, reconfigure, recreate, reimagine, reinvent? If it is against, what is it for? Here literary critics are likely to fall silent：there is a virtual taboo, it seems, on articulating positive accounts of the books we teach and write about. We are badly in need of more comprehensive and compelling vocabularies of value. In two recent books I've argued for a literary criticism that is more attuned to the many different reasons why people read literature；that takes seriously the force of their attachments and the thickness of aesthetic experience.

It is in this context that I talk about "postcritical reading". We've seen a surfeit of "post" words in the last few decades—postmodernism, poststructuralism, postfeminism. Why add yet another to the mix? "Postcritical" refers to ways of reading that are informed by critique while pushing beyond it：that stress attachment as well as detachment, that engage the vicissitudes of feeling as well as thought, and that acknowledge the dynamism of artworks rather than treating them as objects to be deciphered and dissected. "Post" acknowledges a reliance on the thing one is questioning：a dance of dependency and difference rather than a simple opposition. (Post-critique is not the same thing as anti-critique.) One advantage of the term is its openness：a refusal to specify a single correct path for literary scholars. Rather than closing things down, "postcritical" leaves room for differing alternatives to a prevailing ethos of suspicion and skepticism. Yet it is also crucial to clarify what postcritical reading is not.

It is not, for example, nostalgic for a time when the canon was almost entirely white and male, when criticism relied on a purely formalist language of irony, paradox, and ambiguity, and when any attempt to discuss the social or philosophical meanings of literature was waved away as a category mistake. (The point needs to be insisted on；thanks to the grip of the art versus politics opposition, it is sometimes assumed that anyone who questions the sovereignty of critique must be a dyed-in-the wool aesthete. My own background is in critical theory and British cultural studies；I dislike aestheticism, high formalism, and the obsession with close reading as a path to redemption even more than the clichés of critique.) My current work centers on the "uses of literature"—what literature does in the world：how it acts and reacts, absorbs and inspires, transports and is transported across space and time. "Use" should be understood capaciously, in the spirit of Dewey, and not confused with a crass utilitarianism：the uses of literature can include escapism and enchantment, the shock of recognition and the subtle reverberations of semiconscious affinities. I am interested in how literature composes, connects, ties, builds, brings together. Of course, worldly ties are not free of power, as critical theory reminds us—but neither are they reducible to power. We need a critical vocabulary that is more attuned to the complexity of ties—as not just chains of domination，but also indispensable forms of relation. Bonds do not only constrain，but also sustain：they enable，create，make possible.

My argument has affinities with other critics who are currently questioning the orthodoxy of a hermeneutics of suspicion，such as Sharon Marcus，Stephen Best，Heather Love，and Toril Moi—all scholars who are also associated with feminist and/or queer studies. Our concerns are very different to，say，someone like Harold Bloom，whose antipathy toward critique is fueled by a view of art as floating free of mundane social realities. Feminist and queer scholars are highly attuned to the ways literature is tangled up with gender and sexuality：they see it as worldly rather than otherworldly；they think of art and politics as related rather than opposed. Yet they are also highly conscious of how the figure of the detached，critical scholar has been used to devalue or dismiss other ways of reading. Identification，immersion，enthusiasm，the experience of being lost in a book：such responses—portrayed by literary theorists as intellectually naïve and politically pernicious—have especially close associations with female readers（Madame Bovary）. Queer theory also has longstanding interests in affect and attachment：a camp sensibility，for example，blends irony and theatricality with intense affection，devotion，even love.

If the postcritical is not anti-political，neither is it anti-intellectual. Defenders of critique insist that it is synonymous with rigorous thinking；that if we give up critique，we will be left with nothing but mindless reverence，sentimental effusion，or chitchat about fictional characters. And yet ordinary motives for reading can be engaged without shortchanging intellectual depth or sustained reflection. Experiences of identification，empathy，or immersion raise a host of questions whose complexities have barely been touched upon. Postcritique is not anti-theory；but，it leavens theoretical reflections with the messiness of examples and close attention to the differing ways texts and persons connect.

Recognizing oneself in a book，for instance，is a very common experience—yet one that has received a rough handling in literary and critical theory. The usual response has been to demote recognition to an instance of misrecognition. Invoking Lacan and Althusser，critics have insisted that any self-understanding gained from reading literature can only be delusory. Recognition offers the banal consolations of shoring up sameness and denying otherness：it is complacent，conservative，even narcissistic；it sustains the illusions of selfhood rather than dismantling them （literary theory is deeply suspicious of the category of the person，whether real or fictional）；in short，its purpose is to shore up the status quo. Yet such dismissals or denunciations of a widespread response are no less problematic than the humanist bromides they replaced（that we all recognize ourselves in Oedipus or Lear because they embody timeless truths of the human condition）. Critical readings of literary works can be fine-grained and attentive to textual detail；and yet critical accounts of how other readers（lay readers）respond to these works are often remarkably simplistic and reductive.

Self-recognition in literature, as I've argued in *Uses of Literature*, is a complex and multi-faceted phenomenon. "Recognition is not repetition: it denotes not just the previously known, but the becoming known...In a mobile play of interiority and exteriority, something that exists outside of me inspires a revised or altered sense of who I am." Glimpsing aspects of oneself in fictional characters involves sameness *and* difference: to recognize is to know again, but it is also to see anew. It may well involve moments of confirmation: we all need to have our distinctiveness acknowledged and literature can be a vital medium of self-reflection and self-understanding for those with limited access to other forms of public recognition (women; racial and sexual minorities; the working class). But it is also about self-extension across cultural, historical, temporal differences; no-one wants to be *reduced* to their identity; through reading we partake of other realities and inhabit other worlds. Patterns of affiliation are often fluid and unpredictable; aesthetic affinities may cut across or complicate familiar rubrics, social categories, and ways of thinking. Meanwhile, the phrase "shock of recognition" is not just a cliché. We can be disconcerted, even mortified by our kinship with a fictional figure; the result can be sobering self-scrutiny rather than preening complacency.

Such a defense of recognition steers clear of clichés about universal or timeless aesthetic values; cognizant of the lessons of critique, it avoids making assumptions about how we read or what we should read. Readers come to literature with very different histories, experiences, literary tastes, and forms of response that need to be reckoned with. (And here the conservative claim that feminist and minority critics are constrained by "identity politics" has a certain irony; surveys confirm that men are much less likely to read works by or about women than the other way around; there are similar findings with regard to cross-racial identification.) Literature is a worldly thing; reading can serve varying purposes, both positive and negative; readers are fallible beings who are capable, without a doubt, of narcissism, misapprehension, and self-delusion. And yet intense connections can be forged across differences; unexpected affinities come to light; moments of recognition occur that may be self-transformative or eddy out into larger social currents. (That Ibsen's original female audience recognized itself in Hedda Gabler, for example, had a force that surged beyond the personal to fan the flames of the early suffragette movement.) Recognition, of course, is just one of various possible literary responses. (I've also written about experiences of enchantment, shock, empathy, allegiance, and attunement, and there doubtless many others.) Acts of reading need to be grappled with in all their phenomenological complexity and social variety. They are distinctively aesthetic insofar as they involve style and form, language and mood; and yet such aesthetic affinities cannot be quarantined from readers' ethical concerns or worldly affiliations.

As Edith Hall remarks in her review of Jeffrey M. Duban's *The Lesbian Lyre* (2016), it has been a tactical error for progressive critics of literature to place all their bets on acts of demystifying and debunking: leaving a yawning gap that traditionalists have rushed to fill. "By failing to produce a theory of aesthetic value, the literary Left has relinquished the best critical tunes to the devil of diehard conservatism." I am not persuaded we need a (single) theory of aesthetic value, given the differing criteria of evaluation that are in play across genres and forms as well as audiences but Hall is right to argue that we need better ways of talking about *why* people are drawn to literature, or music, or film, or painting. In neglecting such questions, we have shortchanged not just the responses of other readers and viewers but our own. Scholars are also enmeshed, entranced, enlivened by the works they read; they too register sparks of commonality and affinity. Attention to phenomenology, meanwhile, does not exclude sociology, though it requires a more fine-grained form of sociological thinking that is open to the differing uses and purposes of art and that is willing to be surprised. Post-critical reading does not—cannot—forget the lessons of critique, which remains an integral part of contemporary thought. But it is much less invested in knowingness, skepticism, and ironic distance, more willing to acknowledge the overlapping affinities between scholarly and everyday reading. Whether we are academics or lay readers, how we read is shaped by our attachments.

三、《反理论错在哪里?》选读[①]

Introduction: Antitheory and Its Discontents

Antitheory is nothing new. As long as there has been theory, there has also been antitheory. The two fit together in a codependent relationship that has served not to enervate the other, but rather to energize it. The rise, then, of antitheory coincides with the rise of literary and cultural theory in the 1970s. Moreover, just as theory in the new millennium is stronger and more robust than it has ever been in its roughly fifty-year history, so too is antitheory. New directions in antitheory arise on a regular basis albeit with more or less the same mandate: to express discontentment with theory.

At its most rudimentary level, antitheory takes the form of opposition to some of the major mandates of theory. For example, there is a faction of antitheory that opposes the use of race, class, gender, and sexuality in the analysis of literature and culture. There is another that rejects critique and calls for forms of criticism that do not involve ideological analysis. There is still another form of antitheory that rejects the epistemological and metaphysical project of structuralism and poststructuralism and its so-called social construction of knowledge. In short, antitheory has a long and varied list of complaints about theory that can include but are not limited to the commitments of structuralism; poststructuralism; multiculturalism; and race, class, gender, and sexuality studies.

But there are other complaints by antitheorists that really have nothing to do with specific

---

① Jeffrey R. Di Leo, ed., *What's Wrong with Antitheory?*. London: Bloomsbury Academic, 2020, pp.1 - 22.

theories. Rather, these complaints are directed at the general tenor of theory, which is viewed as replete with "inflated claims" "facile slogans", and "political pretensions". There are also complaints from these antitheorists about the lack of "reason and science" in theory, its "paucity of evidence", the "incoherence of certain theorists", its "flagrant identity politics", its neglect of aesthetics, its lack of logic, and, its "fashionableness". Of the last complaint, one wonders though if the zeal of antitheorists would wane, if it were not that theory has a knack for eliciting critical interest and generating scholarly excitement in the humanities. Shiny objects are well known to attract attention.

Still perhaps the ultimate complaint of antitheorists is the alleged way in which theory impairs our appreciation of literature. "All [antitheorists] share an affection for literature," write a couple of prominent antitheorists—share "a delight in the pleasure it brings, a respect for its ability to give memorable expression to the vast variety of human experience, and a keen sense that we must not fail in our duty to convey it unimpaired to future generations". In short, theory destroys our appreciation of literature, and it will continue to do so until it is cast out of the house of literary criticism. By eliminating theory from the academy, the valiant warriors of antitheory will have thereby rescued it from appreciative peril. Antitheory, writes the novelist Mario Vargas Llosa, "returns sanity and rationality to literary criticism, rescuing it from the esotericism, jargon, and delusions under which it [has] been buried by the 'theorizers'"—something he feels that "lovers of genuine literature and criticism" desperately desire.

Nevertheless, to say there are central tenets to antitheory would be misguided. Though its discontentment is generally localized to what it regards as "theory", just as there are many different types of theory, so too are there many different types of antitheory. Moreover, unlike other terms with the same prefix such as antifoundationalism, which refers to a rejection of foundational beliefs or principles in philosophical inquiry, and anti-essentialism, which refers to the nonbelief that things or ideas have essences, *antitheory does not necessarily imply the rejection of theory* or a nonbelief in theory. In fact, in many cases, *antitheory* simply means another type of theory. This is one of the things that make antitheory a fascinating topic for consideration.

One of our contributors, Jeffrey T. Nealon, who self-professedly "has been toiling in the vineyards of antitheory for more than twenty-five years", recognizes well the theoretical nature of antitheory. "Antitheory" writes Nealon, "has long been a venerable brand of theory." His comment might seem odd to those who view antitheory like antifoundationalism, that is, as a rejection of theory. But he is correct in his branding assessment. The only question is what "brand of theory" is antitheory? In Nealon's case, antitheory was initially movements that offered theoretical alternatives to structuralism and poststructuralism such as cultural studies, globalization studies, feminism, race and gender studies, queer theory, postcolonialism, Marxism, and new historicism, but has now in its later stages of development moved on to some new brands of theory.

Nealon's assumption in his contribution is that the "theory" in "antitheory" refers to "structuralism and post-structuralism", which he describes as "a loose grab-bag of movements also dubbed 'the linguistic-turn'". Antitheory, then, is not work that directly follows from the linguistic turn like the

far-reaching revolutions in thinking about everything from the nature of kinship systems (Claude Lévi-Strauss) and historical events (Hayden White) to the workings of political power (Louis Althusser) or sex and gender (Judith Butler), all the way to the workings of African-American cultural production (Henry Louis Gates's "signifyin") and even the unconscious itself (Jacques Lacan's famous dictum that the unconscious is structured like a language is specifically scaffolded on Saussure's relation between the signifier and the signified).

Rather, antitheory is work that takes *another* "turn", specifically, one that is not linguistically based. So, for Nealon (and others) antitheory is theory that does not directly follow from the linguistic turn. Or, otherwise stated, antitheory is work that is more closely associated with the theoretical movements that are not considered part of the linguistic turn, which is, of course, not a small body of theory.

What is interesting about this position is that antitheory is not the rejection of theory. Rather, on this view, antitheory is the *multiplication* of theories—a way to build out the house of theory beyond the constraints of the linguistic turn, or, if you will, beyond the parameters of structuralism and poststructuralism. In effect, then, antitheory from this perspective involves discontentment with only one form of theory and offers, in its stead, other forms of theory. This version of antitheory opens the path to regarding, for example, not only the very long list of "studies" today as antitheory (e.g., debt studies, sound studies and surveillance studies) but also new materialism, object-oriented ontology, and surface reading. On this view, the house of theory is large and regularly expanding through the multiplication of antitheories.

Nevertheless, for some, the rejection of theory does not entail the adoption of another version of it. Rather, it is the simple and categorical rejection of theory—all theory, no exceptions. This rejection holds equally for structuralism, poststructuralism, cultural studies, globalization studies, feminism, race and gender studies, queer theory, postcolonialism, Marxism, new historicism, and so on. Vincent Leitch, who, like Nealon, may also be described as having "toiled in the vineyards of antitheory for a very long time", has said that this group of antitheorists includes "traditional literary critics; aesthetes; critical formalists; political conservatives; ethnic separatists; some literary stylisticians, philologists, and hermeneuticists; certain neopragmatists; champions of low and middlebrow literature; creative writers; defenders of common sense and plain style; plus some committed leftists". I too have toiled in the vineyards of antitheory probably just as long as Nealon and can say too from my professional experience in comparative literature and philosophy departments that some first-generation champions of "comparative literature" as well as most analytic philosophers need to be added to Leich's list. I know all too well their scorn for theory.

But even so, this level of antitheory is perhaps easier claimed than accomplished. It assumes that these so-called antitheorists have no theoretical position of their own or that it is possible to regard them as theory "neutral". Otherwise, they would be in the same boat that Nealon puts his antitheorists, though with one major difference: their "theory" would not be the "linguistic turn". Rather, it would be one of a host of "earlier" alternatives such as philology, stylistics, formalism, aestheticism, hermeneutics, or, even, dare I say, some other version of "philosophy" other than that found in the works of Ferdinand de Saussure, Jacques Derrida, Richard Rorty, and others. So, for example, the proponents of "stylistics" as their preferred theory might argue that everything that comes *after* it is "antitheory".

Still, what if we posited that "theory" is not just the linguistic turn or the structuralism-poststructuralism dyad? And that one of the lessons of theory is that *it is no longer possible to be theory neutral*? Moreover, isn't this just the assumption of folks who call themselves "antitheorists" only to brand their own work as another version of theory? The difference between those who formulate their theoretical positions in comparison to the work of structuralists and poststructuralists and those who do not is merely, then, a historical contingency. Just because the antitheoretical "new historicists" happened to formulate their positions *after* the theoretical work of the structuralists and poststructuralists, it does not make their work any less theoretical than the philologists whose positions were established *before* the theoretical work of the structuralists and poststructuralists.

There are parallels here too with the case of philosophy. Just as we do not believe that pre-Socratic thinkers such as Pythagoras, Heraclitus, and Parmenides were not philosophers because they "preceded" Socrates, the "father" of philosophy, by the same token we should also not contend that pre-Saussurean or pre-Derridean thinkers were not also theorists. Perhaps, as a concession to the formative powers of Socrates, Saussure, and Derrida, we might respectively then dub these thinkers "early philosophers" and "early theorists", but we surely would not dismiss any of them from philosophical or theoretical consideration.

But the point regarding the history of philosophy goes forward too. For example, consider the case of Friedrich Nietzsche, who was widely rejected as a "legitimate" philosopher by many twentieth-century American analytic philosophers because of his aphoristic style. Just as philosophy is not just Socratic philosophy or analytic philosophy, so too is theory not just Derridean theory and its variants. In addition, just because one does not self-identify as a philosopher or theorist, it does not mean that one should not be considered one. Same too with antitheorists.

The discontents then of antitheory are many. First and foremost among them is an inability to escape or make a clean break from theory. This is especially true in the new millennium, where the reach of theory is greater now than at any time in history. Today there is arguably no nontheoretical position from which one can claim to read literature or study culture. Theory now consumes all possible approaches to literature and culture—or at least this is the belief of those who choose to observe the theoretical field as a whole, rather than merely view it from only their own position within it, which can lead to the mistaken view that one's own approach is somehow "outside" of or "beyond" the purview of theory.

Stepping back from our critical practices and reading positions to situate them within the theoretical field is one of the central tasks of those who are committed to a progressive future for the humanities. There are many things wrong with antitheory, but perhaps the biggest one is that it promotes the illusion that it is possible for the humanities to consider literature and culture without theory. Fifty years ago it was still possible for the humanities to consider literature without theory. Twenty-five years ago it was still debatable whether this was possible. Today, however, it is not possible to be a legitimate humanities scholar and at the same time an antitheorist who categorically rejects theory. To attempt the impossible, that is, to claim to be a humanities scholar and categorically reject theory, is at this moment in history to place not only theory in jeopardy but also the future of the humanities. In short, antitheory of this ilk is wrong because it plays dice with both the future of theory and the humanities.

[...]

Antitheory encompasses a wide range of discontentment with theory. Like theory, it exhibits both periods in the spotlight as well as those of relative quietude. Today it is in the spotlight, whereas tomorrow it may not be. Felski and Latour have done a lot to put the spotlight on antitheory of late with their critique of critique just as Knapp and Benn Michaels lit it up decades ago with their clever theory against theory. While it is painful for some theorists to respond to the antitheories of Felski and Latour, oppositional work such as theirs in the end only serves to rally theorists to redouble their efforts to make theory stronger.

Moreover, as an inhabitant of the neoliberal university, which now only attaches value to work in the humanities when it raises the bottom line of the university, I would wager that by drawing millions of grant dollars to their work, Felski may have unintentionally also raised the bar for the next wave of antitheory. The antitheory of Knapp and Michaels only sparked debate, which might have been sufficient in the early years of the neoliberal university, but now that we are well within its heyday, opposition without outside financial support for it will not be good enough when antitheory makes its next move against theory.

What is odd though about antitheory is not the oppositional work it does with respect to theory, but rather that discontentment with theory is viewed the opposite or other of theory—as some way or other against or antitheory. To get a sense of this oddity, again, look at how oppositional ideas are dealt with in philosophy.

In the philosophical world，dualists have long lived next to monists，but no dualist has ever called a monist an "anti-philosopher". Nor have the many rationalists who reside in the big house of philosophy denied empiricists access to it. Sure they fight like cats and dogs over which is the preferable position，but the rejection of proponents of oppositional positions as philosophers is not something that has not traditionally been done. Moreover，not only has materialism long coexisted with its other，idealism，it has also dueled with naturalism and realism for philosophical superiority. So，why should the current internal squabbles within theory be any different? Why are we so quick today as theorists to look at alternate positions as a threat to theory?

But maybe，like philosophy，discontentment in theory will one day just become part of the very fabric of theory. It might even be argued that those who see a family resemblance within the world of theoretical difference fashion it more like the philosophical world than the world of antitheory.

In conclusion，the major questions of antitheory today are not whether theory is "dead" or what comes "after" theory. Those have been *de facto* sorted out by the emergence of robust new forms of antifoundationalist theory that offer novel opportunities and challenges for academe. Theory can no more die than philosophy or literature or rhetoric. Ultimately，the discontentment of antitheorists is not so much from outside of theory but from within. While some might be inclined to view postcritique or speculative realism as battles "against theory"，as we have seen，others view them as local struggles within theory for institutional dominance. Whether we regard theory as the legacies of antifoundationalism or the rise of alternatives to it，the dialectics of theory must be regarded as an essential aspect of its rise and dominance in the academy over the past fifty years. So，what's wrong with antitheory? If we just focus on its role in fortifying theory over the past fifty years，then perhaps nothing. But if we focus instead on its efforts to destroy theory，then *everything*.

四、思考与讨论

1. 史蒂文·纳普和沃尔特·迈克尔斯为什么要反对理论？米切尔为什么说他们要挑战的不仅是一种思考和写作方式，更是一种"谋生之道"(a way of making a living)？

2. 芮塔·菲尔斯基为什么要倡导"后批判"转向？她的主张与 20 世纪末反理论者的主张有哪些区别和联系？在她看来，文学批评应该如何彰显文学之用呢？

3. 迪利奥如何看待反理论运动的本质？我们应如何理解他所谓的(反)理论之争不过是围绕"制度性主导权所展开的理论内部斗争"(local struggles within theory for institutional dominance)？

本章推荐阅读文献：

［1］Bruno Penteado. "Against Surface Reading：Just Literality and the Politics of Reading," *Mosaic: An Interdisciplinary Critical Journal* 52. 3（2019），pp.85－100.

［2］Daniel Rosenberg Nutters. "The Irony of Critique," *American Book Review* 38. 5 (2017), pp.14 – 15.

［3］Elizabeth S. Anker and Rita Felski（eds.）. *Critique and Postcritique*. Durham：Duke University Press，2017.

［4］Jeffrey R. Di Leo（ed.）. *The Bloomsbury Handbook of Literary and Cultural Theory*. London：Bloomsbury Academic，2019.

［5］Jeffrey R. Di Leo（ed.）. *What's Wrong with Antitheory?*. London：Bloomsbury Academic，2020.

［6］J. Hillis Miller. "Presidential Address 1986. The Triumph of Theory, the Resistance to Reading, and the Question of the Material Base," *PMLA* 102. 3 (1987), pp.281 – 291.

［7］Joseph North. *Literary Criticism: A Concise Political History*. Cambridge：Harvard University Press，2017.

［8］Matthew Mullins. "Introduction to Focus：Postcritique," *American Book Review* 38. 5 (2017), pp.3 – 4.

［9］Paul de Man. *The Resistance to Theory*. Minneapolis：University of Minnesota Press，1986.

［10］Rita Felski. "Postcritical Reading," *American Book Review* 38. 5 (2017), pp.4 – 5.

［11］Rita Felski. *The Limits of Critique*. Chicago：The University of Chicago Press，2015.

［12］Steven Earnshaw. *The Direction of Literary Theory*. London：Macmillan，1996.

［13］Steven Knapp and Walter Michaels. "Against Theory 2：Hermeneutics and Deconstruction," *Critical Inquiry* 1 (1987), pp.49 – 68.

［14］Winfried Fluck. "The Limits of Critique and the Affordances of Form：Literary Studies after the Hermeneutics of Suspicion," *American Literary History* 31. 2 (2019), pp.229 – 248.

［15］W. J. T. Mitchell（ed.）. *Against Theory: Literary Studies and the New Pragmatism*. Chicago：The University of Chicago Press，1985.